RANCID PANSIES

James Hamilton-Paterson

RANCID PANSIES

Europa
editions

Europa Editions
116 East 16th Street
New York, N.Y. 10003
www.europaeditions.com
info@europaeditions.com

Copyright © 2008 by James Hamilton-Paterson
First Publication 2008 by Europa Editions

Library of Congress Cataloging in Publication Data is available
ISBN 978-1-933372-62-4

Hamilton-Paterson, James
Rancid Pansies

Book design by Emanuele Ragnisco
www.mekkanografici.com

Cover photo © Hulton-Deutsch Collection/CORBIS

Prepress by Plan.ed – Rome

Printed in the United States of America

In memory of Charles Swann

RANCID PANSIES

1.

Melancholy as it is to stand at dawn and watch one's house vanish over a cliff, I can't deny that amid the attendant dust cloud of black thoughts is a whirling spark of exhilaration, as after the death of a partner or parent. Part of this is natural relief that one wasn't in the place at the time. But there's more to it. A perverse pleasure, even? Yet how could any normal person be pleased to see the precious home they had created with such expenditure of taste and ingenuity (to say nothing of time, money and labour) reduced to rubble in a matter of seconds? No doubt a normal person couldn't, especially not in full victim mode as the frantic householder left holding not so much as a doorknob. Clothes, books, files, letters, CDs, a farting teddy bear named Gazzbear™, *a life*—torn from his grasp and hurled into the abyss as detritus to be exposed to the scrutiny of wild boar and buzzards, not to mention Italian hunters.

Well. The seismic hazards of living in Tuscany. Hollow-eyed, unslept and unshaven, I was by no means my usual neatly groomed self when the following day Virgilio, my friend in the carabinieri, arranged for a helicopter to fly me over the scene. It looked just like one of those TV news pictures of million-aires' homes in Californian canyons after freak rains have pro-voked a mudslide. A pale scar down a steep and forested hill-side; a section of roof lying askew on the slope like a badly pitched terracotta tent; unidentifiable torn material draped over rocks. (*Ha! Even millionaires are not immune, the bas-*

tards!) We flew another slow circuit even lower and I spotted the puckered grey rump of my Toyota Avensis—or Ass Vein, if you share my weakness for anagrams—sticking up out of the churned earth like a mouldy boulder.

"*Madonna cara!*" said the pilot over the intercom. "How did you all get out in time? It's a miracle no one was killed."

Seeing it from above in broad daylight, I had to agree it was fairly unlikely we should all have survived uninjured. An entire slice of mountainside had collapsed. The level acre of grass and trees that constituted a *cordon sanitaire* between my house and Marta's now ended in a ragged lip above a raw precipice. Because it was winter and only the scrub oaks retained some brown, withered leaves I could glimpse between the trees the stout fence I had put up to demarcate my property. It now stood within a mere twenty metres of the edge.

"The Blessed Madonna was surely watching over *you*," said the co-pilot into his microphone. "You see? She even protects foreigners."

"Evidently." My sceptical voice sounds disembodied in my own headset. "Although of course in England we have *la* Diana. You know—the Princess of Wales. She has become our national Madonna. It was probably she who saved us."

"She had terrific legs," said the pilot wistfully. "A tragedy."

I was about to elaborate on my light-headed piece of face-tiousness when our pilot needed to take swift evasive action to avoid a second chopper, apparently from a local news station, that had arrived to gloat over the debris with long lenses. There was talk among the police in my helicopter of setting a guard over the site to deter looters. It didn't seem to concern me. Some unfortunate's worldly possessions, but no longer mine.

For suddenly I didn't care. By the time we landed I had discovered to my surprise that I no longer wished to put that particular life painfully back together again. I had no urge to send in the bulldozers, not even to unearth the battered but tough filing cabinet that doubtless still contained all my insurance papers, my passport, my *permesso di soggiorno* and a bottle of poppers called Kix that Adrian had brought me and which I had forgotten to stash in the freezer. Suddenly I was stateless, shorn of identity, with nothing to insure since nothing of value remained from my former existence. I didn't care if souvenir-hunters found the platinum disc of Alien Pie which the bald boy-band leader Nanty Riah had given me scant hours before the fall of the house of Gerry, in exchange for my having given him this name for his band. And anyone who could be both-ered to dig for them was welcome to my dullish but signed Picasso lithograph and my autograph letter from Oscar Wilde (three querulous lines about a cigarette case to Messrs. Thornhill, Walter & Co. of 144, New Bond Street). I wanted none of it. It even crossed my mind to tear off the clothes I stood up in and walk away stark naked into the world, a born-again atheist aged fifty and a day. I was restrained by natural modesty and anxiety that my underwear might bear signs of the previous night's trauma. Also, it seemed unlikely that the carabinieri still standing around the military helipad at Pisa would appreciate the gesture's metaphorical intention. Not for them the poetry of departures; more a pretext to commit me to a locked ward for observation. (Poor *maestro*! One under-stands: the terrible shock and *lo stress*.)

I now wonder if I shall ever revisit the site of my former home—say in a year's time—like Thomas Hardy in his poem "Where the Picnic Was." I may say that until it was brusquely curtailed by geophysics, my fiftieth birthday party was consid-erably better than any picnic. Hardy doesn't mention what his little group cooked over their wood fire: some grim Wessex fry-up, possibly, or merely a kettle boiled for that horrid British beverage involving stewed leaves. But whatever it was it couldn't have compared to the superb badger Wellington *farci* with gun-dog pâté and the odd psychoactive mushroom that I served my own friends, inducing in us all such a memorable sense of relaxed camaraderie. But a year on, shall I still be able to identify the precise spot, as Hardy did his by fragments of charred wood? Or will the tough Tuscan *cespuglia* of broom and juniper and brambles have long grown over the scarred hillside to obliterate everything? And shall I, like the poet, reflect gloomily on the subsequent scattering of the band of friends who had sat around my hearth that fateful evening?

So far, not much scattering has taken place and as yet none of us has mawkishly "shut his eyes for evermore." Within a matter of days I was forcibly abducted to Suffolk, for all the world like an African foundling swept up in the photo-op embrace of a Hollywood nobody, escorted by the world-famous conductor Max Christ and his scientist brother-in-law, my partner Adrian Jestico. I was installed in Christ's newly renovated house, Crendlesham Hall, in a well-appointed attic suite with a four-poster bed the size of a squash court, and bidden to recover my wits. This I have almost done. In the interim, Adrian has continued to work towards eminence at the British Oceanography Institute in Southampton (BOIS) and these days is a frequent visitor to the Hall, where he is company for his sister Jennifer when Max is away on tour, and an uncle for Josh, her six-year-old son. He also comes as something more than a mere helpmeet for me. Some nights beneath the squash court's duvet Adrian punishes my age with his superior stamina and wristy action. It's all too hideously domestic for words and I've got to get out. Nature did not intend Gerald Samper to lounge around on other people's beds like an odalisque.

Of the other guests at that interrupted dinner party it is my neighbour Marta who most occupies my thoughts, and in her usual infuriating manner. Since her surprise return from America on the night of that memorable dinner, the Voynovian baggage has bravely taken up residence again in her gloomy hovel on the edge of the chestnut forests at Le Roccie. I say bravely because her house is now the lone survivor of our Apennine eyrie overlooking Viareggio and the coast of Tuscany. She is in the position of the last, rather dim, householder of the medieval town of Dunwich who, having watched the rest of the town progressively collapse into the North Sea, in turn finds herself on the brink and counting. Unfortunately for lovers of poetic comeuppance, Martha's dump is still a generous hundred metres from the ragged lip where the dinner was and it would take a serious act of God to send it tumbling to its well-deserved ruin. Don't think for one moment the irony isn't lost on me: that the irritating neighbour who spoiled my solitude (but to whose house I painstakingly acted as caretaker in its owner's absence) is now in triumphant sole possession of the site, while my own vastly more meritorious home lies scattered in the forests below like a shower of Lego pieces tipped from a pail. This is a cosmic injustice and something will have to be done about it. To think of that frowsty creature finally lording it up there, thumping out her film scores on her Warsaw Pact upright, is gall and bile to me. What did Marta ever do to deserve being spared? For the best part of a year she simply abandoned her house and I took pity on it only because I thought its wretched owner had been kidnapped for outsourced interrogation in Poland or Syria or somewhere, like so many other victims of "extraordinary rendition" at the time. I didn't like to think of Marta suspended by her grubby thumbs as the humming cattle prods zeroed in. But it turned out she had been in America all along, messing about with her music and not bothering to get in touch with her loyal neighbour, not even sparing the time for an SMS text message to *farsi viva* and to ask whether I wouldn't mind keeping an eye on her place. I did so anyway because I was properly brought up; and in due course she swanned home and look what happened. Within hours she found herself in de facto sole possession of Le Roccie. My repellent religious stepmother Laura has often been heard to demand querulously why it is that the wicked prosper. I gather she is plagiarising the psalmist, but for once I can't take issue with her.

Meanwhile the slow, healing regime of grappa laudanum and bitter reflection has all but restored my normal spirits. Sometimes when I wander Crendlesham Hall's warm domestic spaces while everyone is out I can definitely feel the earliest twinges of boredom. There is something about the empty day-time shell of a normally active family house that can—when a shaft of aqueous February sunlight catches the remaining tat-ters of Christmas decorations—induce a melancholy fretful-ness. In the kitchen the kettle sighs on the Aga, Luna the cat lies like a fur puddle deep in the only comfortable chair that she shares with several of Josh's rubber dinosaurs and a Transformer toy. I stand at the window and watch wintry lap-wings rowing their aimless way about the grey Suffolk sky. On the wall is one of those office whiteboards covered with felt-tip scrawls and scraps of paper held on by fridge magnets, the memos of other people's lives: "Josh dentist Tues 11.30," "Electrician Friday," "Max Berlin 5th–8th," "Sarah's b'day 15th." It induces a familiar wistfulness adrift between envy and repulsion.

Moreover, after a couple of months in England I cannot ignore the degree to which I have found myself so radically at odds with my native culture. It is only by dint of natural good manners that I hold myself in check when experiencing at close quarters the very horrors that first made me flee the country of my birth so many years ago. Jennifer has often urged me to join her on short daytime excursions, no doubt hoping to "take me out of myself." These outings are kindly meant; but it is in the nature of efforts to cheer people up that they simply spread moroseness and spleen on every side. Josh's kindergarten teacher, who should probably be prosecuted, has evidently brainwashed him into thinking that every home should have a bird table. Why a bird table? Well, apparently bird tables are just what the planet needs to offset something or other—maybe the wretched child's carbon footprint (Barf tonic, pronto! Brr! Non-fat octopi! Or come to that, the great headline Top Fart Icon Born! which, unlike news of carbon footprints, does at least grab the attention). So one morning we set off to buy a bird table at a garden centre a few miles away at Peasewold St. Phocas, a name not even P. G. Wodehouse could have bettered. A rustic notice at the entrance informed us that St. Phocas is the patron saint of gardeners, so we were effectively on sacred ground. We would have known this in any case since garden centres have become the new cathedrals of the secular age, combining as they do the worship of shopping with eco-rectitude. The great thing about Le Roccie (and how the tears spring to my eyes as I think of my lost paradise!) was that there was no garden. It was an eyrie on a mountainside. Who needed a *garden*? Nasty bourgeois things. Post-industrial attempts to buy into some long-dead version of English pastoral.

Between them, Jennifer and Josh chose an object on a pole that was the avian real-estate version of a roadhouse, more a bird motel than a table. It had walls and a pitched roof and was stuck all over with plywood cut-outs shaped like robins and thrushes, just in case these ideogram-literate birds were too dumb to recognise the food as intended for them. Josh remarked that if it was a proper house there ought to be a bird bathroom inside with a bird bath and also a bird loo where birds could poo. He and I lagged behind and had a short speculative conversation about whether birds ought to remove their feathers before having a bath, but the loud anatomical detail he went into attracted attention from other shoppers that he alone welcomed and I hurried to catch his mother as she wheeled her trolley back into the indoor acres devoted to

Green spin-offs where the garden centre's real biz seemed to be done. The place was jammed with products which only a giant leap of the imagination would remotely connect with gardens. As in an Italian cathedral there were candles for sale, but the candles of Peasewold St. Phocas came with scents and names, both calculated to give maximum offence to a person of sensibility: "Aromatherapy," "Harmony," "Seascape," "Warm Embrace" and—the gastric juices leaping up to splash one's uvula—"Beingness." There were also joss-sticks with similar names but even worse smells and, tangling from time to time in one's hair, the clappers of bingling-bongling, dingling-dangling wind chimes.

That day the Samper misanthropy was in full spate and bursting its banks. How detestable to be in a majority! The ideal I aim for is to cultivate an attitude of *impassioned detachment*. I was certainly feeling impassioned, so to achieve detachment I went to sit morosely in Jennifer's car rather than accompany her and Josh to the garden centre's tea room where Josh had been promised a reward for good behaviour. Some reward he was in for, I thought to myself. It was too easy to imagine the fifty varieties of herbal teas, all of them tasting of stewed twigs and fruit but just about the only things on the menu not containing rolled oats or molasses. I could already see the Bizarre Bakery Selection featuring rolls containing oats and lupin seeds, inferior species of wheat that sound Biblical and hence spiritually wholesome—spelt, emmer, wild einkorn, Khorasan—or else flapjacks made of oak galls and molasses ("Traditional Love-Offerings on pre-Christian Lesbos!"). I could foresee the horrid middle-classness of it all, the self-pleased obsession with physical health and spiritual harmony.

I admit I can't easily explain why a mere visit to a garden centre should have had such a curdling effect. It was just that the place seemed to combine a whole series of pet hates I never realised I had been nurturing until there they all were, one after another, somehow a part of my former self as a Briton back in the years before I took the cheerful, lightening step of becoming a renegade and a foreigner. In a mysterious manner Jennifer's memo board in Crendlesham Hall's kitchen seems like a palimpsest which, if I rub hard enough through the layers of her half-erased scribble, might reveal my own mother's identical scrawls to herself that were equally a part of my own childhood. "Floor pol." "Tea." "Order Cash's name tapes." "Pay Sanders Friday." So I stand alone in this kitchen, staring through the window, trying to resist being dragged back and suddenly dismal with a sense that it is all up with Samper, that the act of living has slipped out of my hands and into those of Adrian's in-laws.

And then one morning a phone call from my agent Frankie reminds me that I could have a pretty good life of my own somewhere out there well beyond the plovers. In these withdrawn periods of recuperation we artists forget how much we need these voices from over the horizon. (Had her moated grange been on the phone, Mariana need never have become so run down. At the very least she could have sent out for a pizza.)

Frankie brings me the news that although I may be minus a house, my latest book *Millie!* is selling prodigiously, and worldwide at that. It was always likely to sell well in the UK in the run-up to Christmas since its subject, the appalling one-armed yachtswoman Millie Cleat, was a heroine who had "sailed her way into the nation's hearts" (*Sun, Mirror, Daily Express, Daily Mail*, et al.). In the normal course of events sales would have dropped off quite a bit in the dead season following New Year. But her spectacular televised death in Sydney on Christmas Day had done both my spirits and my book an immense favour. I am now, Frankie assures me, on my way to becoming modestly well off, especially if the film deal currently being negotiated in Hollywood comes through.

Thus it is that one day I awake and *know* that Samper is

back to his old self. I open my eyes and an inner zippiness easily neutralises the grey Suffolk light seeping in from outside. Remember those derring-do novels that always compelled the reader to picture the reality of their flabby old authors? Their heroes, refreshed by ninety minutes' sleep after spending the night hanging by their fingertips from a windowsill to avoid SMERSH agents with poison-dart guns, bounce out of bed in their Mayfair bachelor apartments. To demonstrate their rugged hardihood, ease their bruises and melt the tension out of cramped muscles, they first shower with water as hot as they can stand and follow that with an ice-cold drench, "laughing at the stinging brunt of it." After which, luxuriating in a buzz of superb animal fitness, they do a hundred quick press-ups on their fingertips, tuck a towel around their brown whipcord torsos and go into the kitchen to make themselves a breakfast of six eggs, a pound of toast and several pints of Blue Mountain coffee. Well, it was never thus in the Samper household, I can tell you, and nor is it at Crendlesham Hall. Nobody laughs in the shower here except nervously, taken by surprise by one of young Josh's inventive montages involving a baby ichthyosaur peering quizzically out of a loofah. But on this particular morning I do leave the squash-court bed singing a sprightly aria from the opera the English pronounce as *Donkey Hoaty*.

As I shave, one of my all-time favourite quotations pops into my mind: "Feeling you're whole is deeply refreshing." Many years ago I overheard a Buddhist make this astonishingly frank confession on a BBC World Service programme called *Words of Faith* (broadcast on 31/8/95, if you'd care to check), and it has been with me ever since. I hadn't realised that Buddhists, too, indulged such furtive pleasures. It makes them seem quite like the rest of us. Anyway, today I discover I am myself deeply refreshed, yearning to be up and doing, full of energy. It is like being in my twenties again: a sense that there's nothing I can't do, nothing and no one to stop me. And suddenly—yes!—I'm glad not to be a householder with a life organised by fridge magnets. I am also happy that I no longer have to worry about a lump of property a thousand miles away. I am newly relieved of the burden of a lifetime's accumulated possessions. In short a novel, simplified Samper begins here. Above all, a Samper determined never to write another book for a sports hero. But where to go? What to do?

And bang on cue, another call from Frankie. He is a three-packs-a-day man with a Low Tar voice to match, and this morning he is so gravelly and super-laconic with dramatic news I have to ask him to repeat himself.

"I said 'one and a half million,' Gerry. The film rights for *Millie!* Proper pounds, that is, not wincy little dollars."

"Good God." I lean weakly against the Aga, which sends a comforting glow through my areas of contact. Then, getting to the point, "What's my cut?"

"If you remember, we agreed the splits with Millie's agent when we did the book deal. All quite regular. We've got a twenty per cent share of the sale of film, TV and allied rights in the Cleat life story as told by you. So your take is, um, three hundred thousand, minus this agency's fifteen per cent plus VAT. *Haaargh haaargh*" (hideous coughs shake his phlegm-clogged alveoli and I superstitiously hold the receiver a little away as though a spray of pulmonary flecks might spatter my ear) "*wuuurgh* call it a shade under a quarter of a million."

"For me personally? Golly. And right on the day when I'm feeling at my most irresponsible."

"Oh, we're all agreed in the office that it couldn't have happened to a less responsible person, Gerry. Congratulations. But before you go out and do something to merit arrest, I'm afraid you have to make some decisions."

"Make them for me, Frankie. You're my agent," I say, suddenly distracted by a strong smell of singeing. I discover that the back hem of my natty and elegant jacket has been overlapping the only one of the range's hobs not to have its lid down. Damn. I douse it with the kettle. Never mind, it's only Armani. Cooking couture.

"I can't," Frankie is saying, and again coughs as though trying to uproot his bronchial tree. "Only you can, Gerry. It's you to decide if you also want to write the screenplay."

"Are you serious? Of course I don't. Not in a million years."

"More dosh, mind you." Frankie does not like to see money slipping away from his ochre-stained fingertips.

"I don't need more dosh. Look, Frankie, if you remember I swore to have nothing further to do with that ocean-going old poseuse, and I'm sticking to it. I think we should take the money and run."

"Fine, if that's what you want." Nevertheless he sounds wistful. "Still, my antennae are telling me there's yet more money to be made out of Millie Cleat. There was quite a feeding frenzy towards the end of the film rights bidding, you know. All the big studios were biting. An international sports personality whose dramatic life was followed by a super-dramatic death live on worldwide TV? And, of course, the news that she was going to be Damed in the New Year's honours list but had to be scratched at the last minute because they don't award civil honours posthumously. Can't go far wrong with all that as a story. But have it your own way. *Hucka. Hucka. Harraargh.* Now to another matter. There's still one more book to do for Champions, according to our contract."

"Oh, convert it to a two-book deal or something. Or buy it up, I don't care. Because today is the day I sever for ever any connection with the world of sport. That's it, Frankie. Samper has spoken. I have ghosted my final biography. I have made my very last effort to extract an intelligible thought from creatures festooned with Nike swooshes. The full beauty of this hasn't yet sunk in, but when it does I shall indulge in epic celebration."

This first day of the rest of my life (as we born-again athe-

ists say) has begun so brilliantly I simply have to tell somebody.
Unfortunately Max is in a recording studio in London today,
while Jennifer and Josh are doing mother-and-child things in
Colchester. For some reason the person in whose face I find I
really want to wave my quarter-million windfall is Marta, and I
actually start looking up her number before deciding she might
think it vain of me or identify it quite correctly as vulgar gloat-
ing. In any case, someone whose gangster father has secreted
heaps of money for her in numbered accounts around the
world isn't going to be overly impressed by a mere quarter of
a million pounds. You have only to look at her to realise she's
oblivious to the stuff. If you have oodles of the readies you only
dress like a bag lady and live in a mildew hatchery if you're a
Voynovian composer in your forties.

Not for the first time I reflect on what a peculiar person she
is, and yet again speculate about her erotic life. I once enter-
tained the fantasy that under cover of darkness a simple but
husky woodman's son would occasionally emerge from the forest like a soiled faun to park his axe by her back door and, omit-
ting to remove his boots, leave her bed covered in twigs, leaves
and seed. But then she began keeping the company of a glam-
orous Italian film director's son who was admittedly worth
more than a second glance, and I began to think it wasn't rough
trade she was after. However, Filippo eventually took me for a
spin in the Pacini family's helicopter and I noticed him giving
my exquisitely cut Homo Erectus jeans a knowledgeable once-
over, as well he might. After that it became impossible to imagine him fancying a middle-aged woman with the dress sense of
a moose. To say nothing of the physique. Meanwhile, Marta's
erotic leanings remain as opaque as ever. I suppose we must
assume she takes the odd lover prophylactically, much as people put studs in their earlobes to keep the holes from closing.

So instead of Marta I call dear Adrian in his laboratory at
BOIS. He is satisfactorily bowled over.

"That's terrific," he says when he has recovered from the shock. "I'll just trot along to the Director's office and hand in my resignation. The ocean will just have to get along without me as best it can. I've always wanted to be kept."

"I'm not keeping you, you mercenary old poof," I tell him sternly. "The very idea. Anyway, I shall need the money myself. I'm planning great things. But I shan't mind lashing out and buying you a new set of oilskins."

"Huh, I shall expect bespoke ones, you know. None of your off-the-peg rubbish. We're talking Savile Row oilskins here . . . Heavens, Gerry, what a lot of money. I won't say 'it couldn't have happened to a nicer person' because it might have happened to me."

"No it mightn't. Who's going to pay one and a half million quid for the film rights of *your* book? Just tell me that." It is true, Adrian does actually have a book to his name: an expanded version of his doctoral thesis called *Trophic Interactions among Post-Spring Estuarine Communities of* Pseudodiaptomus hessei *Copepods*. This is not what the book trade calls a selling title, so it's small wonder that if you ask for it in Waterstones they look at you waggishly and say without even consulting their computers, "Oh, I believe we've just sold our last copy of that. We'll have to re-order for you."

"You just don't realise how full of high drama and low cunning the life of a copepod is, Gerry. Brutal and disgusting, too. Show it on the big screen and you'd have people stampeding for the exits."

"Yes, to get their money back from the box office. And now I think your nephew and sister have just come in. Do you want a word with Jen?" I hand him over to her with an aside as she stands there shedding scarf and gloves. "Your brother."

For the next few days I go about cocooned in a warm feeling that an immense problem in my life has been solved. Had I been back in Italy I have no doubt I should have broken into song and invented an expressive dish that would take its place in the annals of celebratory cuisine. But being in this great house with such kindly people leaves me unaccustomedly inhibited. If you share living space with one of the world's greatest conductors you don't spontaneously break into song. This is a man who is on first-name terms with the two tenors. Nor do you artlessly commandeer your hostess's Aga for culinary experiments unless she asks, particularly when she has a dinner party of grandees slated for this coming weekend. I have now been on my best behaviour for the past nine weeks and the strain is killing me, but I shall have to keep it up for a little while yet.

Until two or three months ago I would have allowed a blacksmith to extract my eye teeth with a chisel in exchange for the chance to shine at one of Max Christ's dinner parties. After years of exile in the intellectual wastelands where sports personalities and celebrities dwell I felt like Ovid, banished by Emperor Augustus in AD 8 to what is now Constanţa on the Black Sea, separated from his beloved Rome by a thousand miles of howling barbarian tribes. That my biographees ate muck planned for them by private dieticians rather than real food was their own business. That they drank electrolyte sports drinks instead of decent wine was their loss. But that they knew nothing about anything interesting had me yearning for the company of people who had read, and looked, and listened, and thought, and lived. Naturally this was not snobbery on my part, merely the innate discrimination that draws all species to the company of their kind. Breeding will out, which is why arranged marriages often work so well while those of the ill-bred fall apart. As I say, time was when I longed—and very recently, too—for the society of like minds. But lately even this has become a casualty of a new-found impatience. Despite this, I find I still have pathetically lingering hopes that this imminent dinner party won't disappoint with mere farty glitterati. Max tells me ominously that he is inviting a surprise guest for me so, Samper, *good grace*. Thankfully, Adrian has promised to come up from Southampton. And yes, of course everybody at the table will dutifully rejoice over my piece of good fortune when it is inevitably mentioned. But the truth is these people already have money and simply take it as read that everyone else they know has, too.

So it's really not such a big deal for them that this mysterious, cultured and amusing friend of Adrian's has suddenly come into a bit of cash. How could it be? *They* never had to spend months trying to extract usable biographical data from harridans like Millie Cleat for a living. *They* were never invited to shower with Luc Bailly, the legendary downhill skier, as the price of an interview. This came about ostensibly because it was the only spare time he had. In reality he wanted me to observe for myself what had made him legendary. For Luc had the Lyndon Johnson syndrome. The late American president would sometimes shame visiting male dignitaries into swimming naked with him in his Texan pool in the sure knowledge that faced with his monstrous appendage they would be reduced to shrivelled inferiority. It was a bad error to try the same trick on Samper. Bailly had never had to learn the defensive—and offensive—shower techniques that come naturally to someone who has been to a decent English public school. From the moment we undressed I relentlessly grilled him about his relations with his mother, and it was he who shrivelled at the stinging brunt of it as the water hammered down and the steam billowed up. He soon turned his back and mumbled evasively into the suds. After that he was as good as gold.

The point is that these delightful denizens of the East Anglian arts set have no idea of the awful things I have had to do these last twenty years simply to earn a crust, and what they will inwardly dismiss as just a handy bit of extra cash is in fact my exit visa out of the land of servitude.

The inner excitement provoked by my sudden change in fortune fills me with energy that demands to be dissipated. Since I need to plan my future and have always found walking a great aid to thought, I set off from Crendlesham Hall in an arbitrary direction. Ever since my first visit here, when efforts were made to bamboozle me with obscure Suffolk place names, I have been chary of asking the way. But I have an uncanny sense of direction, as well as the foresight to keep the wonky spire of Crendleburgh church at my back. Pevsner or somebody rated its rood screen; I value its landmark qualities. I passed it the other day: a great pale barn of a place with a notice inside the lychgate posted by the incumbent, the Rev. Daphne Pitt-Bull. She was informing her parishioners that "Pilates is at 10 A.M. on Wednesdays." Obviously the good though ungrammatical Daphne must be planning a Passiontide play and is auditioning for the role of Pontius, a personal hero of mine. I'm amazed they've still heard of him in these illiterate, happy-clappy times. It's cheering for an exile to return to his native land and find that not everything has gone to rack and ruin.

But never mind East Anglicanism; I have my own future to think about. I hop over a stile and set off across a field. As I was adding the final, highly artistic, untruths to my portrait of Millie Cleat I had two other possible assignments lined up. One was to write a biography of my glittering host, Max Christ. When I broached this idea with him he promised to give it his earnest consideration, but that was months ago and he is probably hoping I will have forgotten. Really, he is too distinguished to care about such things, and anyway, at forty-seven he's still too young for anything as retrospective as a life. In fact, Christ is the polar opposite of the sports heroes I've been writing about, who tend to become geriatric at thirty and whose "stories" have to be told before they're old enough to have done any real living. I have always thought it would be far more revealing to write these people's lives when they are sixty or so. I suspect very few would avoid a sorry saga of decline. Sometimes they linger on as commentators or run a chain of sports shops, and sometimes they invest in one of those night clubs where fights break out at night and guests are rushed to A&E with uncomfortably lodged snooker balls. But for most of them it's a long twilight of drink and flab and self-pity, which makes me feel that there may, after all, be some justice in this uncaring universe.

My other project was something I have already made a small start on. This is the biography I mentioned earlier of Nanty Riah, aka Brill, the leader of Alien Pie. Doubtless you will remember how his buttocks were riddled with bullets during an art theft from his private jet—it was top of the world's news stories for at least a week. I've grown quite fond of old Nanty, largely because there's no side to him—other than, of course, his backside with its little perforations that so dominates his conversation. Unlike most pop stars he's under few illusions about his social and artistic value, as opposed to his financial worth which is indeed immense. There's something touching about his Harpenden background, his total alopecia, his devotion to his retarded sister and his sporadic faithfulness to his wife. However, as I tramp along one of the few Suffolk hedgerows that hasn't yet been grubbed up by agrivandals I don't feel any great enthusiasm for ghosting Nanty's story. My finances have improved too dramatically. He can wait, I say to myself; and this liberating thought is enough to break the spell of silence that living with Adrian's in-laws has forced upon me, for I am by nature a singer.

I don't know whether you're familiar with Richard Strauss's comic operetta *Wienerparodien*? It was a little essay in nostalgia he wrote while waiting for Hitler and his SS to blow over and has some terrific stuff for a Heldentenor in the Richard Tauber mould—exactly, as it happens, in the Samper mould too. The dashing but irascible captain of horse, Fechter (a demon with the sabre and whimsically known to his comrades as the Knight of the Long Knives), is about to marry Ernestine, Count Schütterbart's daughter. On the night before the wedding the Count takes his future son-in-law aside with some well-meant but inept advice couched in an aria that generally brings the house down (*"Nach Anbruch gut verschließen! Trocken and kühl lagern!"*). Fechter takes offence and is on the verge of challenging this repulsive old man to a duel. Instead he contains himself with a struggle and makes a bitter riposte with an aria that generally brings the house to its feet. It is a virtuoso tirade. *"Bei sachgerechter Lagerung,"* he begins sarcastically, *"mindestens haltbar bis wann? Wann?"* before hitting his triumphant top C on *"Siehe Prägung!"* Then, their honour restored, the two sit down to a platter of Viennese cream cakes while the orchestra plays a *Rosenkavalier*-ish waltz.

Such is my vocal verve that I notice plovers three fields away taking hurriedly to the air with black-and-white wingbeats. Good: Samper is definitely back on form, even though unwillingly back in the land of his birth. However, amid this tense musical concentration I seem momentarily to have lost my bearings. I look in vain for Crendleburgh church on its low hill— not that there are any other kinds of hill hereabouts. Nothing but a horizon of wintry stalks with some moth-eaten woods nearby. I have an impression of telephone poles beyond a distant hedgerow disappearing behind the wood, which suggests a road. Also, between the trees a vague patch of pale something that might just be a house but will probably turn out to be a swag of old man's beard. Anyway, there's nothing else to aim for so I head towards it, taking a short cut through the woods.

These turn out to be much less moth-eaten than at first glance. They are, in fact, a dense jungle of mouldy willows and ground elder and dead trees held upright by straitjackets of ivy. I lean against one to scrape the mud off my boots and with an awesome groan it topples slowly and crashes to the ground. The place is a death trap. Suddenly a crotchety, fluting voice addresses me out of the jungle.

"You, there! What the hell do you think you're playing at?"

I peer into the tangle of branches and brambles. It is like one of those pictures in children's magazines in which you're told there are five lions hidden and can you spot them?

"Do you realise what you've done?"

Now I see him: a tall, gaunt old geezer wearing what looks like an ancient army battledress jacket and corduroy trousers of an excremental colour, balding about the knees. His hands, I notice, are huge: all veins and knuckles. One of them holds a pair of secateurs. He is fixing me with a glare from washed-out ceramic blue eyes half hidden like a terrier's behind wild white eyebrows.

"I'm afraid I've lost my way," I say in a pacific tone.

"Pity it wasn't your voice. I assume it was you making that infernal row just now? Sounded like pigs being castrated." He bends stiffly to examine the tree I have knocked over. His clothing hints at the skeleton beneath. "I hope you know this marvellous plant you have just vandalised was the last of its kind in Britain? Probably in Western Europe."

"What do you mean, vandalised? The thing fell down. It's dead."

"Nothing of the kind. Allow me to know my own garden. This noble plant is a unique tree with historic connections. It was brought here by T. E. Lawrence as a sapling in 1912. He was excavating at Carchemish at the time, and the shoot was presented to him by the Emir of Aleppo, who had taken a fancy to him. They were both buggers, of course. This"—the old man indicates the corpse with his secateurs—"is *Commiphora byzantina*, related to the myrrh tree. It flourished here for nearly a century despite its Mesopotamian origin, itself a miracle, and it bloomed beautifully each year. And now look at it."

"Obviously we're none of us immortal," I offer by way of appeasement. "I'm sorry, but that tree is defunct. You can't push a live tree over just by leaning against it."

The old man snicks at it with his secateurs and holds up a sprig. "What's that, might I ask? Green, wouldn't you say?"

I am beginning to get impatient with this old bore. "I'm sorry," I apologise again for what I vow is the last time, "but I had no idea this was a garden. You must be a member of Jardins Sans Frontières."

"Never heard of 'em."

"It's a horticultural society dedicated to abolishing fences."

"Don't believe a word of it. You must be blind, anyway." The glare intensifies and a khaki-clad arm sweeps the air. "What do you think that is? *Euphragia monocotylens*. *Aspergilla tradescantii* there. *Dendrofolium physoloides* over there. And look there—Vanessa Bell planted that *Forsythia brucei* with her own hands in 1937. "No idea this was a garden," indeed. Full of rare plants. And very shortly Lytton Strachey's hollyhocks will be coming up exactly where you're standing."

I take a nervous sideways step with an apologetic glance at my feet. All I can see are nettles and ground elder.

"Not there!" comes the squeaky bellow. "You're right on top of the hypericums! Duncan Grant used to paint them. He would come up from Sussex each year. He was living with Vanessa by then although of course he was a bugger, like Maynard. Are you a bugger?"

"I really . . ."

"Thought so. Can always tell. But you're obviously no gardener."

"Tell me how to get to Crendlesham Hall and I'll get out of your garden."

"Crendlesham? Crendlesham? That where that musical johnny lives? The conductor chappie?"

"Max Christ, yes. I'm a guest of his."

"Are you just? I suppose he's a bugger too. They mostly are. Like that Britten fellow. We once gave him an entire flowering branch of that *Commiphora* you've just murdered. Wanted it for one of his operas over at Snape. Never so much as a thank-you, of course. They're like cats, you know. All over you until they get what they want, then just walk away."

"If you point me in the right direction I'll do the same."

A ragged bony arm extends the secateurs. He looks like an illustration by Mervyn Peake. "Down there. Hundred yards, there's the road. Exactly where you'd expect it to be. Turn right. Go on past the crinkle-crankle wall to the junction. Turn right again. Signposted. Only a couple of miles. I doubt even you could miss it. And mind my lizard orchids on the way out, they're very rare in Bri— No! To your left! To your *left*, dammit!"

Eventually the petulant hectorings die away behind me. God, what a place. I'm lost here. This is no longer my country and even to recall that it's the land of my birth makes it feel like a concession to me that they still speak English and drive on the left. Get out while you can, Samper. Italy was never like this. Strange to think Ovid might have gone home after Augustus's death and found that in his long absence Rome had become horrid and incomprehensible. He did well to die in exile; there's nothing so disillusioning as returning to one's native land. Crinkle-crankle, indeed. But I soon come upon a brick wall that waves in and out with sinuous curves and assume this is it. And the old sod's instructions do prove accurate and soon I can see Crendleburgh church in the distance. But out of nowhere it suddenly comes to me, whether via Richard Strauss or this ludicrous encounter: what I'd *really* like to do is write an opera, commission the music and have it performed. Why have I never given this serious thought? It would so perfectly match my talents. Opera was my first love, of course, but the trouble with first loves is that one needs to pluck up too much courage to do anything more than gaze at them from afar. Still, money does wonders for self-confidence and I really think (already singing as I walk along) this is something I simply have to do.

By now I'm well into the celebrated Buggers' Chorus from Act 1: "Balls to his hollyhocks! / Uproot his hydrangeas! / Teach him some manners / To perfect strangers!" Somewhere in my mind's eye the curtain comes down to a storm of applause, while on the road to Crendlesham the startled pee-wits flap restlessly on all sides. It's wonderful what a good solid sum of money will do for the spirits. But foolishly, and for quite some time, I forget a cardinal item of hard-won Samper wisdom. It is *never* safe to heave a sigh of relief.

Adrian 1

email from Dr. Adrian Jestico (ajestico@bois.ac.uk)
to Dr. Penny Barbisant (penbar@labs.whoi.ed)

O K, it's not easy to spot a sick marine bivalve. But have you looked for mitotic suppression and/or nuclear poly-ploidization? I'm assuming you were asleep in my kary-ology lectures. Think chromosome set changes. You'll find that tabulating percentage changes will give you some figures for the sub-lethal effects of pollution.

You asked about Gerry. He is indeed the same Samper who wrote about the awful Millie Cleat ("As told to"). More, you'll be surprised to learn that he and I are something of an item. At least, I think we are. Nothing's ever quite that straightforward with Gerry. I'll certainly tell him you found his book a laff-riot: he'll be dead chuffed, on the grounds that anyone who found it *that* funny will have seen what he was getting at. Almost everybody else has taken it as a kind of sporting holy writ. They've been especially po-faced about the boating heroine since the Sydney harbour episode. Not since the Blessed Diana was wafted to Heaven by teams of bungling French surgeons have such croc-odile tears been shed. You were still at Southampton when Mil-lie screwed up the EAGIS survey, weren't you? (time moves so fast). Don't worry—sooner or later it'll all come out.

As for Gerry, he's just told me they've sold the film rights to the book for 1.5 million, so he's quids in, lucky sod. But in a funny way I'm not sure how much difference it'll make to him underneath. I told you he'd lost his Italian house? It hit him harder than he'll admit, for all his tragic act, and he doesn't know what he'll do next. He really needs something extravagant for him to get his teeth into. I've not known him for that long but he's obviously one of those people who need work, a project, a proper intelligent occupation. These Cleat-style biographies of his definitely haven't filled that need, even though he's been amazingly successful with them. Poor Gerry! For all his high jinks and sheer amusement value he can be surprisingly bleak at times. He has the habit of singing rather loud operatic arias in falsetto when he thinks he's by himself. Personally, I'm not sure it's possible to howl like that without imagining an audience, even just one of inner ghosts. I once asked him whether he thought stranded people, loners, rebels, might sing in the hope of being overheard and rescued? He gave a pure Gerry reply. "Robinson Caruso, that's me," he said. Exasperating though he often is, one can't help being drawn to him. Who else at the age of fifty would embark on a course of penile enhancement that he didn't need & may temporarily have screwed up his endocrine system? He always claims he did it purely in a spirit of scientific enquiry, which you & I would think a likely tale, but with Gerry it really is possible. Awful thing to say about your supposed partner but in some respects he's like a child. He really needs someone to save him from his delusions. If he had somebody living with him who could laugh at him from time to time there's a chance some of his wackier notions might be curbed.

How are things at Woods Hole? You must be well settled in by now. I do envy you—you're on hallowed oceanographer's ground in Cape Cod. Apart from the presiding ghost of Spencer Fullerton Baird you've got that exotic mix of stolid British-sounding places (Falmouth, Barnstaple, Yarmouth, Sandwich) cheek by jowl with those mysterious and beautiful Algonquin names like Sippewissett, Teaticket and Mashpee. I'm always struck in the US by how poetic such Indian words sound to us

(Parsippany, Shenandoah) even though they usually turn out to mean the same as place names anywhere and most were anyway mis-transliterated by immigrants. Well, I hope you're enjoying New England as much as I did. I loved my time at WHOI, as you know, and I'm already looking forward to my next visit. And what of Luke and your own domestic setup? I trust there's more to your life than sick bivalves? Remember me to Peter Millikan.

Cheers,
Adrian

PS: Are you doing b-radioactivity counts on the shells? You should be.

2.

The kitchen presents a scene of peaceful normality, though hardly of the kind that once reigned in my sweet Tuscan farmhouse, despite the heady regressive scent of baking. Jennifer is stirring something on the Aga. Luna the cat is asleep on a tea towel on the work surface next to it, her tail draped across a block of butter on a plate. Josh is sitting on the kitchen table in his underwear, licking the remains of chocolate-flavoured cake mixture out of a bowl. I notice his pants are on back to front, as so often. It's sheer luck whether the little pest puts them on the right way round, as with his shoes: a reminder that it will be years yet before he becomes fully human. At the moment he's really just a collection of more or less noisome valves, though at times he can be quite ornamental.

With her back to me his mother says, "Max still raves about your birthday dinner, you know. He thinks that badger Wellington was superb. I'd have had you do it for this dinner, only we couldn't guarantee to find you a badger in time."

"Alas. But there's also the gun-dog pâté, don't forget. That's an essential filling. I suppose in default of Italian-style hunting accidents I could hang around the local vet's back door and make a quick offer for the bulging bin liner even as the wailing owners retreat to their Volvo out front, leaning against one another for support. All the same, I'm none too smitten by the idea of meat containing a lethal dose of anaesthetic."

"But you are doing us an inventive hors d'oeuvre instead?"

"It's all in hand," I tell her loftily. "You specified something a little out of the ordinary and I'm working on it."

"I was quite hoping it mightn't involve that plastic pot in the pantry fridge with things in gore."

"Very delicious, that will be. You lack faith in the Samper artistry. I'll say no more."

"Promise me it has nothing to do with bats, Gerry," Jennifer-the-hostess says anxiously, turning around.

"Certainly I promise."

"Eeeuwghh, *bats*?" Josh looks up with gleeful horror, chocolate cake-mix glistening in his hair. Blondes really can't afford to be careless in their eating habits.

"Just carry on," I tell him. "When you've finished with the bowl there will still be plenty left on your face. I promise: no bats. But I did wonder for a moment whether an authentic hedgerow broth mightn't be made by gently seething some owl pellets. Do you think? Obviously one would need to strain out the fur and the voles' teeth; but if the Chinese can make soup out of birds' nests held together by avian phlegm, I see no reason why owl pellets mightn't yield an equally interesting stock. I rather fancy chanterelles and a smidgin of fresh ginger would set it off admirably."

"But pellet soup's not on tomorrow's menu?"

"I'm afraid not. One more thing that required notice. But I had a good morning's shopping in Woodbridge earlier."

"Finished!" announces Josh, banging the bowl on the table. Luna stretches and her hind paw gets enough purchase on the butter to push the plate away, leaving a deep footprint.

"I want to know who's coming," I say, "but Max won't tell me."

"Oh, you know him, Gerry. He's just a tease. There's the odd local we owe hospitality to, and a player from Colchester Symphony Orchestra. We'll only be eight. I'm going to do a plain ordinary roast and to hell with it. We look to your starter to add the exotic touch. Josh and I will be off to the butcher to collect the meat tomorrow morning so you'll have the kitchen to yourself."

So next morning, having ruthlessly ejected the cat, I lay out a small but highly select variety of things in plastic pots, ready for their translation into something rich and strange, like somebody's father in that play I did for O-level. Over the years I have, of course, amassed a great number of inventions for teasing the palate, not a few of them themed. (My Men of Violence suite of starters includes Pol Pot Noodles, Somozas, Shin Fein—a divine junior cousin to *ossobuco*—Papa Duck, Kim Jong Eel and my celebrated Mobster Thermidor.) But today I shall stick to a mere three or four little appetisers, one of which was suggested by that wonderful book, *Emergency Cuisine* by Dame Emmeline Tyrwhitt-Glamis. If one needed a glowing example of staunch British gallantry in the war years this little gem of a book would supply it, so practical in the face of adversity and so sunny and uplifting in tone. Winston Churchill's speeches undoubtedly stiffened the sinews and summoned up the blood of his people as they crouched around their sunburst-fretworked wireless sets; but Dame Emmeline would have taken both sinews and blood from novel sources and made of them novel sauces to fill their bellies with fire. The loss of her book in the recent collapse of my house, together with that equally irreplaceable volume, Maj.Gen. Sir Aubrey Lutterworth's *Elements of Raj Cookery*, is a blow that may yet prove serious enough to make me send in the bulldozers after all to see if they have survived.

What *Emergency Cuisine* reminded me was how good field mice can be. Indeed, in the nineteenth century they received a famous accolade from Frank Buckland, who used to supplement his meagre public school diet with such delicacies. "A toasted field mouse, not a house mouse, makes a perfect bonne-bouche for a hungry boy. It eats like a lark." So for some days I set traps in the extensive stables and outhouses that surround the Hall, and these yielded ten—no, eleven on a recount—plump specimens which I kept secretly in a foil-covered pot in the little fridge in the pantry where Jennifer seldom goes. The worst job was skinning and boning them: there's nothing more fiddly. For discretion's sake I did it in my bathroom up in the attic. Even so, Luna must have caught the enticing scent because she came miaowing at the door. The skins and entrails had to go down the lavatory. The result of my labours was what Jennifer had disparaged as the "things in gore" in the fridge. It's true that, when thoroughly unzipped, eleven field mice yield not much meat at all; but if there are only the eight of us that's nearly a mouse-and-a-half apiece. The question is, which way to do them? One can cook the meat very gently with a little butter for a bare minute or two, add the merest dribble of mouse broth and use this delicate hash as a vol-au-vent filling. On the other hand you can cream the meat with a pestle and mortar, ideally with a little goose fat and a teaspoon of the best Armagnac you can find, set out the mixture in blobs on a baking sheet and grill them quickly. These are Samper's justly renowned Mice Krispies; and as a way of teasing the palates of visiting gourmets they are unsurpassed. They somehow manage to give off an aura of warm haylofts and hazelnuts nibbled amid stubble beneath great yellow harvest moons. For the present occasion, though, I incline towards the vol-au-vent solution which it now occurs to me could easily become vole-au-vent with a slight change of its rodent filling.

So that's settled. I put the tiny giblets and skeletons (how touchingly frail they are!) on to boil in a bare cup of water with a quarter of the smallest shallot I can find and a single juniper berry, and turn to the tender Cumbrian lamb I had the butcher mince up fine for me in Woodbridge yesterday. This, too, can go into puff pastry cases, enriched with tiny quantities of chocolate, à la rabbit in chocolate that the Mexicans do so well. Into the mixture go four drops of Fernet-Menta, the Branca Brothers' bid to attract to their exquisite original product a wider public than hollow-eyed topers. A little finely chopped basil and fresh mint will add green top notes, and my betting is that Samper's After Eight Mince will not soon be forgotten. Of course, both these little *amuse-gueules* are savoury. Ideally, I would like an additional dish of sweet beetles for my diners to crunch on—probably the candy-bug *Scarabaeus gastromellifer* that Guatemalan Indians give their boys as a reward for not crying during circumcision, an operation performed by the village shaman using his or her teeth. These yellow-spotted delicacies have the additional advantage (for a dinner party, that is) of being mildly aphrodisiac. But in default of such exotica in Suffolk I think I shall accompany my groundbreaking hors d'oeuvres with my patented liver smoothie (served with a slice of lime, a sprig of basil and a sprinkling of hundreds-and-thousands as a final touch of festive playfulness). It really is just too banal to serve nothing but unrelieved savouries before a main course. Finally—and all those years in Tuscany have clearly left their wholesome mark—some *bruschette* spread with my inventive haddock marmalade, which isn't sweet but is wonderfully confected with sour cream, a pinch of cinnamon and cooked lime peel, carefully de-pithed to avoid bitterness.

Adrian, bless him, turns up for a conventional bread-and-cheese lunch. I am itching to consult him about my grand operatic plan but first he has to play dutiful uncle to Josh. He has brought his nephew a junior microscope which he sets up on the kitchen table. They look at several prepared slides of the sort of unsavoury little creatures one swallows without noticing while swimming. Then he and Josh go outside with a jam jar to sample ditchwater or a puddle and for the next half hour they peer at daphnia and paramecia and amoebae swimming about.

Cries of delight from Josh, who is especially pleased to watch them slow down, dry out and die beneath their cover slips in the heat of the lamp. Then they examine one of Luna's hairs. I am astonished to see Josh, whose attention span is normally that of a grasshopper, diverted for so long without the least sign of boredom. Is this perhaps the eureka moment when we realise we have another Richard Feynman in the making? It would obviously please his scientist uncle but it would probably please his musician father even more, Max having once confessed he wished he'd been a palaeobiologist instead of a conductor. Maybe at the age of six Richard Feynman, too, wore his underpants back to front out of sheer other-worldly brilliance.

Later, while changing for dinner, I tell Adrian about my operatic plans. However, my sketching out a grand future is halted by having to decide what to wear in order to wow these Suffolk grandees. I can't wear my Blaise Prévert suit in chocolate corduroy: it had its first outing right here at Crendlesham Hall some months ago and is for ever associated with an unfortunate social gaffe I inadvertently made in the course of the evening. I also wore the same adorable suit a little later for a crucial dinner aboard an Australian billionaire's yacht and that occasion, too, brings back discomforting memories. The upshot is that this masterly creation of Blaise Prévert's is, through no fault of mine or his, unhappily tainted. My mohair and denim slacks by His Majesty would have done admirably, but fate arranged for me to be wearing them at my last birthday party. The result was that not only did they spend part of that night on a bare mountain and the rest in Marta's sopping slum, but they were all I had left to wear for the next several days. When eventually I retrieved them from the dry cleaner in Woodbridge I realised they were beyond saving. The mud and scuffing of that traumatic night had ruined them. It begins to seem as though anything decent I buy to wear is sooner or later doomed to bring humiliation, ruin and despair upon their blameless owner. But since taking up with Adrian I have had optimism thrust upon me, and it takes more than reverses of fortune to turn a Samper into a sloven. I went to London and did some necessary shopping. Given that practically my entire worldly wardrobe was lying beneath tons of rock and earth on a mountainside high above Viareggio, it seemed a pretty good excuse for doing the January sales.

I now break out a creamy linen and merino suit by Erminio Zaccarelli so drop-dead gorgeous that even if tonight's assorted bumpkins affect to be unimpressed by my financial windfall they will at least be obliged to fall properly silent before such sartorial poetry. Adrian has been wittering on in the background about the sort of opera libretto I might write when he breaks off suddenly.

"Good God, Gerry, are you going to wear that suit?"

"I am. It's rather a masterpiece," I say a little stiffly.

"I can see that. All I meant is that it'll be like putting on tails to do the gardening. You wait till you meet the guests. Have you never seen orchestral players when they're not in black ties in the pit? Think Oxfam. Or better, Millets."

"Well, I can't help that. It's the job of a peacock to make ordinary fowls look dowdy, and all the more so if the peacock has just sold its film rights for a quarter of a million quid. It's very salutary for the rest of the barnyard. It pushes the bar higher even as it lowers their spirits. Anyway, what was it you were saying?"

"About your opera? Just that I think your talents are perfect for farce, Gerry. Try this. Two newlyweds go abroad for their honeymoon. Their plane is hijacked and they're held captive by the modern equivalent of Barbary pirates in one of those pretend countries like Mauritania. A sort of *Il Seraglio* parody but full of topical zingers. Their captors are extremely radical. In fact—yes—they're the militant gay wing of Al Qaida, *that's* how radical. They're demanding th—"

"No, Adrian. That's not at all the sort of thing I have in mind. I'm aiming for the grand and the serious, not a satirical musical." I zip up my gorgeous new trousers decisively.

"It can be called *Has Anyone Interfered With Your Bag?*"

"No it can't. I admit that's a great title but no, Adrian. My ideas are running more along the lines of something lofty and sad. I'm toying with the *Epic of Gilgamesh.*"

"What's that?"

"*What's that?* Honestly, you scientists. Where have—"

But at this moment there's a hooting from the drive down below. We go to the window and glinting in the porch light is the roof of a taxi. Standing next to it is a mountainous man in furs, one arm thrust through the driver's window. When he turns to go into the house the light from the open front door falls on his face, revealing him to be wearing a full gorilla suit. When eventually I fly downstairs to make sure my hors d'oeuvres will be in readiness—it being elementary etiquette that one does not keep gorillas waiting for their food—the creature is sitting at the kitchen table with a gin and tonic in his furry fist, chatting with Max. Josh is in his dinosaur pyjamas by the Aga, his arms entwined in its chrome rail for safety, one pink foot standing on the other, nervously entranced. Max introduces me to the man in the ape suit, who is a clarinettist with the Colchester Symphony Orchestra that Max has so brilliantly built up to be one of the world's best by luring just such instrumentalists away from the Berlin Phil. and elsewhere. When you're in the market for the best available talent it doesn't pay to be overly fussy if it turns out eccentric.

"Nice suit," the gorilla says to me, raising his glass. His mouth looks obscenely wet, like that of a bearded man.

"Thanks. Ditto." One tries to be civil to these wind players.

"I was telling Max that I've just been molested by my taxi driver. He wanted to feel my perineum."

"Ah. If he was a Pakistani it was the same fellow who drove

me out here last year. He suggested we stop and explore the local scenery, which he pretended to know intimately."

"Khurshid," says Jennifer from the stove. "So he should. He was born in Suffolk, which I imagine is more than any of us in this room can claim. His parents were from east Pakistan as was, which I suppose makes him a Bangladeshi by descent. But he's entirely East Anglian. I know all this from the local paper. He did six months in Colchester for feeling men's bottoms, or similar. But he's a good reliable driver, for all that he's a fantasist about the landscape hereabouts. He told Gerry that a low hill on the way here is known as "the Crendle" and was where they used to execute horse thieves. Something like that, wasn't it?"

"Exactly that," I say. "Whereas when I arrived you told me the Crendle was a stone monument that figures in one of Constable's paintings."

The gorilla empties his glass. "According to him just now, the hill is named after an Anglo-Saxon monster who lives underneath it in a huge cave, sleeping until the sea rises to wake him, which this driver seems to think will be soon, what with global warming."

"East Anglia must be the sort of landscape that begs you to invent stories about it in order to give it some interest."

"Mummy," interrupts Josh, who is tying himself in embarrassment-displacing knots while hanging from the Aga's rail, "why does this man feel men's bottoms?"

"*What* a good question," I breathe, with all the insouciance of one not obliged to answer.

But at this moment there's more banging on the front door and Jennifer hustles her son off to bed. His question floats with piercing clarity on the air behind him like a waft of Chanel Number Five or some other equally identifiable scent. Max takes the ape off into the sitting room so I can get on with some serious dishing-up. I'm beginning to worry about my mouse vols-au-vent. It's hard to know when to transfer them to the top oven: they can so easily dry out. At this moment a stocky workman wearing a faded blue boiler suit wanders in.

"Evenin,'" he says. "Name's Spud. Did the missus tell you where she'd left me beer and butties?"

"Beer and . . .?"

"Me sandwiches. Corned beef, usually."

"Corned beef? Are you quite sure you've come to the right . . .? I mean, I doubt if . . . *Corned beef?*" I repeat faintly. Even in dear Emmeline Tyrwhitt-Glamis's recipe book, penned as it was in the depths of wartime, there is not a single mention of this substance. Maybe like pemmican and biltong it retains a sort of gritty chic among the unshaven adventurer set as they fan up the camp fire to keep the jackals at bay. There again, there is a Protestant continuum in Britain and her ex-colonies— including the United States—in which a perverse pride is taken in elevating crisis fare to the status of national delicacy. Baked beans spring to mind. Salad cream is another example, bearing the same relation to gastronomy as Brylcreem does to hairdressing. At this nonplussed moment Jennifer returns.

"Oh, hullo, Spud," she says. "I didn't realise you'd arrived. I was just getting Josh to bed."

"Evening, Mrs. C. I'll be getting out of your way."

"There's a crate of your favourite in the cellar, if you wouldn't mind? And I'm afraid we may be out of corned beef. Can you make do with cheese and pickle? And onions?" And soon Spud is settled at a table in the scullery with bottles of Greene King ale and enough bread and cheese for a gang of ploughmen with tapeworms. Producing a rolled-up tabloid newspaper from a deep pocket in his boiler suit he looks all set for an intellectual evening with the *Sun* crossword.

"Who on earth?" I ask Adrian sotto voce when he comes in for some olives, and nod towards the scullery.

"Spud? He's Dougie Monteith's driver. Or factotum. Partner, really. They've been together thirty years at least.

Spud's a Wykehamist, as I expect you could tell. He's only ever called Spud, but I imagine he must have had a surname at school. You'll meet Dougie shortly. He's Sir Douglas Monteith, Bart. A real baronet, ancient family, total black sheep. Passed over for Lord Lieutenant of the county, probably for cohabiting with a Winchester man and much, much more."

"And Spud doesn't eat with us?"

"No, no. He doesn't do formal. He lives quite happily in garages and sculleries and garden sheds and, we presume, used to make himself available in the master bedroom before Dougie got too old."

"Golly. So that's what Lord Chatterley got up to that drove his wife into a gamekeeper's arms."

"Presumably. It's pure Suffolk. One foot in the twelfth century and the other in the thirteenth. One day someone's going to wander into one of these villages and find them drawing up a list for a children's crusade. How are your hors d'oeuvres?"

In deference to my artist's temperament Adrian hurries off to get everyone to the table while I briefly finish off my precious savouries in the top oven.

There is something about the magic moment when one enters a dining room bearing fuming dishes of one's latest creation that can never quite be equalled. Alone, we artists know what it is to make an entrance. The great pianist who walks impassively through a heavy shower of applause towards his waiting instrument; the superbly starved supermodel who sets off down the catwalk, her eyes bright with cocaine; the actress who stalks imperiously from the wings in time for the Act 5 dénouement: all relish their professional moment of glory. But tonight I dare say Samper gives his public that little bit extra when he sails into the Christs' dark-panelled dining room wearing Erminio Zaccarelli's linen and merino suit and with a huge tray of original masterpieces. Which, I may say, I come within an ace of dropping when for the first time I have a look at tonight's guests. Even though I know he will be there, the sight of a gorilla sipping a pre-dinner sherry is still disconcerting, and all the more so because the man inside the suit is making no concessions and is evidently prepared to dine with his costume's head on. And the rangy aristo in the moth-eaten Norfolk jacket is . . . good God! . . . that appalling old buffer who only a few days before so rudely drove me out of his jungle domain full of Bloomsbury plants. Tonight his faded blue eyes hold not the least sign of recognition as he fixes his gaze on my crotch while politely inclining his head to hear his neighbour, who is . . . *Marta!* I don't believe this. What is the frowsty old buzzard doing here, if not come to torment me with crowings over my fallen nest?

"*Gerree!*" she cries from her perch at the far end of the table. "You're looking *so* much better than when I last saw you. And what a lovely suit!"

This disarms me, of course, just as she intended. Crafty as ever, that's our Marta. "Marta, darling," I greet her. "You're looking wonderfully well. I've so missed you this last couple of months." I begin distributing the dishes. As I do so Max gets to his feet and introduces me graciously as a friend of the family and the author of the recent bestseller, *Millie!*, whose subject died so dramatically at Christmas aboard her yacht in Sydney harbour. He also mentions that the film rights of his book have been sold for "a substantial sum." He then sits down and people make obligatory clapping gestures. I expect I blush prettily.

"This substantial sum of yours," observes a man with a costermonger's face and a dreadful gold Rolex, "I'd hang onto it with both hands if I were you. Otherwise old Max here will have it off you toot sweet."

Amid sycophantic laughter Adrian introduces the costermonger to me as yet another knight: Sir Barney Iveson, who seems to have been the CSO's principal financial benefactor and all-round good fairy while Max was building up the orchestra. I suppose transfer fees are high these days and I wonder how much Max had to fork out to lure the ape away from the Berlin Phil. or wherever he talent-scouted him. "You know Barney's the inventor of the Shangri-Loo?" Evidently my expression conveys bafflement because as I hand around the last glasses of liver smoothie Adrian explains to the barrow boy that I've been living abroad in Italy for years, otherwise I would surely be familiar with the huge success story of the Shangri-Loo, the exotic lavatory that has become an indispensable part of the modern British bathroom. "The new millennium's equivalent of the jacuzzi," he finishes, provoking in my imagination images not wholly compatible with gourmet dining.

An ape, a lavatory manufacturer, a nonagenarian black sheep and Marta: is this really the dazzling gathering of intellectuals with whom I was hoping the Samper wit might cross swords? And Adrian was spot-on about my being over-dressed. If the lavatory king's trousers aren't polyester I need my eyes testing. Even old Marta seems to have forgotten what little dress sense she acquired in America and has reverted to her old babushka chic, being bundled up in a shapeless frock of midnight blue netting sewn all over with glass beads and sequins. She looks like the wife of a Communist Party official on holiday at a Black Sea resort in the 1960s. I feel I should write a note to Signor Zaccarelli apologising for his beautiful suit's exposure to such ignominious slumming. And as I finally take my seat I'm further annoyed to find I must have mis-counted somewhere and have no mouse vol-au-vent of my own. Presumably I've given somebody two by mistake since I seem to have two After Eight Minces. It's in the nature of things that chefs often never get to eat their own creations and must rely on less discerning palates to learn how successful they are.

The full irony of this last statement only becomes apparent some twenty minutes later when the second course, two magnificent roast legs of lamb, is well under way. Beneath the influence of my brilliantly inventive starters, whose ingredients I refuse to divulge despite all entreaties, conversation has been animated and convivial. Given the peculiar and ill-assorted company, however, it has been less than intellectually dazzling. The creaky old baronet who chivvied me off his patch of Eden has been giving Marta some detailed reminiscences of his Bloomsbury friends of seventy years ago, and serve her right. Judging by overheard snippets of the Bart.'s conversation his set were people of excruciating inconsequence and I can't imagine Marta has the vaguest idea who they were, any more than we would be familiar with the leading lights of Voynovia's Vorticist movement in the 1930s. But having to listen to the old buffoon with a semblance of interest will be good for her manners. Meanwhile, the Samper etiquette has itself been under strain as the costermonger tells me exactly how the Shangri-Loo "Dream" model differs from the carbon neutral "EcoTwirl" model, not to mention the "Arabian Nights," whose "gossamer fingers" feature pursues hygiene entirely too far for any dinner table.

Over the last five minutes I have noticed the general conversation flagging somewhat, doubtless on account of my informant's graphic descriptions of advanced sanitation techniques. People are eating more slowly and with increasingly thoughtful expressions. I am just trying to think of a way to shut the costermonger up when the Baronet decisively puts down his knife and fork and is clearly about to hold forth. All the better: he has the immunity of old age and can be as rude as he likes. Abruptly his huge gnarled hands clutch the edge of the table as though to push himself to his feet. As he rises, he begins "I . . .", but his sentence is cut off by a sudden hawser of blue-brown vomit that stretches wide his mouth and hurtles across the table, hitting a Wedgwood bowl of roast potatoes at least four feet away. He collapses back on his chair and heaves again, this time swamping a pot of mint jelly. And as if this were the trigger that releases everybody else's inhibitions, the others promptly follow suit. Stomach contents empurpled with Max's superb '97 Bolgheri Sassicaia and launched at projectile speed knock over wine glasses and even salt cellars. Several diners retain enough control to attempt to stem their torrents with hasty wads of napkin, but such is the force that subsidiary jets spurt out at the sides, in one case upwards into the diner's own hair, in another into a neighbour's neck. In a matter of seconds a perfect dinner table is splattered with liver-coloured lumps and froth, the reeking air full of the sound of retching. Not since the grosser feasts of Ancient Rome can there have been such a scene of mass gastric ejaculation. Gleaming strands now bow down the innocent spring flowers that comprise Jennifer's charming centrepiece, drool joining the snowdrops' heads to the drenched tablecloth. I notice the gorilla is particularly under the weather. Presumably the costume's designers overlooked the possibility that its wearer might be overcome by violent regurgitation. No doubt the mouth wouldn't open widely enough and the inner contours of the moulded plastic must be redirecting a good portion of the flow internally. This would explain the lumps of sick pouring from both eyeholes and the luckless clarinettist's frantic but blind attempts with his paws to find the Velcro straps that will release his head.

My first instinct was naturally for the safety of my Zaccarelli suit, and I sprang up and backed away from the table even before my costermonger neighbour exploded into the gravy boat and beyond. I reflect that it's all very well making a private fortune out of bringing dernier-cri luxury to the nation's lavatories if you're then reduced to publicly blowing chunks into a bowl of perfectly braised leeks. It is a tribute to my self-confidence as a cook that even now it doesn't immediately occur to me to suspect my own handiwork behind all this.

Nonetheless, I do seem to be the only person unaffected, although the sight and sound and smell are making it likely that if I stay I, too, will shortly succumb. Leaving behind a chorus of groaning and splashing I dash for the kitchen with some vague idea of fetching paper towels and pitchers of cold water. Off to one side I glimpse Spud in the scullery munching stolidly on a doorstep of bread and cheese.

"How's it going, then?" he calls, banging crumbs off his newspaper.

"Equivocally." Carefully I remove my lovely jacket and hang it out of harm's way. Over the roar of tap water I add: "I think we may have problems. The phrase 'throwing a dinner' has just acquired a new level of meaning. Perhaps you'd better come, if you wouldn't mind."

By now the possibility that Samper might somehow be to blame is beginning to sink in and provides yet another reason for my reluctance to return to the dining room. Not for the first time while dining in Crendlesham Hall I feel a real urge to sidle out of the front door and start running. But my Norman forebears were not called "Sans Peur" for nothing and anyway a gentleman must take responsibility for his actions, no matter how well-intentioned. So back I go with a large jug of water and a roll of kitchen paper, albeit not with any real enthusiasm. I can hear Spud's heavy footsteps and jaunty workman's whistle behind me. Little does he know.

The scene is awesome, the smell worse. A few, their worst spasms over, are struggling weakly to their feet. Marta looks as though she has been at the epicentre of a cataclysm involving industrial quantities of porridge. I think her outfit may have intercepted some of her neighbour's early heaves. Her great, sodden, muslined bosoms sparkle in the lamplight, though the sequins are dulled. Max, too, is on his feet, leaning heavily on the table and occasionally spitting. The ape is now headless, and the small gingery face of the clarinettist within glistens with mucus and clots beneath thin plastered hair. The fur on his chest is matted and dripping.

"Bleedin' Nora," says Sir Barney Shangri-Loo feebly, also beginning to stir. "What the hell was *that*?" To judge from one side of his coat he appears to have taken much of Jennifer's liver smoothie in his left ear. And yes—the way things are sliding and plopping off his jacket confirms that it, too, is polyesterous. It's odd what secrets these little crises throw up. Meanwhile, over on the far side of the table it seems from Spud's hoarse cries of "Dougie!" that all is far from well with his baronet, who is slumped back in his chair with his eyes shut.

"Don't just stand there," Spud throws at me as he feels the old man's neck. "Get an ambulance, quick! Get ten! They'll all have to go to hospital, the lot of them. *Now!* Get your skates on!"

The clear, incisive tones of Winchester suddenly give him the authority he lacked as a boiler-suited Man Friday. Obediently I go out into the hall and dial 999, stressing that the house is that of the world-famous conductor Max Christ and that he himself is one of at least six other victims. Back in the dining room I find that everyone bar the Baronet is now walking wounded. I open the French windows and let in some welcome cool night air. People totter out to the terrace with glasses of water and there comes the sound of much gargling and rinsing and spitting. Jennifer comes back in and leadenly begins stripping the cloth and its gastric load off the table.

"Leave that, Mrs. C," Spud tells her. "It's evidence. You've all been poisoned. They'll want to know what it was. Help me get Dougie on the floor, if you can. I need to do heart massage."

Standing here amid the debris of what until only five minutes ago was a staidly tasteful dinner party, the discrepancy between my intention to pull off a culinary coup and the awful outcome is too huge to be plausible. It still feels like nothing to do with me. "What hath God wrought!" was the phrase Samuel Morse sent to congratulate God on having invented the first practical telegraph. I am inclined to employ the same phrase right now, the whole thing clearly being God's doing and not Samper's. My insufferable pious stepmother Laura once told me that Morse had borrowed the phrase from the Bible, which being itself the Word of the Lord makes it just the sort of self-praising utterance the Almighty favoured. I feel very strongly that if He could take credit for the Morse code, He can jolly well do so for this carnage in Crendlesham. As to whether any-one else will agree is another matter. The coroner, for instance, I think as I snatch a glance at the ancient Baronet who, flat on the floor with Spud pumping on his chest, looks as though he may already have gone the way of T. E. Lawrence's myrrh tree.

Perhaps because like his sister he is young, Adrian seems over the worst. In the kitchen he grabs a tea towel and douses his head under the tap. Then, drying his hair, he pushes me none too gently into the comparative privacy of the scullery.

"Okay, Gerry," he says. "You've done it this time. Out with it! What did you put in the starters? And don't fool around, we haven't time. As it is, Dougie may not make it, he's ninety-three or something. They'll need to know in A&E. What was it?"

"Scout's honour," I say, "I've no idea. I bought most of the stuff in Woodbridge."

"'Most.' What was the rest?"

"Er—just the odd field mouse. Good fresh country fare."

"We've just eaten field mice?"

"Quite small ones. Eleven of them. I trapped them myself."

"You're sure they were all trapped?"

"Honestly, Adrian."

"Using what for bait?"

"Cheddar from the fridge."

At this moment—and welcomely interrupting the sort of cross-examination one scarcely expects from a lover twelve years one's junior—the first ambulance arrives and Dougie with Spud in attendance is swiftly removed and whisked off into the night with flashing lights and braying sirens. A second ambulance comes after five more minutes. In addition to its two-man crew this one carries a medic with a mobile phone.

"They say it looks like food poisoning, right? I need to know: were there mushrooms in any of the food?"

"None in my dishes," I say, and Jennifer equally firmly says no.

"Okay, then, no mushrooms. Is there anyone *not* affected?"

"Well, er, me I suppose." How is one expected to say this with regret?

"What didn't you eat that the others ate?" the doctor asks me while busy assuring himself that the rest of the guests will live, at least in the short term, before they are led off to the waiting vehicle.

"Just one of the starters," I say. With tedious inevitability the subject of mice crops up once more. Obviously this unpleasant young medic fancies himself as a bit of a thesp and grossly overdoes the "registering incredulity" bit.

"You've been eating *field mice*?"

"Yes, yes," I say wearily. "Why not? People said they were delicious. It so happens that—" But what's the use? I needn't go into further details of being quizzed by a succession of people wearing uniforms of one sort or another who sooner or later strike attitudes of morbid rectitude. Honestly, the dim *moralism* of the British! The various sufferers are meanwhile carted off to hospital for "observation" after I've promised Jennifer faithfully that I will look after her son. "You'd better," Adrian adds quite unnecessarily. At last silence falls and here I am, in sole charge of Crendlesham Hall and its other human occupant, Josh, who has presumably remained blissfully asleep throughout the various comings and goings.

By tradition, survivors at a scene of tragedy either howl hysterically or sit listlessly. Neither is the Samper way. I direct my energies into clearing up the mess. The tablecloth, heavy with evidence, has been removed in a plastic sack, ditto the greasy oven tray in which the mouse vols-au-vent were baked. Samples have also been taken of the liver smoothie and the After Eight Mince: I only hope that whatever analysis the scientists contrive will not enable them to filch the recipes of my still-unpatented masterpieces. Even in the absence of all these items there is still no lack of things to purge, quite apart from the washing up. If atonement is supposed to afford humiliation on top of decent apology, then doing the washing up at Crendlesham Hall on this night of the Great Puke has to be reckoned atonement at its most abject. By the end, the dining room looks more or less its old self and no longer like the Augean Stables after a prolonged bout of equine flu, although the faint scent of disinfectant lingers in the air from where I had to scrub the carpet. Incredibly, I even found a pea stuck to the panelled wall at shoulder height and there may yet be others. The kitchen, too, is back to normal.

I promised Jennifer I would look in on Josh in case he woke and was frightened to find no one about. I don't feel much like sleep myself but on my way up to the attic I find Josh wandering with the crushed, drugged look that woken children have. I gather he's thirsty and wants his mother to bring him some water *now*. I explain that everyone got a bit ill suddenly and had to go to hospital for a few hours but that they're quite all right really and will be back in the morning. So for the moment we two men are in charge of the house and the cat. He says he had a bad dream about gorillas and I assure him the gorilla is also in hospital and there are absolutely no gorillas on the premises. Seeing he is unconvinced, I reluctantly agree to his proposal that he share my bed upstairs while I keep any stray apes at bay. So he brings along his favourite stuffed dinosaur, who is apparently deadly to gorillas, and is soon asleep in a distant corner of my vast attic bed in which at length I also manage a few hours' oblivion.

My many weeks of being a guest at Crendlesham Hall have, in Josh's eyes at least, accorded me the status of a member of the family, or at least someone he can feel free to whack with a stuffed dinosaur at six in the morning because he's hungry. Why anyone *elects* to be a parent I can't imagine. So we are both long up and about when, at seven-thirty, the first taxi-load arrives with people wearing clothes still spattered with dried flecks of the evening meal. It is nice to be able to hand Josh back into his parents' charge, but not much else is a pleasure. I have been dreading this moment from the instant I was bullied awake. It had always seemed inevitable that there would be some quite nasty recriminations, but it turns out that things are even worse. Sir Douglas Monteith is now recumbent in a mortuary freezer, the result of a massive overnight heart attack brought on by convulsive vomiting, which in turn was due to . . .

". . . but you get my drift," Adrian ends grimly. "However you look at it, Gerry, last night you murdered a baronet in the dining room of Crendlesham Hall. And the rest of us have had a fucking awful time. Anyway, the police will be here shortly and you can try bad-taste Cluedo jokes on them if you like."

I am contritely brewing coffee as a peace offering and I must admit this news upsets me to the extent that I allow the milk to boil over, something I haven't done in years. Jennifer, bless her, comes to my rescue and is a good deal more conciliatory than her brother.

"Come on, Adrian, be fair. Gerry didn't *deliberately* poison anyone. It was obviously a horrible accident."

"Well, okay, I know that," my loyal lover grudgingly concedes. "But all the same, you've got to admit there's something about it that's typically Gerry. Extravagant, irresponsible and just generally misplaced. Even Josh would have had more sense."

"Might somebody kindly explain what this poison is that I'm supposed to have administered?" I ask with commendable quiet dignity but inevitably sounding like a defendant at the

Nuremberg trials. "In my irresponsible and generally misplaced way?"

"They think it was rat poison," Jennifer explains, "but they won't know for certain until they've done more tests. But they do say the symptoms are a good pointer."

"Specifically," her brother adds with his not very charming air of technical omniscience, "they said it was probably red squill, which is extracted from the bulb of some plant or other. It works on rats because they can't vomit. Luckily for us we can, as you may have noticed. That is, if 'lucky' is an appropriate description for what happened to poor Dougie," he adds.

"But it makes no sense," I protest. "Obviously I don't have any of this stuff. I caught all my mice using ordinary mousetraps and cheese. So where did the poison come from? It might have been in any other part of the food last night. I don't see why everyone immediately suspects me and treats me like someone in an Agatha Christie novel."

"Think 'probabilities,'" says Adrian. "The entire meal, apart from your contribution, was perfectly standard fare. Yours was most definitely not. I can't speak for the rest of us, but personally I'm finding the time-honoured way of trying to pinpoint exactly what gave me food poisoning isn't working in this case. *All* the starters seem nauseating in retrospect."

This is deeply wounding. "Others, including yourself, were full of praise at the time," I point out with some asperity. "I seem to remember you called my little hors d'oeuvres 'inventively sublime.'"

"That was before I knew they were lethal. Also before I'd tasted the liver smoothie. God, *no*. I don't even want to think about that."

Here, Max shambles in with a couple of policemen and shambles out again to go to bed. The great maestro appears to have aged overnight. He complains of feeling too weak to go into a recording session, which he has had to cancel. That will cost somebody something. The policemen politely but firmly refuse my offer of coffee, no doubt thinking it will be laced with arsenic or strychnine, and things quickly become very boring indeed. Their ponderous opening sally sets the tone. "Obviously, the death of Sir Douglas Monteith has made this a very tragic affair, sir. There is not the slightest suspicion of anything other than a terrible accident, but you will understand why we need to ask you a few questions, sir, as the person who prepared the food but who alone was unaffected by the poison." And much in the same vein, with undercurrents of forensic menace. Oh, what am I doing in this benighted land? Why am I not still up in the blissful seclusion of Le Roccie? And why is my house there not still standing? What malign fate has had all this in store for me?

So I go over it yet again and show the policemen the outhouses where I set the traps. I describe how I made all three starters, concealing only the exact quantities from them. One doesn't give priceless recipes away to the police, especially not to men philistine enough to express incredulity when I describe the dishes. Suddenly, I'm very relieved that in the general excitement of my financial windfall I clean forgot to mention my inauspicious first meeting with the Baronet. I had intended to tell Adrian about my encounter in Monteith's jungle, but by the time he arrived with Josh's microscope there were more pressing things to think about. Now I realise how important it is that the police never find out that Sir Douglas and I exchanged tense words some days ago, even if the addled old buffer appeared not to recognise me last night. Certainly I don't wish to give the police the least impression that as far as I'm concerned, the Bart.'s demise is one of those human tragedies that make one's sides ache. Now, in the course of our explorations, we come across the potting shed where the Christs' gardener—whom Jennifer describes as "a treasure"— has his lair. Here the policemen poke about and become excited over an ancient bottle with a corroded cap on a shelf. The label reads "Squillo-Death" and has a faded picture on it of a rat in terminal agony. Using plastic gloves they drop the bottle into an evidence bag.

"And you say you've never seen this bottle before, sir?"

"Absolutely not. In fact, I've never even been into this potting shed. The kitchen garden is not somewhere I visit frequently."

At last they go away to interview the gardener, also taking with them all my new "Little Nipper" mouse traps. And in due course it is confirmed that the bottle of red squill is indeed the culprit—or rather, the gardener is, the dear old Suffolk treasure who without telling anyone blithely put down bait laced with a banned rodenticide around a house with a six-year-old child in it. There remains the conundrum of how a poisoned mouse wound up in one of my traps. It is assumed that because squill doesn't act instantly the luckless rodent was able to move on for a second course of excellent cheddar cheese before falling victim to an old-fashioned spring. Thus the amount of this highly emetic substance actually ingested by Crendlesham Hall's luckless diners was very small, and fatal only to a very old man with a dicky heart. The police do not return, and things slowly revert to normal, at least on the surface. It is acknowledged that I am not directly to blame for the disaster, the gardener is fired, and in due course we all dutifully troop over to a draughty church to see Sir Douglas's mortal remains buried beneath six feet of earth but with, we are implausibly assured by a robed comedian, the lively expectation of his eventual resurrection. The grieving Spud is plainly unreconciled to the idea that I am not guilty of his aged partner's death. He is but distantly civil, while I do my best to express sincere regrets without implying the least degree of responsibility, like a Japanese politician when obliged to comment on the War in the Pacific. For me the most distressing part of the proceedings is being unable to wear my Zaccarelli suit. The jacket is saved but the trousers are ruined. In my urgent efforts to bring Crendlesham Hall back to normal on that fateful night I forgot I was wearing them as I knelt and scrubbed and disinfected. One cannot kneel on patches of wine-tinged vomit in linen and merino mixture without irreparable damage, as I later discovered.

For Jennifer and Max the whole episode has been something of a social disaster in that news of a fatality at your dinner party inevitably gets around. For a while there is even some loose talk of the costermonger suing. This is mere rumour and, being friends, all the guests amiably agree to write it off as just one of those unfortunate things. Nevertheless I can't help feeling a line of sorts has been drawn beneath my welcome at Crendlesham Hall. It simply makes still clearer a conclusion I myself have already reached: that it is high time for Samper to move on.

I do, however, have a valedictory conversation with Marta, with whom I haven't otherwise had a chance to swap news. She is a little pale but otherwise seems undamaged. There is stout stuff in these Voynovians. I suppose after occupation by the Soviets everything else must seem minor by contrast. In my usual guarded fashion I'm genuinely pleased to see her, although apprehensive of what new indignity I am about to suffer at her hands. I am still touched by the memory of her bedraggled state last night, her Iron Curtain finery plastered by vomit to her ample body. It gave me no pleasure to see my old neighbour so miserably reduced, poor thing.

Yet as usual Marta manages to wither my sympathy with an artless piece of news. By one of those brutal little ironies I seem to attract, it turns out she is herself engaged in writing an opera! She is over in the UK to see her librettist, Sue Donimus, whose name makes me groan with vexation. She is a literary prizewinner who feels the world is clamouring to hear coma-inducing details of her private life, such as exactly how much she recently spent having her teeth straightened. A bullish creature in tartan trews, she was elected a Fellow of the Royal Society of Literature mainly because the panel was too intimidated by her to turn her down. She is most famously the author of an unusually disgusting flagellation novel, *Heavily Tanned Men*, a book widely seen as stylish and liberating. Overnight it made her the darling of the sort of people who have darlings, starting with herself. The only thing one can't blame her for is writing under a pen name, since my agent Frankie has assured me the name on her passport is Wendy Marsupial. I now dread to imagine what the attraction is between Marta and this "doyenne of transgressive literature" (*London Review of Books*).

This news that Marta is writing an opera casts an immediate pall of doubt over my own nascent plans. Blast her! Why should her project have the least influence over mine? Especially as I assume any libretto by Sue Donimus will involve distasteful and even fashionably gross scenes onstage, whereas my own ideas are jelling fertilely around the timeless dramatic themes of love, heroism and grief. Yet at Marta's casual announcement I feel enthusiasm for my own grand project beginning to wilt. Does this mean I have unconsciously been hoping that Marta might write the music to mine? Might I actually have wanted to lay myself open to an artistic partnership with this increasingly successful musical frump?

But now the frump breaks into my uneasy speculations with news from Le Roccie. It seems the Italian authorities are viewing the remains of my poor house—which they laughably claim they are guarding from looters—as a potential source of pollution. They cite cooking gas cylinders that will corrode, oil and fuel leaking from my half-buried Toyota Ass Vein and a ruptured septic tank as endangering the environment and the town's artesian water supplies. Also, the *Corpo Forestale dello Stato* are considering taking out an action against me for fly-tipping, would you believe, on the grounds that my protracted absence indicates "the intention permanently to abandon, in a protected area of the rural patrimony, unsorted debris and refuse contrary to environmental statutes currently in force." Marta is reading this from a note she took to make sure I get the full majesty of the phraseology. I particularly love "unsorted." The implication that I might be prosecuted less rigorously had I taken the trouble to separate the ruins of my house into categories as for the correct rubbish bins—paper, glass, iron, non-ferrous metals, organic waste and the rest of it—is the final ludicrous straw, given Italy's generally cavalier way with rubbish.

And here's another strange thing. After my initial relief at being freed from the burdens of home ownership and personal possessions, these very things start to make a case for themselves at the back of my mind, like an exasperating lone councilman who at the last moment makes the trenchant objection that stops a motion going through on the nod. My recent experiences as a guest at Crendlesham Hall are no doubt contributing to the suddenly alluring prospect of once again having a space of my own *to myself*: one in which county deadbeats and jokesters in fancy dress don't come to dinner, disgrace themselves, and lead to my being interrogated by policemen as though I were Dr. Crippen or Graham Young. And for the first time since the awful night of my fiftieth birthday party, I actively begin to miss certain items buried beneath the collapsed hardcore littering a far-off mountainside. One such item is my independence.

In short, it's back to Italy for Gerald Samper just as soon as I can book a flight.

Adrian 2

email from Dr. Adrian Jestico (ajestico@bois.ac.uk)
to Dr. Penny Barbisant (penbar@labs.whoi.ed)

It sounds to me as if your data are fine. The chromosome set changes correspond nicely to the reported pollutant bioaccumulation. Good work. I agree the phosphorus readings are odd. You say they've eliminated industrial sources/outfall within range of the site. But have you considered a wreck? It's going back a bit, but I remember hearing that quite a tonnage of US merchant shipping was sunk off the New England coast by German U-boats in WW2 and I bet it wasn't all accurately charted. A munitions ship whose cargo is breaking up and decaying might easily account for your phosphorus levels locally. See if you can find out, if only to eliminate it. Munitions are not my thing but a few years ago someone at Aberdeen (I forget who but you can easily find out from Marine Lab.) did great work on dumped explosives in the Beaufort's Dyke disposal site after phosphorus shells etc. began washing ashore in N. Ireland & the Firth of Clyde & even as far as Islay.

By the way—& this is just an idea—do you have figures for *Eurythenes*? I know it's not a bivalve but it's pretty voracious even for an amphipod, & as it scarfs up practically any organic detritus that comes its way you might get higher P concentrations from it & a quicker pinpoint on your grid for a possible source. Assuming a fairly constant demersal current (which of course there may not be) you might be able to establish a transect. I'm sure you've thought of all this & more & what do I know about it? Just a thought.

*

I'm glad you're licking Luke into shape, if that's the correct metaphor, and that he's turning out to be fully domesticated. I only wish I could be as cheerfully uncritical about Gerry. He's not the flavour of the month at present, and not just with me. This follows a dinner party at my sister's last Saturday that went badly wrong. So wrong, in fact, that it actually caused the death of one of the guests. OK, the guest in question was 93 and had a bad heart, but I thought before dinner he looked good to make his century. We were all poisoned—all of us *except* for Gerry, that is. What happened was that we were overcome by violent puking of a kind I've never experienced before. It took us completely by surprise. One minute we were tucking into Jennifer's excellent roast leg of lamb and the next we were upchucking for Britain. What was odd was there was no real nausea beforehand, just a slight feeling of unease. Then suddenly you opened your mouth and out came vomit instead of words. When you have seven diners at the table all doing it at the same moment you're talking major barf-fest. I'll spare you the details. Except for poor old Dougie Monteith we're all fine now, though it makes me a bit queasy just remembering it.

It turned out that Gerry had prepared some "special" starters of his own bizarre invention, one of which he hadn't eaten. This was—and you'll have to get a grip on your credulity here, Penny—*field mouse vol-au-vent*. He said he'd trapped the mice himself, but it seems at least one of them had already eaten bait laced with something the gardener had put down for rats. So we all spent a night in hospital, where poor Dougie succumbed from heart failure. Luckily the poison was something called squill, which comes from a plant and isn't supposed to be toxic long-term once you've got it out of your system. And boy! did we ever get it out of our systems, and all of us at exactly the same moment. It was like community singing.

Upshot: Gerry grilled by police & grudgingly exonerated of murder, manslaughter & deliberate mayhem, but his reputation has taken a severe knock. I actually feel sorry for him but I was majorly pissed off at the time. It was so typical of his irresponsibility. He's got this anarchic streak that makes him think the ordinary laws of common sense simply don't apply to him. His sense of humour is equally suspect. Who else helps someone tottering with nausea into an ambulance with the murmured encouragement "Queasy does it!"? The person who has found it easiest to forgive him, oddly enough, is my illustrious brother-in-law Max, even though he was quite poorly for a couple of days afterwards. Maybe Max has a bit of Gerry in him that I've never suspected before. (If my sister's worried by this possibility she's decent enough to say nothing.)

Anyway, it sounds to me as though your Luke is a good deal more of a regular guy than my Gerry is. I can almost hear you thinking this guy's beginning to sound like the partner from hell, and I wouldn't blame you. To tell you the truth I don't even know if he's a partner at all. Partner, lover, friend, ex: how can one ever distinguish between them except over time? And I've only known him 18 months or so. But as I've said before, Gerry can be exhilarating company—totally unlike anyone else I've ever met. Funnier, more extravagant, determinedly incorrect, yet strangely vulnerable. I can never forget that when he was a kid his mother and elder brother were swept off Lyme Regis Cobb by a freak wave right in front of his eyes. Gone in an instant, their bodies never found. A thing like that has to have made its mark. He was left with his father, who he's reasonably fond of, & a stepmother he detests. Who knows how relevant all this is to his character & behaviour? I've even wondered whether he mightn't have been attracted to me because I'm an oceanographer, though not being a psychoanalyst I can't imagine how that twisted logic might work. Certainly he's got a thing about the sea. It was one of the reasons why he bought that remote house of his in Italy. He liked its distant view of the sea, he told me, *because* it was distant. And although he talks down his *Millie!* book as trash, nobody else could have written it half as well as Gerry. He showed a real feel for the maritime aspects & picked up the technical stuff on navigation & sonar surveys etc. very quickly.

I'm sorry, Penny, I'm rabbiting on and it's not fair of me to take advantage of an ex-graduate student even though you were kind enough to ask for "as many details as I care to send"—words you may yet live to regret. What the next stage in Gerry's life will be is anybody's guess. He is completely unpredictable, but then after he's gone & done something the first thing you think is "how predictable!" when I suppose one really means how typical of him. But it's always retrospective. Anyway, all I can do is be supportive & allow him all the room he wants, which he'd take in any case. I must admit I'm a bit ruffled over the other night. It's not often you attend a family dinner with a few locals & find it turning into a medical soap with guests being stretchered off to a waiting fleet of ambulances, paramedics doing heart massage, defibrillators pinging away. And bloody Gerry worried about keeping his new suit clean. The awful thing is that now it's over & we've done the funeral & everything I can see there's an element of comedy in it. It isn't every day you see a vomit-drenched gorilla being helped into an ambulance. I just wish Gerry hadn't pointed this out quite so soon after the event. One might say that tact isn't his thing. Neither is remorse, come to that.

Glad Peter M.'s doing well.

Cheers,
Adrian

3

My flight is, of course, delayed (the evergreen excuse, "due to lateness of the incoming flight," is trotted out by uniformed drudges too bored to care whether we think they're lying). The upshot is that, disembarking in Pisa at twenty minutes to midnight, I have no option but to take a taxi into town and spend the night in one of the hotels near the station. A wintry rain is falling and I'm not choosy. I check into one where I know just by looking at it that the crimson-carpeted marble staircase will go up from the foyer only to where it becomes invisible behind the lift shaft, whereupon it will revert to being a cement emergency stairwell signposted with icons of a running figure pursued by flames. I surrender my *carta d'identità* and the night clerk returns to his under-the-counter DVD.

Old and jaundiced—that's what Samper is in danger of becoming, I think when I resume consciousness at six-thirty the next morning, blinking woozily at the ceiling. Time was, when waking early in a foreign hotel would fill me with the excitement of possibility. These days I know too much about probability. Still, I'm back in Italy, and that alone is cause for rejoicing. I switch on the TV and find the BBCNN channel, which in itself shows how addled I've become. It immediately reminds me that what I dislike is not so much my native land but Anglo-Saxon culture in general. Between them, American and British TV broadcasters somehow manage to imply that they have a semi-divine right to interpret and mediate the world for the rest of its six billion inhabitants. This cocky assumption is immediately implicit in the familiar (not to say over-familiar) mateyness that now booms from the TV set.

As though to share some cosmic in-joke exclusive to themselves, BBCNN newsreaders are specially trained to grin and speak at the same time, which is how they introduce their weather seers and prophets who are also grinning insanely while waving vague hands towards a map of Africa in gestures that, by the time they are half completed, cross China while a farrago of pop meteorology comes *sweep*in in there from the Atlantic an *push*in those rain shahs ere over towards the west coaster Denmark which spells a largely sunny dye ere in Ukraine but over in Sarf America well, still a few otspots left from that depression centred on norfeast Brazil over the last few dyes . . . Hectic blank smiles, spastic gesturings, maps, images and symbols blinking and collapsing one after the other in wild cascade. The screen is a loony chaos of dizzying junk masquerading as information. Running straps top and bottom about sports, stock exchanges, President Bush shoots himself in the foot while hunting terrorists on his Texas ranch, while in the middle of the screen two presenters made of high-impact plastic carry on their grinning knockabout act while their mouths babble about a baby polar bear born in a zoo, Guantánamo Bay, a car that runs on Coca-Cola, a small earthquake in Chile, a White House aide who fucks penguins for charity, torture, car bombs etcetera, and now it's exactly seven o'clock Southern Pacific time and time for the News but just to keep up BBCNN's famous irritation quotient here instead is a stream of advertisements aimed at drumming up visitors to countries no one has ever wished to visit and that thousands have died trying to escape—like *Voynovia*! Whirling images of travelogue guff, national costumes, sun-tanned cleavages, all-purpose *Zorba*-esque music, ecoparks (formerly the hunting preserves of the late dictator-for-life Bashir Mohammedov)

and hotels . . . God, how many hotels! . . . those vile cara-
vanserais of the jet set that resemble an architect's idea of what
Nero would have liked, all pools and palms and mother-of-
pearl-inlaid foyers exclusively sited on yet another piece of the
world's previously unspoiled coastline, now forever ruined, the
images syruped together with words supposed to convey pitiless luxury: *pampered, beyond, paradise, dreams, palace,
deserve, exquisite*—but abruptly the screen dissolves into share
prices and a Chinese-looking Dax-hound in shirtsleeves and
glinting horn-rims is reading some supremely resistible information about the equities market in Bonn off the autocue and
strings of figures spool across the screen in arbitrary directions
and so it all rolls on and around in a great flashing blather of
interglobal garrulous garbage brought to you by BBCNN 24/7
and don't forget it's all there too on our website and also
beamed direct to your mobile phone and hearing aid and
equally accessible on your prosthetic limb or electric tooth-
brush thanks to instantaneous XP Vista chip satellite technology because we know how important you are and how vital
time is to you and how as a top executive you absolutely need
up-to-the-minute information about White House aides plea-
suring flightless birds because otherwise some beady-eyed bastard who's leaner and meaner and has the world's biggest blad-
der will steal a march on you while you're away from your desk
taking a leak. And yes—see what you missed when you took
your eye off the ball there as that high-pressure area came
*push*in in from Mongolia where the Genghis Khan Nirvana
Palisades Mansion awaits your exclusive and demanding custom, the first and cutest ten-star hotel ever born in captivity
while nuclear crisis talks loom grinning and grinning all over
your kaleidoscopic, epilepsy-inducing flickering screens, faster
and faster until we whimper prayers for the failure of the
global power grid and entertain fantasies of the pampering,
pitiless luxury of solitary confinement and total sensory depri-

vation. And all we ever actually wanted, of course, was footage of the White House aide lying back in his double bed, arguing with the penguin about whose turn it is to make the coffee. That would have set us up nicely for the day.

A lot of this drivel is visible, reversed out in the bathroom mirror, as I shave. If this is how millions of people begin their day it's small wonder they're full of stress and ill informed. I leave the hotel without breakfast, knowing too well what awaits me. Amazing to think that in my lifetime we've sunk so low that even in supposedly good hotels guests are now expected to fetch their own breakfast, not to mention put up with a miniature dustbin in the middle of the table for all the nasty little plastic pots, butter wrappers and pieces of foil— and, what is more, join a conspiracy to pretend that this is gracious living. I cross to the station and in the bar have a blissful espresso (why *is* Italian coffee so distinctively good?) that sends a glow through me and makes me feel I'm home at last. I salute a stalwart group of dungaree-clad workmen beginning their day with croissants and Fernet-Branca and commandeer a taxi to drive me to where I belong. The driver, relieved at not having to do the five-minute run to the airport that he could do—or give a realistic imitation of doing—with his eyes closed, warns me that he expects the trip to cost €90, depending on whether I want him to go via the autostrada where I will also have to pay the toll, or the old Aurelia coast road, which is slower but free. I tell him airily that since I'm an eccentric millionaire I don't care which way he goes. I then slump back in silence to contemplate exactly what I need to do. First, find a suitable local hotel as a base to work from, then set about discovering what the position of a homeowner is whose house has been reduced to rubble—rubble that I increasingly feel I should search to see what of my former life has survived. There is also the pressing question of insurance. Suddenly having abundant money seems to be making me less fatalistic about

Le Roccie. From time to time I glance up from my reverie and finally notice that whenever I have done so I have seen the Leaning Tower, now on our left and later on our right, sometimes leaning towards us and sometimes away.

"Had you maybe thought to *leave* Pisa at some point this morning?" I ask with amiable restraint.

"It's the one-way traffic system." The driver unwraps a stick of gum and places it on an extended grey-coated tongue the colour and texture of mouldy bread. We watch one another in the mirror. "Also, I'm an eccentric taxi driver."

Touché, I suppose. Normally this would provoke Samper to stinging repartee but I am still fighting the influence of BBCNN's breakfast television. I very much want to be calm. The rest of the world may, if it wishes, dissolve into schizophrenia, frantically whirling to confront a madcap slurry of voices and images. But this is not Samper's way, especially not after a spell in the cool backwaters of East Anglica where, as we know, feeling you're whole is deeply refreshing and the Rev. Daphne Pitt-Bull is quietly auditioning her Pontius Pilates. I therefore renounce all contentiousness with taxi drivers and concentrate instead on my silent plans, which may yet turn out to encompass a certain amount of mayhem and revenge.

As we approach familiar terrain the air becomes hazier until it is almost foggy. The town itself is shrouded in a muffling grey sea mist. Or mountain mist? Adrian would know. But it is familiar enough at this time of the year to be nostalgic. I experience a pang of pleasure immediately swamped by melancholy. It is three months since I was last here and the sheer familiarity of the wet mountain smell coming through the driver's window feels like homecoming. Ordinarily, I would stop here and lay in provisions suitable for some astounding and inventive dishes before heading out past Mosciano and up to Greppone, beyond which is my private eyrie. But today I view the place through a grey lens of sorrow, brimming with the irony of a homecoming without a home to come to. Unavoidably adding to my rue, I have the taxi stop outside a hotel. Nothing feels quite so wrong as checking into a hotel in one's home town. Owing to a bizarre set of circumstances I once had to stay overnight in a hotel at Liverpool Street station and couldn't rid myself of the idea that, because I was a Briton living and working in London, I ought to have been able to stay there for free, or at least pay a fraction of what it was costing foreigners and outsiders. As I disembark on the pavement the taximeter shows exactly €90, strangely enough, and I wonder if my gum-chewing chauffeur hasn't fixed it somehow. However, I derive a certain bleak pleasure from staying within my role. Many years ago Nubar Gulbenkian, on a whim, commissioned Rolls Royce to build him a London taxi. "I'm told," he famously observed, "that it will turn on a sixpence. Whatever that may be." In this same spirit I now hand my driver €120, saying "Do keep the change. You might find a use for it." Everyone ought to allow himself a little vulgarity now and then, and the driver's expression makes it all worthwhile.

Once checked in and my bag dumped, I head off along the Corso to my favourite bar. It feels both inevitable and right that before I can reach it I nearly collide with a misty figure briskly rounding the corner and suddenly I'm face to face with my old Moriarty, signor Benedetti, the dapper, shifty little estate agent who sold me my house some years ago. Because he had assured me that my sole neighbour was almost never there and was anyway mouse-quiet, I bought the house from him without a qualm. More fool I. When I tell you that the neighbour turned out to be a piano-bashing Voynovian in permanent residence—to wit, the egregious Marta—you will understand why relations between Samper and Benedetti have at best been distantly civil over the years. It turned out that the unscrupulous little rodent had told Marta exactly the same thing about me and it was not long before she was countering my polite remonstrations about her piano playing with gratu-itous remarks about my singing: an impasse that led to all sorts of unpleasantness. Ever after, the difficult civility that Benedetti and I have maintained has been based on a kind of parody of elaborate Renaissance manners such as Castiglione's ideal courtier would have approved. On my side it has also been inspired by the enjoyment I get from watching his losing battle with male pattern baldness, a field on which *noblesse* and chivalry are sadly powerless. Benedetti's startling new tactics in his trichological campaign are, in fact, the first thing I notice as we courteously side-step before recognising one another as old foes. Gone is the old hair-weaving ploy. In its place, exactly as I predicted, is a glossy, shameless rug. It's a very good rug, and must have cost him a lot of money. It reminds me that this man ought really to be cherished for the gaiety he brings to our lives. I had similar feelings about Jerry Falwell, the late American evangelist. Anyone who can accuse one of the Teletubbies of being homosexual, and do it with a straight face, is a priceless asset to the human race. Benedetti's rug is perfect in that it is very slightly wrong: just a shade too black, just a little too full, and only barely avoiding the pompadour look of Elvis Presley or President Marcos, which makes me think he hoped to add a much-needed inch to his stature. The sight of it gives me immediate strength.

"Signor Benedetti!" I cry. "Dottore! How is it that the pleasure of running into you always exceeds my liveliest antic-ipation? And how young you're looking! Truly, you must allow me to say there is something almost uncanny about your refusal to age like the rest of us. Sometimes it crosses my mind that you may have sold your soul to Satan in exchange for eter-nal youth. If you have, I would be much in your debt for an introduction to His Infernal Majesty."

"Signor Samper! Maestro! How greatly I have missed that wicked English humour of yours—so piquant, yet so urbanely expressed! As you know, we do have a few other English residents here, including a couple with a blind daughter who arrived last year. But where the art of conversation is concerned they're simply not in your league. As an honest man I tell you, this winter has been all the drearier for your absence, and no less so for knowing its cause. I have been counting the days until at last I would be able to commiserate with you on the loss of your beautiful home. Believe me, even when I heard you were safe I felt a shaft pierce my heart in sympathy."

Brilliant! Well up to the little weasel's usual standard of florid insincerity. He has even managed to suggest the image of the statue in a church only a few hundred metres away of the Virgin with her heart transfixed by a ring of gilded tin swords representing seven distinct dolours, any one of which would have been enough to spare her the other six: the Baroque version of overkill. We both smile at the same moment, happy to be sparring partners once again.

"In confidence, I was hard hit myself," I admit. "As a gentleman of your exquisite sensibility may imagine, the shock was life-threatening." (I use the word *micidiale*, which can cover anything from the unwelcome attentions of a mosquito to assault by a knife-wielding maniac.) "To lose one's entire house and very nearly several dear friends with it—not to mention one's own life—in a whiff of brimstone, how can mere words do it justice? The incident provoked in me the gravest medical repercussions. I was prostrated for many weeks." That's enough dramatic pathos. Time now to give him a taste of Samper *redivivus*. "For endless hours I lay and contemplated the dire event. Yet do you know, in all that time it never crossed my mind that even so brilliantly qualified and experienced a property surveyor as yourself could have guessed that the site at Le Roccie hid a fundamental geological weakness."

Benedetti gets the point at once. His raven plumage may be borrowed but his mind is still very much his own. "Naturally not, maestro. There was, of course, a meeting in the Comune only days after the tragedy because the tremors were also felt down here, although thanks to the Blessed Virgin we were spared damage. As a courtesy you were invited to attend this meeting yourself, but we gathered that you never received the invitation, being by then back in England. It was our loss. But the region's geological assessor gave evidence, recorded in the minutes, stating clearly that any suggestion that such a weakness could have been suspected in advance would amount to slander and misprision. The truth is we were all taken completely by surprise, and new geological surveys are now urgently in progress. There is of course concern for Greppone. As you know, there have been several landslides up there in the past, although in general these were caused by heavy rain rather than seismic tremors. But, signore, if I may presume to enquire: what are your plans now?"

"I was going to a bar for coffee."

"But what a coincidence! So was I. I pray you would not think it presumptuous if I joined you and had the privilege of offering you the coffee? I feel there are still matters we might profitably discuss."

Obviously the crafty bastard wants something from me. He has certainly been quick to soften me up. To find out if there actually was a previous geological survey of the area that he could have known about I shall probably have to go to the central records in Lucca and dig them out. He must also know I could never be bothered. Meanwhile, I badly need coffee.

The surprised barman gives me a welcome reassuringly free of hyperbole. Indeed, he manages to make me feel something of a local celebrity. I suppose I am, really, but it's nice to know at least one of the tradespeople is pleased to see me. Benedetti elects to sit at a table instead of standing at the bar, and the barman duly brings us our coffees and chocolate-filled croissants.

"You must forgive me for harping on it, maestro," Benedetti dabs at his lips with a tiny square of tissue paper, "but I feel myself privileged to be sitting here not merely with an esteemed client and valued friend but with the authentic beneficiary of a miracle. I remember in one of our previous conversations you were, dare I say it?, somewhat *Protestant* in your scepticism about the powers of Our Lady. But I understand that the ex voto intercession of the Blessed Diana was your salvation. It is my firm belief that she is simply another aspect of the maternal principle embodied by Our Lady who watches over this sad world of ours. At some level they are surely indivisible."

Huh? What nonsense is this? I have come prepared for coffee, not for a theological discussion. "You must forgive me, dottore. I hadn't taken you for so profoundly religious a person."

"Oh, I am, signor Samper, I truly am. For a while as a student I even wondered whether I might have a calling. But as scripture soberingly points out, many are called but few are chosen. I, alas, was not chosen."

I resist saying this showed a novel fastidiousness on the deity's part. "My stepmother assures me that anyone may serve, regardless of profession. Even a humble prostitute or estate agent or"—I add hurriedly, for I like to be fair—"a mere *writer* can, I gather, be an instrument of glory. But I'm puzzled by your mention of a Blessed Diana. I'm afraid I'm not very well up on your Catholic saints. Is this to do with hunting? The Roman goddess?"

"Oh, but surely?" Benedetti raises his eyebrows and I am intrigued to see how his rug almost (but not quite) imperceptibly floats like a dark continent above shifting tectonic plates. "The newspapers here were full of it. A police helicopter pilot reported you as saying that you and your friends were saved by an apparition of the Blessed Diana, the late British princess, the wife of *il Principe Carlo*. It was all in *Il Tirreno* and other newspapers. Did you not see it? You told the pilot she appeared in your kitchen surrounded by a halo of light and warned you to leave the house at once. Already, I believe, her followers are visiting the place, and not all of them British, either. Many Italians are—"

"*What?* Signor Benedetti, this is utter nonsense! This is truly the first I've ever heard of it. No such thing happened and I assure you I said nothing of the kind. I'm afraid the entire incident is a complete invention by the pilot and the press. A total fabrication. What I think I said was—" But although I'm in full expostulatory mode I now can't remember exactly what I did say at the time. It had hardly been a moment for great coherence, dangling underslept and overwrought above the ruins of my house. "Whatever I said, I most certainly didn't claim we saw an apparition. I've never heard such rubbish. And I'm quite sure that if I were going to see an apparition it wouldn't be of a public figure I never met and who, at best, moved me to utter indifference. In any case you can't possibly describe her as 'Blessed' as though she were a candidate for sainthood. She was a Protestant and certainly no saint."

It's infuriating how difficult it is to deny something vehemently without incurring the suspicion of over-protesting. I hope that in these chronicles I have painted a self-portrait of Samper the inflexible rationalist. Quirky and passionate on occasion, maybe, as befits an artist; but someone who has no truck with the sordid cop-outs and infantile comforts of religious belief and similar superstitions. I generally treat transcendental assertions with pained impatience, hoping to get back quickly to a subject worthy of intelligent conversation. But this tactic can also be overplayed and appear too casual by half, just a little too studiedly indifferent. Here and now, back in my favourite hometown bar and hearing outrageous lies imputed to me by a weasel in a wig, I can't stop myself from lapsing into furious denial.

Meanwhile, the bewigged weasel is looking rather shocked. He collects himself enough to begin blustering, "Of course, signore, these are matters for the individual, and I'm sure in the confusion of that terrible night . . ." But then he changes gear as though he has suddenly thought of something. "Might I humbly suggest it would be to your advantage if you didn't express such views too widely?"

"You think it might put me on the Vatican's hit list? Papal assassins stalking me and lacing my coffee with polonium?"

Benedetti turns around and with a graceful gesture indicates to the barman that he should bring us fresh supplies. Turning back, he says in a suddenly businesslike tone, "*Rompo il discorso.* To change the subject ever so slightly, my friends at the post office tell me there are a good many letters waiting for you that they were unable to deliver. I would expect some of them to be the usual tiresome bills from ENEL and Telecom Italia since here one still pays for services like electricity and the telephone even if the cables are snapped off and dangling in space. One has a vision of volts and voices just dribbling out into the void," he adds with a surprising flight of whimsy. "You know how it is with these companies: if you wish to discontinue a service you are required to give suitable notice in advance. They are relentless."

"I'm sure a good lawyer will sort that out in thirty seconds."

"Oh, then there's nothing for you to worry about. An agent of your insurance company has also been trying to find you quite urgently. In her frustration she was even reduced to calling on me to see if I could give her your address. But alas! Still, I'm sure a man of your astuteness will long since have had such matters in hand and I have no business even mentioning them. No doubt your good lawyer will easily be able to cancel whatever financial penalties accrue from a failure to notify a loss as soon as it has occurred. I am impertinent even to mention it."

"No, no," I say magnanimously, while sipping hot espresso cautiously. I don't suppose polonium has any taste. "These are all things I shall be attending to now that I'm back."

"I'm relieved to hear it. As one familiar with your house as well as someone who esteems you greatly, I naturally have only the well-being of your affairs at heart. So I need not allude to other concerned parties such as the carabinieri, the Forestale, and the Comune itself."

"You may set your mind at rest, dottore. La signora Marta has already apprised me of them."

"Ah, you have seen her?"

"In England. And only last week."

"What an estimable person! I believe she is destined to be a great artist."

"So does she." Estimable, my foot. Not long ago, Benedetti was spreading the implausible canard that Marta was either a call girl or a madam, a calumny for which he was later obliged to apologise. There is craftiness in the wind here but I can't yet make out its direction.

"Because you and I are such old friends"—Benedetti's eyes guilelessly take in the flyblown ceiling overhead that still bears signs of the exuberance surrounding Italy's last World Cup win—"I will tell you something you will not have heard me say once I've said it. It is that gossip in our small world suggests la signora Marta has already made enquiries about the status of your remaining land at Le Roccie."

"*Ahh.*" Not to me, she hasn't. Devious bitch. Wants to expand her little empire, I suppose.

"Yes indeed. I expect you are wondering about property values and so on."

"Suppose I were. What would you say my remaining land is currently worth? In round figures?"

"In round figures? Precisely zero, I'm afraid. The roundest figure of all." Benedetti darts me an intense glance as if daring me to protest that only a few years ago he had promised me its value could only ever go up in leaps and bounds. "How could it be otherwise, signore? You would never get planning permission to rebuild a house up there even if you wanted to. And if by some miracle you did, no one would insure it for you."

"I suppose not."

"Definitely not. As *terreno* it is valueless. It is not agricultural land, nor is it proper forest. At best it is merely *sottobosco*. And blighted *sottobosco* at that."

It's dreadfully upsetting to hear my treasured patch of Eden so described. "You mean I might as well give it to Marta?" I exclaim bitterly.

"Ah, but would the signora want it? Don't forget that from the moment of the earthquake, the value of her own house halved."

"Really?" I perk up a bit.

"Of course. Who else would want to live there when one day a slightly bigger tremor might drop her house into the gulf as well? I fully understand your predicament, maestro, and I am overwhelmed by sympathy. Both you and la signora are artists. You must have silence and solitude. However, I promise you need not search out wildernesses above the snow line in order to find an ideal house for yourself in this area."

Good God, I do believe he's going to try and sell me another house! The *nerve* of the man! One really has to admire his chutzpah. "No doubt you have somewhere in mind?"

Again Benedetti scans the ceiling. Some of the adhering flecks may be the dried toppings of ice creams that were hurled heavenwards at the moment of Italy's winning goal: peppermint and chocolate sprinkles and the like. For the first time I notice that the little round grey marks are actually dimples in the plaster, no doubt impacts from the metal-topped corks of shaken spumante bottles. "But when I say your property is valueless," he says as though I hadn't asked the question, "that is true only in terms of the *terreno*."

"Oh? So what else is there? Don't tell me the landslip has exposed an Etruscan hypogeum full of treasures? Or an unexpected vein of gold, perhaps?"

"I'm afraid not. No, I am still thinking of your Princess Diana."

And suddenly I get it. Of *course*. How dumb I've been! So fixated have I become on the demise of my beautiful home that I have been blind to alternative possibilities. Seeing my expression Benedetti nods, the lights gleaming in his jet black thatch where only a few months ago they would have glistened pinkly on his scalp. Does he take it off at night and put it on a stand? I wonder. Or does Mrs. Weasel like to run her fingers through it when hormonally urged? And why does this make me feel marginally more softly disposed towards him?

"You see?" he says with a smile. "But it will need quite careful management. How much need I tell *you*, maestro, of all people: a local resident of such exquisite knowledge and perceptiveness? It has long been a cause for regret that our little town, though richly historic, lacks the somewhat obvious attractions that cause tourists to flock to our neighbours. Viareggio is an important town with excellent beaches and a major yacht-building industry. Lido di Camaiore and Forte dei Marmi have even more perfect beaches. Pietrasanta has its grand piazza and an international community of sculptors taking advantage of the proximity of the marble quarries of Carrara, where the immortal Michelangelo himself chose his stone. But we, tucked away as we are among the splendours of the Apuan Alps, need to work a little harder to entice visitors. All these things we can acknowledge without for a moment undervaluing our beloved town."

"But."

"But I have no doubt as to the possibilities opened up by

your recent experiences. They could be, shall we say, a way of turning misfortune into fortune? *Porto un esempio.* A little while ago you were perhaps toying with the possibility of buying or even building another house. You might, for example, discover a plot of land that is ideal for your purposes but that turns out to be classified as non-residential or has some other regulatory impediment. So let's just say I feel sure you would find your path made remarkably smoother provided that . . . But I hardly need labour the point to a man of your exceptional intelligence."

True, my intelligence *is* rather exceptional, although I think by now anybody who didn't live in a hollow tree and grunt would have got the idea. It's not polonium I need fear as the wages of indiscretion so much as penury and homelessness.

"*Rompo anch'io il discorso*," I say, it now being my turn to change the subject. "It occurs to me that a little earlier when we were discussing your religious beliefs I may have given offence by implying that my own position is one of intransigent scepticism. No, no"—I hold up a hand although Benedetti hasn't moved a muscle—"it has been preying on my conscience this last half hour. You must remember that my memory, which you yourself were once generous enough to call 'a gem,' was badly affected by my experiences, as my doctors will testify. Yet do you know, in the last few minutes the block caused by the trauma has miraculously begun to lift? I think this superlative coffee may have helped. At last I'm beginning to remember what I told that helicopter pilot about the apparition of the Princess that we all so clearly saw."

Now the weasel is nodding. "I knew you would," he says, exposing his canines in a rapacious smile. Then in a surprising gesture he reaches a manicured paw across the table to me. Recklessly—and is there any other way for a Samper to do something momentous?—I take it. As we leave the bar we step into brilliant sunshine. While we have been murkily plotting inside, the mist has vanished. The familiar towers and fountains and archways glitter in Mediterranean light. Greedily I drink it in. Suffolk is a merciful million miles away. My adoptive home town is laid out before me with the air of one of those trays full of objects one has to memorise quickly before a cloth is dropped back over it. My co-conspirator gives a little bow and twinkles away towards his office, sunlight gleaming off his mirror-finish shoes and striking pomaded highlights from his Stygian wig. Whoever would have thought a fastidious artist like Gerald Samper would find himself further thrust into the company of his erstwhile estate agent, a scheming tradesman of high polish and low cunning? My life is at present dogged by menials and functionaries (with a shudder I recall the recent quizzing of police persons) and this must definitely stop. Somehow, I must regain my creative solitude where only the muses are fit company. And I now realise that means right *here*. It is another of those decisions that take themselves.

After this encouraging start to the day, the rest of the morning unfolds in layers of bureaucratic monotony. I need hardly say that Benedetti proves to have been perfectly informed about my affairs. There are bills waiting for me at the post office, faithfully promising escalating fines the longer I postpone paying them. The companies behind them are not to know that their final sanction, the threat to cut off their services, merely makes me laugh. And in the offices of Assicurazioni San Bernardino da Siena, the agency that unwisely insured both my house and my car, I encounter the expected thicket of small print and unread clauses designed to let the company slither out of any obligations it once implied it would honour. A horrid glued-on fingernail gleaming with crimson lacquer draws my eyes to the clause, in print a bacterium would need a magnifying glass to read, stating the company's grudging preparedness to reimburse me the current value of the house as it presently stands.

"Unfortunately, signore, it no longer stands, does it? Regrettably, therefore, it has no current value." The creature raps her claws on the policy as though the whole matter were settled. She has a lot to learn about Gerald Samper. A wedge-shaped piece of wood on her desk announces her as Dottoressa Paola Strangolagalli, a name that gives you some idea of her family's antecedents. They probably had to make their own furniture.

"Preposterous," I tell her. "I can't be bothered to argue here and now. I shall have my solicitor handle the entire business. This is a perfectly standard Act of God for which I am covered and indemnified. Houses are always falling down, often on their owners' cars. You agreed to insure mine sight unseen, and that was your own look-out. Do you really think the saint whose name this company has adopted would have tried to wriggle out of such a moral commitment? I notice your letterhead presumptuously includes San Bernardino's famous IHS plaque, which he devised so that the crowds who heard him preach would venerate the Holy Name of Jesus. Undoubtedly you know that this native of Massa was celebrated all over Italy for restoring stolen or defrauded property? I rest my case." It really pays to do your homework. These proliferating Catholic saints often have considerable ironic value. I doubt if I know a single Maria who is a virgin.

"I shall need to confer with our head office."

"As opposed to your conscience?" On this tetchy note I leave. But there's nothing to lose. My solicitor will do the don-key work, after which I shall not again be putting my custom into the hands of Assicurazioni S. Bernardino da Siena, espe-cially not when they wear glued-on talons the colour of fresh blood. I spend the rest of the day visiting old acquaintances, not least of whom being my solicitor. I also hire a car.

The next morning, having avoided switching on BBCNN, I am drawn irresistibly back to the scene of my tragedy. I drive up through Greppone along the winding mountain road that eventually peters out in a realm of crags and buzzards. Just before it does there is a short track leading slightly downwards to the left. I bump along it. The view of Le Roccie is at once warmly familiar and painfully strange. The immediate trees seem unchanged but the expected roofs beyond them are gone. Someone has closed my barrier with a bright new chain, wound it with police-style dayglo tape and hung a medley of notices on it: *Proprietà Privata. Attenti al Cane. Zona Proibita Senza Esclusione. Via Interdetta, Sia per Veicoli o Pedonali. Pericolo di Morte!* In addition, panels of rusty builder's mesh have been secured across the track. The effect of all this drama is spoiled by a clearly trodden path off to one side that simply avoids the whole caboodle and gives easy access to what is left of my property. With misgivings I note a car cavalierly parked halfway down the track leading to Marta's house. I prepare to deal mercilessly with intruders.

Feeling almost like an intruder myself, I pick my way between the trees and in past the barricade. It really is very strange, the huge gulf that now yawns to the left: a pit of sky and blue panorama where until so recently stood my beautifully refurbished garage apartment and my house. Now someone has officiously—and probably officially—erected a lengthy chicken wire fence along the raw edge of the precipice plus further notices: *Zona Frana! Si Avvicina a Pericolo di Morte!* More skulls and crossbones. On the right, the copse that once acted as a cordon sanitaire between my house and Marta's now seems much too close, and the fence I put up beyond it as a cordial expression of legal demarcation is a bare twenty paces away. Behind that, Marta's house glows in the morning light and seems deceptively less like the hovel I know it to be. As the sole surviving residence at Le Roccie it has taken on an impertinent air of being lord of all it surveys. Given its new-found solitude, it even looks faintly desirable. Only I know its fungoid interior will be concealing heaps of unironed laundry and quantities of lethal Voynovian delicacies such as *shonka*, a sausage that induces paralysis, as well as its owner's flea market cosmetics with names like Randy Minx. Still, to the unaware passer-by the house would suggest the estate agent's adjective "unspoilt," which means something marginally better than a ruin. I'm not surprised the lady of the manor has been making discreet enquiries behind my back about the status of my surviving land. I just hope she has discovered that her manor has recently halved in value.

I am distracted from these tooth-grinding reflections by movement at the edge of the copse roughly where my patio once ended and the washing line began. A strange alien structure has been erected there, around which two figures are moving. They are badly dressed in bulky fleeces and look like the sort of people who haunt shopping centres in Britain muttering "Gotny spare change?" As I approach they seem faintly familiar although I can't place them. Suddenly the anger I have been suppressing at the way fate has trashed my lovely house and allowed Marta to gaze placidly out over the remains bubbles up. What the hell are these ragamuffins doing on my land, in complete contempt of fences and notices? I hail them in steely Italian from ten paces.

"Good morning. I trust you are aware that you're trespassing on private property? I need only to whistle for my Dobermans."

The two figures turn with a start. They now look even more familiar.

"Oh, bon jawno," says the woman. British and no mistake, even had their clothes and dentistry not given them away. "But surely we know you?" she continues in English. "Aren't you . . . Good heavens! You're the owner of the lovely house that fell over the precipice! You used to live here. We met last summer. *You're* the one saved by the miracle!"

And now I place them: a couple of prospective buyers whom Benedetti had shamelessly shown over Marta's house one day during her absence last year. I see them now as I did then, as Baggy and Dumpy. I can't remember their surnames. Barton? Ringworm? They were sniffing about for out-of-the-way properties, aided by a collection of keys that Benedetti had thoughtfully held on to after his agency had sold the houses.

"Ah yes, I remember now. Mr. and Mrs.—?"

"Barrington," says Baggy. "Chris and Deirdre. Well, this *is* an honour. You're a truly celebrated survivor."

"Gerald Samper," I say, not much moderating my steely tone. "Survivor or not, miracle or not, this is still my private property, you know. And what in God's name is that?"

"We mean no harm," says Dumpy soothingly. "We just came to put fresh flowers on the shrine."

It is an affair about shoulder height, cobbled together out of dressed stones—*my* dressed stones—into a solid plinth with a large recess. Inside the recess are coloured stalagmites of candle wax, sundry burnt matches, a chipped vase, faded bunches of flowers and a photograph of the late Princess of Wales protected by a crinkled sheet of plastic.

"Who built this?" I demand in a tone that goes with a riding crop being slapped against twill trousers.

"We don't know," says Baggy. "I think it sort of grew spontaneously round about Christmastime when all the stories came out. You mean you didn't know about it?"

"This is the first time I've been back since the night of the earthquake," I admit, easing my tone somewhat. This is a test, Samper. Can you go along with the fiction as rashly agreed yesterday with the crafty Benedetti? Or to put it another way, can you afford not to? I'm beginning to be aware of the sheer horror I've let myself in for: the awful strain of maintaining a lie that goes against every principle I hold. Not that I hold many, of course; but feigning a belief in apparitions is right up there with the taboo against humping the help and giving cash to beggars.

It is a classic dilemma; and like just about every other human dilemma there is a precedent for it in Italian opera. Those of you who sensibly resisted Glyndebourne's production last season of Handel's four hundred and fifty-second opera *Muzio* could have attended the revival in Cremona of Dario Maringiotti's brilliant *Il confessionale*. This minor masterpiece, produced in 1887, was banned after its first scandalous night and both librettist and composer were threatened with excommunication unless they recanted and promised never again to stage the work. This was still a big deal in 1887 but in the twenty-first century the Cremonesi had no such hang-ups.

The story of *Il confessionale* concerns a young, idealistic priest named Gioachino who is posted to a backward rural parish in Calabria. Shortly after he arrives a young girl, Tiziana, claims to have seen a vision of the Virgin sitting, as virgins will, in one of her father's olive trees. The priest visits the spot and declares he can sense the lingering presence of this blessed visitation. Both Tiziana and the olive tree become locally famous. But one day she comes to the confessional in a fit of contrition and admits to the priest that she made up the whole story for a bit of celebrity and to attract Valdemaro, one of the few lads in the village without acne, whose romantic interest is apparently fixed elsewhere.

Gioachino is horrified by this deception but feels he can't now repudiate his own validation of the olive tree as a sacred site without risking both his and the Church's credibility, and nor can he explain his change of heart without betraying the secrets of the confessional. So even as Tiziana penitently goes about the village denying her vision, Gioachino continues to encourage the pilgrims with tales of the apparition until he almost comes to believe he saw the vision himself. Yet he knows in his heart it is a lie, even though one whose revenue is swelling his church's coffers. There are some good subplots of rural cunning, rivalries and superstition. The climax of the story approaches with a terrific aria by Gioachino actually in the confessional with Tiziana. In a fit of remorse the tormented priest is revolted by his deception and condemns Tiziana for her fictitious vision and for impiously using the Virgin herself as a cloak for her own sordid romance. Tiziana then turns the aria into a duet by confessing that she also invented the tale of her affair with Valdemaro: it is the young priest himself whom she loves so passionately, and has done since he first arrived in the village. (It was at this point that the original production began to be booed on the grounds that for an audience to over-hear a confession, even a staged one, implied a de facto breach of sacred confidentiality.)

By now young Gioachino is completely out of his depth although with compassion he recognises that Tiziana is the least-favoured girl in the village, being bandy-legged and lightly moustached, which is motive enough for her intrigue. Feeling pity but threatened by her advances, he begins to panic and tries to drown out her shouted declarations of love with stern Latin reprimands and exhortations to say innumerable rosaries in penance. Meanwhile, hearing raised voices, the village elders gather in the church just in time to see Tiziana emerge stark naked from the confessional with a beatific smile of satisfaction. Is this her brutal attempt to incriminate the lover she cannot have, or are the villagers' coarse peasant suspicions justified that Gioachino has finally yielded to carnal temptation?

From this point on the melodrama admittedly becomes a little crude, although Maringiotti's score is sensationally accomplished. The solo oboe weaving around moments of spiritual tension is especially adroit in its vulgarity, suggesting the Holy Spirit's Tinkerbell-like habit of alighting mysteriously here and there amid the hurly-burly of human affairs. Whatever you thought of the score, if you were in the audience of *Il confessionale* in Cremona last year you could not possibly have emerged afterwards feeling you had been short-changed dramatically. On the other hand had you been nearly a thousand miles away in Sussex you would have discovered that Handel's *Muzio* concerned Mucius Scaevola, the Roman hero who penetrates the Etruscan camp but is captured while failing to kill the enemy king, Lars Porsenna. Porsenna condemns him to be burnt in a furnace but when he hears the sentence Mucius merely laughs, boasting that no Roman fears death. To show his contempt he holds his right hand unflinchingly in the flames until it is reduced to a blackened stump. Impressed, Porsenna frees him and Mucius is henceforth known as Scaevola or "Lefty." This is the only dramatic scene in the opera, and needless to say it takes place offstage. Better luck at Glyndebourne next year, you may think, when they are staging Handel's four hundred and fifty-third opera, *Physippides in Tartary*, whose plot can be viewed as an early experiment in anaesthesia. Spies tell me the production will be set in Wall Street, complete with stretch limos and mobile phones: the essential furniture of twenty-first-century ennui.

In any case, you will readily understand Samper's predicament here as he stands before this ad hoc shrine with Baggy and Dumpy expecting him to attribute his miraculous survival to the direct intercession of Barbara Cartland's step-granddaughter. Taking a leaf out of Gioachino's book I assume a rapt, far-away expression.

"I'm sure you can imagine how impossible I find it all to talk about. It's just . . . you know . . . one of those intensely *private* things."

"But she really did warn you to leave the house and it collapsed immediately you were all out?"

"We certainly got out in the nick of time." From their expressions of awe and devotion these two mugs are ready to believe anything I say. Despite the tragic outcome I find it hard not to smile as I recall the very unspiritual atmosphere that night last December when Adrian and I, considerably the worse for drink and hallucinogenic mushrooms, had tried to stop giggling long enough to convince our guests to forsake the warm kitchen with its log fire and hurry outside for their lives into freezing mist and pitch darkness. The only unexpected appearance that evening had been Marta, much too solid (and probably sullied) in her flesh to be anything as ethereal as an apparition, who had suddenly returned after the best part of a year in America. Even then, once we were all standing outside shivering we kept remembering essential emergency articles such as passports and overcoats that were worth dashing back indoors for in an elaborate game of "chicken," daring ourselves to get in and safely out again before the steadily crumbling ground at the front of the house carried away the entire building. The effects of the mushrooms, cunningly incorporated into my award-winning badger Wellington, persisted for hours and surrounded objects with shimmering haloes. They cast a dreamy, surreal air over the entire night so that even the eventual vanishing of my house—weirdly, in near silence—seemed phantasmic and illusory. Equally so are the present activities of Baggy and Dumpy, who strike me as implausible acolytes in this particular sect. "But I still don't understand what you're doing here," I put to them in the tones of a magistrate still far from won over to their case.

"Long story," says Dumpy.

"Oh, we live here," says Baggy.

Why is this so unwelcome? "You mean you live in Italy?"

"Yes—right here, down the road in Greppone. Last year

Deirdre and I bought a house just this side of the town. We'd been looking to move for ages. I mean, Britain has changed rather a lot, hasn't it?"

For the better, I should imagine, since they moved. To think: but for the providential destruction of my house I would have had this ineffable couple as neighbours a mere five kilometres away. It turns out I even know their very house, down past the path leading to the cemetery. It gets very little sun after noon, especially in winter, and has an unrelieved view of a menacing mountainside opposite that looks as though it might topple forward across the dark gorge and obliterate everything. It is indeed a peculiar sensibility that could have stood on their terrace and said "Darling—we're never going to do better than this." But then, they probably thought the same thing on the altar steps some fifteen years ago in an equally self-fulfilling prophecy.

"When there were all those articles in the newspapers last year about the earthquake—which, by the way, we also felt down in Greppone—we read about how the Princess had saved your lives and we just knew, didn't we, darling? It was *meant* that we should have moved to almost the exact spot where she manifested her love for her subjects. But that was Diana all over. Ridiculed and outcast in her homeland, she chose to appear abroad to rescue distressed Britons."

I can't help making an exasperated inventory here. "Three of us weren't Britons at all. A Voynovian composer, a Russian pianist and Max Christ himself, who is Bavarian."

"Diana spread her light equally around the world, as I'm sure you remember, Mr. Samper. She was oblivious to nationality."

I am about to ask tartly why, in that case, Dumpy had singled my houseguests out as distressed Britons but caught myself in time. Never argue with the devout: another in my short list of axioms. After more conversation—desultory and resigned on my part, intractably fervent on theirs—I gather these two exiles are leading members of a Diana cult that is rapidly spreading among British expatriates and local Italians. The Italians always were sentimental about her, of course. On the day of her death my barber observed how tragic it was. "She had adorable legs," he said soulfully as he wound crêpe paper around my neck. But more than that, Diana was really a figure straight out of . . . straight out of Italian *opera*. Of course! Romantic, melodramatic, tragic . . . What a perfect, camp . . . *No!* What a perfect, *tragic* theme! The simple, English-rose step-granddaughter of a serial romance writer, unhappily married to a prince, cold-shouldered by her husband's family, alternately pilloried and fawned on by the British press, adored by the afflicted and downtrodden of the rest of the world, driven for affection into the dusky arms of a foreign tradesman's son, immolated in a Paris underpass with her lover to incredible rumours of Secret Service assassination plots . . . Forget the *Epic of Gilgamesh*. This is surely the only possible operatic subject for Gerald Samper, mischievous tragedian! Send 'em away with a tear in their eye and a faint, indefinable feeling that creeps up on them later that they may have been sent up.

"You find it amusing?" Baggy is asking, faintly aggrieved and defensive.

"Absolutely not," I tell him. "Far from it. No, just an idea I've had. Not funny at all. In fact, I want to know more." An inner voice of caution is warning me that once again I'm putting my head into a noose of pure hokum. Too bad: this is an operatic *gift*. But right now I need to get back to town and organise a bulldozer because I want to see how much can be saved from the rubble of my former home. I leave Baggy and Dumpy unwrapping sheaves of gladioli and preparing to dress their shrine. I suddenly feel rather cheerful. It has occurred to me that the presence of hordes of pilgrims on my land ought to remove the last vestiges of peace and quiet from Marta's property. Truly, it's an ill wind.

Adrian 3

e-mail from Dr. Adrian Jestico (ajestico@bois.ac.uk)
to Dr. Penny Barbisant (penbar@labs.whoi.ed)

S orry about the gap, Penny. Like almost everyone else in this department I've become the victim of temporary institutional paralysis. We've had our work disrupted or suspended by the government's sudden brainwave to dust off— yet again—their ancient plans for a Severn Barrage. So we've all gone into lunacy mode, with fifty-nine thousand committees trying to work out how many Environmental Impact Assessments they'll need to cover all political eventualities. Everyone knows, of course, there can never be enough EIAs for a thing this size, or well enough done. It's guaranteed that if the project does eventually go ahead (oh! that delicious gravy train of EU & taxpayers' money!) somebody at the very last moment will discover a community of five specimens of something called Showalter's Banded Snail (previously thought extinct) in the Vale of Berkeley, or a nesting pair of Gloomy Petrels or some other unknown bird of vast emotional significance to the middle classes in Notting Hill Gate, & the entire thing will grind to a halt amid recriminations & backbiting.

I'm glad the idea of following up on *Eurythenes* has paid off. With those P concentrations you quote I'm willing to stick my neck out all the way & say you've definitely got a wreck or a dumped cargo out there. I can't think of anything else that would come close to accounting for such quantities. Any wreck ought to show up on the GLORIA scans USGS did for the 200-mile EZ, depending on how much sediment is getting dumped out there.

You might eventually have to do a search through some print-outs if you can bear the tedium.

As you say, it was probably inevitable that Gerry would return to Italy, & not just because of what happened at Crendlesham. He seemed to suffer from a kind of paralysis in the UK as though completely out of his depth: moody, on edge, generally baffled. Often not even very good company, which really is unlike him. I suppose it's simpler to think of him as a displaced person, he's lived so little of his adult life in Britain. In fact, he often describes himself (with some pride) as a professional foreigner.

Quite why he's so disenchanted with the land of his birth isn't clear to me. I don't think it's anything to do with that accident at Lyme Regis when he was a kid: a freak natural event like that could happen anywhere. It's more as if he felt let down, as though he expected England to live up to some propaganda version he inherited from his parents. The war and all that. He once told me the tiny straw in the wind that finally made him realise he would need to leave Britain permanently was the slogan "You Know It Makes Sense" that the government used in one of its public campaigns. It's over things like this I'm most aware of the age gap between us. And no, your questions aren't improper at all—they're highly pertinent. It's just that I don't know the answers. I don't know Gerry well enough & suspect I never shall. He manages to maintain no-go areas in his private self that he polices with great subtlety & humour so you're hardly aware they exist. It's only later when you're trying to explain his behaviour to somebody who doesn't know him that you realise how little you actually understand yourself. He's the archetypal god of the gaps. And as I know to my cost, it's pointless trying to quiz him as part of a plaintive demand for more intimacy. One relates to Gerry on his terms or, I'm afraid, not at all.

If you want a tale out of school, it's something I heard him once hint at in an unguarded moment. It dates from way back in the Seventies when he was working in London as an apprentice scriptwriter for Curzon TV. (Curzon TV? You're far too young to remember it.) All I know for certain is that it involved his friend Derek, who was at his birthday party on the night of the earth tremor & with whom Gerry maintains a strange relationship based—as far as I can see—equally on affection & contempt. (If I say Derek's an ebullient little hairdresser you'll get at least half the picture, but he's also surprisingly sharp & steely underneath. Quite a street-wise creature, if you ask me.) Something happened back then & they were both quite badly burned. I get the impression they may even have narrowly escaped jail. Actually, I quite like to think of Gerry having been caught up in something fishy. It's so much at odds with his current image as grandee aesthete. At any rate I suspect each has something on the other; & whatever it was is enough to keep their relationship going. I thought at first they were ex-lovers but they're so not each other's type. No, I feel sure they share a history as ex-conspirators or as the seared survivors of a scandal. It's yet something else that shows me how little I know about Gerry but I do quite like the mysteriousness.

Exactly how much hold he has over Derek now becomes germane. Gerry is making an extraordinary request of everyone who was present at that birthday party of his. No, not a request—more a demand. Take a deep rationalist breath, Penny, because you won't believe this. He wants us all to back a story that we were saved from death that night by a vision of Lady Di, who is supposed to have appeared in the kitchen & warned us to get out of the house. Apparently it's something the Italian newspapers concocted at the time & it has caught on to the extent that there's now a sort of St. Diana cult involving pilgrimages to Gerry's land—what's left of it—& miraculous healings & all the other stuff you'd expect them to invent.

*

Well, of course we all know it's garbage & to judge from his phone calls Gerry's own brand of combative scepticism is unimpaired. However, it seems the local authorities are keen that nobody issues any actual denials because they sense a boost for their tourist industry. But what's in it for Gerry, you acutely ask? Broad hints, apparently, of massive concessions over planning permission for a new house. He says he wants to stay in the area & find himself somewhere to live that is as private as his old house was (his ex-neighbour Marta aside) but not so hopelessly inaccessible. So he's put us all in quite a fix. For his sake, how can we not go along with this bogus vision story? But for the sake of our own self-respect, not to mention reputations, how can we possibly agree to it? My brother-in-law Max Christ is extraordinarily good-natured & loyal, even though as a Bavarian he must be wondering what on earth kind of nutty English family he has married into. Despite everything he clearly has a genuine soft spot for Gerry. But I can tell he's pretty exasperated, all the same. We had a sort of family confab last weekend at which both Max & I agreed that if asked we will simply answer any questions with a firm "No comment." However, it goes against the grain. I don't know about you but it costs me nothing to keep quiet about things like Creationism or Intelligent Design. I've no more quarrel with them than I have with Santa Claus or the Tooth Fairy. But helping to maintain the fiction that you've seen a vision of the Princess of Wales feels like a serious cause for shame. I suspect these dilemmas only ever happen to people who associate with Gerry.

And so back to BOIS & a meeting in half an hour with some bearded geologists moaning about erosion if the Severn Barrage doesn't get built. Small wonder I burden you with long emails: it's such a pleasure to be reminded there's life outside this institution. I had a similar pleasure at the weekend introducing my young nephew Josh to tardigrades (I bought him a beginner's microscope recently). It's great watching a bright kid catch on to the idea that there's so much going on in the world he can't see with his naked eye. He now badgers anyone who'll listen to go up a ladder & pull lumps of moss out of gutters so he can find his "little bears." He'll soon be risking his own neck but I still think it's better than sitting inertly in front of a TV.

I hope things with Luke are progressing satisfactorily. Even satisfyingly?

Cheers,
Adrian

4.

Among the many grim things about living in a hotel is the lack of a telephone of one's own. In terms of cost, hotel phones are like restaurant wines: simply the proprietor's way of hastening his early retirement to the Virgin Islands. Mobile phones, especially abroad, are equally ruinous. Nevertheless, a mobile phone is what I am using to keep in touch with the indispensable Frankie. He calls me as I am leaving the office in the Comune where I have just received their gracious permission to engage a bulldozer to search the ruins of my house for my buried personal effects. I am now on my way to the offices of the Forestale, where I need to obtain yet another *permesso*, when I answer my mobile on the steps outside. A fusillade of coughs identifies the caller.

"Do you know who I mean by Leo Wolstenholme?" asks Frankie eventually.

"No. Who's he?"

"It's a she. Leonora. Pretty famous here in the UK. Lots of tabloid interest in her various affairs, a boob operation that went wrong, etcetera, but best known as a regular presenter of *Global Eyeball*. No?"

"No."

"TV investigative series a bit like *Panorama* used to be but much less political, *harrucka-rucka-rucka errgh*, as befits the twenty-first century. Long on personalities and short on theory. They're doing a series of occasional programmes about sports heroes and the economics of commercial endorsement. Quite good, actually. I saw one they did about that golfer, Justin McPeach. Now *there's* a shit, incidentally. You did well not to write about him. What Wolstenholme wants is for you to take part in a programme about Millie Cleat."

"Oh Christ, Frankie, not *her* again? I'm still relishing her demise."

"I'm afraid you're considered as the world's leading Millie expert, Gerry. Just about everything anyone knows about her comes from your book. And now the film rights have been bought she'll go on being news for quite a time yet, at least until someone still older and missing more limbs breaks her records. Trust me, Gerry, you should do this interview. Leo's very popular and it'll help the book. And talking of which"— here he interrupts himself with another coughing fit so explosive that the tinny clacking the mobile makes as I hold it safely away from my ear actually causes a passing shopper to glance up in surprise—"Champions want to bring out a new edition of *Millie!* and they want an Afterword from you to take in her death and the investigation in Sydney. They also want you to concoct some kind of summing up. Her legacy, and all that. It needn't be long: fifteen hundred words at the most."

"For heaven's sake, Frankie." But I'll do it, and we both know I will. If I'm going to be buying a house shortly I shall need all the dosh I can earn. Movie deal or no, the book's an important part of my exchequer for as long as it can be made to last. A new edition's like a re-tread tyre. One takes something that's basically clapped-out and with judicious tweaking ekes out some more mileage. In the meantime I suppose I shall have to take part in this TV thing for much the same reason. According to Frankie this Leo creature is still "putting it all together," doing preliminary research and getting some "core interviews" lined up. Thanks to my brief long-ago stint in television I know this means that a team of baby research assistants and PR flackettes with names like Sappho and Poppy will be doing it for her in their slangy posh-cockney drawls. Frankie tells me Leo's quite happy to fly out and interview me here if I'm not planning on being in London. I tell him to relay the proviso that they may have to do it in snatches while a bull-dozer turns up precious relics from my former home.

"She'll love that. She's got an Action Woman reputation to keep up. She doesn't like studios, they're too tame. She's always on location. The more shells whistling overhead and pillars of oily smoke in the background the better. I realise you won't be providing those, but how many authors does she film pulling chests of drawers full of their underwear out of a Tuscan landslide? Knocks studio shots of talking heads for six, ditto tubby old ex-pats wearing panama hats slumped in a deck chair, maundering on about I Zingari and their cricketing heydays."

"Oh, and Frankie," I say before he can ring off or a pulmonary seizure supervene, "I need a contact number for Marta. She's supposed to be in London at the moment working with the awful Sue Donimus. No doubt in Voynovia they're still using pigeon post but after last year in the States she may actually have a mobile by now. Might you see what you can do, please?"

"H'm. Someone else I thought you never wanted to see again."

"Unfortunately she's got something I want."

"I'd rather not know."

"No, it's an almost impossible ambition. I want her silence."

Hours pass, during which I succeed in obtaining my *permesso* from the office of the Forestale. Faintly incredulous, I'm beginning to wonder whether Benedetti may not after all be putting in a word for me in various quarters. Generally speaking, the norm when applying for even the most trivial piece of paper in an Italian bureaucrat's office is that after queuing for an hour one will be sent smartly away for not having brought

RANCID PANSIES · 103

one or more of the following: a notarised copy of one's late mother's birth certificate, one's passport, one's *permesso di soggiorno*, one's medical records translated into Italian by a certified translator, one's *codice fiscale*, half a dozen passport photos, a sheet of *carta bollata* (from the nearest newsstand), one's inside leg measurement as taken not more than three months ago and duly attested by the Carabinieri, and anything else the bureaucrat can think up on the spur of the moment. In the good old days before the "Clean Hands" initiative of the Nineties that tried to do away with the bribery of officials, the only known way of getting anything out of chronically underpaid Italian bureaucrats was to turn up with a *mazzetta*: a "bunch" of banknotes or similar. I found a bottle of Chivas Regal would generally ensure the processing was over in a medium jiffy. True, they would still require you to return in three months to collect the relevant *permesso* ("Alas, the dossier has to go to Rome, signore, and you know what Rome is like"—hands spread in an expressive gesture of amused resignation), but at least the worst was over. In this brave new post-Chivas Regal era, though, bureaucrats are still underpaid and there's no knowing what vital document you may have left behind. ("But naturally, signor Samper, we require a notarised copy of your parents' marriage certificate." "In order to be connected to the town's *sewerage* system?" "Of course, signore. It is the law." And that's another hour's waiting down the chute.) All of which explains why native supplicants in Italian government offices wisely come armed with bulging portmanteaus containing every conceivable document detailing their family's history and activities back through several generations. Even so, the chances are they'll be sent away again for forgetting to bring a post office counterfoil proving they have already paid €31.83 for the *permesso* they're still months away from getting.

So the effortless speed with which I have just cleared the

bureaucratic hurdles required before I can go digging in the remains of my own home makes me wonder if the weasel's paw may not be behind this. Over the years I have deduced that Benedetti is very well connected in this town. I imagine it's impossible to be an estate agent in a place this size without being in touch with the movers and shakers, not to mention the makers and shovers. After all, he was probably at school with half the town council, if not the mayor himself. Come to that, I dare say I am myself not wholly without friends in the sort of places that count; so maybe our humiliating plot can be made to prosper long enough to see Samper once again ensconced in a suitable house, with grounds spacious enough to sing in and a kitchen designed for radical creativity. Cheered by the thought, I ring up a bulldozer man of my acquaintance and book his services in three weeks' time, which is the earliest he can manage.

And finally, now armed with her mobile number, I call up Marta in London from a bar where for old times' sake I am cautiously sipping a Fernet-Branca.

"Gerree!" comes that familiar cry that only a little over a year ago used to make my blood run cold practically daily.

"I hope I'm not interrupting a work of high art?"

"Not so." She giggles. "I am eating my lunch in the nude here."

Oh God. "You're fading, Marta. I didn't catch that?"

". . . in Danubya. Danubya's a new Voynovian ristoran. The first in London, it opens only last year. The *shonka* is *mm!* but not so good as ours from home. The manager and chef they are city men from Voynograd and do not understand country food so well. Do you remember *mavlisi?*"

Do I ever? Marta once called these "national delicacies" the Voynovian equivalent of Florentines, but having eaten them I can emphatically state that this description is far more misleading than helpful. True, both are pastry-based, but thereafter all similarity ends. One variety of *mavlisi* resembles testicles on the half-scrotum: a pigeon's egg pickled in spearmint, nested in a milky jelly and cupped in a wrinkled shell of dough. Another kind is like a tiny jam tart spread with a mulch of capers ground up with lavender. A third is a deep-fried ball about the size of a marble stuffed with chillies, garlic and horseradish. It explodes in your mouth like a depth charge and leaves your head hanging by a hinge for the rest of the day.

"My poor Gerree, you were so fast to eat them! There is a right way for eating *mavlisi*, very special and historic. The *mavlisi* of Danubya here are very *mm!*, as good almost as those of Mrszowski's in Voynograd. When I eat them I have tears in my eyes."

When I ate them even my underwear became damp, but I assume she is talking about tears of homesickness in her passionate, Slavic way. Frankly, Marta's a bit of a puzzle to me. Despite having had our misunderstandings in the past, affording both of us a fair old laugh from time to time, I can never quite disabuse myself of the apprehension that in her sly, peasant way she may be after my body. I know, I know—it sounds immodest. I'm hardly one of those men who delude themselves that they cause every woman they meet to go into a permanent state of rut, even though I've met no end of ladies who have been far from impervious to the urbane, artistic type. I must be a welcome change from business boys with boxer shorts and Boxster cars whose gift for music comes into its own on the terraces of Tottenham Hotspur. But I did give Marta a good deal of neighbourly help and generally took pity on her, and such things can be misinterpreted by romantically inclined girls. She was a stranger in a strange land who initially spoke no Italian and a brand of English that only I could understand. And frankly, no one could have been more sympathetic than I towards her drink problem and her weight problem and the fact that she comes from a family of millionaire racketeers based in the Carpathians—or wherever Voynovia is, I've still not looked it up in an atlas. As a Shropshire Samper whose family roots go back to Norman times it is hard not to view Marta as basically of gypsy stock. In a society like hers which surely sets great store by making upwardly mobile marriages, it's impossible to overlook that someone like myself with a proper pedigree would represent a considerable catch.

Small wonder, then, that I'm a little nervous. As friends were kind enough to remark on my fiftieth birthday (although not Derek—failure noted), I could easily pass for forty, being blessed by good fortune with one of those enduringly trim physiques that seem never to get badly out of shape (unlike, for example, Derek's). But poor Marta is really nothing but a great lump with hair that makes her look like Struwwelpeter's sister. When in her cups she has a habit of leering suggestively and becoming *tactile* in a way that quite frankly rather puts the wind up one. Unfortunately I now need her connivance. The importance of her going along with the Diana story outweighs everything else.

"The reason I'm calling," I tell her after an emboldening slug of Fernet-Branca, "is to say that I'm really worried about your lovely house."

"You are saying the ground is still moving, Gerree?"

"No, no, nothing like that. Structurally, it's fine." For a mildewy old barracks, that is. "I'm talking about the visitors up there. You must have noticed them when you were there after Christmas?"

"Sure. Rubber knickers."

I was forgetting her year in America. "But these people aren't just rubberneckers, Marta. They're pilgrims. It's hard to explain over the phone. They are going to grow in number and soon they'll make it impossible for you to work in peace. They'll be up there all the time. And once they discover you were at my birthday party that night they won't leave you alone, I promise you. They'll be banging on your door in a constant stream. Believe me, Marta, your days of quietly working at your music up at Le Roccie are numbered."

"No, Gerree, I can't believe this. Surely they just want to see the place where your house fell over. I would, if I am them."

I'll bet. "No, Marta, they want a lot more than that. You'll have to come out and see for yourself. And it's not just the value of your house as a retreat that is dropping. So is its market value, according to Benedetti."

"He is a *mustelje*, that man. A what do you say?"

"Weasel. Of course he is. We've both known that for years. But he's an expert weasel when it comes to local house prices. Look, will you come? I really think you should. Besides, I've a great favour to ask you and I can't easily explain it over the phone."

She perks up. "A favour, Gerree? What is that?"

I thought that would get her interest. Expecting Marta not to rise to the idea of having me indebted to her for a change would be like imagining Dracula walking past a blood bank without salivating. "We need to pretend that we escaped from my house before it fell over the cliff because the ghost of Princess Diana warned us to leave. I know it sounds silly . . . For God's sake, it *is* silly . . . But it's terribly important that you don't tell anybody it's untrue."

"But nobody says it is true, Gerree."

"Not over there in London, no. But they do here. These people who're ruining your house's peace and quiet believe that's what happened. They're religious maniacs and there are sound political reasons why we mustn't deny the story. I'll explain it all when you come over. I promise you, Marta, it's in both our interests. Even *financial* interests."

"Well, if you say, Gerree. But I don't believe in ghosts."

"Neither do I. But if anyone asks you if it's true that the ghost of Princess Diana saved our lives that night you must just lie and say yes . . . Oh, I wish you were here. It's so difficult explaining from a thousand miles away. Incidentally, how is work with Ms. Donimus going?"

"I think perhaps Sue and me, we are washing up."

"I thought you were writing an opera together?"

"That was our plan. But it's not going so good."

"Washed up? Oh, you mean the project's over?"

"She is very violent, that one. There is much whipping even in Act 1, Gerree. I cannot write music for whipping. We in Voynovia have enough tortures when the Soviets were occupying us. I want loving, Gerree! I want to write passion! I do not want to write people in pain from their *vudel* parts whipping and burning. We're talking wall-to-wall S&M," she ends surprisingly in Bay Area leather-bar style.

Crikey, what kind of an opera is that? It sounds like a cheap way of evoking those staples of classical tragedy, pity and terror. Maybe it's a comic opera, a sort of upmarket musical tailored to suit the degraded tastes of modern Britain? After all, the common horde is for ever having holes drilled in its *vudel* parts in order to insert rings and studs and pins. And not just there, either. Also in its nasal, labial and auricular regions. We have finally become the sort of people *National Geographic* photographers used to go to Papua New Guinea to record, allegedly for anthropological purposes. Tattooed, pierced and infibulated, Britain's tribespeople are now the vanguard of a new Stone Age. So possibly this Sue Donimus libretto would admirably suit Glyndebourne (Nun orgy bleed, One bulgy nerd, Nylon bee drug or—as I often refer to her among operatic friends—Beryl Dungeon).

"Poor Marta. That doesn't sound at all like your sort of thing. Apart from that, is the lady hard to work with?"

"She is like many writers, Gerree. She has no music. It is the concept she likes, the idea to make an opera so many people will give her claps."

"Applaud her."

"Oh yes. Applaud she likes very much."

"Well, look, if you come out here I think you'll find there's a perfect story just waiting for you. Do you remember when we first met you told me you admired the British royal family?" (What she had actually said was "I love you British queens and kings tradition," a phrase that stuck in my mind as an indication that this was someone not destined to become a soul mate). "This story has high romance, high farce, high tragedy and absolutely no whipping. It's made for you."

"I may go back to the States, Gerree. Perhaps Max is trying to commission me."

"It's your life, Marta. But it's also your house and I urge you at least to pay a visit to Italy before you run off to America again."

With that I leave her to the joys of the cuisine in London's first (and I'd bet last) Voynovian eatery. Such has been the strain of conversing with her that I seem to have consumed rather more glasses of Fernet-Branca than I'd intended and my thoughts have taken on that floating quality I normally associate with early afternoons in Italy. I idly wonder what sort of a place the Danubya is. I can readily imagine its kitchens might surprise a health inspector by their lack of mice and cockroaches. What mightn't cross the inspector's mind is that these creatures are probably essential ingredients in the *plats du jour* and are therefore not allowed to go to waste. Still, as students of the Samper philosophy of food will know, any adventurous cook should indeed think seriously about rodents and insects. The industrialised world is only gradually waking up to the ecological soundness of tapping food sources that are plentiful and require no "food miles," in the current cant expression. Above all, in a grotesquely overpopulated world I think we should definitely be looking speculatively at our own species as offering real gastronomic potential. I am sorry that pioneering

German gourmet, Armin Meiwes, is unjustly languishing in jail for an entirely consensual culinary act, although if I may say so it was a blunder to sautée his friend's *vudel* part with garlic, salt and pepper. No wonder its owner found it too tough to eat. It would obviously require slow, juicy cooking as cock au vin. However, these are mere details. Anthropophagy would definitely be a small but decisive gesture towards dealing with the population explosion. We could start by putting environmentalists into the pot. They are multiplying at an alarming rate and are easily outbreeding and endangering more traditional natural science species. "Eat up your Greens!" could once again become a nursery injunction.

Although nobody would feel sentimental about environmentalists, let alone miss them, it's possible the old taboo against cannibalism might occasionally deter even venturesome diners. And it is here that modern science will shortly come to the rescue. If culturing stem cells will enable us to grow new body parts, then it is surely only a matter of time before slabs of boneless human meat can be grown in great vats: meat that was never part of any individual and so required no slaughter. This opens up all sorts of possibilities. The alimentary raw material could be grown from the diner's own stem cells, heralding a glorious new era of autophagy. Better still, at really expensive restaurants it would become possible to dine off the famous. Fans could eat steaks cultured from the film stars of their choice. Flushed with hero worship, young groupies could bite into hamburgers whose patties were made from the *vudel* parts of their pop idols and favourite sports personalities, drawing an ancient superstitious strength from the idea of incorporation . . . At this point, however, the thought of facing a plate of Millie-and-chips makes me come all over faint and I'm obliged to retire to my hotel for a lie-down, much as the late W. G. Sebald was always doing in his books.

On awakening with a slight headache I find a note waiting

for me downstairs. It is from Benedetti, who begs to inform me that he is in a position to show me a property that, he humbly ventures to suggest, might satisfy my exacting requirements for a domicile. I believe it's the first written message I've ever received from the *mustelje*, as Marta called him, and it's nice to see his written communications are as florid as his speech. There's much to be said for consistency of manners, even when we both know it's based on amused contempt. I'm perfectly certain he doesn't affect this sort of language with any other client. I suppose in a quaint fashion it amounts to a kind of intimacy. Once again I find myself wondering about his home life. As with his dumbfounding revelation a little over a year ago that he was a keen amateur plane-spotter, I feel sure there are aspects of Benedetti's private life that would readily incite both pity and terror.

Instead of immediately replying, I take myself off to the Farmacia for a packet of *paracetamolo* tablets. This late winter weather of early chill mists and brilliant sunshine seems to be having a slightly headachy effect on me. Then I go to my favourite bar to give the whole question of Whither Samper? some serious consideration. The problem of buying a house that is not merely a holiday home is it throws into question the whole business of why one chooses to live in any particular place. Most people can answer this by saying they want to be not too far from where they were brought up, or they need to be near their work and their children's schools, or else they understandably require a minimum distance of several hundred miles from their in-laws or ex-partners. In short, there are usually compelling circumstantial reasons why the average person is pretty much tied to a particular area. This makes house-hunting both simpler and more difficult, especially if everyone else wants to live in the same place.

I, however, can do my work anywhere. I have no relatives whom I wish to live near, nor any relationship that crucially depends on geography for its future. I am a free spirit, which makes house-hunting both more difficult and simpler. Theoretically, I could live just about anywhere I choose, and this constitutes a real problem. If like me you happened to read English Literature at a proper university—i.e. one founded before 1600 that does not offer online dating or origami as special subjects—you will doubtless recall having to study things with titles like *Sir Gawain and the White Night*: dreary mediaeval texts where knights and ploughmen alike lie awake in the small hours wondering whether their souls are sufficiently shriven (answer: *no*). If so, you may be surprised to learn that although he entirely lacks a soul, even G. Samper has the occasional white night in which a chef's panic about running out of thyme somehow takes on a disproportionate and dismal urgency. I'm also reduced to compulsively playing with words, which appear in my fevered mind as large white letters on a blackboard that re-shuffle themselves unstoppably. The anagrams take on an aura of spurious significance that fades even as dawn strengthens outside. Thus Lyme Regis is turned to Grey Slime, just as it has reduced my life to that of a Sly Emigré; while Lyme Regis Cobb cries "Come, grisly ebb!" and "Go, sly ebb crime!" or simply remains for ever a chill Iceberg Symbol of my past.

It's exactly in these small-hours moods that one wrestles with the question of where to live. The imagination proposes locations in copious variety. Each has advantages, each drawbacks. At the end, in fretful impatience with my irresolution, the white-night questions come: "Why live anywhere in particular? *Why live at all?*" And suddenly the simple, practical problem of buying a house takes on existential proportions and swamps the mind with desolation. This may be connected with eating Gorgonzola before going to bed. Certainly the utter futility is overwhelming once we have truly seen ourselves in the hours of darkness as plankton adrift in an ocean of time, each microscopic organism pathetically calling "Remember me!" before winking out. I review all this from my bogus marble table in the bar, drinking coffee with a Fernet chaser, both of which cast a deep umber pall over my mood. I can see Nico the owner occasionally giving me a sardonic head shake. I can read him like a bad paperback. He thinks I'm brooding over the loss of my house at Le Roccie. He can't imagine why I should be sitting glumly alone when I'm a local celebrity whose life was saved by a vision. Any Italian who had had such a sensational write-up in *Il Tirreno* would long since have worked out a way of capitalising on it, even if only to get other people to pay his bar bills. It would be a complete waste of time trying to explain to Nico that yes, the loss of Le Roccie was grim; but equally though differently grim was the confirmation in Crendlesham Hall that I ought never again to think seriously about returning to the land of my birth. It seems that even crafty old travellers manage to shut themselves out of places without a key to get back in. Does it matter? Maybe just occasionally, when I recall some vivid childhood pleasure such as the deep reassurance of a particular food or the associations that the seasons (four of them in those days) carried with them. People never hear me saying this, of course. I assume a scoffy radicalism in company but I'm often nostalgic when by myself. Nostalgia is my private default position.

But this will never do. I am surely not the sort of person who falls easy prey to introspection. My present task is to recognise that I wish to go on living *here*: here in hospitable Italy, right here in Versilia, even though a house in this area is going to cost me an arm, a leg and probably even a kidney if it's to be somewhere acceptable that I shan't need to renovate with my own two hands. Well, so be it. But even if re-establishing Samper in a house that befits his superior style will mean some years of having to eat fried grass and woodlouse paste, I am *not* going back to Champions Press. As I keep telling myself, never again will I ghost the biography of Millie Cleat's successor or the next Formula One pin-up goof or anybody else wearing a baseball cap and making those learned-from-TV gestures of punching the air and snarling. They are unfit company. Nor will I extend my range, as the nicotine-pickled Frankie has suggested, and write the life story of one of those celebs-for-fifteen-minutes or TV cheffies. He defends himself by saying it would have given me the opportunity to write a comic masterpiece. That's all very well, except that Gerald Samper is destined to write a *serious* masterpiece and it's time Frankie knew it. I don't need to be sidetracked by daft suggstions, all the less so now that I'm moderately affluent. There's a grand opera waiting to be written, and despite our slightly weird relationship I think Marta might actually be the right person to do the music. Her score for Piero Pacini's aborted last film, *Arrazzato*, did genuinely surprise me by its originality and skill, although it costs me something to admit this because of the brutal way in which she used it to lampoon my singing. I personally feel that a cruel musical parody whose target is instantly recognisable constitutes a kind of libel, although Little, Gidding LLP of Lincoln's Inn have advised me otherwise. It has taken almost two years for the pain of this betrayal to diminish to a dull ache, but over this period my scrupulous sense of fairness has enabled me to appreciate how good the rest of her score is. The film itself was never completed and, since the great Piero Pacini's untimely death, is destined to remain a torso that will only ever be watched by dedicated cinéastes. Marta was well paid for her work but I gather she has cannily retained the copyright. It strikes me that some of the music could well be adapted for an opera. God knows it's melodramatic enough, but it also has a neo-Prokoviev astringency that is brilliant for portraying sleaze. I think with her avowed romantic leanings tempered with her instinct for down-and-dirty Marta would produce a sensational score for my Princess Diana libretto. The libretto I have yet to write, that is. I shall try to keep the whippings to a bare minimum.

However, I can't do anything without somewhere of my own to work in. That means finding a suitable house as quickly as possible. So with a sigh I pay Nico for sundry coffees and walk down the Corso to Benedetti's office. This turns out to be in the sole charge of a love-bitten teenager who tells me his boss is out with a client and won't be back until six-thirty. So I leave the weasel a message suggesting we look at this property of his in the morning. Back at the hotel I find I have been asked to call a London number which turns out to be the *Global Eyeball* office. I am speaking to somebody named— what else?—Saffron. In Marlborough tones she tells me Leo Wolstenholme is delighted I've agreed to be interviewed because it would be impossible to make the programme without me. (Like hell it would. These people are ready for all contingencies. They would cheerfully cobble the entire thing together out of library footage if they had to.) Unfortunately Leo's not in the office just now but she does want to know if I can suggest someone they could contact about Millie's seamanship skills, especially somebody who knew her personally. This, too, is standard procedure: to use a patsy who has already agreed to be interviewed to do some unpaid research. For a moment I contemplate sending them off to Salcombe to track down an ancient salt who might remember Millie on holiday there at the age of six messing about in boats, as she had once claimed, the lying cow. As her husband Clifford remarked to me, she hadn't put bum to thwart in so much as a funfair rowing boat until she learned to sail on Ruislip Lido as an adult. But instead of maliciously proposing this fool's errand to Saffron I really try to think of somebody useful.

"It's hard to come up with a suitable name at a moment's notice," I tell her apologetically.

"It is," she agrees (although what she actually says is "i' *is*," with two rapid glottal stops).

But at this moment I do think of somebody: the redoubtable Joan Nugent. Joan is a hard-bitten ex-Royal Navy lady with a penchant for gaspers and pink gin who was a splendid ally to me when Millie was being drawn into the wacky world of marine mysticism. She was an old sailing chum of Millie's who lived near her somewhere between Chichester and Portsmouth and was distressed to see her friend sucked into a form of extreme environmentalism that was only ever going to make her look a total idiot. Indeed, Britain's national heroine barely scraped out of it with her reputation intact. I now think Joan will be the ideal person for this *Global Eyeball* malarkey. To counteract the inevitable sentimentality her rasping, down-to-earth assessments will be exactly what the programme needs.

"I *can* think of someone," I now say. "She and her friends used to sail with Millie in the old days. Believe me, she's just what you're looking for. She'll provide an alternative view."

"Oh wow! Sounds great. Who is she?"

"I think I'll contact her first, if you don't mind," I tell the eager Saffron firmly. "It'll be better if it comes from me."

So I sit on the edge of the bed and call up Joan. I realise I haven't spoken to her since Millie's death; but although I've known her for less than a year she already feels like one of those rare people with whom one can be out of touch for ages without it having the least effect on the friendship. She'd been an instant ally last year when we first met aboard a yacht at a dinner thrown by Millie's Australian partner, Lew Buschfeuer. Hitherto whenever I've rung Joan she has answered from a maelstrom of yapping dogs at the other end. For once, her nicotine-pickled rasp comes unaccompanied by canine bedlam.

"Gerry!" she cries when I've identified myself. "What makes you call this ancient mariner in her time of woe?"

"Why woe? Poor Joan, are you still grieving for Millie?" Well, they were old friends.

"Not right now, no. But last night I had to do away with the Bo'sun, poor old sod."

I remember the Bo'sun as ringleader of the doggy chorus that usually accompanied Joan's phone calls. "I'm sorry," I say insincerely.

"Don't be. He was twelve. Good age for them. Kidneys packing up. Could happen to any of us and probably will." A mirthless, deep ochre chuckle.

"Unfortunately no one's going to take us to the vet for a quick, merciful end."

"Huh, I certainly didn't take the Bo'sun to any vet. What do you think I am? Disgraceful idea, handing someone you love over to a total stranger to be executed. Any pet owner worth her salt ought to do it herself, and if she hasn't the guts she oughtn't to keep an animal. It's the least you can do for an old friend."

"I see." I picture Joan's stocky figure swinging a baseball bat or pouring barbiturates down the animal's throat through a funnel.

"Shot him with a flare pistol. A distress shell to the head, instant death, just like that. The old boy went out in a glorious blaze of red, you should have seen it. Twenty-five thousand candelas."

"You surely didn't do it at sea?" I imagine Joan and her yacht being impounded by coastguards for sending out a marine false alarm.

"Christ no. Did it right here in the back yard. Ha, it lit things up, I can tell you, but only for five seconds. Grand show while it lasted. God knows what the neighbours thought, but sod 'em. I gave the old Bo'sun a nautical burial this morning. Sank him off Hayling Island with a fathom of chain. We'd done a lot of trips together, he was a proper shipmate, bless him. A real old sea dog. Now, what can I do for you?"

118 · JAMES HAMILTON-PATERSON

I explain about *Global Eyeball*'s forthcoming documentary about Millie and ask whether I could put Joan's name forward. There is a silence.

"Oh fuck it, why not?" she says at length. "They may as well have someone on the programme who knew her and can cut through some of the crap."

"That's exactly what I told them. Without naming you, of course."

"I really miss the old girl, you know. I didn't say it before, Gerry, but I think you did her proud in that book of yours, even the cheeky bits. I know you never took to her much but you didn't know her in the early days when she was so happy to get away from that family of hers in wherever it was, Pinner. Believe me, she was a different person then. We were all sailors together, used to have some smashing nosh-ups out there in the harbour, just us girls. All that success did go to her head a bit, though. Mind you, it'd be a pretty rare person who wouldn't have her head turned. Talk about national adulation. It was ridiculous, really. I'm afraid she did go a bit potty towards the end, poor old girl, but of course you know that better than most. Still, what a way to go, eh? Prime-time Christmas TV, a rogue hoist and bingo! Strangled at her own masthead. By the way, did you hear the Aussies have nailed the company responsible?"

"No?"

"Turns out it wasn't the boatyard's fault. There was a defective batch of hoists with gears the wrong way round or something. The others were recalled. Curtains for that particular marine supply company, I'd think."

"Right." I've had enough of this boating backchat. There is a delicate Samper agenda to pursue. While Joan has been talking I've suddenly seen how she is exactly the person I need for some practical help. The truth is, I'm daunted by the horrid and arduous prospect of unearthing the contents of my house. It's too much for a refined English aesthete to do on his own, no matter how sprightly and resourceful he is. Adrian can't come because he's apparently up to his eyes in some panic at BOIS. So I'm wondering . . .

"Joan?"

"Yup."

"I suppose you wouldn't fancy a trip out to Italy would you?"

"*Italy*? Why, when are you leaving?"

"I'm here already. This is where I'm phoning from. This Leo Wolstenholme says she'll come out here to film an interview with me, and it just struck me that if you were here too they could do us at the same time, maybe even both together for some of the bits. I'm sure we can wangle your air fare and expenses. A programme like *Global Eyeball* will have an exes account dribbling at the seams with cash. But also . . . I hardly like to ask this of you since I don't really know you that well, but I'd be awfully grateful for a hand."

I explain the problem, during which I can hear the unmistakable sound of Joan lighting up one of her high-tar gaspers with a Swan Vesta. She thinks lighters are effete. How is it I know all these hard-core smokers? At least she doesn't cough like Frankie.

"I remember now," she says. "Of course, it was all in the newspapers before Christmas, wasn't it? About that famous conductor nearly getting killed in an Italian earthquake but you all got out of the house in the nick of time? You mean that's *your* house still buried out there, Gerry? You poor bugger. Well, why not? We Service pensioners don't get much fun. I'll need to do some arranging, though. The dogs'll have to go into kennels and I booked *Navy Lark* to have her hull cleaned next week. But she'll keep."

"You're a star. All your costs will be on me, of course. Meaning anything I can't induce these TV people to pay."

The next morning dawns grey but dry. After elaborate pleasantries in which Benedetti and I each vie for the preference of not being driven by the other, I find myself sitting fatalistically in the passenger seat of his late model Range Rover being whirled through ever-narrowing lanes above the town. He has not driven me since I was negotiating to buy my late lamented house many moons ago but I haven't forgotten his distinctive combination of competence and lack of imagination. It is not really the devilish élan that is so Italian as much as the absence of apprehensiveness. Whereas I *know* that when I hurtle around a blind corner there will be a tractor with a huge trailer full of logs chugging in the opposite direction, Benedetti is equally certain that the road will be empty. It simply doesn't occur to him that it could be otherwise. Presumably he is right in at least nine cases out of ten. One's disinclination to be with him on the tenth occasion is what is keeping my knees locked and my fingerprints imprinted in the leather of the armrest. In the breeze from his half-open window his borrowed tresses wave like weeds on a river bed. Strange to think that hanks of hair from the same Chinese peasant girl who grew them will be waving on heads all around the world at this very moment. Today, possibly in my honour, Benedetti is dressed in what the clothes shop in the centre of town calls "stilo English gentlemans" in its window displays: brushed cotton shirt with a discreet check pattern, grey slacks and a light tweed sports jacket with an ivory silk handkerchief tucked into the top pocket. By his own lights he undoubtedly looks convincingly "*snob*," which in these parts connotes a fashionable retro Englishness vaguely associated with old leather, horses and monocles. To me the overall effect—by no means discounting the wig—is that of a slightly caddish prep-school master of forty years ago who will soon be leaving the school under a cloud. But what the hell, I'm hoping to buy a house from him, not staying behind after class. At this rate, with his refulgent brown brogue pressed so firmly on the accelerator, we may neither of us live to see the *compromesso* stage.

Yet before long, after a suicidal turn up an unmade track with small stones popping and pinging beneath the car's fat tyres, we come to a halt in a cloud of dust. As this drifts away a view of olive trees slowly clears. We are on a level patch of weedy land of maybe an acre, behind which a steep grove of olives clings to the mountainside with bundles of orange plastic netting tied to them. The same continues on the downward slope, falling abruptly away to a view of the town's red roofs far below. And behind those slumps the distant sea, flat-lining across the horizon, grey and unmoving like a patient beyond resuscitation. In the foreground, amid tangled briars and nettles, stands what I take to be the shell of a substantial stone farmhouse incongruously capped with a corrugated iron roof.

"No," I say decisively. "Nice position, but no. Too much work."

"Ah, but . . ." begins Benedetti. This is his métier, of course: the salesman for whom the word "no" is always equivocal and reversible. "Allow me, maestro, to tell you why you ought not to be hasty. For a start the position, as you have just spontaneously volunteered, is quite sensational. I know of no other house so close to town with a view like this, and I can assure you there is scarcely a property in this area I haven't visited. Now, I grant that at first sight the building itself is very slightly *unpropitious*, shall we say, but first impressions can be cruelly deceptive and besides, there's a story behind this place."

There always is, of course. Benedetti takes a heavy stick out of the back of the Range Rover. Muffling an inward sigh I allow him to slash a way through the nettles to the back door of the house, which is surprisingly new and solid-looking. He produces a set of keys and lets us in. He disappears into the semi-darkness to throw open some shutters and suddenly the interior gloom is dissipated and to my slight surprise I'm looking at a tastefully restored farmhouse kitchen. Old but re-laid and sealed *mezzani* gleam dully on the floor. Overhead the beams have been sand-blasted clean of the whitewash once tra-ditionally applied to ceilings in this region. The old wood has come up the shade UK colour charts usually describe as "tobacco" (but probably won't for very much longer out of abject political correctness. The Italians are a good deal more robust about such things, as one can deduce from their own charts which unabashedly retain "*testa di moro,*" or Moor's head, a phrase that not only translates as "nigger brown" but also denotes an old-fashioned type of bristly, rounded lavatory brush). Between paler new chestnut rafters the *mezzani* form regular strips of terracotta. A big open hearth, raised a couple of feet from the floor, dominates the rear wall. On the other side of the room an ancient door leads to a stone-flagged pas-sageway. Along this to the right is the front door and across the passage is the *salone*. More brick floors and beamed ceilings.

For once Benedetti keeps silent as though calculating that my own wordless surprise is best allowed to speak for itself. Despite myself I am already trying to visualise how this space can be best adapted to the Samper style of living, my initial resistance to the house admittedly lessened by finding it in such good internal repair. Going ahead while opening win-dows Benedetti leads the way up the staircase to the first floor. This, too, has been unfussily restored. The plasterwork on the white walls is obviously all new, and without any of the tricksy "antiquing" lapses of taste such as individual stones arbitrarily left unplastered and carefully picked out. There are three bed-rooms, the principal being spacious enough to accommodate easily even a bed the size of the one in Crendlesham Hall that Adrian and I shared at weekends and in which the sleeping Josh practically disappeared on the night of the Great Puke—as I now think of that literally fatal evening. The two bath-rooms are unfinished, presumably awaiting somebody's choice of tiles and fitments. The floor is cement, the plumbing connections all ready. A smaller flight of stairs leads to the attic. Great stretches of raw cement floor. The walls end abruptly just above the lintels of the window frames. Around them stands a rusty line of "cristi," the extensible builder's props whose shape suggests crucifixion to the jocular mind, supporting four-by-twos of rough pine to which the tin roof is nailed, pitched slightly higher at the back to shed the rain. Here the walls' stonework is hidden behind the modern ribbed terra-cotta slabs called *tabelle*, but to judge from the window embrasures without increasing the thickness of the walls. H'm.

"Okay," I say at last as we go back downstairs. "What's the story?"

"A tale indeed. A builder from Lucca bought this house at about the same time as you bought yours. I believe he was a distant relative of the old *contadini* who owned it. He had no intention of living here himself. He bought it speculatively when house prices in this area were beginning to rise rapidly. It was in pretty shabby condition. Shall we say in that respect it was not unlike la signora Marta's house before she took up residence at Le Roccie?"

What does he mean, before? On that illicit visit last summer with Baggy and Dumpy Benedetti must have seen for himself that Marta's residence in the house had changed nothing. A couple of rooms had been whitewashed and a few sackfuls of cobwebs had been removed, but only because the place had been used as a set for shooting some interiors for Pacini's film. "I can imagine," I say.

"So this builder was hoping to restore it and sell it to foreigners but unfortunately . . ."

". . . he ran out of money?"

"No, although I agree that's what so often happens. He simply did the project without getting the necessary planning permissions. He claimed he was just doing some necessary repairs."

"Expensive, but not particularly fatal."

"True. But then he fell foul of the Belle Arti, or the Beni Culturali as we have to remember to call them these days. He added that top floor, which is inauthentic."

"I thought those *tabelle* upstairs were suggestive. The stonework up there's just cladding."

Benedetti eyes me with mock admiration. "I pity the poor agent who tries to pull the wool over signor Samper's eyes. He stands no chance. When we go outside I think you'll agree the builder did a pretty good job of matching the stonework of the top storey with the rest of the house but yes, when you see those modern *forati* on the inside up there you realise at once what he's done."

"So basically he did everything *abusivamente*."

"Exactly."

"And the inevitable moment came when the Comune stopped him working?"

"Correct. The whole site was embargoed four years ago. *Bloccato*. He was allowed to put on a temporary roof to protect it, that was all. They gave him the opportunity to demolish the top floor and restore the original roof but he must have thought he'd already spent too much. He decided to leave everything as it was and hope for an amnesty."

Ah, that made sense. Like everything else the builder had done, it was a calculated risk. Every so often the Italian government declares an *amnistia* on illegal buildings and they acquire a *condono edilizio*, or a pardon. At the cost of a token fine the building suddenly becomes legal. In this case the builder had no doubt reckoned the time he might have to wait until the next amnesty against the money he'd already spent and the ever-increasing theoretical market value of the property itself, and decided to bet on it. Since there hasn't been an *amnistia* recently and I'm here as a potential buyer, he has obviously lost his wager.

"But if the place is still embargoed," I point out in a musing sort of way, "he can't sell it and no one can buy it."

"*Teoricamente*. In theory, that's true." Benedetti eyes me again, a prep-school master attempting to disguise an indecent proposal behind a meaningful hint. But old lightning-brain Samper has long seen it coming. Almost from the start the air has been laden with the gamey scent of a deal.

"Mm," I say. "So I officially endorse the Diana story, the Comune lifts the embargo on condition that the builder sells—which I bet he will since his money's been locked up for a good few years now and he must be sick of the trouble this place has caused him—and I get first refusal. Probably several refusals. What's he asking?"

"Four hundred thousand."

"Euros? He must be joking. An entire floor to demolish, a new roof to put on, a *pavimento* to lay outside, a garage to build, bathrooms to install, kitchen to equip. What about services? I can see it's plumbed and wired."

"Well, of course they all have to be connected. There's mains sewerage and even gas in the middle of the road."

"Yes, a good hundred metres away. Phone? No visible landlines. You're talking a lot of money and a great deal of time and bureaucratic nightmare to make this place fully habitable. And still he wants four hundred thousand?" Cool hand Samper, playing the seasoned expert, chooses the right dismissive tone. "Not a cat in hell's chance. Shall we go back to town and get a coffee?"

In silence Benedetti locks up and leads the way back to his monster wagon. "I'm sure the sum being asked is *trattabile*, by the way," he adds.

"Negotiable? I should hope it was."

"But a person as enviably *aggiornato* as yourself," he says as

I once again strap myself fatalistically into his all-terrain juggernaut, "will of course be aware how much in demand isolated properties with a stupendous view like this one are." The prep-school master, his initial advances rebuffed, resorts to wheedling and threats.

"If by up-to-date you mean that I'll have heard the wild rumours about Russian mafiosi buying properties around here with attaché cases stuffed with cash, then yes. But people to whom money is no object don't buy unfinished houses with tin roofs, do they? They go upmarket for grandees' villas with swimming pools and tennis courts. And most of the prospective buyers of houses like this one have just enough sense to work out that there will be a long way to go before they can finally let themselves and their kids through the front door for a family holiday. And they also may not know there are ways of minimising costs and hustling things along." Now it's my turn to give him a meaningful look, schoolboy hinting that he might come across if it were made worth his while in terms of exam results. We all have our price, do we not?

We are barging back down the mountainside along the narrow winding lane with dangling brambles from the high banks on either side slapping the car's flanks like quirts. For one appalling moment, just as we are about to enter a blind S-bend, Benedetti takes his eyes off the road to give me a placid leer.

"I think you'll be pleasantly surprised, signor Samper, at how relaxed and easy this process could be. These little transactions are two-way affairs, aren't they? A bit of give and take on both sides?"

I begin to wonder if at some time in the past Benedetti might actually have been a schoolteacher. He has all the moves.

Adrian 4

email from Dr. Adrian Jestico (ajestico@bois.ac.uk)
to Dr. Penny Barbisant (penbar@labs.whoi.ed)

So it *is* a munitions ship, eh? Does your old supervisor not merit a small prize for inspired guesswork? Anyway, you're right: it will probably foul up your fieldwork unless you can get your department head to change the remit so you can work specifically on mapping chromosome set changes in bivalves at graduated distances from a WW2 munitions ship wreck. Anyway, have a look at the Beaufort's Dyke data I mentioned last month. All those ancient incendiary devices coming ashore on the Scottish and Irish coasts. There was a mini-panic about it in 1995 when I first went to BOIS (which is how I remember the year). You might also glance at the data on a WW2 Liberty ship, the *Richard Montgomery.* It's also a US munitions ship but wrecked in the UK off the Isle of Sheppey. The MoD has decided the cargo's too unstable to risk touching so the whole area around it is buoyed off. There may be some existing studies on chemical contamination in the surrounding sediments & biota but there probably aren't because of the prohibited area. They say if the remaining cargo explodes at low tide it could flatten Sheerness. One's mouth waters.

You admit to being homesick from time to time but take it from me, Penny, you're well out of Southampton. This Severn Barrage thing's shaping up to be another Great British Farce. There are two reasons for building a barrage across the Severn. Number one: tidal power generation. Good strong tidal flows there, lots of whizzing turbines. The other is that serious erosion of the N. Devon & Somerset coastlines is proceeding apace & with rising sea levels it's getting worse by the year. They predict that unless the barrage is built the Somerset Levels will flood in the next 20–30 years. So?

I can't remember how many Severn barrage schemes have been proposed since 1849, when they wanted it to create harbours for their fishing fleets & to serve as a road bridge. 14? 16? And that includes plans by the dear old Nazis in the 1940s who decided they would need one after they'd conquered Britain. Anyway, it's now time for yet another barrage scheme so Defra & the Dept. of Trade & Industry have duly commissioned a zillion Environmental Impact Assessments, a lot of which fall to BOIS. It's seriously getting in the way of normal work. In addition we're bombarded with fierce or whingeing notes from municipalities in South Wales who write in to tell us that a barrage will dramatically change their coastline's sediment budget. All this crap is turning us into bureaucrats. I became an oceanographer because I actually love the sea & its creatures. I do not love the DTI & its creatures, some of whom make holothurians look multi-talented. I had one in my office the other day who, if you'd upended him, could probably have ejected a stream of water & sand particles from his anus in vague protest, but that would have been about it.

As for dear Gerry, I'm afraid he's miffed with me because I can't go & give him a hand rescuing stuff from his house when the bulldozers go in. I just can't get away at the moment, we're all knee deep in these endless meetings. He *says* he understands but his tone says he doesn't. That's the trouble with being self-employed: you imagine that everyone else is as free of timetables as you yourself. And what's more, because everyone else has a salary (as opposed to your own unpredictable pittance) you assume they must have the financial freedom to be able to take time off on a whim. On the phone Gerry's voice gets a slightly petulant edge to it when I say I truly can't drop everything & come. He's such an egotist but I do feel sorry for him. It will be no fun unearthing his belongings (embarrassing, too, now & then) & I wish I could be there if only to lend moral support.

However, he says he's going to be interviewed for a TV documentary about Millie Cleat, which he'll enjoy. I gather it's for *Global Eyeball* & Leo Wolstenholme's going out personally to interview him, so our Gerry's clearly on the way to becoming a mini-celeb in his own right. He has also raised an interesting point. I can't remember if you were still here when there was the fuss over that EAGIS survey in the Canaries two or three years ago? Sorry if I'm telling you stuff you already know, but the EU funded a seismic study of the roots of Cumbre Vieja, that volcanic peak with the crack in it which, if it collapses, they say will cause a tsunami that could swamp New York. The survey was in full swing when Millie was doing one of her around-the-world races. To save time & catch a current one night she cut across four brilliantly lit survey vessels close enough to make them take violent evasive action. Needless to say, this completely screwed up the leg & it turned out that in about 5 minutes flat Millie had ruined a vital part of the survey. As usual, they were on an ultra-tight time budget & it took them the best part of 24 hours to disentangle a cat's cradle of streamers & air hoses—£80,000's worth of equipment damage—after which they had to abort the survey & head home. The gap in the seismological picture turned out to be critical so we still don't know how unstable Cumbre Vieja really is. Gerry always claims Millie remained to her dying day (which we all remember so vividly) blissfully unaware of the havoc she caused. Meanwhile, there was a conspiracy at BOIS & all the other participating institutions in Europe not to leak the fact that the survey vessels had got the whole episode on video. They were so mightily pissed off at her they were saving the film for release at a moment when she could be made to look a complete idiot. Unfortunately they waited too long & it never happened.

Gerry's now suggesting Leo Wolstenholme ought to be told about the Canaries caper—the other side of the Millie myth, sort of thing. So he has asked me to sound out various people who were on EAGIS & ask what they think. All the video stuff's here at Southampton. It's not edited or anything, just webcam files, but the TV people could easily put it together if they wanted. If *Global Eyeball* does run the story I'm afraid I don't think it will have the impact a lot of scientists (as well as Gerry himself) imagine.

Other than that, Gerry says he's thinking of buying another house in the same area of Italy though obviously not on that same bit of mountain. From the point of view of our relationship, such as it is (whatever it is), I'm sorry he's so far away. From his own point of view it's logical. He's more than fluent in the language—verbose, one could say—& the place feels like home to him, so why not? It's a pity house prices in that part of Tuscany are so ludicrously high he's probably going to have to spend a good deal, if not all, of his film rights windfall. Our lavishly salaried hearts bleed for him.

I must now apologise for being gratuitously rude about the man from the DTI. He's just been back & he's actually from Defra. He came to remind me there's virtually no aspect of a Severn Barrage that can't fall under the heading of the environment or food or rural affairs. Exercising his department's interest in food he stayed to lunch, & I wish to state that like any sea cucumber he can ingest nourishment even though his mouth is fringed with a moustache rather than tentacles. It remains to be seen whether he can eject sticky white threads when irritated. I'm hoping to give him plenty of opportunity to display this faculty but until he does holothurians still win on all-round performance. Especially their conversation.

    Cheers,
    Adrian

5

In pursuit of background information for my nascent opera I have just paid a mental visit to the Vatican, specifically to that administrative area around the Cortile del Triangolo. Here is the sixteenth-century palazzo jocularly known as Castel Birbone whose ground floor houses a large office with "De Reliquiis Sanctis" on the door. These days it is generally pandemonium, being full of short-tempered American novelists of no great literary talent. They are trying to track down that Holy Grail of the popular American novel, the Holy Grail. They have, however, scarcely a word of Latin or even Italian between them, so are reliant on official interpreters with whom they soon run out of patience. The booming voices demanding access to archival evidence spill out into the hall and pursue one's hurrying heels as they mount the glorious staircase (by Baldassare Bernucci) to the first floor's comparative hush. There, at the end of a corridor, is a heavy wooden door marked "De S. S. Manifestis."

This is the office that deals with holy apparitions, mostly of the Virgin. Time was when it was regularly besieged by Irish, Portuguese and French peasants dressed in rusty black, staking their claims to a personal visitation. But as their countries' economies improved and folk acquired a rudimentary education, the numbers of supplicants coming to this room fell off sharply. It was almost as if the Mother of God, whose own education had stuck at counting to five and learning mnemonic rhymes for knowing when to plant olives and mate sheep, was nervous that She might be asked her opinions on gender theory or economics. Of late, therefore, those to whom She had appeared were almost exclusively children from the remaining wilds of Catholic credulousness: Poles, Bosnia-Herzegovinans, Voynovians and the like, hailing from villages where oxcarts still have solid wooden wheels and suspected homosexuals are periodically burned. Here the Virgin can alight with complete intellectual safety, surprising children on hillsides as they go about their humble tasks of watching olives grow and sheep tup.

On the day of my visit, however, there was no one in the high, beamed room except a young priest with remarkable curled eyelashes. He was sitting behind a desk playing *Grand Theft Auto: Vice City* when I entered after a respectful knock. The priest zapped the game with a guilty look and as 1980s Miami faded from the screen he sprang to his feet, offering me a chair. His screensaver, I noticed, was a stately swirl of golden Paschal Lambs with their shouldered banners of St. George revolving against a velvety blue background.

"You have come to report a vision, signore?" he enquired. The attractive thing about robes is they always make one wonder what's under them, something modern secular clothing practically never does. One day couturiers will wake up to this.

"In a way," I said. "That's to say, it's more of a second-hand report."

"I see. And the individual who saw the vision is still too overwhelmed to testify in person? That is often the case. It was of our Blessed Queen of Heaven?"

"More a princess. It was of Diana, the wife of—"

"—*il Principe Carlo*? Yes. Remarkable. Only a few days ago in this very room I had a visit from a British couple who likewise reported a visitation by *la Principessa*, although again it was not a first-hand account."

"Signori Baghi e Dampi?" I exclaimed in surprise. "Or

rather, Signor e Signora Barrington?" It was strange enough meeting them again as they were dressing the shrine at Le Roccie; but their already having paid a visit to the Vatican was downright disturbing. What possible motive could they have?

"Ah yes. Yes—countrymen of yours, if I may presume? But they didn't enjoy your excellent fluency in our language, alas. They were accompanied by an Italian friend who I gather is intent on establishing a shrine on the spot where the apparition occurred. Unfortunately I had to tell them what I have to tell you, too, signore. You want Room 21."

"I do?"

"Room 21 deals with applications for non-Catholics to be considered officially as having lived *vitae sanctae* or holy lives. As the wife of a man who might one day become head of the Church of England, the Princess was surely of the Protestant faith? No one here doubts that over the centuries several Protestants may have lived quite saintly lives, but that is unfortunately not the same as being eligible for inclusion in the Catholic Calendar."

"Surely a bona fide apparition carries some weight?"

"Even if it did you would still be in the wrong room. Regrettably," the priest added gently, as though lamenting some undefined pleasure for ever forbidden us. He may have been itching to get back to his computer game but if so he betrayed no hint of it. "Here in 'De Sancto Spirito Manifestis,' as our name implies, we deal exclusively with instances of the Holy Spirit made manifest as apparitions. Under a ruling of 1889 this is understood to refer only to saints, the Apostles, members of the Holy Family and individuals of the Trinity itself. No one else falls into this category. Candidates for some kind of ecumenical canonisation, such as *la Principessa* may conceivably be, would still be as it were in an anteroom of sanctity. Their apparitions would likewise be accorded a slightly lower status in hierarchical terms but not, I stress, in terms of miraculous value. If in the distant, unforeseeable future a Holy Father were to grant the late Princess sainthood, then her apparitions before that will acquire, retroactively, the same significance as if they had occurred after canonisation. That of course also goes for anything she might say, any message she might impart during a vision. Did she in fact leave a message?"

"I believe so. 'Get out.'"

"'Get out'?"

"She was supposedly warning some people to leave a house that was in imminent danger of collapse."

"Ah yes, I remember, your compatriots mentioned it. Not a very spiritual saying, on the face of it, but as it narrowly saved lives it would surely count as a miraculous utterance."

I was not, unfortunately, in a position to tell my curly-lashed informant that mine was one of the lives saved by this timely but quite imaginary command. "So—informally speaking, of course—what would you say her chances were? I mean, in the distant, unforeseeable future?"

"I'm afraid I couldn't possibly say. The first step, of course, is to be considered a Servant of God, and on a Papal decree of heroicity or martyrdom the subject is pronounced Venerable. Only then can beatification follow when His Holiness declares that she is blessed in Heaven. The basic procedures were all laid down quite clearly in Benedict XIV's *De Servorum Dei beatificatione et beatorum canonizatione*. I'm sure you're familiar with them. First, the life of the candidate is examined. Only if this is found worthy are the miracles then assessed. At least two miracles are essential. The event you allege would undoubtedly qualify as one of them, theoretically speaking. The majority of miracles involve cures, of course. The paralysed being enabled to walk, that sort of thing."

At the dinner party on the night in question we had been as close to paralysis as leglessness entails, what with alcohol and hallucinogens, but I decided to spare this charming young priest's sensibilities.

"Then there is a systematic examination of the candidate's virtues. It used to involve a quasi-legal process with a 'prosecution,' the *promotor justitiae* popularly known as the Devil's Advocate. However, that office was abolished by the late Pope John Paul II in 1983 when he streamlined the whole process, enabling him to achieve four hundred and eighty-two canonisations during his Papacy. These days, opponents of the candidate are simply called in to give any negative testimony. Against these voices a defence is mounted in which the candidate's writings and the testimony of sworn witnesses are put forward as evidence of his or her consistent virtue."

The candidate's *writings*? It was already beginning to sound like a pretty long shot. The evidence, inevitably thin, might include a school essay, "What I did in my summer holidays," plus several postcards from places like Biarritz and Klosters. But then I reflected that there must be plenty of saints who hadn't left behind any writings whatever, who might not even have been *literate*. There was hope yet.

"I can tell you," the young priest added, "the Vatican does occasionally receive proposals for recognising a Protestant as a saint. Dietrich Bonhoeffer's name is quite frequently put forward. I believe he was technically a Lutheran pastor. He may indeed have been a remarkably saintly man but in my personal view he could not under any circumstances be eligible for canonisation. I'm afraid any opponent would easily win the case against his being deemed a martyr for the faith. The Nazis hanged him in 1945 not for religious reasons but for high treason since he had taken part in plans to assassinate Hitler. My Church considers that plotting to kill people, for whatever reason, is an insuperable impediment to canonisation."

"Oh, well, bang go my own chances," I said lightly. "Anyway, you've been most helpful."

"Not at all. I'm only sorry to disappoint you. Incidentally, I'm afraid I did make a slightly whimsical suggestion to your compatriots when they were here last week. I told them they might find the Princess's chances for recognition better in the Russian Orthodox Church, which also creates saints. In fact, not long ago I believe it canonised Tsar Nicholas the Second's family. Since there are blood ties between the British and the former Russian royal families, might it not be possible to argue a kind of honorary Russian Orthodoxy for the Princess as the basis for a plea? Failing that, there are always the Greeks and much the same reasoning."

"H'm. Rather scraping the bottom of the barrel of sanctity, I'm afraid."

"Well, do urge the Princess's supporters not to give up hope. The restrictions I've been quoting are, after all, very worldly. It's the fragrance of the life itself that rises furthest," said the young priest with an encouraging smile of intangible sultry import. "One must never despair."

"I never do. Something always comes up. Room 21?"

"Room 21."

As I closed the heavy door I thought I could hear the streets of Miami burst back into life behind me.

Such is the imaginary scene I am now toying with for an important episode towards the end of my opera. I see it as an exalted version of a courtroom drama, taking place in a Vatican office where the merits of a potential saint's case for canonisation are thrashed out. These will start in the normal way, with testimony from Diana's family, friends, African AIDS victims, etc., being read out. And then—*coup de théâtre!*— Diana herself appears in order to answer her own case. Consternation! This is unheard-of in the annals of the Vatican: an actual apparition of a soul on day-release from Purgatory to answer her critics in person! News of this drama quickly spreads and people crowd in from the rest of the building. So beautiful is her visionary appearance that everyone is instantly swayed, and cries of "A saint! A saint!" can be heard, while her prosecutor, sticking to his guns, tries to make his voice rise above the din, appealing for caution and scepticism. (I have just the heroic bass in mind for his role.) And as the unerring Mozart showed in *Don Giovanni*, tragedy may mysteriously be intensified by a pinch of comedy so there is even a walk-on part for a lost American novelist ("Your Blessed Majesty, all hail! / Just tell me, where's the Holy Grail? / I gotta deadline I must meet and / Gee! Your hair looks real neat!"). For as you can see, I have begun serious work on the libretto at last. If the impression I've given so far is of something between *Parsifal* and *South Pacific*, I beg you to suspend judgement. These are early days yet. Trust me: this is going to be *grand*.

Elsewhere, other matters have been moving quite briskly and Samper's life is fast regaining some of its former purposeful shape. First, Benedetti found me a small flat in town that I'm renting on a short-term lease. It belongs to a Belgian sociologist who is apparently studying voting irregularities in Italian local elections and has disappeared. But Benedetti says he has the man's authority to let the flat when he's not there, so here I am amid furniture that causes me severe anguish, in particular the shade of the bed linen, a sort of Zsa Zsa Gabor peach. It's no fun being an aesthete; one's sensibilities are constantly being outraged. But I shall have to put up with it. At least the place is quiet, being over the back-street annexe of a nuns' retirement home. When I meet them on the stairs—midget creatures like worn-out bats—I look in vain for signs of grace and serenity. They have rumpled little grey faces like unironed school laundry and I reckon they could do with a visitation from the Blessed Diana to cheer them up, poor dears. A lifetime's service to Mother Church has left them looking sour and battered. But maybe their presence below me is beneficial to my muse since I am making progress with the opera and getting back to work is doing wonders for my spirits.

I needed the flat also because after several more inspections and much wrestling I have decided to take that house Benedetti showed me. Well, of *course* the seller dropped his price, what did you think? We have agreed on three hundred and ten thousand euros. It's still an absurd sum but one has to be realistic, the house being in an area estate agents describe as "exclusive" rather than merely "much sought-after." But for me the clincher is the site. Benedetti's right: I'm never going to better the position, not in this region and hardly anywhere else. It's not as dramatically panoramic as Le Roccie, which provided more of a cockpit view, but it's more authentically "Tuscan," with forested foothills folding and unfolding on either side and pines and villas sprouting half-hidden among them. From a bathroom window there is even a dramatic prospect of Monte Prana, its rocky peak topped by a cross. At the front of the house the partial view of the town's distant roofs and towers beyond the olives' headlong plunge manages to suggest both apartness and inclusion, which I think will suit very well the life I am hoping to lead here.

The first steps of the purchase are now going ahead. Provided all the usual legal stuff about the seller's right to sell is as straightforward as Benedetti promises, the *compromesso* and the *contratto* ought both to be routine. What isn't routine is a document he is drawing up to the effect that I will be bound not to recant the Diana story the moment the house is mine and I'm safely installed. I'd already thought of that possibility, of course, and had expected him to insist on formalising our deal in some way. Somehow I'm not surprised to discover that Benedetti is a qualified lawyer as well as an ordinary *ingegnere*. All this document will stipulate is that I don't repudiate the official account. I shall have a perfect right just to remain silent. The Comune has also drawn up an agreement to buy up the rest of my land at Le Roccie "for reasons of public safety." If their hopes are fulfilled and some sort of tourist industry based on pilgrimages does flourish, I'll bet they're planning to build an official shrine up there. I envisage an Apuan version of Lourdes ("Dr. Louse"), complete with a grotto. For some reason grottoes seem to be an essential part of Marian cults: some nonsense that elides mothers, the earth and wombs, no doubt. I'm sure a Diana cult will require a similar mise-en-scène. Of course if they do develop the site they may even make a bid for Marta's house, itself dark and damp enough to be a grotto without much in the way of fundamental alteration. With luck this will give the old girl a chance to sell it dear when in normal market terms it's virtually worthless. I feel a sudden burst of generosity towards her since no matter what she does, she will never again be a neighbour. The nearest house to mine is four hundred metres away, and that's as the crow flies across olive groves and jungly crevasses. But my experience of living cheek by jowl with her over the last few years (my cheek, her jowls) surely justifies caution, even though a horror of neighbours is sometimes taken as particularly British and can even lead to accusations of stand-offishness.

In fact, you will scarcely credit that a few months ago a critic in London's *Independent on Sunday* described me as "an insufferable snob." I can't imagine why. Some remark in *Millie!*, maybe, that he wilfully misunderstood? At any rate it's rather a wounding thing to see in print about oneself and I ought really to take such an accusation seriously and consult my old friend Patrick Little of Little, Gidding LLP of Lincoln's Inn. A charge of snobbery certainly has a sting to it, especially when made by a member of the British press, a respected and high-minded body of people famously indifferent to stories involving royalty, the rich and the fleetingly famous. Still, one admires the way their democratic credentials sometimes oblige them bravely to overcome their nausea and deal with the aristocracy. After years of consistently lampooning the late Princess of Wales as a thicko Sloanie scrubber who couldn't scrape up a single O-level, it took them less than twenty-four hours after her death to discover that she was actually the Princess of Hearts, an icon of selflessness and purity suddenly sacred to the British public.

Luckily, some of us can fight back. It is a comfort to know that my particular accuser almost certainly thinks Caravaggio plays for Arsenal and *Les fleurs du mal* is a new cologne by Stella McCartney. Meanwhile, my original point about one's neighbours in Tuscany remains unassailable. Unlike most British visitors, I actually *live* here. My house is not a second home and neither am I buying it as a canny investment ("Bricks and mortar, mate. Can't lose, canya?"). And thus the question of neighbours becomes paramount. Imagine finding oneself living next to Baggy and Dumpy. Inconceivable.

I'm glad we've got *that* settled.

I have now reserved a room at a nearby hotel for Joan Nugent, who arrives the day after tomorrow. She at least is one Briton I'm very much looking forward to seeing. I can't tell you how supportive she was during the traumatic later stages of writing *Millie!* We hardly saw one another, but over several long phone conversations she managed to reassure me that not all the yachting fraternity consisted of vilely rude egomaniacs. Her nicotine-toughened vocal cords gave an edge to what at the time seemed like a lone voice of sanity. Because she had known Millie Cleat for years she was able to convey both what she loved in her and what she abhorred. At a time when abhorrence had become my dominant emotion it was good to be reminded that Millie had once been not only less loopy but nicer. Joan was refreshingly dismissive of the mystical airs and graces that the Great Helmsperson, under the influence of various groupies dedicated to Deep Blue ecological claptrap, was beginning to give herself. What with millions of devoted fans viewing her as an ocean-going combination of Donald Campbell and Mother Theresa, and my publisher bullying me to deliver a hagiography worthy of such a figure, I was often reduced to wondering if I was the only person left immune to the spell cast by this salt-stained old harpy. Luckily I then met Joan, who was even more salt-stained and proved a sterling ally.

A few days after she arrives the bulldozer will start excavating my former home. An old though young acquaintance of mine, Silvano, who before the juvenile court's unwarranted decision used to frequent the Piter Pan games arcade and billiard rooms on the outskirts of town, has put at my disposal a cavernous unused garage beneath his parents' apartment. This should be amply big enough to store temporarily whatever poor relics seem worth rescuing from my previous life. Strange it is that now I'm in the process of buying another house my interest in the corpse of its predecessor has considerably dwindled. And to think that only a couple of months ago I was inconsolable . . . Our great advantage is that we're such fickle creatures, our attention constantly grabbed by the ever-sliding present. Dead friends, last year's lover, a lost recipe, long-vanished muscle tone—with a slight grinding sensation we move on as tragedy turns to seemly regret and finally flattens out into vague recollection. It very seldom calls for bulldozers. And speaking of bulldozers, you're probably wondering why I'm not having Joan stay with me here in the Belgian's flat, since there is a spare room. But although we took to each other from our first meeting, she does have quite a pungent presence. I refer not merely to the aroma of dogs and fags that clings to her but more to her forceful *projection*. We Sampers are sensitive souls, especially first thing in the morning, and self-preservation made me reflect that sharing a breakfast table with someone whose personality seems to come through a loud-hailer might prove trying. Besides, I expect she also would prefer not to have a comparative stranger thrust domesticity upon her without consent. She must surely have had enough of that in the Navy.

I just wish old Adrian were here as well. It would make all the difference to me to have his calm, rational support, not to mention some affectionate company between the Zsa Zsa Gabor bed linen. I do miss a bit of epidermal contact from time to time. Not that it's primarily about sex, of course. What could be more lowering than procuring dutiful orgasms as alike as hiccups and just as irksome? Unfortunately, as far as Samper is concerned the erotic and the domestic go together about as naturally as lions and early Christians, affording pleasure only to the spectator. All my attempts at companionable domestic relationships have been frank disasters. In any case Adrian does promise to come as soon as he can, swearing he daren't take so much as a day off at the moment. I believe him, as anyone would who knows anything about today's academia, which Jobsworth bureaucracy has long reduced to a state of terminal paralysis. Farewell to those cinematic memories of brilliant boffins each beavering his or her way towards a revolutionary breakthrough! The sheer *pathos* of modern Britain can be read in the career advertisements at the back of the various professional journals Adrian takes, offering to applicants of no particular race, gender, creed, physical mobility or age an equally chimerical career in Never-Neverland.

A creative thinker, you will be joining a highly motivated group of team players with a proven track record of consistently meeting deadlines. Championing operational excellence, you'll thrive in a fast-moving environment where you need to think on your feet and be prepared to run with the ball. It is your models that will shape the health of Britain's coastal systems.

Blimey, as Nanty Riah would say. And if you did ever manage to come up with an individual idea and attempt to run with it in this zingy, jockstrap environment, you might make it as far along the corridor as the first committee room before you were tackled by the rat-faced harridan from the HSE office or the guy with no roof to his mouth from Project Funding. That is, of course, if your team supervisor hadn't already claimed your idea as his own and gone running off with all three of your balls. But then, what else would you expect for £18,000 a year plus a discounted membership at the local Sports Village?

Thanks to Adrian's influence and after years of intensive research I should modestly like to announce that self-starting, out-of-the-box-thinking Gerald Samper PhD has finally established the real cause of climate change. Don't forget when you're drawing up your list of Nobel nominees—you read it here first! Global warming (or as we scientists know it, Big Grown Llama) is entirely the fault of Mrs. Elfriede Keilberth of Lolling, Upper Austria. One fateful morning in the summer of 2002 she gave her sitting room its customary blast of fly spray. One of the windows was open and a peacock butterfly (*Inachis io*) innocently passing by flew through the poisonous mist and died eight minutes afterwards. It had long been known to the world-famous research laboratories of *Reader's Digest* (*Readiest Dregs* or *Dead Registers*) that a butterfly flapping its wings in Europe causes typhoons in South East Asia. Had this particular peacock butterfly been allowed to flap its wings for another half hour it would in fact have brought about a record-breaking storm a year later that would have struck the Philippines with waves big enough to bring up cold water from below the Pacific's warm surface current. What nobody knew at the time was that the "great ocean conveyor belt" (as the Intergovernmental Panel on Climate Change calls it) was in a critical state. By the summer of 2003 the slightest cooling effect in the surface waters of the Western Pacific could have brought this vital current system back into its

96,000-year-old equilibrium. Unfortunately, in the absence of the right typhoon at the right moment this didn't happen, and the Earth's ocean currents are now doomed to run amok and endanger life everywhere *and it is all the fault of Mrs. Elfriede Keilberth of Lolling* (although she has since moved to the near-by village of Pfisting for family and erotic reasons). We only hope she feels proud of having single-handedly changed the course of the planet's history. The rest of us, meanwhile, can go back to driving our Hummers and flying to our dive holidays in Palau with a clear conscience since there is nothing now any-one can do to reverse the trend already set in motion. We may as well enjoy our luxurious lifestyles for as long as we're able—those of us lucky enough to have them, that is.

The instant I meet Joan at Pisa airport I am reassured that I haven't made a sentimental mistake. She really is the sort of person one needs to have around when there's rough work afoot.

"Whew!" she bellows as she bursts from the "*Arrivi*" gate like a bull newly released onto the streets of Pamplona. "Am I well out of Blighty! As much as I could do to get here without being lynched. Take a gander at this," and she thrusts a copy of the *Chichester Observer* into my hands and thumps a nico-tine-stained forefinger onto a headline. "Backyard Funeral With Flair!" it reads. "'Flair,' geddit? Basically, I've been shopped."

"The neighbours?"

"The buggers. They've got one of those adolescent kids who spends most of his time dozing in bed, like—"

"Rip Van Wankle?"

"—Ha! Exactly. But that night I put down the poor old Bo'sun, their bloody boy must have been awake long enough to go snooping and prying and now he's claiming to have watched it all through a hole in the fence."

"You didn't think letting off a twenty-five-thousand-candela distress flare in a suburban back yard at night was likely to catch someone's eye?"

"So? What damned business was it of his? And now look at this"—and she produces a copy of the *Portsmouth News*. "This is today's edition. 'Flare-Up Over Pet Death.' In a few days I've gone from being an amusing eccentric to a dog-torturer. Tomorrow the story will go national, bet you anything. Even as we speak I presume my house is besieged by reporters trying to get a shot of me toasting kittens with a blowlamp. They won't drop by the local kennels and check my other dogs, as friendly and well-nourished a bunch as they'll ever have seen. Oh no. Of course they won't; no sensation there. I tell you, I'm out of it in the nick of time. I shall have to stay here until the lynch parties turn their attention to some other blameless citizen. Anyway, bollocks to the lot of 'em. How are you, Gerry?"

"All the better for seeing you, Joan," I tell her truthfully. By now she has blasted a passage through the mass of reunited couples shamelessly embracing so as to block emerging travellers, as well as past the usual doleful, sweaty men holding aloft squares of cardboard bearing felt-tip legends reading "Mr. Ali Muntasser." "As one exile to another, I'm happy to be able to offer you asylum. We victims must stick together."

"It's either me or the old country that isn't what it was."

"It's not you," I tell her. Joan is possibly the last person in Europe to carry her own luggage. Not for her the wimpy little wheels and embarrassing *clackety-clackety* noises of suitcases that modern urbanites haven't the strength or dignity to carry. She refuses my help and soon we are stowed in my rental car, her respiration rate unchanged. Mine, though, starts changing as soon as we're aboard the sun-heated car and an astonishing canine bouquet builds up. But I turn the air-con on and soon we're pounding northwards along the motorway and catching up on events since Millie's death. Clips of her fatal attempt to shorten sail that resulted in a lengthened neck have been regularly shown on satellite TV and Internet sites. It has been prime-time for ghouls of all nations during these last months. As her friend, Joan mourns her with seemly restraint. "Daft old girl!" she says fondly. "But you know, Gerry, it felt to me as if there was something almost inevitable about the whole thing. She had probably gone as high as she was destined to go."

To the masthead of her career, I think, but tastefully do not say. "You mean she'd peaked?"

"I reckon so. And knew it, too, which was why she was so easily suckered into heading that Deep Blue caper. This around-the-world racing lark—you *can* only try to beat your own record, can't you?"

"Or look for novelty. The first unmarried mother to do it in a yacht going backwards. The first lone quadriplegic to do it with a parrot trained to peck at a keyboard to set the course and the sails. Stuff like that. The way all extreme sports are going, actually."

"Well, Millie did do it one-handed, bless her. But it really left her with nowhere else to go, especially as she was knocking on a bit. Late fifties. I ask you."

"But having acquired a taste for the limelight, she couldn't bear the thought of it moving elsewhere and leaving her in the dark."

"Too right. Fame and Millie went together like vinegar and chips. But what about you, Gerry? All these film deals and things. How's the limelight suiting you?"

"Huh! I might ask you the same question. People like you and me only ever emerge from obscurity when we're briefly lit by distress flares." And then, despite all my resolutions, I find I can't resist telling her about the ghostly—or maybe saintly—apparition of the late Princess of Wales that is alleged to have saved my life and that of my guests last November. Joan reacts in reliable fashion.

"A load of festering testicles."

"Of course. But all that festers is not mould, you might say. There are wheels within wheels here. Welcome to the land of plots, deals and stealthy accommodations."

"Sounds just like the Navy."

Then, even more against my better judgement, I add that I'm working on an opera about the Princess. To my amazement Joan turns out to be something of a Diana fan. Maybe there weren't too many republicans in the armed forces in Joan's day or—more likely—there could be some sort of sexual undercurrent here.

"Perhaps you'll do her a favour and leave out the crap about visions. Then you can concentrate on what made her so fascinating, poor wee thing," she says. "I tell you, me and the girls watched her progress with keen interest. You know—how she started out as a naive kid working in a nursery school who could be bullied into anything, gradually took charge of a foul marriage and ended up telling the world what it ought to be doing about AIDS victims and landmines. Bloody admirable, actually. But here's the thing. If you wanted a visual yardstick of her progress you couldn't do better than watch her wardrobe. I'd think that would be ideal for an opera. As she gains in confidence and becomes her own person, you could have her costumes evolve from the gauche early days of Laura Ashley and Benetton to the full fuck-off Versace kit, just as they did in real life."

"Golly, Joan, I had no idea you were so fashion-conscious."

"Just because a girl's no clothes-horse herself it doesn't mean she mightn't have wanted to be," my companion says with what fleetingly sounds like regret. "I just turned out to look my best in rubberised canvas, neoprene and a diving helmet. That's the way it was and I've no complaints. But I like my gals feminine, and I've always been interested in what they wear. Still, what the hell do *I* know about operas? You're the writer, Gerry. Sorry I mentioned it."

"No, mention it as much as you like. I would never in a million years have thought of moving a story along by means of clothes. Cooking, possibly, but never clothes. It's brilliant. A visual counterpart to her developing character . . . Yes, I can see it now. Oh dear, I'm afraid I'm going to have to pick your brains quite a lot in these coming days."

"Happy to be of service. Do you mind if I smoke?"

Well, of course I *do*; but in the circumstances I simply boost the ventilation and put up with it. After all, the car belongs to Mr. and Mrs. Avis. But apart from that, I dislike the fashionable new priggishness even more than I dislike smoking, and her need plainly outweighs mine. Before long we reach town and I see Joan safely installed in her hotel. I'll give her time to recover from the flight and adjust to her new status as Havant's Most Hated Woman. Then in an hour or two we will have an early dinner in some nearby restaurant. I just wish I could cook for her myself. Under normal circumstances it would be the most natural thing in the world for me to devise a sumptuous and inventive dinner to celebrate our reunion. But I'm hopelessly inhibited by this Belgian's kitchen, which would be paltry for a timeshare cottage in the Lofoten Islands. There is a three-burner stove designed for a small caravan; an assortment of cutlery that would allow two students to dine modestly out of opened tins; and a chipped pile of those egg-yellow plates, apparently made of plaster of Paris, that seem to haunt holiday homes. This is no workshop for a culinary genius.

You may also be expecting me to add that some of my inhibition stems from what happened at Crendlesham Hall when I last cooked for others. Well, it doesn't. A misfortune out of the blue like that can strike even the greatest chef at any time. The more I think back to that evening the more I wonder whether it wasn't an example of mass acting-up rather than mild food poisoning. It's well known that the sight of someone being sick can induce nausea in perfectly healthy people. All it took was for that ancient turtle, Sir D. Monteith, to have a heart attack—as is perfectly normal when you're a hundred and twenty-seven and have sent your blood pressure up by chivvying innocent walkers off your land. I'm sure I read somewhere that heart attacks can induce vomiting, and all the other guests simply followed suit out of a kind of hysterical politesse. Later, all those dim-witted Mr. Plods having "Aha!" moments with bottles of alleged rodent poison was just so much post-hoc rationalisation.

And while we're on the subject, I realise it's a long time since I last gave the world some of my recipes that, I dare to believe, will one day ensure my name survives. However, until once again I have a kitchen of my own to play about in I can't perfect the details; and as any cook knows it's the exact quantities, temperatures and timings that make or break the greatest recipes. Still, creativity will out, and from time to time I divert myself with theoretical dishes, much as scientists conduct thought experiments. My current batch involves the linking of a public personality with a particular food so that it becomes associated with that person's special glamour. If one can have *Oeufs en cocotte* Rossini, Peach Melba and Pavlova Cake then I suggest one can equally delight in Mutton Victoria Beckham, Stewed Ham O'Toole, Roly-poly Prescott, Thai Chicken Gary Glitter and Liver George Best (this last a new departure in offal cookery, involving a lengthy marinading in Scotch whisky). I am also toying with a Medlar Fool Blair that will be remarkable for its smoothness.

Our dinner is a happy occasion. We have no difficulty in agreeing that Italian cuisine is immeasurably more satisfying than the last meal we had together. This was aboard the private yacht of Lew Buschfeuer, Millie Cleat's Australian partner, when the food consisted largely of vegetation: Korean waterweed, Papuan tubers stuffed with moss, steamed sago balls. Even now I can still taste the Balinese goat-berries. Despite being hungry Joan and I dined frugally that night. The other guests seemed to eat the stuff with pleasure but I suspect they were heavily influenced by a belief that it was full of rare, cancer-targeting vitamins, plus a snobbish assumption that toasted Amazonian pitcher-plant was bound to taste better than something ordinary like cauliflower, even though it patently didn't and soon demanded advanced techniques of sphincter control. A sense of virtue must never be brought to the table. It is the death of good eating.

Having seen Joan back to her hotel I let myself into the Belgian's flat, whose decor as well as kitchen is seriously beginning to undermine my normally sunny disposition, and eagerly jot down some operatic notes. Our dinner conversation has triggered ideas for all sorts of new scenes. It's amazing how a casual nudge from an external source can stimulate a surge of creativity. I have definitely reached the point where I need a name for this opera project. Most of my awful biographies of sporting heroes acquired working nicknames as I wrote them, names that predated the final title and functioned merely as handy labels for folders of notes and computer files. They tended to be ironic or just plain rude, expressing a deep disenchantment with both the subject and the job. For instance, I privately knew the burnt-out downhill skier Luc Bailly as "Lily" since one anagram of his name is "A club lily," which exactly described his priapic après-ski presence. Millie Cleat just became "Malice" after her name yielded the entirely appropriate "I tell malice." Until now I have been thinking that this opera of mine might be called *Princess of Hearts*, so with a nightcap of Fernet-Branca at my elbow I get to work. Some splendid phrases soon emerge. "I refract poshness" seems apposite, "Horse-penis crafts" rather less so, while "Preacher Fists Son" has a tabloid grossness which, though I like it, is irrelevant. *Poshness* will do nicely as a working title; but just for interest's sake I doodle around with *Princess Diana* instead and at once come up with "*Rancid Pansies*." Oh yes! It may or may not turn out to have relevance but I can't resist the assonance. And so to bed, where inevitably my brain refuses to shut down and spends half the night compulsively churning out anagrams. Some time after "Princess of Hearts" has shuffled itself into "Free crap hits sons," I at last fall asleep.

The day before the bulldozing is due to start I take Joan up to Le Roccie. She has expressed an interest in seeing not only where I used to live but the seat of this new Diana cult. I've not been up here for some time myself and there are ample signs that my old exclusive domain is well frequented. The footpath through the undergrowth that avoids the official barrier is now trampled flat and there are cigarette ends embedded in the mud. But the most telling indication is that the improvised shrine has grown considerably. Something like half a rubble igloo is beginning to take shape. Stones, rocks and the odd brick have been piled up and lengths of rusty iron secured with strategic blobs of cement support an unstable-looking sketch of a grotto roof. What it really resembles is the ruined stable in one of those Renaissance Nativity paintings where there are so many holes in the roof that the only real shelter over the subjects' heads is provided by their haloes. The Princess's photograph now stands on a proper little altar covered in a clean but elderly linen pillowcase. Next to it is a new vase with a spray of quite expensive plastic flowers to supplement the improvised bunches of wilting spring flowers scattered about. Propped on the altar is also an announcement in Italian, neatly printed and framed behind glass. On closer inspection it turns out to be a prayer, presumably composed by a supplicant.

"Hey, get this," I say to Joan, translating it out loud as I read. "'O Glorious Diana, mother misunderstood and wronged, you nevertheless reached out to the unhappy and sick children of the world who laughed in your embrace. You transcended this life's mortal stain and dwell now like a flower in the radiance of the Blessed Virgin, the archetype of all mothers. This very place witnesses that by Mary's grace you do not forget to extend your hand to save your children from certain death. Intercede for us, we beg you, even as we pray for your matchless soul. Amen.'"

Silence. No birds sing.

"Bleedin' 'eck," Joan says at length. "Talk about over the top. I mean, they're treating her as if she's already one of their saints. But she couldn't be, could she?"

"Not officially. But I'd say she's well on the way to becoming a local one, wouldn't you? Like one of those *sufi* saints in Islam. Popular appeal is its own form of canonisation. Believe it or not this place is still technically my property although you wouldn't know it. Obviously it's already been annexed by anyone who feels he can wander up and beg heavenly favours. Look at that tree."

Just behind the shrine is a fine old stunted pear tree that until last year supported one end of the Samper washing line and provided a hardbitten variety of fruit that became the principal ingredient of an extraordinarily delicious and subtle pear and ginger relish I perfected some years ago. It goes wonderfully well with slightly dull, crumbly cheeses like Caerphilly. One day when I'm less preoccupied and properly settled in a house of my own I'll give you the recipe. Today I'm touched to see my old pear tree dressed in new leaves, but less so to observe that its low spreading branches are now also hung with all manner of ribbons, pieces of material, cards with messages on them, plastic necklaces and trinkets. Even a few miniature teddy bears dangle here and there like unseasonal hairy fruit.

"And all this derives from some pleasantry I apparently exchanged with a helicopter pilot last November," I say. "You've got to be impressed by the seriousness of human lunacy, haven't you? It's easy to see how entire religions arise from hearsay. All you need is the right rural gossip at the right time and people's superstitious desire to believe any old cock-and-bull story does the rest."

"What do all these say?" asks Joan, examining the notes nearest her.

"They seem to be the usual requests. 'Gracious Princess, please cure my paralysed son and I will never doubt again.' 'I beg you to let me win the Lotto or I shall be homeless. I am in despair.' 'Merciful Diana, my child is dying, you are her only recourse.' Oh, here's a good one: 'My bastard neighbour Raffaele is an adulterer and a deflowerer of children and mer-its your sternest vengeance.' The simple outpourings of des-perate people. I tell you, all human life is here. Except my own, of course," I can't help adding bitterly. I turn to stand at the fluorescent tape strung behind the lip of the precipice and gaze over a panorama so familiar it could almost make me weep. Tears of sternest vengeance, naturally.

Joan joins me. "Hell of a spectacular place. It must have been a fantastic house."

"That it was. Round about *there*"—I wave my hand at a patch of air some twenty feet away—"was the terrace where I wrote much of *Millie!* I've half a mind to post a note to Diana myself. 'Kindly restore my house. Signed, a homeless admirer.'"

"The whole damn thing simply vanished, just like that?"

"Pretty much. First the garage with a self-contained flat above it. Then the main house. Finally the terrace. Piecemeal but effective."

"You can say what you like about the hand of Diana but if you ask me you were all pretty lucky to get out."

"Everyone says so and I don't deny it. Yet oddly enough, if I owe my life to anybody it's probably to Marta. She's my neighbour. That's her place over there behind the fence— Tuscany's answer to the Bates Motel. The night of our party she arrived back unannounced after months in America but couldn't get into her house because I was acting as caretaker and I'd locked it up good and tight. So she left her bags outside her door and came over here. Later, Adrian and I went out to fetch her luggage across so she could stay the night with us. It was just as well we did because it was then we suddenly noticed the absence of the garage."

"I'll bet you all made a hurried exit."

"As hurried as possible, impeded as we were by badger Wellington, alcohol, magic mushrooms and a general feeling of unreality."

"So this opera of yours is really about Marta in disguise."

"It most certainly is *not*." It isn't often that Samper is shocked. "The opera I'm working on isn't about angels flitting down from heaven to save people from death, either. It's about this numbskull yearning to invent religious heroes to stuff the remaining chinks of life not filled by soap opera. It's about myth and glam. It's about credulousness."

"So tell me about her."

"What?" I'm distracted from an interior vision of a grand operatic *scena* with a choir of satirical angels all dressed by Marks & Spencer like a lightened-up version of the chorus of demons in *The Dream of Gerontius*.

"This old neighbour of yours, Marta. You talked a lot about her when we first met. In fact, you seemed a bit obsessed."

"That's because she was a protracted pain in the arse. For one thing, you never knew when her East European mafia family weren't going to drop by in black helicopters. They used to land just over there beyond those trees next to her house. It was one damn thing after another when Marta was here. I couldn't get any work done. And she was always coming over here on some pretext or other. Drink, usually. She was addicted to Fernet-Branca."

"You mean she wasn't after your body?" says Joan, I hope mischievously.

"If you go on like this I shall faint with horror and then you'll be sorry."

"Huh. In the Navy we'd just bring you round again with a bucket of seawater. Anyway, I hate to distress you further but there's someone over by that gate there trying to attract your attention."

And of course you win no prize for guessing who it is. The devil you talk of is frequently, I find, already present. But have I mentioned that Adrian has passed on the news that the great Max Christ himself says he would be interested to have a good look at any opera whose composer is Marta? You will see why, if she really has fallen out with her flagellistic librettist Sue Donimus, I must woo her as a potential collaborator. The idea is that together we will make wonderful music (as ingénue lovers once told each other in bodice-rippers back in the days when any insertions took place off the page). I step forward manfully to introduce Joan.

"Gerree!" Marta hails me from a distance. "I never know you're here."

Oh God, those tenses. Can I really face months of close-range Voynovian syntax? But the show must go on. "Snap!" I call.

"'Snap,' Gerree?"

"It means I didn't realise you were here either. May I introduce my friend Joan, an old yachting chum of Millie Cleat's? Joan, Marta. Marta, Joan. Well, what a surprise."

"But it was you who tell me on the telephone I must come to Italy and see my house because of the earth tremble and the pilgrims to the Princess. So I've come. And everything you say is true. Not so good, no. But *bentornato*, Gerree. I will kiss you. *So!* Please, you will both come in and I will offer you a little Voynovian speciality. It is the best moment of the morning."

I was afraid of that. As soon as I saw her standing there at the gate in the fence with the spring breeze lifting the unclotted portions of her hair and she so clearly the owner of the only house for miles, I had a reflux of the memory (as one might say) and my mind went shrinkingly back to a previous episode of this ex-neighbour's ethnic hospitality. "Not *mavlisi*?" I ask, trying for a tone of polite anticipation but achieving one more like pleading.

"No, I have something even better, something even more—" and she performs that loathsome gesture of hers when she kisses the bunched fingertips of one hand and rolls her eyes up in their sockets to indicate ecstasy. She ushers us in through her back door. I feel like a child being led into the doctor's surgery for another of those little injections they claim don't hurt.

Marta's kitchen is exactly as it always was. The same piles of unironed sheets dumped on chairs, the same aura of bohemian chaos. The same low-beamed ceiling and great damp flagstones. There is her old Iron Curtain upright piano, and there the electronic keyboard hitched to a dusty computer given her by the late Piero Pacini when she was writing the score for his last film. Everything is completely familiar to me, down to the cobwebbed sheaf of porcupine quills in a handle-less mug on the mantelpiece above the hearth. I used to visit this place regularly in my capacity as good neighbour while Marta was in the States most of last year. The only difference I can see is that she has acquired a new fridge. This might explain the absence of the crypt-like stench that resulted from ENEL cutting off the electricity while she was away and the contents of her old fridge brewing up into something the germ warfare boffins of Porton Down would once have been proud to own.

Marta fettles up the coffee percolator and then lifts a large jug out of the fridge. Into three glass dessert bowls she pours what looks like—and I apologise for this, but one must be accurate—diarrhoea. Sloppy brown gloop with knobs and bobbles. Over the surface in each bowl she scatters multi-coloured flakes and then cocks her head on one side, considering her handiwork. She adds a dollop of white substance to the centre of each bowl and actually claps her hands, for all the world a kindergarten teacher summoning her charges to elevenses.

"This is purest Voynovian, very special," she announces. "It is made by the chef of Danubya, our first restaurant in London I tell you about, Gerree. It is our famous *varminty* which he makes the best outside Voynograd. Come, you will try."

"It looks scrumptious." I was very well brought up, just as I'm glumly expecting my *varminty* to be shortly after I've eaten it. I pick up my spoon like a guest at a dinner party thrown by the Borgias. I have to admire Joan. Without a moment's hesitation she sets to with gusto.

"Hey, this is all right," she exclaims. "Can't put my finger on what it is but my tongue tells me it's pretty decent stuff."

Marta positively beams at her. "It is very old plums purée with salted *kisi*, um, cherries. It must be five years old at least in store and dark, with herbs and spices like *kimunyi*—I don't know that in English. Then on top is our Easter speciality, dry ram."

"Well, it's delicious," says Joan stoutly.

"Dry ram." I toy with my spoon. "And in the middle?"

"That is just plain yoghurt also from the ram."

"Ram's yoghurt. I see." I dab the white substance with the tip of my spoon. She *can't* mean . . .? Surely not even *Voynovians* would . . .?

"Sheep's yoghurt," says Joan.

Marta beams some more. "I'm sorry, yes of course, sheep. This is dried sheep on top also. At Easter we always make like this. We in Voynovia love colours."

Unlike everywhere else that prefers monochrome, I suppose. Why do foreigners say these damnfool things? Samper may lack patience but never let it be said he lacks courage. I try a mouthful. As usual with Marta's "specialities" I have an immediate mental image of my taste buds withdrawing defensively like coral polyps when touched. It is basically very sweet and yes, I can taste the hundred-year-old plums and things and the salty knobs that might conceivably be wizened cherries. I can also taste the dyed shreds of jerked sheep impregnated with an unidentifiable spice reminiscent of turpentine. For all I know they could be flakes of desiccated jackal. The sheep's yoghurt, to my surprise, tastes exactly like sheep's yoghurt.

"I can tell you, Marta," I say, wishing my eyes would stop watering, "what you call *kimunyi* is cumin."

"Oh yes, now I remember. Cumin. So what do you say, Gerree, of our *varminty*?"

"Fantastic. And you brought it all the way from London?"

"Well worth the trip, I should say." Joan bangs her spoon down beside her empty bowl. "I haven't tasted anything like that since I last put into Port Said. Exotic and interesting. Tip-top nosh."

At this moment the coffee comes through and while Marta deals with it at the stove Joan surreptitiously helps me out with my *varminty*. What a trouper, I think; but then it occurs to me she may be doing it less for me than to avoid her hostess's feelings being hurt. At any rate by the time Marta hands us our welcome doses of caffeine there are three empty bowls on the table.

"So you've seen the Diana shrine over the fence?" I ask.

"Oh yes. It's terrible, Gerree. Awful. And the people, they come all the time and sometimes they sing together. Can you believe this? How can I work when—?" She breaks off—tactfully, I imagine, given that she always claimed my own singing used to disturb her work to the extent that it provoked her into cruel parody in her film score. It sounds like poetic justice to me. Whatever these pilgrims sing they surely lack the artistry I lavished on Rossini and Donizetti arias. Good on them, I say. A worthy comeuppance for the last Queen of Le Roccie.

Suddenly I notice a large tear slide down beside the nose that emerges from the tangle of hair that always covers Marta's face when she leans forward. Her cup, tilted at an unregarded angle, is also leaking coffee onto the table.

"Oh, Gerree!" she exclaims in woeful tones, "I am so unhappy. I don't know what I shall do. Your house is gone and these singing idiots are changing everything." Liquidly she sniffs.

"Poor Marta. It's all gone wrong up here, hasn't it?"

"It's a bloody tragedy if you ask me," rasps Joan, and leaning sideways she slips a beefy arm around Marta's shoulders. The anchor tattooed on her forearm glows in the sunlight from the window.

Adrian 5

email from Dr. Adrian Jestico (ajestico@bois.ac.uk)
to Dr. Penny Barbisant (penbar@labs.whoi.ed)

First, well-deserved congratulations on having talked your man into agreeing your new remit! A quick search tells me virtually nothing's ever been done on seabed fauna specifically around wrecked munitions ships & certainly not at the genetic level you're proposing. The field is yours. And what a fantastic bit of luck having a survey vessel in the area that could divert for half a day & send an ROV down to identify it. I wonder who's still alive over there who can remember the *Hattie MacAllister*? When you know exactly what the *Hattie M.*'s cargo was & specifically what of it was damaged at the time of the sinking you'll be able to guess what are the most likely contaminants to have been seeping out into the local chromosomes these last sixty-four years.

Duh! Sorry, Penny—you hardly need me to tell you that. But stating the obvious is becoming second nature here at BOIS. There's a right & a wrong way to put together reports for Defra, & the wrong way is to assume they already know some elementary facts about the environment (or food, or rural affairs). Most fatal of all is to imagine they understand anything about the sea, such as that it can both erode *and* deposit, even on the same tide. To be fair, as individuals with doctorates they mostly know these things, but as a Department they don't. I suppose they need it all spelt out Janet-&-John style for the benefit of the politicians they have to show the reports to. Nothing can be too simple for *them*.

News from the home front, you ask? Nothing spectacular. My illustrious conductor brother-in-law Max is in mourning for his principal clarinettist, who was arrested in an Ipswich shopping mall for patting children on the head while dressed as Winnie-the-Pooh & led off to be sectioned. The wretched fellow has a history of such episodes & at first they didn't seem to matter, given his brilliance as an instrumentalist. A couple of years ago Max recorded the Weber clarinet concertos with him dressed as a raccoon. It was a great recording that went on to win awards, but only that morning he'd been detained in the same costume for waving his tail at a crowd of kindergarten kids & Max only just got him out in time for the recording session. Since when it has reached the point where he will only play while wearing an animal costume. Tricky, really, as there's no mention of a dress code in the CSO's contracts. But the sight of a panda taking its seat in the woodwind section excites comment in the concert hall, not all of it favourable. Though that being said, his example did lead Max to give a TV performance of Saint-Saëns' *Carnival of the Animals* where the whole orchestra wore animal costumes & it was a massive hit last Christmas. It sold I don't know how many DVDs. But the poor man became a liability & is now obviously too ill to function. Did I tell you he was a guest at Crendlesham at our fateful dinner the night we had Gerry's hors d'oeuvre of poisoned mice? He came dressed as a gorilla. Why? Hard to tell. Maybe he hoped it would please or divert young Josh, but the kid was actually slightly scared & who can blame him. Gossip now talks of the man having become "eccentric" ever since he lost his own daughter, a cot death or something. So, sad rather than sinister. At any rate Max is quite depressed about it & goes around muttering that you can't replace the equivalent of Jack Brymer & Karl Leister rolled into one (I gather they were ace clarinettists of yesteryear). And he'll now be adding a dress clause to all CSO contracts.

Gerry called me last night to announce that his ex-neighbour Marta—who, poor lady, quite unwittingly lurches between being his bête noire & the one composer he must have to write the music to his opera—is back home in Italy. But her place has been fatally compromised by the landslip and subsequent geological uncertainty about the whole of that little plateau, which I have to say is as spectacular a site for a house as I ever did see. A sort of Space Shuttle's view of north-western Tuscany. A shame. And now of course it's further blighted by pilgrims of this weird Diana cult. Apparently they come at all hours & hold vigils & sing hymns on the spot where, six months ago, Gerry was still hanging out his socks & boxer shorts to dry. The result is Marta is plunged into gloom because although she now has the sole surviving property up there its future is in doubt & her work is constantly interrupted. Gerry, never the most accomplished dissembler, is cock-a-hoop over her misfortune. He says it serves her right for inviting him in for coffee the other day & forcing him to eat what he describes as a diabolical Voynovian laxative made from fermenting prunes with ram's sperm topping. He's probably just jealous that she came up with something as inedible as one of his own inventions.

Of course I don't mind your asking questions about Gerry's & my "relationship," Penny. It's just that I don't think I can give you any satisfactory answers. I guess in that respect I'm a typical "guy," as you unkindly put it. We guys tend not to ask ourselves about our relationships unless we've been feminised by all that dismal gay propaganda about marriage and long-term responsible blah blah. Whether he & I have any future as an "item" is not something we give much thought to, I'm afraid. At least I don't, & Gerry's been a professional bachelor far too long to be capable of any domestic relationship with man or beast (since living with someone & not living with anybody can both become habits). Besides, as we live & work in 2 different coun-

164 - JAMES HAMILTON-PATERSON

tries & that isn't likely to change for the foreseeable future, there's scarcely any point in looking at things long-term. So speaking for myself I pretty much live from day to day & take things as they come. And I think Gerry does the same, except with him it's more a matter of lurching from crisis to crisis, which suits his temperament. What does it matter in any case? Things will turn out how they turn out & in a few decades it won't matter a damn to either of us.

Since you ask, I think what I most admire in him is his conviction that one can only be truly light-hearted & amused in this world if one is a total pessimist and misanthrope. I still get gloomy & contemptuous about e.g. politics & our infliction of slaughter & suffering on millions of Iraqis under the pretext of replacing one man as head of state—now long dead anyway. Gerry just says I should be ashamed of such remnants of youthful idealism & ought just to laugh because "laughter is the whole of wisdom"—his phrase. It's a philosophy you'd think would make him horrid but for some mysterious reason doesn't. Sure, he's capable of saying mean things (especially about Marta) but they're usually said out of wit & for momentary effect & because he likes to express himself extravagantly. In actual fact he has been rather good to her. All the time she was away in the US last year he looked after her house, fitted new locks & generally acted as a caretaker, completely unbidden & without her knowledge. Beneath the quite genuine misanthropy he's an often kind person with that peculiar gentleness that goes with resignation. I remember him last summer reading a story about a gang of drunken British teenagers kicking an innocent passer-by to death while good citizens hurried past. His comment was "if you expect precisely zero from your fellow man you'll never know disappointment." A quintessentially Gerry remark.

Perhaps I should now ask about you & Luke, except that we guys don't know quite what to ask. We have to rely on you to tell us. Pathetic or what?

Cheers,
Adrian

6.

Once again I imagined myself in the hot, labyrinthine corridors of the Roman Curia, this time searching for Room 21. It would not have surprised me to glimpse the shade of Franz Kafka flitting ahead. At every level there was a background susurration, very faint, as of great numbers of people talking somewhere far away. Regardless of where I went it never grew any closer, neither did it fade. I saw not a soul. All the doors I tried were locked.

At last I came upon a janitor seated on a misericord that folded out of the dark wood panelling. He was reading a dog-eared book of Mickey Mouse cartoons. He courteously directed me up a flight of stairs to yet another corridor where eventually I fetched up outside a heavy oak door with the number 21 painted on it in faded gold figures. I knocked. Silence. I tried the handle. It would not turn. I stood back to look at the door in the way that one does, acting out bafflement as though for an invisible watcher. Only then did I notice the heads of large brass screws spaced regularly around the door's periphery. It was unquestionably screwed shut.

"True," the janitor said when I went down to tell him. He inserted a brown finger in his book. "It always has been like that. I have never seen it otherwise."

"You might have mentioned that."

"You didn't ask, signore. And even if I had told you, you would still have gone to make sure. Maybe now you should try

Monsignor Ricci on the ground floor." He smiled and resumed reading, his lips moving silently to Pluto's repartee.

Mgr. Ricci was an iron-grey elderly man in a black soutane. His face wore the expression of slightly bitter amusement common among Italian bureaucrats whose job it is to give the same explanation to endless supplicants, an explanation that studiedly explains nothing but which needs to be given anyway. However, he was neither playing *Grand Theft Auto* nor reading "Topolino," and the fact that his large desk was piled high with files and dossiers inspired in me a faint confidence that here, finally, was somebody who might know something. I introduced myself and told him about my visit to the room called "De S.S. Manifestis" and the young priest's redirecting me to Room 21, a piece of whimsy that now made me feel a little less warmly towards him.

"He was doing his job," Ricci said. "Enquiries involving non-Catholics are always referred to Room 21."

"Which is screwed shut."

"Which regrettably is not at present open." He laid his reading glasses down on the text he had been studying. "You must understand that his office, like this one, is merely one of several dozen that all serve the Congregation for the Causes of Saints, Congregatio de Causis Sanctorum." Like most Italians, he couldn't pronounce the Latin word "sanctorum" without slipping a pared-down vowel sound between the *c* and the *t*. "As I'm sure you know, the Congregation is the part of the Curia that supervises the complicated process of canonisation, although nowadays it is admittedly simpler than it was before the late Pope John Paul II revised it. Might I enquire as to the Cause you are hoping to pursue?"

"I'm not pursuing anybody's Cause," I said with the confidence of a rational and sceptical outsider. "I am simply trying to establish the theoretical position of the late Princess Diana."

"Of course. You are following in the footsteps of"—he

broke off to uncover a desk diary—"Signor e Signora Barrington. A British couple who were here very recently."

I groaned. I might have guessed Baggy and Dumpy would have got here first again. "I can imagine. And you, of course, told them that the whole idea of Princess Diana being canonised was ludicrous because apart from anything else she was a Protestant. End of story, except I bet they told you some tale about an apparition."

"It wasn't true?"

"Not the way they told it, I shouldn't think," I answered carefully.

"I can see you know these people well," said the priest. "They were making difficult progress because they had to bring an interpreter with them but I hope I did my best to set them straight. We are dedicated to the truth in this place, the truth of Christ. We have an old saying here in the Vatican: 'One vision does not make a saint,' and this I told them. As one would have expected, they were disappointed. Without presuming on your own faith, signore, I have to say it constantly grieves me to see the burden of ignorance under which so many non-Catholics labour who come to this room. I think they must long for the simple clarity that is the essence of the Mother Church. Let us pray that for many of them this may become the first impulse towards conversion. And speaking of which—" Ricci got up and crossed over to a table where he pawed some files. "Here we are. I should have sent this back to the archives after their visit, but conveniently here it still is."

"Maybe the Holy Spirit knew I was coming."

Ricci glanced at me from beneath stern eyebrows. "It is not for us to secondguess the *inscrutabilities* of the Holy Spirit. Now, this file contains a tiny part of the evidence used for the beatification—and what must surely be the eventual canonisation—of the Blessed Teresa of Calcutta, or Mother Teresa as she is still known to millions. I do not have the authority to show it to you directly, still less give you a copy of any document in it. However, I can tell you it includes certain notes and entries in the Blessed Teresa's spiritual diary following meetings with *la Principessa* Diana in the 1990s.

"The gist of it is that in three private audiences Diana expressed a keen interest in converting to Roman Catholicism. It was evidently her opinion that the Church of England, far from being a spiritual entity, was nothing but a social club for the English middle classes and that it would soon die out in the United Kingdom because a majority of its members was now aged fifty or over. The Blessed Teresa expressed sympathy with this view without, of course, venturing an opinion. In her diary, though, she wrote that she rejoiced as she always did when anybody showed a longing to step from darkness into the radiance of the True Cross.

"However, er"—Msg. Ricci turned over some sheets of paper rapidly—"yes. The Blessed Teresa did tell Diana she should be very watchful of her own motives. She ought to guard against being seduced by the inverted glamour of charity work with slum dwellers, lepers and AIDS victims and not to forget the eye of the news camera cannot see what God sees in the heart. Above all, she must be absolutely certain in her own mind that she would not be embracing the Catholic faith in order to score off her husband Charles. It would undoubtedly make his constitutional position as potential monarch quite difficult and might even be a deciding factor for his mother the Queen never to abdicate in his favour. As you can see," Ricci said, closing the file, "the Blessed Teresa had a remarkable understanding both of the Princess and of British constitutional affairs. But then I hardly need tell you she was a quite remarkable person in her own right, as well as a handmaiden of Jesus Christ."

To say I was surprised at this news is not enough. I am an artist, not a journalist, and I was elatedly assessing the exciting implications for my opera. Maybe there *was* plausible hope of a canonisation for Diana—if not by some future pope then at the hands of Gerry Samper, librettist of genius. I was already beginning to see an ascent into heaven in Act 3: a grand finale to stir the blood and bring in its wake a tempest of applause from an audience with tears streaming down its face, standing and clapping until its hands were numb. However, we weren't there quite yet. One or two points still to clear up.

"That's fascinating," I told the Monsignor. "So, assuming there is nothing recorded on paper to show that the Princess *did* convert, would it theoretically have been possible? I mean, could a woman like Mother Teresa, a nun, have secretly received Diana into the Church? Or could only a male priest do that?"

"I take your point, but it is quite irrelevant in the light of Teresa's beatification. After all, if a future *saint* couldn't receive someone into the Church, who could? Diana wasn't hoping for ordination. She showed an interest solely in converting, an interest the Blessed Teresa ultimately judged to be genuine and fervent." He re-tied the file with its purple ribbon and replaced it on the table.

I couldn't resist letting a trickle of holy water out of this urbane priest's stoup. "I have heard it said that Mother Teresa's journal also tells of her being plagued by doubts. I'm not sure the average layperson associates sainthood with doubts."

"My son," he responded unfazed, "doubts are to Christians what erections are to adolescents. They come unbidden at unwelcome moments and simply have to be lived with and dealt with as they arise. That is what we call faith. The struggle to keep this faith is part of what *makes* a saint. And now I must beg you excuse me. You happily chanced to catch me between appointments and I see I have a meeting in a few minutes."

I took my leave of the Monsignor, expressing gratitude for his time. Little could he have guessed the artistic consequences of his dry summarising of archival data. Descending the building's broad steps into the sunlit courtyard in which the cheeping of sparrows was suddenly loud I felt life streaming back into me. Even here, in the heart of the bureaucratic Vatican, I could smell espresso coffee and garlic frying. Italians have a genius for getting life's priorities right. It is something we British completely lack.

On my way out I passed through another courtyard with a fountain at its centre—the entirely dreadful *Delfino e Fanciullo* by Federico Corvo, who had only won the commission by being Pope Hadrian VII's former catamite. It really ought to be scrapped for its bronze and replaced by something modern. Around it, clearly oblivious to its aesthetic deficiency, was gathered a disgruntled knot of arguing foreigners. From my previous visit I recognised them as the American authors in search of the Holy Grail. Since then they seemed to have banded together for mutual support. Obviously they were hardcore traditionalists and not subscribers to excitable modern theories such that the Grail was actually Mary Magdalene's womb—which if true would surely have made the Last Supper (aka Repast Plus) a bizarre and racy occasion that only Aleister Crowley could have enjoyed. These questers had spread maps on the worn stonework and were arguing animatedly about the cost of shuttling around Europe and even into Asia Minor in their hunt. Their voices went ricocheting about the surrounding buildings' impassive façades. It struck me that the railways of each European country ought to issue a specially reduced season ticket—I fancy it might be called a Student Grailcard—to promote such tourism, which is clearly a growth industry.

"Fucking Italians," one was saying bitterly. He wore a jacket with a tan suede yoke over a snap-front shirt down which a string tie dangled. "They just give you the royal runaround here. Polite as all-get-out but they're not about to give up a single damn piece of hard info. Nada. Zilch."

"Hey, lemme tell you it's no better in Malta," said another. "Those Templar Knights of the Grand Doo-Dah, whatever? Those bastards wouldn't—"

"Look, what it is, it's a conspiracy, okay? It's simple. These Europeans are in it together. It's a conspiracy aimed at the heart of American literature."

It turns out the *Forestale* and even the Comune's Department of Works insist on sending representatives to attend the excavation of my collapsed home, so this event has been further delayed by several days. Joan doesn't care a hoot, not least because she has phoned her brother and learned that she did indeed hit the national press for a single edition. Apparently she is suspected of conducting satanic rituals in her back yard in Havant that have resulted in the death of at least one dog. A neighbour claims to have seen her kneeling with a gun and when the gun went off the whole yard was bathed in unearthly red light that was visible from as far away as Warblington. He also saw naked figures dancing around the corpse of the dog. The RSPCA are investigating.

A yet better reason why Joan seems in no hurry to leave Italy is—well, to put it bluntly—Marta. To say they have hit it off would be an understatement. To say that Joan has already moved out of her hotel and into Marta's hovel up at Le Roccie would be a good deal more informative. This is a wholly unexpected turn of events and I'm still trying to work out the possible consequences for G. Samper. It would never have occurred to me to imagine they have anything in common other than a taste for *varminty*. Can it be that my fantasies about Marta's nocturnal visits from the simple woodcutter's son with his hefty chopper were wide of the mark? I'm astounded; I don't normally get things like that wrong. I now have to imagine rather different scenes taking place in that attic bedroom of hers with the iron-framed peasant *letto ma-*

trimoniale in which I once, in dreadful error, woke up next to its owner with the mother of all hangovers. But let's not go there. I absolutely must see Marta to talk about the opera but I haven't wanted to intrude. It just never seriously occurred to me that she . . . I mean, I swear she used to leer at me in a way that . . . Naturally it's none of my business. It's absolutely of no consequence to me what two grown ladies do in their spare time. Why should I care? It's not even interesting, for heaven's sake. I just hope if the woodcutter's son ever finds himself at a loose end, it's mine.

Today is excavation day and I am up bright and early. Searching the Belgian's TV for a weather forecast that can tell me what to expect, I hit the ineffable BBCNN where a generic tart is doing aerobic exercises in front of a map of the Caribbean. Her whirling arms and jabbing gestures are supposed to show the course of Hurricane Rupert, *sweepin* in there an just clippin the toppa Haiti while over ere in suvvun Europe these ot winds from Africa are *drivin* up Italy an there'll prolly beesum thunderstorms developin later over the Hapennines though the picture over in central Mongolia ere is very different with these cooler winds pushin dahn from Russia an easin those igh temperatures, thirty-eight, look, *forty-four* over there in Riyadh so take plentya sunblock there, any of you travellin in that, er, region. It's already Thursday nah in Australia, so . . .

Eventually some news items reach me in garbled fashion as I shave, and very disgusting one of them is, too. A grinning ninny with gelled hair says that half the target survey of people between the ages of fifty-seven and seventy-five claimed they regularly had oral sex, while 26 per cent of those polled at the ages of seventy-five to eighty-five reported having had sex with a partner in the last year. I have to rest my razor for some minutes while waiting for my heart rate to subside. What one marvels at is not the statistics, repellent as they are, but the willingness of these elderly people to answer such revoltingly intrusive questions. Have they *no* self-respect? These are just the sort of old geezers who bang on about their right to die with dignity, yet they're perfectly content to live without it. Surely nobody of any breeding, of whatever age, would actually respond to these impertinent oafs with their clipboards? The only proper reaction to such questioning would be to behave like a character in a Terry Southern story, come prancing out in an ancient silk bathrobe and hit the oaf a stunning blow over the head with an immense black dildo the size of a vegetable marrow while exclaiming "Take that, sir!" or "Try *this* on your pianola!" One of several matters of pride I shall take with me to the grave is that I have never once told the truth when quizzed in the street or door-stepped. It is a rare instance of Samper's having shown a glimmer of social responsibility.

Two hours later Joan and I are standing at the edge of a jungle some miles out of town. In front of us an excavator is snorting and rummaging about like a yellow boar in the steep slope of scree on the side of the mountain. It is one of those immense machines with a scoop at one end and a blade at the other, and earlier it had led the way here by bulldozing a trail uphill through the dense undergrowth. Behind it was a solemn convoy headed by the *Forestale*'s Fiat Campagnola. Behind that were the Comune Works Department's Land Rover and a battered Ford Focus bearing a reporter and a photographer from *Il Tirreno*. Joan and I had brought up the rear in a cavernous hired van that already felt freighted with my misgivings about the entire venture. I had never envisaged this circus. I should have thought that searching for one's personal belongings at a scene of tragedy was best conducted in discreet privacy, but such is not the Italian way. I suppose I ought to be thankful that so far there's no procession of robed choirboys and a firework display. On the other hand it is extremely unfortunate that yesterday Leo Wolstenholme and her *Global Eyeball* colleagues announced their imminent arrival. If they arrive today their hotel is supposed to be directing them up here to interview Joan and me about Millie Cleat. I'm banking on their never being able to find this place. Still, I have taken care to dress in a style that might best be summed up as "casual rugged": a plaid shirt and an old but beautifully cut pair of Man2Man jeans that I bought in Aspen to cheer myself up while following Luc Bailly in the waning but still erectile days of his skiing career. I also have on a pair of new black boots that were the only things I could find locally. I really wanted something along the lines of Doc Martens, though more navvy than chavvy. What I found, now that I'm wearing them, do have an air less of a building site than of a Seventies' NHS orthopaedic department, being somewhat bulbous in odd places. But all in all, I daresay I cut a figure of no little masculine dash and competence that will show up to advantage on camera. I certainly detect what must be admiring glances from the two *Forestale* men.

I don't wish to give a misleading impression of the *mise en scène* here. You mustn't imagine that we're at the foot of a vertical cliff as though standing on the shore beneath Beachy Head. Hereabouts the Apuan Alps have forested lower slopes and Le Roccie is roughly a third of the way up a mountain. The section of the plateau on which my house once stood broke off and slid down a steep wooded hillside avalanche-style, breaking up as it went, clearing trees and everything in its path. It came to rest about a hundred metres lower than it started, in a vast moraine of boulders and mangled trees among which a few remnants of my home are still pathetically visible. As I have indicated, reaching this remote place from below required much trail-blazing on the part of the excavator and now that we're here I quite wish we weren't. Surveying the immense boulders, the sheer volume of stuff, I'm suddenly convinced the task is too huge to be worthwhile. Whatever lies buried has already been here a good five months, exposed to winter rains and melting snow. It seems hardly worth the effort to launch a salvage operation at this late stage and particularly not in front of all these inquisitive witnesses.

However, here we all expensively are and I must make the best of it. The house's roof that had still looked vaguely intact from the helicopter has since acquired gaping holes. I borrow a torch from the crew in the Land Rover and peer around inside it, but it's just a roof that bobbed like a bubble on the general surf of collapse and I can see nothing under it but rocks. Fifty yards away the excavator is making a start clearing rubble from around the rusting rump of my Toyota Ass Vein, which sticks up obscenely in the spring air as though hoping to be inseminated by its yellow rescuer in some rite of mechanical rejuvenation. The teeth on the lip of the huge bucket hook themselves delicately through the smashed rear window and with a heartfelt groan the car's length emerges from its tomb, shedding rocks and soil.

"Bang goes your no-claim bonus, I'd say," remarks Joan, lighting one of her gaspers. "Did you leave anything of value in it?"

"Just the usual junk, I think." We walk over to look. There will be the insurance documents and log book in the glove compartment since in Italy it's obligatory to have them on hand, but all that paperwork has now been settled, the car no longer officially exists and they're worthless. However, I'm still not sure about the legal implications of what we're doing today. That's to say the San Bernardino da Siena agency did eventually cough up for both car and house, though not before *la dottoressa* Strangolagalli had fought my lawyer for every last euro. (I trust little St. Bernard will one day lean out from the gold bar of Heaven and strike the crimson-clawed hag with boils, goitres and prolapses for the way her unscrupulous company continues to take his name in vain.) But now that I've been reimbursed—as much as one ever is by insurance companies—what happens if I manage to recover some of the items I've been reimbursed for? Would I effectively be stealing? Is the agency now the de facto owner of my buried property?

They're certainly welcome to the car, whose interior smells of rotting upholstery and fresh earth. I manage to get the glove compartment undone and there are the vehicle's papers, damp with mould, together with the sort of rubbish that collects in such places and which now looks as though it belonged to someone else. Come to that, the entire site is a reminder of how well one can get by after a few months without one's treasured possessions.

"There's no way of making sense of the way the house fell, I suppose?" Joan muses, looking up at the ragged lip of the plateau far above.

"So we might make a reasonable guess as to where things are? None whatever. That's why I'm afraid I've brought you all this way under false pretences. It's hopeless. Anything we find will be by sheer chance."

"Never mind the false pretences, I'm damned glad I came. It's not just that if I was back in Havant I'd run the risk of being burned alive by righteous pet-owners. If I hadn't come I doubt if I'd ever have met Marta. She's a right shipmate, is Marta."

"I've never sailed with her but I'll take your word for it. She's certainly making a name for herself as a composer."

"She's a genius," says Joan confidently. "She just needs someone to look after her and manage all the day-to-day running of a house. She's not a practical person at all."

Practically useless, actually. One has only to observe the bohemian squalor in which Marta habitually lives, a squalor that I suspect has to do with having become used to the services of the ancient family retainers her father's clan managed to re-engage in Voynovia's post-Soviet era. As the eldest daughter of a godfather of international crime, what need did she ever have to deal with humdrum domestic practicalities? In due course she went off to Moscow Conservatory, where no doubt they had armies of babushkas to clean up after the students. I shoot Joan a sidelong glance. She is examining the corpse of my car with an expert eye, the other being scrunched shut against the smoke from the gasper clenched between her lips. She is wearing a boiler suit faded with age that she probably inherited from the Navy and has long since rolled up her sleeves. The anchor tattoo blazes on a forearm that looks like Popeye's. Can it be, I wonder, that this old salt is becoming broody? Or at least entertaining thoughts of domesticity? And might it turn out that Marta is receptive to this idea? At this moment Joan manages to prise open the car's hatchback and pokes around inside. As I've already said, it is none of my business. But it might have consequences for the plan I have yet to broach with Marta, which is that she writes the music for *Rancid Pansies*. I really must have a serious conversation with her in the next day or two.

"The spare tyre and toolkit are probably worth saving," Joan is saying, hauling them out.

"Not to me." I've already lost interest. I have also noticed that we have acquired some unofficial spectators far above on the edge of the landslip. "Who do you think they are up there?"

Joan removes her fag to follow my gaze. "Christ knows. Pilgrims, I suppose. The very people who are making Marta's life hell. With any luck they'll fall over."

And suddenly I realise how much I've been taking for granted. I still haven't had a proper conversation with Marta about the story of Diana's ghost. I merely asked her over the phone not to deny it. This is doubly remiss of me because not only can one never be certain how much Marta understands anyway, but time has gone by and she may already have forgotten or think it no longer matters. I remember telling Joan the story when I picked her up from Pisa airport but I have never explained to either of them the true nature of the deal I've done with Benedetti. Seeing the distant figures up there on the edge of the precipice reminds me that Marta is obviously going to have to move because living next to a sacred grotto is intolerable. I owe it to her to keep her fully abreast of the political shenanigans in the background. She could at least make the price of her silence a decent sum for her house which is, as Benedetti ruthlessly pointed out, pretty much worthless except to a local council eager to manage the site as a tourist attraction.

There and then I decide to ask Joan if she could explain the whole deal to Marta. It's not so long ago that she proved her worth to me as a co-plotter in her friend Millie Cleat's best interests and I suddenly think she might prove a persuasive advocate. So we sit on a boulder in the pleasant warmth of the spring sunshine and follow with our eyes the excavator's industrious rootings as I tell her about my pact with the Comune.

"You crafty bugger," says Joan at the end.

"Hardly. I was over a barrel, wasn't I? Anyway, I think it's kind to pander to people's delusions. Think how happy it makes all those credulous folk like Baggy and Dumpy to feel that from some mysterious but immanent dimension Princess Diana is watching out for them, shielding them from life's little landmines. I look on myself as a humble agent of good cheer."

"Exactly what I mean by crafty. You've even squared yourself to this monstrous fib. Well, well. I'll tell Marta tonight, of course. The poor lamb's got her own housing problems to worry about."

"Not so poor, as lambs go." I trust I don't sound overly bitter. "Quite a wealthy lamb, actually."

"Oh, she's told me all about her awful father. It's not the expense of buying another house that worries her, just the upheaval of finding somewhere else and moving to it. I can see we've got to go along with this apparition nonsense. We all need somewhere to live and I certainly think we've a perfect right to make local politics work in our favour. Crazy to shoot yourself in the foot just on a matter of principle."

"Almost as daft as shooting your dog in the head with a flare gun."

Joan sighs. "A girl's gotta do what a girl's gotta do. The flare gun was all I had to hand. But I agree it wasn't very discreet."

While we have been chatting the digger has unearthed what looks like bed sheets. Everybody converges on the trove and what might be intimate remnants of the master bedroom undergo immediate public scrutiny. Both sheets and burst mattress have inevitably acquired fungal stains and brownish smears of mud at which everybody stares with horrid know-ingness like Jane Cotter, the Savoy Hotel chambermaid who gave evidence at the second Wilde trial. One of the *Forestale* officers looks me up and down in a saucy fashion and makes a remark to his colleague that I don't catch but which I assume is opprobrious since they both laugh. They're probably both a bit upstaged by my boots. At that moment I'm distracted by the emergence from the ground in the excavator's bucket of what looks like a squashed orange box. I recognise it as my bedside cabinet, once a charming little cupboard from the eighteenth century that has just about made it into the twenty-first. I hold up my hand and go to inspect it. The giant machine waits, exhaling the purposeful scent of hot diesel and hydraulic fluid. Between us Joan and I lift out the flattened relic and carry it to one side. I can just feel the eyes of the *Forestale* men and the journalists waiting to pounce on titillat-ing evidence of bachelor living. I couldn't care less. I know there'll be nothing incriminating in it but I'm hoping against

hope that— *Yes!* My two most prized and inspirational cook-
books, my favourite bedtime reading, have survived! A little
damp, certainly, but essentially intact.

This find thoroughly redeems the day after all. These two
volumes are quite irreplaceable. The older is as much an
adventure book as a cookbook: Major-General Sir Aubrey
Lutterworth's *Elements of Raj Cookery* (1887), printed in
Hyderabad. How very much more readable the recipe books
of today's winsome TV cheffies would be if they included
detailed instructions on how to catch the ingredients, as well as
asides on the language and grosser habits of the natives in the
area where the ingredients once thrived! The one thing the
Major-General seldom did was go around the local market
hoping to find interesting cuts of bandicoot, although he
would regularly send his batman down to the bazaar for fresh
spices. "'The animal we know as the bandicoot,'" I read out
aloud to Joan, "'the Teloogoos call *pandi-kokku* or pig-rat, and
a deuced intelligent little beggar he is, too, often requiring
quite a measure of ingenuity to trap. It is almost as if he knew
that his own flesh, lightly seethed in the juice of green man-
goes, attains a delicacy as perfectly suited to the discernment of
a crowned head as to a rough-and-ready camp fire repast. In
truth he is fit for any table although it has proved best to con-
ceal his true identity from the Memsahibs by means of harm-
less misdirection. Trubshawe, our Colour Sergeant, informs
me that the phrase 'Malabar Mutton' passes muster and has
never yet been enquired into closely. To take Master Bandicoot
you must lay your springes well before dusk and bait them with
new leaves of *khati-sakhi*, which he has little enough mind to
resist. Your artificer having also procured you an ounce of
ordinary black powder . . .' Oh, you've no idea how many
times I've read myself to sleep with old Aubrey"—and in an
unbridled moment I kiss the book's mildewed cover. "It's brilliant to have him back." I notice the onlookers now gazing at

me in surprise and disappointment. No normal man goes into ecstasies over a mouldy old book, *per carità*, not even the Bible (although possibly a woman might). At the very least they were hoping for one-handed magazines depicting criminal acts or even a box full of gold watches and other heirloom trinketry. Old books simply don't hack it. Losing interest, they start to move away.

"And this other one—" I hold out Dame Emmeline Tyrwhitt-Glamis's *Emergency Cuisine*. "It's just as heroic in its way. Terribly rare, too."

"'HMSO 1942,'" Joan reads. "It can't be that rare, Gerry. The Stationery Office had huge print runs even with the wartime paper shortage."

"True. But the first edition was awaiting distribution when it was virtually wiped out in an air raid. I've no idea how this copy survived. I like to think it was Dame Emmeline's own, of course. In its way it's every bit as much a gem as the Major-General's book. She was the one who invented Victory Paste, made from puréed cockroaches. She was full of splendid morale-raising zeal. I see her as a sort of Joyce Grenfell figure but grander. Wait a bit . . . Yes, here we are: 'Threats from abroad cannot make a true Briton quail, but they certainly ought to make him look more closely at the generous defences Mother England has provided for her children in time of need. When we look in awe at a noble English oak we may reflect how its forebears supplied the 'hearts of oak' for our naval and merchant fleets that won us our Great Empire. But time moves on, and today's ships have hearts of steel. Yet we would be badly mistaken if we thought our English oaks were thereby demoted to mere symbols of past glory. Not a bit of it! Did we but realise, they provide a way to beat rationing and help the fighting housewife eke out her family's food with recipes that tease the palate and fortify the nation.

"'You probably thought acorns were mere food for mediaeval

pigs, or for Hitler's Germans in the form of their despised 'ersatz' coffee. But they are much more than that, as England's sturdy peasantry once knew, although the modern swain has misguidedly abandoned this valuable form of commons in favour of 'labour-saving' foods with half the nutritional value. I have frequently had words with the workers on my estate about this very subject. There is something about tied cottages, I find, that goes hand-in-hand with stubbornness and the wrong sort of conservatism. The truth is that British acorns can enable us fighting housewives to tap the strength still abundant in the very veins of Old England. Probably as a child you once tried to eat a raw acorn, as I did, only to reject it outright on account of its bitterness. This is due merely to the presence of *tannin*, a major ingredient of our national drink, tea, although in concentrations too high for our taste. But this bitterness is easily removed if you follow these simple instructions . . .' And on she goes about leaching and grinding before giving us a recipe for Acorn Polenta with Sparrow Sauce—and very good it is, too. I made it a few years ago. Anyway, Dame Emmeline's a darling and I love her dearly. I just *know* we'd have got on. Honestly, Joan, finding these books has made my day."

"I'm glad. I think your lady would be a bit long-winded for today's housewife, though, if that species still exists at all."

"But that's exactly what I like about both her and the Major-General. They weren't just writing about food. And I also like their determination to treat virtually anything as edible and make an adventure out of doing it. Vastly preferable to those spotty cheffies telling us about the only shop in London that sells *mozzarella di bufala* worth dying for, don't you think?"

"What I think," Joan observes, "is that your film crew have arrived."

"Oh, *no*?" But there is a new car parked with the rest, from which are emerging people wearing those beige waistcoat things with about twenty-five zippered pouches that TV correspondents affect when on assignment in foreign danger zones. An American friend of mine calls them flack jackets, with a *c.*

"I'm so glad I put on my best boiler suit," says Joan as we stroll over to meet them. "I should hate to shame anyone. And with that shirt you look as though you might be about to break into the Lumberjack Song at any moment."

"I was hoping the boots might distract that sort of attention."

"In a way they do. Do you remember those old three-wheeler invalid carriages with a two-stroke engine? Of course you don't—you're far too young. But somehow your boots remind me of them."

"Thanks, Joan," I say a little stiffly. "They were all I could get at short notice. Actually, I can barely walk in them. They're giving me frightful blisters."

"Don't worry. You've got the authentic labourer's slouch, even if he'd be the sort of labourer who calls for a lager-and-lime."

"I do hope our relationship isn't going to degenerate into vulgar butcher-than-thou competitiveness."

"Not a chance, sport," says Joan, merrily giving me a whack between the shoulder blades.

But we have now come up with the TV party, who are unloading equipment from their car. The lead flack does in fact have a face I vaguely recognise despite my practically never seeing British TV. The celebrated Leo Wolstenholme is quite short and stubby with a radish nose and an expression of mulish equanimity like that of a garden gnome used to being lied to. Her lack of glamour seems a hopeful sign. Nobody looking like that could possibly flourish in television these days unless she had genuine talent.

"Leo Wolstenholme? I'm Gerry Samper and this is Joan Nugent, the close friend of Millie Cleat's I mentioned. You've done well to find us up here in the wilds."

Hands are shaken. A girl in her mid-twenties with fashion-ably butchered hair and a face bristling with pins and studs is presented as Leo's personal assistant, Sappho.

"Not Saffron?"

"No—Saffron's in London. She's the one you spoke to on the phone." The same Marlborough tones, though.

"Good name, Sappho." I suppose I'm hoping to cheer up this dour and charmless creature. "I mean, in the circum-stances." The girl looks blank. "Your name? It's an anagram of 'Posh PA.' Rather appropriate." But she goes on looking blank even as her lips mime a baffled smile.

"And this is Jonti." Leo presents a lean young man with what looks to the eagle Samper eye like a half-smoked spliff parked behind one ear. Jonti is obviously sizing up the site for suitable locations and the sun's direction. He looks as though he'd tried it all by the age of twelve and been bored by every-thing that didn't involve electronic technology. "And Olly." Olly is a puppyish elf who at a guess has tried nothing other than being a sound-man in a TV company. He is already wear-ing a pair of cans around his neck.

"And *this* is what's left of your house?" asks Leo incredu-lously. "They warned us at the hotel that there wouldn't be much left to see. They were right."

"It did fall from right up there," I point to where a few onlookers are still visible at the plateau's edge. "It's quite a way."

"Shit. Your *whole house*?"

"The lot. Everything I owned in the world. It's all under there, somewhere." I indicate the moraine with a suitably casual gesture. The four from *Global Eyeball* are silent, evi-dently awed by the idea of material belongings being so quickly and impressively annihilated. "Except for my car." They take in the battered hulk of the Ass Vein and the excava-tor still snorting away busily behind it.

"That's pretty tragic," says Leo thoughtfully. "Good job you weren't in the house."

"I thought so."

"At the hotel they said something about your having got out by a miracle. I think they mentioned the ghost of Princess Diana, but the desk clerk's English was a bit iffy."

"Oh, one of those local bits of superstitious gossip," I say dismissively. "Typical republicans: they're obsessed with royalty and tragic glam. Beautiful mothers dying young, apparitions, Catholic kitsch with erotic overtones, all that stuff. We are in Italy, after all." I do feel a bit disloyal, not to say hypocritical, but these people are here to talk to me about Millie Cleat. Nothing else need concern them.

"Mm. So let's make a start, if that's all right by you? We'd like to be done and dusted by tonight. Our flight's tomorrow morning early. Jonti?"

"I was thinking over on those rocks? Sun's right and you've got that busted roof on the ground behind with the excavator coming in and out of the frame in the distance. Obviously we can vary the shot, pan around as you're speaking."

"Yes, I like the idea of some action going on behind me. Otherwise this film is going to be all shots of yachts plus some newsreel footage. We can't afford to have the talking heads too static. OK Gerry, you're the writer—brilliant book, by the way. Best I've ever read of that kind of thing—do you want to go first, or what about Joan here? I'm hoping you can add some details about Millie that don't appear in Gerry's book, Joan. Especially towards the end when she seems to have lost the plot over those Deep Blue environmentalist fanatics. However, I do want to make it clear to both of you: this isn't going to be a knocking film. Millie's a heroine and she'll stay one. But I've read enough to realise she was a complex and fascinating character. We're trying to investigate why she captured the public's imagination to such an extent.

I want some warts to go with the normal picture. She wasn't a saint, after all."

For a bizarre moment I have to remind myself it's Millie and not Princess Di Leo's speaking about. As we all move towards Jonti's favoured site our attention is distracted by shouts in the distance. It appears that something else has come to light. Joan and I excuse ourselves and hurry over. There's now a rather depressing heap of old rags piled up on one side that I recognise as part of my wardrobe, sadly aged. But they aren't the centre of attention. They are not what the boys from *Il Tirreno* are busily photographing as one of the *Forestale* officers holds it up. It takes me a moment to recognise it as an object I've clean forgotten I owned. You know how it is: you get so used to certain things in your house that you no longer see them. Wives, children, pets, of course, and pictures. Especially pictures. After a few years on the wall the only way to see them again is to re-frame them and hang them somewhere else. This object being held up is a piece of campery that Derek gave me as a joke years ago when it became briefly notorious: the twelve-inch tall porcelain doll of Diana wearing that high-collared "Elvis dress" studded with fake pearls. It was marketed by the Franklin Mint, the American company the Diana Memorial Fund later unsuccessfully sued, in the process making an ass of itself besides losing thirteen and a half million pounds. And as soon as I see it I realise this is one of those potentially awkward moments when it's necessary to think on one's feet, even if they do hurt. The two from *Il Tirreno* come hurrying up, the eager hack-light gleaming in their eyes.

"Excuse me, signor Samper," the elder addresses me in Italian, "but can you confirm that this exquisite statue of *la Principessa Diana* was in your house when it fell?"

I take it from him gingerly as though it were a little antipersonnel mine that had been unearthed. "Er, well, yes, I suppose it must have been. It's just, you know, an ornament."

"Ah, like a household god? Like *i Lari e i Penati*?"

O-level was a long time ago and I'd forgotten about the Romans' gods, Lares and Penates and Vesta the goddess of the hearth watching over their elegant villas with courtyards and pools and those bedrooms with improper friezes. But I must club this hare he's started before it can run another step. "No, absolutely not. It's just one of those bits of junk that gradually accumulate in everybody's house. A mere *ninnolo*: it has no significance whatever, although by now it may be a collector's item for all I know."

"But you can't deny its survival is pretty miraculous," the hack perseveres. "Just look at it. *È porcellana, è fragilissima*, yet it's not even chipped. It's perfect, even after falling at least a hundred metres in a shower of rock and rubble, lying buried for nearly half a year and being brought to the surface by an excavator. Don't tell me that's not miraculous."

"It's remarkable, certainly," I concede. "Even wonderful." Now, Samper, be careful here. Your new home depends on it. "But I'm not sure I'd dare call it a miracle. We're not priests and it's hardly for us to make judgements of that kind. And as a matter of fact it isn't perfect. She was holding a ghastly silk rose in her right hand—the stem went through here, look. I'm glad to see that's gone."

"*Eh be'*, *signore*, a detail. A missing rose, though? Some would see that as significant. My judgement tells me that Princess Diana is somehow bound up with your life and, miracle or not, here you are and here her statue is, both of you intact. I can assure you, very few of my readers will have any doubts."

"That I can well imagine. After all, a good percentage of them believe they'll win the Lotto each week." Suddenly I notice the saturnine Jonti has his camera on his shoulder and is filming this little scene. "Hey, stop that!" I cry. "Come on, you guys, you're not here to film this stuff, you're here to do an interview about Millie Cleat." I turn to Leo for support. "Can't we get started?"

"Oh, Jonti was just getting some light and sound levels. General location shots. Anyway, it's interesting, Gerry. This statue really came from your house?"

"Yes, yes, yes. It's just one of those silly camp gifts that friends give each other as a joke. I bet you've got plenty of similar things at home. I mean"—I swing around and sweep an arm over the boulder-strewn scene—"somewhere under this lies a farting teddy bear I was given. If that had survived, would these goons be calling it a miracle? Of course not."

"Still," Leo says musingly, "it does rather tie in with what they were saying in the hotel this morning. Maybe you really are under the protection of Lady Di's spirit even if you don't know it."

She laughs, but not as though the whole things is as risible as I find it. A weight of irritable hopelessness envelops me like a leaden cape. All at once the excavator stops and falls silent with a wheeze. People begin drifting towards their cars. Midday already. Leo agrees to send her crew down to the nearest bar to have some sandwiches made up for us and also bring us back something to drink while she stays behind with Joan and me to prepare the interviews. I wander off and kick moodily at my heap of ex-finery. I notice it includes my famous pair of Homo Erectus jeans that a mere two or three years ago were denim couture's equivalent of a Vacheron Constantin watch and now look as though they'd been used to stuff a drain. Strangely, I feel no pang. Since I'm hiring its driver by the day, the digger can carry on this afternoon but if nothing else turns up I shan't bother to continue. What's the point? I'm sorriest about my books and CDs, many of which (if I could ever remember their titles) would require a good deal of money and effort to replace. All the rest is just stuff that can be bought anywhere. Of all things it *would* be Derek's blasted Di doll that should have come to light. True, ten years ago I was happy to have it as a piece of topical kitsch. In her bobbly bolero she used to stand behind the bath taps and gaze down at bathers' languidly floating genitalia with her curiously American, Pepsodent smile. She kept dropping her rose into the bathwater and after sundry immersions it was looking faded and tatty. Still, I do wonder at the physics involved not only in the statuette's freakish survival but in its complete isolation. There was not a shard of broken hand basin nearby that I could see, nor even one of the sundry Floris bottles that had shared her perch. Strange indeed.

The film crew returns, we eat our lunch, the day wears on. As the excavator comes to life again Leo interviews me perched on the rock in an uncomfortable posture that reminds me of Copenhagen's mermaid readying herself for curettage. My boots will, I hope, go some way towards dispelling this image. Even as my feet throb I wonder whether an important part of my decision to halt all further excavation after tonight isn't down to my determination never to wear these things again. I'm equally determined never to be interviewed again. Leo's questions are disappointingly the tired old stuff of someone who is afraid of eliciting responses that imperil the line she has already decided to take. What was the great Millie Cleat like to work with? (Grim.) How close was she to her family? (Not.) Do I think she had mystical experiences during her lone voyages? (If you *knew* how I'd prayed for her to try walking on water.) When things appear to sag I at last break the story of Millie's yacht *Beldame* cutting across the bows of that EAGIS survey in the Canaries and confirm that the scientists have it all on video. This promise of some enlivening drama is just what Leo wants to hear. It means being able to show footage the viewing public has never seen—unlike the newsreel shots of Millie's death in Sydney harbour which constant repetition has rendered no longer visible, along with the fall of the Twin Towers or the wives, children, pets and pictures in our own homes. Leo becomes quite red with excitement. She looks like a gnome on hearing it's going to be a bumper year for toadstools.

"Obviously a perfect instance of a natural-born sports-woman being competitive to her fingertips. It's that killer instinct: *Go for it!*"

"It was certainly a perfect instance of an egocentric and ignorant sportswoman ruining a major European scientific sur-vey of vital interest to half the countries in the northern hemi-sphere with an Atlantic coastline."

"You do exaggerate, Gerry. I mean, come on, what people want is to see their heroes make those daring, split-second decisions that break records."

"I was afraid of that."

I think Leo's interview with Joan goes rather better. I assume Joan comes up with plenty of human-interest details about Millie's relations with her fellow sailors in Britain's south-coast yachting community, tales of all-girls-together fish barbecues while moored in Langstone harbour and Hayling Bay. I believe at one point I overhear Leo asking if maybe Millie had been attractive to gay women. I suppose a rule of thumb for broad-casters is the same as that for barristers: that they never ask a question to which they don't already know the answer. This would certainly account for the air of utter predictability the news media seem to cultivate almost as a point of honour.

Eventually, though, it is over, Leo saying she has "some sen-sational stuff from both of you." They are just starting to pack up when another shout announces a fresh discovery. This one might actually be useful, I think, as I see reposing in the exca-vator's muddy bucket my battered beige filing cabinet. Battered it may be, but it turns out to be locked and faithfully impregnable. I no longer have a key so I shall take it back to town and have a locksmith open it. Joan fetches the van across and the excavator lifts the cabinet up and tilts the bucket so we can slide it in. It is remarkably heavy.

As we close the van door Joan pauses like a beagle sampling the air and says, "Do I smell poppers?"

"Oh lor'." I now remember Adrian's present. "Well, if we've suddenly made it leak it'll soon evaporate."

"I'm thinking of the drive back to town with our heads pounding and our blood pressure bottoming out and us both reeking of guardsmen's feet."

"It's not amyl, it's butyl. That doesn't smell so cheesy." I call up to the excavator driver that he can now knock off. Meanwhile the film crew have loaded their car and are poised for hand-shakings and, I hope, an offer of dinner tonight at *Global Eyeball*'s expense. Suddenly Jonti, who seems habitually to be scanning the horizon, gives a cry. "Christ! Look up there!"

A dark bundle is falling, bouncing, sliding, rolling down the mountainside. From above it drift thin wisps of screaming, and gesticulating figures are visible on the lip of the precipice. Limply flailing, the bundle comes to rest in a cloud of dust, limbs asprawl. I experience a brief moment of paralysis in which a small sick feeling is embedded before the admirable Joan banishes it as she sets off at an elderly lope.

"Bets, anyone?" she calls out gleefully. "First aid or last rites?

Adrian 6

email from Dr. Adrian Jestico (ajestico@bois.ac.uk)
to Dr. Penny Barbisant (penbar@labs.whoi.ed)

Amazing about your *Hattie MacAllister* being a Liberty ship. So it's exactly like the *Richard Montgomery* stuck in the Thames estuary. Ancient Mariner in the Archaeology Division here tells me the Americans churned them out for us in WW2 at breakneck speed to replace all our merchant ships sunk by U-boats in the N. Atlantic & it was a good job they did. But the vessels weren't a brilliant design & they were hardly put together like Swiss watches. Do keep me posted, Penny. I'd be interested to know if the *HM* went down in a storm or from structural failure or was torpedoed. According to Ancient Mariner the U-boats used to wait all up that coast which is why in addition to a crew of 50 those Liberty ships usually had about 30 gunners & torpedo crew aboard.

Meanwhile, high drama over in Gerryland. Really, his life seems to have tapped into a vein of sheer wackiness—was this what Jung meant by synchronicity? When things just go on happening as though some offstage entity was trying to make a point? Gerry & and an ex-naval friend of his called Joan spent a day with an excavator going through the ruins of his house (they didn't find much, tho') & they were also interviewed by that poison dwarfette Leo Wolstenholme from *Global Eyeball* who had flown over specially. You know—the one whose boob op. ended up in court along with that unfortunate journalist who'd referred to her ubiquitous cleavage as "Silicone Valley" in his column? Just as they were all packing up to leave, a kid falls over the

194 · JAMES HAMILTON-PATERSON

edge of the cliff up where Gerry's house used to stand. It's not actually a vertical drop but a very steep slope covered in scree & rocks & tree trunks felled by the original landslip, & the poor kid (she's only 10) came tumbling down about 100 metres in a small avalanche of her own. But—& get this—she's OK! Bruised all over & covered in minor cuts but nothing broken. Everyone stands around saying it's a miracle & really meaning it. But it gets better still. After the initial tears she's acting oddly, staring around her & naturally everybody thinks she's a bit concussed, no surprise there & an ambulance has already been called, when suddenly it turns out not only that she speaks English but that she was blind from birth & can now see!!!

Well, that does it. The bulldozer driver and some local officials practically fall on their knees. Have you ever seen those primitive ex voto paintings in Italian churches? They're often quite touching & depict dramatic accidents that people have survived. They're painted as a mark of gratitude to the Virgin, who usually appears in a little cloud in one corner. This kid falling, surviving and being cured of a lifetime's blindness is pure ex voto stuff. Then it slowly sinks in that this time the Madonna might have had help. Where did the kid fall from? Why, right by the Diana shrine where her parents had just been posting a prayer that her sight might be restored. I mean crikey, Penny, I'm so glad I'm not there at this moment trying to preserve a calm, sceptical demeanour as supposedly befits a scientist. There had already been a very minor "miracle" earlier in the day when the excavator found an undamaged but awful camp statuette of—you've guessed—Princess Diana that Gerry had banished to his bathroom for laughs. So you'll see what I mean about synchronicity. Everything is suddenly conspiring to point fingers at Gerry and Diana as though they're spiritually joined at the hip. Poor Gerry is spitting blood when he's not busy working out how he can profit from it. And I forgot to mention that this little ex-blind English girl isn't just some nameless catspaw of fate. Her name's Darcie & Gerry has known her parents for some time. They're a couple he calls "Baggy & Dumpy" who came out to Italy, bought a house a year or so ago & now live much lower down but on the same road as Gerry's old house.

Yeah (I hear you say), so how come two loving parents allow their blind daughter to play on the edge of a precipice? The answer seems to be that they're not the brightest buttons in the box & they'd ducked under the warning tape strung along the edge to find out what all the people and excavators were doing down below. I gather they each had a firm grasp on the belt at the back of their kid's coat, & when the ground beneath her suddenly gave way her weight tore the thing loose & they were left holding a strip of navy blue wool as she bounced down the side of the mountain accompanied by parental screams. These things happen. Of course with the folly of hindsight they now realise it was all for the best & was *Meant*, because such are the mysterious ways that lead to miracle cures & theirs not to question the method which, I should point out, family doctors and opticians everywhere strongly oppose even though it occasionally works. It's a bit like thumping a TV that's on the blink: once in a blue moon you get a decent picture.

So how about that for excitement? Gerry tells me his first thought on seeing this dusty bundle come rolling down the mountain in a flurry of limbs was huge relief at having signed over his remaining land to the local council only days earlier so he was no longer legally responsible. At the time he was naturally thinking in terms of corpses & being sued for not having put up a proper fence or something. But far from blaming him, people are now treating him like a species of holy fool: about as spiritual as a slab of cheddar, granted, but nevertheless one of those people around whom profoundly mysterious things just *happen*. And of course he's also regarded as being in virtual communication with the late squeeze of the Son of Harrods. He tells me Leo W. got her camera unpacked again within seconds & captured the little girl discovering she could see for the first time in her life, possibly the only such occasion ever filmed. Apparently Leo has now decided that this Diana cult & Gerry's association with it is ripe for investigation. Despite his howls of anguish I'd guess he's adoring the attention. It certainly hasn't made him moderate his off-colour remarks. Apparently he told Leo on camera that he felt rather sorry for little Darcie since it would be awful to regain your sight & discover your parents looked like Baggy & Dumpy. At least this kind thought will never be broadcast.

Thanks for your brief run-down on your friend Luke. Choosing my words carefully I'd say he sounds, well, normal. Nothing to do with sex, of course; I'm just comparing him to Gerry, somewhat enviously. I should think an ornithologist would make an excellent companion for someone like you who spends hours staring down a microscope. Patience is a good quality for two people to share. Bit of an age difference, I agree, but hardly disastrous. As for Gerry, in your last email you astutely wonder whether he's the genius he thinks he is. A pertinent question, even if applicable to most of us. It's unfortunately true that the thing at which he really does excel—ghosting the biographies of sports celebs—is also the thing he most loathes & disparages. Why? Because he's convinced he has far greater talents, hitherto unexploited & hence unacknowledged for reasons of financial necessity. Talents for what? we may ask, even as we note it's his very qualities as a ghost writer that have turned him into a minor celebrity himself, fit to be interviewed for TV, as well as earning him a living the rest of us salaried peons can only envy.

There's no doubt he does have other talents, including the ability to make an entire dinner party throw up at the same moment. This is a gift which none of us who were present is likely to forget even though it's something Gerry himself has long since put out of his mind, accusing the rest of us of faking and exaggeration. He's unquestionably musical in a bizarre sort of way & knows a lot about it although he doesn't actually play any instrument, & this seems to be behind his weird relationship with Marta which I've mentioned before. It looks almost like rivalry on his part, yet that's preposterous because Marta's a bona fide conservatoire-trained composer with all sorts of stuff including two film scores under her belt. My conductor brother-in-law thinks she's genuinely outstanding & one of the 2 or 3 younger contemporaries he's eager to watch & promote. So any idea that Gerry could rival her is as absurd as suggesting Marta would make a good ghost writer. Yet until recently he was for ever mocking her musicianship behind her back while to her face he was just plain patronising. It sounds unforgivable—it *is* unforgivable—but as so often with Gerry one forgives him because he's usually very funny with it & because you suspect it's born of a complicated repressed admiration. He's actually far fonder of Marta than he lets himself believe, but heaven help you if you say so. He'll go off into a tirade about "that Voynovian bat" or "the Iron Curtain bagpiper."

Right now he's moderating all that because she has at last agreed to write the music to this opera of his he's become obsessed with. I gather he has just about finished the libretto & it really is about his new alter ego, Princess Di. Honestly—an opera about *her*, of all people! To me I'm afraid she's just another dim Royal, but I listen to Gerry with what I hope sounds like proper enthusiasm. He's paying Marta to do the music but I don't know how much & don't quite like to ask. I do know she has vast private means of her own, thanks to her criminal family.

But the important thing is that Max is enthusiastic & provided he likes the finished article he's proposing to première it at Crendlesham. If it's a success Gerry will at last feel vindicated. He'll have proved he has the right to mix & mingle with the international arts glitterati on his own terms. He may well become quite insufferable as a result.

I *think* it's kind of you to ask about things here at BOIS though as I've said before, part of the reason I like writing to you about munitions ships & Gerry is to take my mind off work. At present I can sum my professional life up with the plaintive question "Why me?" You know me, Penny: I'm just a typical boffin who's attached to cope-poda, never happier than when in the little beasties' company. OK, so I'm head of a small department, but why does the director choose me of all people to deal with these special interest groups who come down to Southampton to petition us? I have the public relations skills of Kim Il Sung. These people turn up here daily, each clamouring to be heard on the subject of the Severn barrage & each convinced that their "input" is the one make-or-break factor that will finally decide whether the damn thing ever gets built, even though they know all the real decisions are taken by politicians 80 miles away in Whitehall who can't tell a shrimp from a sea-cow.

On that sunny note—token of a grey day here in S'thampton—I shall sign off.

Cheers,
Adrian

7.

The scene is the drawing room of Balmoral Castle, nearing teatime on a rainy afternoon around the year 1990. Present are the Queen, on her knees on the hearthrug tempting a corgi with the sort of things corgis find tempting; the Duke of Edinburgh, who is listlessly leafing through a magazine devoted to field sports; Prince Charles in a kilt, who has just found Sir Stamford Raffles's *History of Java* in the Castle library and is reading passages from it aloud to a potted banana plant to make it feel more loved; and Princess Diana, a downcast presence who, as the orchestra begins its lead-in, leans back on an overstuffed sofa with her exquisite arms thrown wide along its back. It is a posture both of despair and of transcendence. Wearing an outfit by Versace, she is outstandingly the best dressed person in the room with the possible exception of the corgi, whose au naturel look is unassailable. The Duke's wardrobe, in particular, appears to have come from a Range Rover boot sale. Diana sings:

DIANA: This place is gloomy as a tomb
I really feel I'm dying here
So far from London and its pleasures.

Heads of dead animals everywhere
Slaughtered for the leisure
Of heavy men in heavy tweeds.

DUKE (*speaks*): Oh Christ, here we go again!

DIANA: The rain outside just falls in sheets.
In darling Gianni's clothes I shiver
And Manolo's slingbacks melt in this rain.

QUEEN (*speaks*): One can buy perfectly good Barbours in
Ballater. Wellies also.

CHARLES: Oh why must you be so difficult?
Marrying me was your own choice,
No one twisted your delicate arm.

You only had to raise your voice,
Put your foot down, sound the alarm.
But making history turned your head.

DIANA: Oh why must you be so boring?
It's no secret that you never
Loved me, even though I shut

My eyes and thought of England twice
And twice became my country's slut
Though proud to be their mother.

DUKE (*speaks*): A nice sort of squabble for your wretched
in-laws to have to listen to! Damned bad form, frankly. My
God, this place: weak tea and moaning women. I'm off to the
gun room for a Scotch.
  [*Exit*]

I just thought I'd run a draft of the opera's first scene by you
to give you a foretaste of my libretto and to convey its dramatic,
slightly foregone tone. Diana's liberation is close at hand, when

with her boys at boarding school and her husband busy with
the organisational minutiae of shoehorning adultery into his
tight ceremonial schedule she can devote herself to charity
work and a fun time. No longer is she the "Shy Di" of her
engagement ten years earlier: the demure, biddable kindergarten teacher who innocently allowed press photographers to
pose her like a Bendy Toy against the light so those 24-carat
legs were outlined against the filmy white background of her
dress. Now, through her amazing wardrobe (requiring two
full-time staff to manage) and the confidence that cult status
confers, she goes her own way, disco dancing and hobnobbing
with lepers and other outcasts such as far-flung British Army
units. I'm afraid I daren't divulge the two arias I have written
for her and Charles when their respective extramarital affairs
become revealed via eavesdropped conversations. I'm pinning
great hopes on these "Squidgy" and "Tampax" *scenas* and it
would be a shame to spoil their effect by giving the game away
in advance. Suffice it to say they employ a device that as far as
I know is novel in opera although not in gynaecology. I'll say
no more. Marta has promised me she will devote her best energies to match the brilliant words with equally brilliant music.

Oh dear, though—there are so many good things. I long to
quote them so they will send you scurrying to buy tickets
before they're all sold out. For instance, Diana's tragicomic
number on learning of her friend Gianni Versace's death not
long before her own. It begins:

Today's glitterati
Are tomorrow's obliterati . . .

and if you think you catch a whiff of banality there you
must remember that the very *essence* of opera (not to mention
musicals) is cod philosophy and stock human emotion. The
words alone shouldn't try to express anything too deep other-

wise they push the music into second place, and vice versa. I'm sure you'll remember Richard Strauss and Clemens Krauss thrashing all that out pretty thoroughly in *Capriccio*, based on the old parody by Casti, *Prima la musica e poi le parole*. In Strauss's opera Flamand the composer and Olivier the poet are constantly trying to decide which comes first, the music or the words. This question was to remain open until decades later when the lyricist Sammy Kahn settled it by saying "The cheque."

Again, I don't want to give away too much but at the start of my final Act, following Diana's death and just before the scenes of her dramatic apotheosis in the Vatican *and beyond*, the stage will be completely dark except for a single spot. A voice with piano accompaniment will sing an old ballad that she loved, the nineteenth-century folk prototype of "The House of the Rising Sun" called "Dilated Wench Inn." This is a very moving moment and I worry about the sort of smartarses who might think it funny to make anagrams of this classic song's title such as "Wild, thinned acne," "Dent-chinned wail" and things involving candles. In order to remove the temptation I have re-titled it "Much adieu about nothing":

Goodbye English flower
Deep-rooted in our soil
You blossomed in fabulous dresses
While gossip came to a boil
You appealed on our newsreels
And tattled in interviews
Now you belong to Althorp Park
With nothing more to lose

And it seems to me your life was like
A condom in a gale
Puffed rigid by publicity's wind

And shrivelling when it failed
Yet even before the day fate spilled
A career so short in years
Its reservoir of love was filled
By all your people's tears

"Bad taste" do I hear? The tutting of the petits bourgeois?
At the risk of sounding immodest by implied comparison, I
remind myself that Beethoven was shocked by Mozart's choosing to set the libretto of *Così fan tutte*. The deaf prude from
Bonn thought it in execrable taste. Reaching a friendly hand
across the centuries to little, farting, periwigged Mozart I can
reassure him that there are worse things than being accused of
bad taste. Being praised for good taste, for one. And writing
lyrics full of grammatical howlers for another (the Brown Dirt
Cowboy please note). Oh—and as a final note for now, I've
written a quite spare speaking role for the Duke of Edinburgh
who appears in several scenes. He acts as an irascible, pithy
version of a Greek chorus and is often silently onstage in one
corner, cleaning a 12-bore shotgun. I confess I've shamelessly
tailored this part for myself. As many people will know, my
singing voice is rather exceptional but, alas, not professionally
trained and I don't think Donizetti-like roulades would fit well
with Marta's music, which to me sounds like an idyllic marriage between Prokoviev and Jonathan Dove. So I've written
myself a largely silent but always expressive part in my own
opera. Sometimes I think my whole life has been nothing but
an overture to being onstage at last.

And prematurely onstage I already am these days, though it
is causing me nothing but chagrin. *L'affaire* Darcie Barrington
has produced world-class hysteria. Led by the Italians, the
whole of Europe's media have converged on Le Roccie these
last weeks. Leo Wolstenholme's footage of the child discovering she can see has been shown and re-shown until, like the

Twin Towers standing and falling and standing and falling over and over again, it no longer feels like before-and-after so much as a permanent state of indecision. Like the pornographic freeze-frame it has become emptily iconic of nothing but itself, although for Leo and Co. it must surely be iconic of a large sum of money. Things have eased a bit now but at its worst, when the town was practically besieged by newshounds wearing some of the most abominable deodorants you ever smelt, I dared hardly stir out of the Belgian's flat for fear of being buttonholed by complete strangers demanding I cure symptoms so disgusting I marvelled they could still be alive. For the first time ever I began to feel a sneaking degree of sympathy for the late Jesus Christ, who must have encountered similar problems— and he was operating in pre-Judaean National Health Service days. I had become so easily recognisable because *Il Tirreno*'s stills of me examining that Diana statuette were syndicated everywhere over absurd and lying copy claiming that the late Princess was "channelling" through me which, like tunnelling through Paris, must equally be a doomed activity for her. Still, the nuns in my building drop creakily to their knees when I pass them on the stairs, and sheer embarrassment as well as *noblesse* obliges me to raise a hand in vague benediction.

Up at Le Roccie it became such pandemonium I put on a large pair of dark glasses and went and fetched Marta and Joan, bringing them back to the Belgian's spare bedroom where they crammed together for a night before I found them the last hotel room in town. They stayed there a week until the worst was over. Despite all the upset and subterfuge Marta seemed oddly unperturbed. I don't know what's got into her: I've never known her so sunny. Resignation? Love? The days go by and Joan is still very much in residence with her. At least they accept their love nest has now been terminally squatted on by the huge smelly vulture of cult religiosity and are resigned to leaving for good. This has privately cheered me, as you may

imagine: Marta's reign as Queen of Le Roccie has been amus-
ingly brief. Complete strangers with vile diseases knock at her
door demanding to use the lavatory or to be healed. What they
get is Joan's tattooed, muscular forearm barring the way and
some rich English naval expletives.

Yet despite all this disruption Marta's mood remains defi-
antly merry. She has spent her time down here in exile reading
my nearly completed libretto and now tells me it is "brilliant."
To be strictly accurate, what she said was "Gerree, never I have
laughed so much. It is brilliant *satjriski*, yes?" This is no less
gratifying, of course, since she told me a long time ago that
because of their post-war history of Soviet occupation
Voynovians take satire extremely seriously as an art form. For
them it always floats as a wafer-thin layer over great tragic
depths, like an iridescent film of tanning oil on a fathomless
ocean. I am completely certain that she recognises my opera's
fundamental high seriousness. She is, after all, a serious artist
herself and would hardly waste her talents on setting anything
but the best texts. And if I needed further assurance, the great
Max Christ himself says that if she finishes the score in time he
will première the opera next year in his own prestigious Haysel
Festival. If it succeeds there it will naturally become squabbled
over by Covent Garden, Glyndebourne and the Met. I draw
the line at Garsington.

I should explain the origins of this festival. Some time in the
past I alluded to Max and Jennifer's early days in Crendlesham
Hall when they were still in the throes of renovation. One of
the reasons they chose the house was because of its immense
and ancient barn about a hundred yards away known as "the
Haysel," one of those daft Suffolk dialect words dating from
the days when the peasantry couldn't pronounce "haymaking," which is what I'm told it means. Apparently, when haymaking was finished the sunburned swains used to occupy as
much of this barn as wasn't stuffed with hay for the sort of

drunken revelry that kept the local birth rate soaring. In 1521, only the other day by Suffolk standards, the bawdiness became so unbridled that Crendlesham's rector was himself erroneously inseminated in the prickly depths of the mow. For many years thereafter an effort was made to conduct the haymaking festivities with a little more sobriety although it was noticed that the rector himself never missed a haysel, presumably in order to quell any immorality as soon as he saw it. But eventually he died and the annual celebrations in the great barn returned to their former licentiousness and according to parish records continued pretty much unchanged until twentieth-century prudery, the mechanisation of farming and the diminishing need for hay brought this venerable tradition to an end. After that the barn became little more than a shelter for rats and decaying tractors and fell into an advanced stage of decrepitude. Max's ambition had always been to restore the huge old building with its oak timbers salvaged from tall ships down the ages. He planned it as a concert hall where he could hold a summer festival to showcase his now-famous Colchester Symphony Orchestra and introduce young composers and instrumentalists. Thus the Haysel Festival, which after a bare couple of seasons in the beautifully refurbished hall has already become a fixture in the diary of anyone who fancies themselves in touch with music. So Max's promise to première *Rancid Pansies* (memo: find a proper title!) at the Haysel will ensure it the best possible launch for an international career.

Tonight I am once again behind the wheel of a Toyota Ass Vein: a "new second-hand" copy of my original found for me by a minion of my insurance company, probably under a deal I should wish to know nothing about. What I do know is that it is a better bargain than if they had simply given me the cash value of my junked vehicle. I may perhaps now moderate the curses I've been requesting little St. Bernard to call down on

Dottoressa Strangolagalli. Perhaps after all boils, goitres and prolapses were a bit on the harsh side. Incurable rectal itch should do it; and I like to think of her having to squirm through meetings, business lunches and Sunday Mass with those blood-red talons unable to dig in for relief. People will think she's harbouring widow's mites or something.

If I gave you three guesses as to where I'm off to this evening I doubt if you would divine correctly, just as until very recently I myself would have been aghast at the idea. I am in fact going to dine at the weasel Benedetti's own home; and what is more, his other guest is to be *il sindaco* himself, the mayor, which will show you the sort of circles Gerald Samper is obliged to move in these days. Not by choice, mind you. These things are about politics, and no doubt both Benedetti and the mayor would privately agree that if it weren't for politics they themselves would have little enough incentive to fraternise with foreigners out of hours.

In idle moments over the years I have occasionally wondered what sort of house an estate agent like Benedetti would choose for himself, much as one wonders what the wife of a professional pornographer would look like. Probably quite ordinary in both cases, I have assumed. Certainly Benedetti's house is attractive enough and not at all flamboyant. On the edge of town with a good-sized garden and a splendid view of the mountains, it's a typical square house in the local style with grey stonework interspersed with two or three horizontal courses of bricks, all beneath a tiled roof. Probably a hundred years old, it is a handsome, solid family house spoiled only (in my view, though not according to local taste) by being surrounded by stone walls set with railings and an immense pair of electrically operated wrought-iron entrance gates. Such are de rigueur in these parts; and the old saying about an Englishman's home being his castle, when compared with the imposing ironwork and electronic security measures with which Italians surround quite ordinary houses, acquires a certain pathos by being exposed as purely metaphorical.

Unsurprisingly, Benedetti in his leisure hours is as sprucely turned out as when he's in his office or disguised as an English prep-school master of yesteryear. Tonight he is in a beige pair of moleskin slacks by Carisma that can't have set him back less than €300. His borrowed Asian plumage looks as though he has coiffed it with hot asphalt, so richly black it gleams.

"Maestro!" he greets me with a passable display of warmth. "I am honoured that you have stretched your precious time to include a visit to this humble house."

"Who could resist an opportunity to deepen a friendship hitherto regrettably confined to office hours?" I riposte, reclaiming my hand which now smells agreeably aromatic: Lorenzo Villoresi's "Piper Nigrum" if I'm not mistaken, revealing that the weasel has better taste in eau de toilette than I would have given him credit for. I follow him into the *salotto* where there is a large black retriever lying on the floor that I suspect might have been acquired to go with the Range Rover. There is also a middle-aged lady with a kindly, shrewd face whom my host introduces as his wife Bettina in a resigned sort of tone that suggests she might have been acquired to go with the house. This is someone I've been looking forward to meeting for some years: the unseen person who sends her husband out into the world each morning as dapper as a beetle, his shirts and handkerchiefs blindingly white and flawlessly ironed, his trousers pressed hard enough to squeeze the dye out of them, his shoes burnished. This polished man must have an equally polished partner, I thought. But Bettina is not at all in the mould I have invented for her.

"I've heard such a lot about you," she says as we shake hands. "What with all the publicity I had no idea what to expect. I've never met a lightning conductor for sanctity before."

"And I've never been one before. The whole thing's absurd. However, the good thing about lightning conductors is that whatever current passes through them leaves them quite unchanged."

"I'm glad to hear it," Bettina says. "So I needn't pretend to believe everything the newspapers are saying?"

With some pleasure I notice this good lady's informal outspokenness is not going down too well with her husband. Benedetti is frowning in a way that betrays his wig's independence from his scalp.

"Nonetheless, *cara*, there are undoubtedly mysteries involved—" he begins pompously but just then there are sounds of arrival outside and he bustles out almost at a run.

"Have you met our mayor before?" Bettina asks, her voice conspiratorially dropped.

"Never. I'm just a foreign writer who until recently lived a long way out of town and spent his time quietly scribbling. What's his name again? Orazio something?"

"Giardini. To tell you frankly, I am not of his party and I pray daily for his arrest for the scandal of the cement at our public swimming pool. Remind me to tell you some time," adds this admirably indiscreet person hurriedly as male voices approach. I'm fast warming to Bettina, who seems very much my sort of gal.

The old-fashioned English phrase used to be "a gentleman of full habit," but the modern epithet "obese" at least starts off on the right foot when it comes to describing the man Benedetti is ushering into the room. Had his habit been any fuller he would surely explode, showering us with tripes and trouser buttons. One could with accuracy describe Mayor Giardini as terminally fat, and with assonance as mortally portly. He has hooded eyes that make one think of a corrupt Renaissance cardinal. At once I begin to wonder quite how wise it is to be doing deals with a man like this, no matter how indirectly. With a familiar weasel like Benedetti it all seemed a bit of a game but seeing in the abundant flesh exactly where this town's buck stops is sobering.

Novelists often describe very fat men as having dainty feet and small hands, which presumably just means these appendages appear small by contrast with the bulk they're attached to. If Mayor Giardini's feet look quite normally sized, his hands are actually rather large. The same novelists also claim that such men move "with surprising lightness and delicacy"—again, one assumes, compared with the lumbering progress one would expect. Mayor Giardini unquestionably lumbers. I vaguely recall that his last election slogan was "A Big Man for a Big Job." Having greeted Bettina he turns to me and envelops my hands with a strangler's grip. He has the politician's trick of making it seem as though we are old friends rather than a couple of complete strangers who, left to their own devices, would never have wished to meet.

"It was a happy day for us when you decided to take up residence in this Comune," he announces while ensuring that no blood is still circulating in my fingers.

Never let it be said that signor Samper can't do the formalities. "It is an honour to meet you, Mayor," I lie.

"Orazio, Orazio," he corrects me. "We're all friends here."

Bettina, who vanished briefly, reappears and announces "*A tavola!*" As we move into the dining room I automatically translate the mayor's name as Horace Gardens and with a shock remember this as a quiet residential road near Kingston, Surrey, where an early boyfriend of mine used to live, lo! some thirty years ago. Thirty! It seems impossible. For a moment pungent memories flood back and swamp the present so that I can't think what I'm doing on this film set with its refectory table spread with enough food to stock a small supermarket. How did I get from Horace Gardens to Orazio Giardini? On what inscrutable, unforeseeable road? And is young Terry—

well, middle-aged Terry now—at this very moment reduced by a similar social commitment to wondering whatever became of me? No, I guess not. Maybe I ought to track him down and invite him to the first performance of *Rancid Pa*—

—but Benedetti is graciously showing us into our baronial chairs, whose choice is wise if the alternative is the set of antique rosewood chairs ranged around the walls. Mayor Giardini's voluminous rump would reduce any of them to matchwood. Golly, the Italians do like their dining tables massive! This one is typical: a gigantic polished slab of oak a good ten centimetres thick supported on legs the size of small tree trunks. The thing could seat twenty and must weigh half a tonne. It wouldn't be out of place in a medieval banqueting hall where, according to Hollywood, troublesome knights were wont to ride their horses up and down the tables, trampling pewter platters and upsetting the ladies in their wimples. (For all I know this may still pass for table manners in Southern California.) But now, as the stout chair beneath the stouter mayor half stifles its well-bred moan of protest, I discover to my surprise and disappointment that only the three of us will be dining. Bettina has done her bit by spreading the table with food and withdraws to leave the menfolk to their important talk. I have encountered this before in Italy. It always seems more than merely old-fashioned and to hark back to a time when Arabs occupied Sicily and the Moslem ladies knew their place.

She has certainly done us proud. There are plates of *salumi* of every kind including blood pudding, a home-cured prosciutto from which Benedetti is carving wafer-thin slices to drape over oozing melon, bowls of delicatessen goodies, cheeses on wooden platters and a collection of bottles neatly ranged at the end of the table like a set of tenpins awaiting someone's triumphal strike. There is also a huge dish of golden *panzerotti* so freshly fried I can hear the batter giving little squeaks and gasps as they cool. All very conventional, of course. Not a mouseburger in sight.

"Gentlemen, you must forgive this scratch meal," our host says, heaping our plates with crumpled satiny rags of prosciutto. "But I thought we could all do with a change from formality and have a more down-to-earth evening with true peasant fare. All the meats here come from Bettina's father," he explains to me, "who raises, butchers and cures his own products himself. You probably know him already. Nicòla the butcher, down by the fountain?"

"The best in town," I say. "I've patronised him for years but I'd no idea he was Bettina's father. This prosciutto is quite amazing."

"'Na favola," says the mayor indistinctly, the compliment escaping wetly from a mouth stuffed and leaking. "Superlative."

There follows some topical and local chit-chat which I recognise as the hors d'oeuvre to the main meat of the evening that is surely the reason for my invitation. I listen more or less curiously to the small talk of these small-town grandees. The mayor mentions the trouble a professor friend of his is having with an Islamic student at Pisa university. This triggers a peculiar and passionate outburst by Benedetti that reminds me of the claim he made to me of having once had priestly leanings. He suddenly puts down his fork and says, "It's all wrong, Orazio, and everybody senses it. We Italians, we *Europeans* don't want to be dragged back. We don't *want* any more Middle East, thank you very much. It has taken us two thousand years to Europeanise our scripture: to blanch Christ a decent asparagus white and set him in Renaissance landscapes and have snow fall at his birth. We've had quite enough of deserts and camels and the sickening cruelties of Arabian tribalism. We'll keep our bourgeois little Saviour and they can keep their scimitars and stonings and implacable deity baying for blood and vengeance. But we don't want them here. I don't mean the people. I mean their quite alien cultural beliefs."

"Well of course," the fat mayor says placatingly. "I've got churchmen in my family who would whole-heartedly agree with you. But as you know, we have Moslems in this town and if they go on breeding like rabbits they'll soon be asking the Comune to build them a mosque. And what then? Build it, obviously. If those *Testimoni di Geova* can have their "Kingdom Hall" or whatever the damn thing's called up there by the cinema on the old Bartoli land, why shouldn't the Moslems have their mosque? At least they'll use it, which is more than you can say of our churches and the Catholics in this town. They're still happily fornicating in bed while Mass is being said."

Interesting. I had no idea such arguments raged in private in the world of Tuscan town councils. Giardini fixes me with his turtle-lidded eyes and asks me: "Well, Mr. Samper? Are you a religious man?"

"No."

"I thought not. Eros here wasn't so certain. But then he's more attuned to mysteries than I am. Maybe it's the failed priest in you, eh, Rosi?"

Eros Benedetti? Incredible. Until this moment I'd no idea he even *had* a Christian name—not that Eros is remotely Christian. If I'm touched it must be the alcohol. This house—or I'm the proverbial Dutchman—is surely childless. No signs of toys anywhere; no rusting basketball hoop fixed to a tree outside or over the garage door; no indefinable feeling that in distant rooms upstairs small children are asleep or morose teenagers are playing computer games and doing their homework. Eros. The Greek version of Cupid. An old weasel disguised as the god of love in a gleaming black wig, pouring me yet another glass of a wonderful complex Chianti Classico (Castello di Ama's Bellavista '99 in case you're interested, as you certainly should be).

"Hard words, Razi," chides Benedetti, but with a distinct glitter. "Since you know I never became a priest you can hardly say I failed at it. My failure, if you insist on calling it that, lies elsewhere entirely. As again you know."

I can't read the mayor's expression because his gaze, fixed on the food he is shovelling into a mouth as loose and capacious as the top of a Wellington boot, is hidden behind his heavy eyelids' scrotum-like wrinkles. But something is undoubtedly going on here between these two rogues Razi and Rosi and I have the startling impression that it is Benedetti who holds more power. He turns to me apologetically.

"You must forgive two old schoolfriends bickering, maestro. It's the eternal problem of small towns. We all know too much about each other."

"But we don't know enough about you." Giardini raises chill eyes to me, his chins glistening. "I don't mean that inquisitively, of course, just that your presence here is bringing about certain changes and it behoves us to understand how far indebted we are to our benefactor. Our host quite naturally sees more behind these recent events—these so-called miracles—than maybe I do. The hand of God, possibly. But an earthbound creature like myself tends to be interested in the machinery rather than in the cosmic mechanic. Strictly between ourselves, then, how many of these incidents are your invention or at your instigation?"

"None of them," I say firmly.

"Don't worry, whatever you tell me won't change any deal you have entered into with Eros. A bargain's a bargain. But you understand that if at some future date a piece of evidence emerges that proves you somehow engineered the Diana myth from start to finish for your own ends, this poor town of ours will become the laughing-stock of Italy, Europe, probably the entire world. As its mayor, I am not prepared to countenance that."

Oh good Lord, how pompous and dreary these functionaries become when they try to "talk turkey" or "lay it on the line" or some such cliché. I didn't agree to dine with men in suits merely so they could grill me at their leisure. I catch my host's bland eye.

"How can I put it more clearly? I and some internationally distinguished guests were celebrating my fif–, my *birthday* up at Le Roccie when something happened that we all of us still find hard to describe. I was just serving my guests with wine— a Chianti, I think: yes, a Cellole Riserva 2000—when I became aware of somebody standing behind the guest at the far end of the table. It was a woman in a sensational blue-grey gown. I remember noticing that her blonde hair seemed to sparkle as though dusted with frost or tiny diamonds. I ought to explain that by this stage of the meal we were none of us stone-cold sober so I wasn't particularly alarmed. Actually, I think I forgot where I was for the moment. It was like being at a party where you suddenly notice someone hovering on the outskirts of your group and feel obliged to bring them into the circle. In my role as host I believe I said something like "Can I help you? A glass of wine?" But immediately I'd said it I recognised her. It was unmistakably Princess Diana. There was no question. What's more, my other guests must have realised I wasn't addressing them because one by one they broke off their own conversations and followed my gaze. I can remember the scene with the utmost clarity. There was total silence, and then Diana spoke. She said very urgently and clearly: 'You must all leave this house at once. Get out now, this instant. Don't wait.' We all heard her, and then she was gone. She didn't gradually fade or anything. It was as though we all just glanced away before focusing again and finding with a small shock she just wasn't there. But we knew she had been and we'd all heard her speak. Even more convincingly, there was suddenly a very strong smell of 'Mitsouko' in the room.

Everybody smelt it and no one else was wearing anything like it that night."

The mayor has been listening with enough attention even to suspend chewing, as evinced by a motionless sprig of watercress dangling from a corner of his mouth.

"Remarkable," he says, his freezing eyes fixed on mine. "And in obedience to this spectral command you all immediately left the table, the food, the fireside, the warmth, and went outside on what I remember was a chill and misty winter's night that must have been even colder up at Le Roccie. I see."

"That's exactly what happened," I say. "The strange thing is how unanimous it was. No one hung back saying it was just a mass hallucination. We all felt a sense of emergency because of the Princess's tone. And as a result we have all lived to tell the tale." I allow myself a gulp of wine, like a lecturer on reaching the end of a particularly dense paragraph read to a particularly dense audience.

"And *what* a tale," observes the mayor as he resumes eating. The ignored watercress retreats into his mouth in jerks before vanishing, reminding me of a guinea-pig I once had as a child that used to eat dandelions in similar fashion. Without warning he begins to heave like magma, his face glowing furnace red from wine and high blood pressure. Suddenly we are all three helpless with laughter. It feels both surprising and inevitable. Nor is it ordinary dinner-party jollity. It has the element of hysteria that comes of ditching solemnity and breaking taboos. Anyone who can remember their schooldays will recognise it. Nothing short of Alzheimer's will make me forget an English lesson one morning when we were doing *Macbeth* for A-level under a rather serious-minded, even slightly priggish teacher. Someone in our class had found an old copy of an acting edition of the play with stage directions added in a nineteenth-century hand. Those for the sleepwalking scene ran: "Enter Lady Macbeth with candle right upper entrance" and

"Exit Lady Macbeth with candle left upper entrance." The ensuing collapse of twenty adolescent boys was so complete the class had to be suspended. The memory can still afford me pleasure at low moments. Some thirty-four years later in Italy our laughter is not quite as immoderate but we have still drunk a good deal and it's quite a while before we sag back in our baronial chairs, wiping our eyes on our napkins, the mayor making dangerous gasping snorts. I have particularly relished the sight of Benedetti's toupee holding itself aloof from its wearer's shakings and heavings, noticeably detached from such worldly displays of emotion. I suddenly feel a bizarre pang of fondness for the man.

"A most interesting account, maestro," says Benedetti at last. "Orazio needed to hear it from your own lips. Although I knew the outline of the story myself I have never heard you tell it with such a wealth of convincing detail. We're greatly indebted to you. So indeed is the Comune. There's no question that the late Princess did us a very good turn."

"And she didn't leave it at that, either," I point out. "Don't forget she also threw the Barringtons' little girl over the precipice—Marcie or Darcie or whatever she's called. A wonder the kid wasn't killed and a wonder she regained her eyesight: two miracles for the price of one. Short of returning in person to sort out your parking crisis I can't see what else Diana can be expected to do for this town."

"No, no, we mustn't be greedy," says Mayor Giardini, his wattles shaking again. "The point to remember is that this version of events is now holy writ. The, er, gospel according to Gerry." He wipes his eyes. "Have you by any chance ever run for public office?" he enquires.

"Certainly not."

"I believe you might do it quite successfully. You seem to have grasped the vital element of fantasy. One expects the brutal calculations and the dirty tricks but one never quite bargains for the success of flamboyant untruth. No doubt it's what Hitler meant by the Big Lie. Your present gospel is a surreal masterpiece. My worry is no longer that it will be disbelieved but that it may be actively countered in some way. Never forget the dirty tricks! I agree, Le Roccie looks well on the way to becoming a major site of pilgrimage. I gather there are already some smelly friars hanging about up there and they're often a reliable indication that there's money around. They're the pit canaries of scams. In any case, you may be sure none of this will have gone unnoticed by our neighbours up and down the coast. They will enviously be trying to dream up ways of equalling or upstaging our town's increasing celebrity. They will also have people looking to explode Gerry's gospel. We need to be seen as a Comune that is playing host to a remarkable manifestation but in all innocence. Our story needs to be bombproof. I assume," the mayor adds with a brief glimpse of his old glacial manner, "that the other guests at your dinner party are not likely to suffer from lapses of memory?"

"Oh no."

"A personal account in a London newspaper that was greatly at variance with your own would provide our enemies with all the ammunition they'd need."

"There won't be one," I say confidently. "If I were you I'd be more bothered about what the Church might do."

"The Church?" says the mayor scoffily. "Who cares what the Church thinks? By now the cult at Le Roccie surely has a life of its own."

"You may be right, Razi, but the maestro's point is a good one all the same," says Benedetti as he gets up to pour us yet more of his fabulous wine. It is a pleasant thought that this meal must be costing him. "The Church still has considerable power in certain quarters, as you know very well. Our opponents would be only too happy to exploit an official denunciation if one were given. Our bishop is a notorious sceptic and supporter of the Vatican's modern demystification policy. This is, that such popular but unverified manifestations of religious hysteria—their phrase, not ours—ought not to be encouraged. You will remember the Church authorities have recently inveighed against the craze for cutting up the late Pope John Paul's papal vestments for sale as relics, and he is not yet even a saint. Our bishop preached a sermon last Sunday saying the Church has an urgent need to return to its doctrinal and scriptural roots and can only be weakened by 'charismatic sideshows.'"

"But surely you can have the bishop assassinated?" I ask with a guilelessness that becomes me.

For a moment Benedetti looks genuinely shocked. The mayor merely rolls his eyes regretfully. "If only. Unfortunately, times have changed. Besides, he is my cousin."

"I don't think, Razi, that our friend is being entirely serious. It's that famous English sense of humour of his. It can be disconcerting until one gets used to it."

But Benedetti's prim caution is quite unnecessary as we all spontaneously start giggling again. Suddenly my case for the Church as a plausible threat seems absurd. When he gets his breath back our host says reflectively: "You know, what I like best of all about this is that nobody gets hurt and nobody loses. That's almost unheard-of in politics."

"It's not quite true," I say. "There is one loser: my poor neighbour Marta, who now badly needs another house. She was, of course, a witness to Diana's apparition," I add meaningfully.

"Of course," Benedetti corrects himself. "La signora Marta. I agree, there is an injustice here. I think there's no doubt the Comune is anxious to help her, Razi, wouldn't you say?"

The mayor is noisily chomping pecorino and fresh figs and merely nods.

"I bet it is," I observe pointedly. "Sooner or later you're

going to need a visitor centre up there, a souvenir shop, God knows what else. That old house of hers would be ideal, to say nothing of her land."

"As a matter of fact an outline planning application has already been filed for a hotel in the meadow behind her house should she decide to sell," admits the mayor. At this, Benedetti flashes him one of his cautionary glances and I suddenly wonder which of these two rogues put in the application.

"I'm glad to hear it," I say a little untruthfully. I can't deny I'm piqued to think that since Marta has oodles of her family's ill-gotten gains behind her she hardly needs the tidy profit her squalid dump is undoubtedly going to net her. Typical. To those that have, still more shall be abundantly added. "To jump to an almost unrelated topic, dottore, might I ask how my own house is progressing?"

"Do forgive me, maestro. I completely forgot to tell you earlier that all the services are now installed and working, except for the telephone which will be connected this week. Essentially, your spectacular new house is already habitable so long as you can make do with a *telefonino* until your landline is usable."

"I'm impressed. Also very grateful. I can't wait to get my own roof over my head at last."

"Just as well," says the mayor around an oozing bolus of fig and casein. "Before I left home this evening the police rang me from Puglia to say they've found your present landlord's body. So I imagine the apartment you're living in will have to be vacated. He was a Belgian, I believe."

Benedetti looks shocked yet again. "How dreadful. Whatever happened to him?"

"Who knows? Apparently he was found floating in Taranto harbour. I believe there was severe damage to the body from ships' propellers but he had *documenti* on him including his press card. He interviewed me some months ago about how I won the last election. He seemed a pleasant enough fellow, perhaps a little green. Having nothing to hide I was naturally happy to tell him everything he wanted to know. Although at the end I warned him that not everyone would feel the same way, he evidently didn't take the hint and carried on regardless. It is the problem of the journalistic profession, especially with foreigners, as I'm sure you will agree, Gerry." His eyes swivel towards me with the dispassionate panning of a CCTV camera. "How can one ever be certain of the full implications of even the most innocently asked questions unless one knows a culture from within? In which case one would know not to ask them. Politics is a touchy subject everywhere. I'm afraid our Belgian must have been naïve as well as an indifferent swimmer. Being out of one's depth often proves fatal."

"You're beginning to sound like a badly scripted noir film, Razi," says Benedetti. "Not only is the maestro here superbly experienced in his profession, he is so wonderfully at home in both our language and culture that I can never remember he is not by birth one of us. Besides, I'm sure that poor Mr. Swanepoel's death was a complete accident."

The mayor is licking fig seeds off his fingers. "Even so. One can't be too careful."

I can't get the hang of this evening at all. Something in the dynamics between Benedetti and Giardini remains baffling. More and more I'm convinced that of these two rogues it is the weasel estate agent rather than the mayor who calls the shots, but I couldn't say why. With all this talk about floating corpses I can scarcely be blamed if my mind turns to thoughts of organised crime. I remember hearing someone allege that places like Lourdes and Fátima and Santiago de Compostela are run by mafias attracted by the constant stream of desperate pilgrims with money to spend on anything that might somehow be translated into miraculous cures. Maybe even here in Tuscany the racketeers are beginning to lick their lips in anticipation of a steady source of income and some fiefdoms are being staked out? Could it possibly be that beneath Eros's shining and lux-uriant wig there sits a made man, an *éminence grise* who helped put his fat old schoolfriend Orazio into office? It would explain how it is that a mere local estate agent has been able to do deals with me on behalf of the Comune. And most convincingly of all, how he has been able to arrange for the services of my new house to be connected in record-breaking time.

After another hour or so, and having paid my various well-feigned respects, I drive away from Benedetti's house still puzzled about the precise purpose of the evening. However: suppose I'm wrong and it *is* still possible to scupper the cult up at my former home? Suppose this time the Vatican were to take more effective steps to protect itself from accusations of pandering to popular superstition by launching its own investigation, one that extends to tracking down and grilling all the guests at my birthday party on that fateful night last year? I sounded confident enough when I assured the gross mayor that my other guests would unfailingly support my gospel, but I wonder if some of them might not have their limit. For instance, Adrian has already told me that Max Christ is a Catholic and comes from a devout Bavarian family. He might well prove susceptible to Church leverage. And if a man of Max's international eminence were to recant and admit the apparition story was untrue, a sensational exposé across Europe's news media hinting at corruption might very well be enough to destroy the cult at Le Roccie and with it the Comune's (or the Mob's) plans to get rich from it. And I hate to think what the press might do to my reputation as I take up residence in a house whose acquisition has been not entirely free of rule-bending.

But this is surely mere paranoia. That's what comes of dining with splendidly corrupt and scheming men, I think as I let myself into my deceased landlord's flat. After an evening at

Benedetti's sumptuous place I am struck afresh by its aesthetic squalor. Somehow Mr. Swanepoel's taste in bed linen and decor foretold a sticky end. But the casual tale of his sudden demise has made its point. I vow that just as soon as I'm installed in my new house I shall never mention any of this ever again to anyone.

I spend the next few days frantically buying the basics for my new home: kitchen stoves and washing machines and beds and suchlike. For the first time in my life I have enough money not to agonise over the cost. Just get it *done*, Samper, is what I tell myself; then you can move in. The only thing to which I devote real care is the *batteria da cucina*: the all-important pots and pans and general kitchen equipment. We artists concentrate on the things that really matter. I'm sure Picasso was far more particular when selecting new brushes and easels than he was over choosing a new girlfriend. At last there comes the wonderful moment when I can lock the late Mr. Swanepoel's door behind me, salute the last doddery nun on the stairs, drop the key off at Benedetti's office and drive up to my very own house.

As I have intimated before, the place lacks Le Roccie's panoramic view which now strikes me as a shade too aerial, a little too detached and godlike. The new vista of adjacent wooded hills, the town's far-off roofs and beyond them a coast-less slot of sea suddenly feels appropriate for someone who, willy-nilly, has descended to being embroiled in local politics. Yet I can still sing up here without risking the complaints of a testy neighbour. On the other hand I can also drive a mere five minutes down the road and come to an outlying *alimentari* for basics like flour and sugar and lavatory paper. As far as I can discover my house has no name but the site is known informally to the locals as Sciupapiedi or "feet ruiner": no doubt a reference to the days when ill-shod peasants named landscapes according to the different kinds of anguish they inflicted.

How can one describe that sublime evening when one pours oneself a large g-&-t and for the first time sits outside one's own house, looking out across a froth of olive trees over a new domain? So many dice have been cast one can no longer be bothered to think or worry about them. It's even possible to ignore the fact that this otherwise bijou residence is still wearing a tin hat. The main thing is that Samper is finally *here*, at home once more, breathing juniper fumes in the sunset and hoping never again to move house until it's time to be carried down to the local cemetery with its discreetly hidden rubbish heap of dried flowers and the empty red plastic cylinders of grave candles. Meanwhile, there's much to be done. The one outstanding alteration to the house is the removal of its illegal top floor and the restoration of the original roof. This is to begin at once, and I have arranged for the entire upper storey to be sealed off and for the workmen to have access to it— together with their rubbish chutes and hoists—from outside at the back. It shouldn't take long for them to demolish the unfinished walls, and putting the roof back on ought to be equally straightforward since it turns out that the speculative builder who removed it stored most of the original timbers in his yard in Lucca where they still are. The point is, I shan't need to have workmen traipsing through the house with their bags of cement and rolls of *carta catramata*. A pity in a way, since from earliest childhood I've adored the smell of workmen: that manly, capable scent of dust and fresh sweat and linseed oil. What I don't like are their cigarettes and transistor radios. All would be forgiven if only they smoked Egyptian rather than Virginia tobacco and listened to Haydn string quartets. But alas.

What I'm really looking forward to is fitting my kitchen up as I want it. My natural creativity has been badly frustrated over these interminable homeless months, although I have managed to concoct a modern version of humble pie that I shall try to induce the St. John restaurant, down by Smithfield, to take up. There is nothing wrong with deer's entrails, liver and heart, and the St. John has a wonderful way with umbles of all kinds. However, inventing "thought recipes" is simply not satisfying. I am a hands-on cook par excellence. I need to get my fingers into the ingredients; that's when the saliva and ideas start flowing. You would think this was a most basic human pleasure but I recently learned a shocking thing: that residential flats are now being built in London that *don't have a kitchen*. Can you believe this? Apparently they don't have a kitchen because their overpaid, philistine owners eat all their meals out. One can't even begin to guess what sort of creatures these are. Imagine delegating one of life's great pleasures to total strangers! If you can't be bothered with your own food, what *would* you take trouble over?

Two days later history uncannily repeats itself. Years ago at Le Roccie when Marta first came to call I was up a stepladder in the kitchen. So I am today, busy fixing the hood of the extractor fan above the cooker, when the door opens and that well-known squeal "Gerree!" turns my blood to ice. This time, however, history has added a twist. Marta is no longer a neighbour but a collaborator in the grandest artistic project of my life. With an inward sigh I carefully balance the screwdriver and felt-tip marker on the edge of the hood next to the glass of prosecco that I find aids concentration in these fiddly DIY jobs. Then I descend the ladder while fixing a courteous smile of welcome to my face.

"Marta!" I exclaim. "Welcome to Casa Samper. And Joan too," for that lady is even now coming in behind her, tucking the car keys into one of the pockets of her dungarees. "How inspired of you both to have arrived in time for a late morning celebratory glass." Thank goodness the prosecco, which I've only just opened, is not very special. There's nothing more galling than having to waste a really good wine on people who can barely tell it from Coke. I quickly retrieve my own glass.

"Gerree, your house is so lovely!" Marta is saying. She is looking far less frumpish, I notice. In particular her hair has emerged from its Struwwelpeter phase. It has been cut and styled and, most important of all, *washed* so it has lost that aura of pristine undergrowth that would once have made a field entomologist's pulse quicken in anticipation. What's more, she's even wearing a dress instead of one of her baggy old shifts that gave her that characteristic Bedouin traffic-warden look. In fact, she appears to be dressing like the sort of girl she now regrets not having had the nerve to be twenty years ago. For the first time since I have known her Marta looks, well, practically *feminine*. Even Joan seems not to have brought with her the trademark reek of dogs, for which I am grateful.

"I was forgetting you've never seen this place," I say, handing them glasses of prosecco.

"Never, Gerree. But it is so big! I think you have many rooms here, more even than at Le Roccie with your garage together."

"Yes, there's certainly ample space for little me. And a bit too much land outside, unfortunately. Three hectares of olives. But there we are."

"Smashing position," says Joan. "But I have to say the corrugated iron doesn't look very Tuscan."

"That's all coming off in a day or two and the original roof will go back on. That's how I managed to get this place at an affordable price, among other things." It's clear the girls want to be shown around so we top up our glasses and bring them along as I give them the obligatory guided tour.

"Once the new roof's on it'll be sensational," says Joan approvingly at the end.

I notice she seems to be smoking less and the absence of canine bouquet is quite startling. "Have you been back to the

UK since I met you at Pisa?" I ask. "And if not, how are those dogs of yours managing?"

"I haven't, no. Too much to do here. The dogs are fine. I rang the kennels the other day and far from pining away in my absence the rotten bastards are putting on weight. The hullabaloo at home seems to have died down and they say I could go back without getting lynched. So I may do that and bring the hounds over here."

"Bring them over? You'll be staying here for longer, then? That's good."

"Well," says Joan a little awkwardly, "I've been meaning to tell you but with all the bloody hubbub recently there hasn't been a proper opportunity." She glances as Marta who . . . *simpers*. The only word. "Cutting through the bollocks and the lovey-dovey stuff, we've discovered that we're natural shipmates. We go together like bacon and eggs, don't we, Matti?"

Matti? I suddenly remember that Marta's younger sister Marja called her by this childhood nickname. By now we're sitting on the terrace under a brand new awning out of which the June sunshine is beating a textiley smell of fresh waterproofing or something. Normally these admissions of romantic partnership merely make me raise a pair of cynical inward eyebrows while maintaining a bland expression of indulgent goodwill. Couples, for heaven's sake. Dinky little dyads. One can't take them seriously. Whenever I read that some creature like the brindled titmouse or the Pripet vole "pairs for life" I am possessed with an immediate yearning for its extinction. I've always assumed this is perfectly normal for single people, regardless of gender. But now the idea of Joan and Marta becoming a domestic item does actually give me pleasure, although I expect the prosecco helps. I've grown rather fond of old Joan, and as for Marta I'm anxious that as composer of the moment she should be as settled and contented as possible. I even go and fetch a bottle of almost-the-best champagne to celebrate.

"Crikey, Gerry, we didn't come here to get slewed, you know," says Joan when we have all toasted each other's new houses, new romances and ageing livers.

"Still, now that you're here . . . Though I think I'd better scratch us together some lunch otherwise we'll get completely sozzled. But what news of your own house, Marta?"

"Ah, the *mustelje* Benedetti comes to me the other day and says he has a very good offer if I am thinking to move."

"Which you bloody well are," adds Joan. "There's no way a composer like you can go on working up there. The place is a frigging madhouse. Honestly, Gerry, if you thought it was bad a couple of weeks ago you should see it now. A constant stream of people, cars parked any old where so Matti can't even get out of her own drive, hymn-singing and chanting and Christ knows what else. Can you believe an actual monk in a dressing gown came knocking on our door asking for a meal and a bed for the night? A complete twat. He kept on talking about *carità* and flashing his rosary. I soon sent him packing and he was a lucky monk not to get a swift kick in the beads for good measure. The nerve of the bloke! I'm glad Matti was busy with her music at the time because her Italian's wonderful and she's so kind she would probably have invited him in and wound up giving him our bed while we slept on the floor somewhere. Talk about a heart of gold, old softy here. I'm a much tougher proposition and it certainly helps not being able to speak much of the lingo. I've always found saying "bugger off!" works well in any language."

Before the champagne renders me legless I excuse myself and go in to get us some lunch. Luckily I have some home-made soup on the go—tomatoes, tarragon and nasturtium leaves, a very refined combo—so I pour it into a saucepan and set it down none too gently on the hob. Immediately, the for-gotten screwdriver and uncapped marker fall off the edge of the hood and plop into the soup. Suppressing a chef's giggle I fish them out and bin the marker, which has left some black streaks on the soup's surface. If I allow my eyes to drift out of focus in a post-champagne sort of way it looks like one of those Second World War aerial photographs of the aftermath of a submarine sinking. I almost expect to see tiny people struggling in the slick. Behind me I hear somebody coming in from the terrace so I hastily give the soup a good stir and the black disappears. Every good cook has secrets from his guests that have nothing to do with recipes and techniques and everything to do with damage limitation. Soon we're all eating outside under the sunshade, and with plenty of hot rolls and butter and another bottle of champagne nobody notices a thing.

"So go on—what *was* Benedetti's offer?" I ask Marta bluntly.

"*Duecentomila.* Two hundred thousand euros."

"Ludicrous!"

"That's what I said," agrees Joan. "I don't trust that fellow, do you, Gerry? He looks like a ferret that's been through a car wash. All gleaming and glistening, but still a sodding ferret. It's a no-brainer. As a structure so close to a recent landslip the dear old place isn't worth half that. In fact, it's probably unsaleable. So if your signor Ferretti is offering two hundred thou, he's obviously got a buyer with a specific purpose in mind, which means he'll go a lot higher."

"Benedetti tells me he's already had an offer for the land behind the house. Someone wants to put up a hotel, presumably for pilgrims and people like that ecclesiastical derelict you chivvied away."

"You're a hero, Gerry. This is vital info . . . How did you get this lovely almondy taste in the soup?"

"That's a trade secret." I have already noticed the flavour she means, which although very pleasant has nothing to do with the official ingredients. It can't possibly be prussic acid: they'd never allow cyanide in felt-tip ink, surely? "So what will your new asking price be? Half a million?"

230 · JAMES HAMILTON-PATERSON

"Not on your nellie. A cool million but prepared to go as low as eight-fifty. I'm not having Matti taken for a ride. If they're going to develop that site someone's aiming to make a fortune out of it and they can ruddy well pay for the privilege."

Marta is looking doleful. "Is sad. I love my house but now is impossible to work there and the music is going so well, Gerree, I think. I have just written your song 'Don't cry for me, Kensington' which is very beautiful. The audience will go away singing this. Also that little beggar girl in Pakistan who is singing to Diana 'There's not much Versace / Here in Karachi.' At the end the audience, Gerry, I promise they will be clapped out."

"It sounds wonderful, Marta. I can't wait to hear it."

"You can if I am not longer in Le Roccie."

"What Matti means," says Joan, covering her friend's hand with her own square-nailed paw, "is that we really must get out of that house as soon as we can, Gerry. It's interfering with her composing. Renting a suitable alternative at short notice may be tricky although I shall have a go. I suppose we're obliged to do it through signor Ferretti, dammit, since he seems to have the biggest agency in town."

"He does. So long as Marta's not a Moslem," I add jokingly.

This provokes an outburst from Marta that reminds me very much of our first meeting when she engaged me in a passionate lecture about Voynovia's long history of Christian resistance to godless Slavs. I was quite right about her religious affiliation. Marta's nothing, but she's a Moslem even less.

"Anyway," says Joan, "in the short term she badly needs a workroom where she can put her piano. So we wondered if it would be possible to have a room here, Gerry, just as a temporary measure? You do seem to have a lot of spare space you're not using. And as it's your opera, too, it might be an advantage if both of you could work together under the same roof for a bit. You know, cross-fertilisation of ideas or whatever it is. It's all a bit beyond an old sea-dog like me."

"Well, why not?" I hear myself say even as a pocket of cells hiding out in a corner of my brain where the alcohol has still to penetrate is telling me I'm completely mad. Invite Marta to move in with that Iron Curtain upright of hers? Wasn't that the very instrument of torture that first made my life hell up at Le Roccie? On the other hand this opera *is* a bid for international credibility and we artists often have to work in collaboration. Da Ponte and Mozart worked side by side on many occasions while *The Marriage of Figaro*, *Don Giovanni* and *Così fan tutte* took shape. Surely Samper and Marta can follow in the same grand tradition for a strictly limited period? Especially now her new hygiene regime means my chances of catching head lice off her are much reduced? Also, of course, I'm paying her to write this music so it makes no sense to risk not getting my money's worth. All in all, Marta's temporary status as composer-in-residence at Sciupapiedi is one of those bullets made to be bitten.

"Anyway, Gerree, have you yet the title? I don't understand this '*Rancid Pansies*' and it does not sound to me so good."

"Not yet," I tell her a little shortly. "How about *Dodi and Aeneas*?" To say I have forebodings about the domestic arrangement to which I have just acquiesced would be one of those ludicrous understatements like "Some assembly required" or "Item may not accord with model illustrated." "Upheaval may be expected" pretty well sums up the future I am resignedly foreseeing.

Adrian 7

email from Dr. Adrian Jestico (ajestico@bois.ac.uk)
to Dr. Penny Barbisant (penbar@labs.whoi.ed)

'm sorry to have taken so long to answer yours, Penny.
There's probably a p.c. excuse for falling behind on one's
emails or else a judicious lie that nobody really wants to
investigate—such as claiming to have just had a piles operation
that precludes sitting. I can't offer this although I did make a brief
field trip a fortnight ago to the Severn estuary to see how a couple of my PhDs are getting on with a copepod survey. I'm
pleased to say the little fellows are doing fine—the copepods, I
mean. Anyway, the trip set me back a bit in terms of keeping up
with correspondence, which included an invitation to give a paper
at next year's 10th International Conference on Copepoda. Will
you be going? It's being held next July in Pattaya, Thailand. The
last one in 2005, you may remember, was in Hammamet,
Tunisia. I like it. The more that global alarm & despondency
about the environment escalates, the more conferences & sym-
posia the scientific community holds in tropical & subtropical
resorts. At least it's honest in recognising that with entire ecosys-
tems already out of kilter a few more hundred tonnes of jet
exhaust in the upper atmosphere's just pissing in the ocean.

Luckily, things here at BOIS are suddenly quieter. Everyone's
now waiting for the results of sundry inquiries and feasibility
studies and EIAs due on the Severn bloody Barrage. The cap-
tains & the kings have departed, likewise the Darwin Advisory
Committee, the Millennium Ecosystem Assessment Panel & the
Advisory Committee on Business & the Environment. FoE is

dead opposed to the Barrage & suggests a system of tidal lagoons instead. The Sustainable Development Commission is about to report. Greenpeace astutely observes that "the jury's still out" (out cold with boredom, at a guess). The Labour Party has launched its own feasibility study. And everybody else you can think of, including the North Somerset Wreckers' Association ("will the Barrage threaten our Members' livelihoods by reducing shipwrecks?"), is "looking at all the options." Except me, that is. Since the pressure's now off me to meet-and-brief I'm slowly resuming a normal life.

This normality—to stretch the definition a tad—has included a quick visit to Italy to inspect Gerry's new house. He was getting a bit shirty with me for my non-appearance in his hour of need & I can't blame him. But it was all OK as soon as we met at the airport. On the way back he warned me not to expect total solitude at home. You won't fully appreciate the irony but he has been obliged to give temporary house-room to Marta and her new official partner, this old RN girl Joan. Marta's own house is no longer hers. She was obliged to sell up because Le Roccie— which I'm sorry you never saw, Penny, it was such a fabulously remote & silent place—has now become a madhouse milling with pilgrims & quack healers & dubious characters having ecstatic moments & wearing bogus robes, all hoping for miracles & demanding alms with menaces. Gerry told me Marta held out for an incredible price—€615,000—because she got wind of plans for a hotel up there. She had to have somewhere quiet to work on her music so Gerry offered her a room upstairs on the far side of the other half of the building he's not living in. This one room has now expanded to include a double bedroom & a bathroom. Small wonder Gerry's panicky.

The house is lovely & the site is hardly less secluded than Le Roccie yet it's barely ten minutes from town & surely better for

Gerry as it's more accessible. It's huge for one person, rather less so for three when one of those is Marta. The poor man has acquired a slightly hunted look. Marta keeps odd hours & may well start playing the piano at 3 in the morning although Gerry has largely (but not infallibly) prevailed on her to use headphones with an electronic keyboard that was given her by an Italian film director some years ago. On my first night we were woken in the small hours by a series of distant lugubrious chords. We thought she & Joan were about to break into Voynovian sea shanties. Meanwhile Joan is doing her best to find somewhere suitable to rent or buy so they can move out but she's hampered by not speaking much Italian while Marta—who speaks it fluently—is too busy with the score of Gerry's opera to spend time on the task. So nothing looks like changing much & the girls have already been there over a month. Gerry fumes & mutters darkly when Marta's not within earshot, advising her under his breath to remember Gesualdo—a sixteenth-century madrigal composer, it seems, who had his unfaithful wife & her lover murdered & may even have done the job himself. So this much-heralded masterpiece of theirs may yet be launched by a televised double funeral & a sensational court case.

Their obsession with this opera is something to behold & reminds me of those young couples whose entire life gravitates around their baby. In a weird sort of way Marta & Gerry are more married than Marta & Joan, & looked at retrospectively their union must surely have been fated from the moment they first rather crossly discovered they were neighbours up at Le Roccie, back in the days when I didn't even know him. On my last night they ran through the opera for me, as much as it's composed. Because Marta has worked on different numbers at different times & not in consecutive order it's sort of patchy. But between her piano renderings with Gerry's vocal acrobatics—now falsetto as Diana, now tenor as Prince Charles, now bass as

Mohamed Al Fayed—& the fully orchestral stuff she's done on the synthesizer, I did get an overall idea of something that really is quite impressive. God knows it's deeply odd, but how could it not be when Gerry wrote it? The "Squidgy" & "Tampax" arias are sensationally strange. Yet it was all rather affecting & that was unexpected because I'm not often touched by a new piece of music the first time around, let alone modern music.

What's it about, I'll pretend you're asking? Not too sure. Gerry tells me it's less a full-out opera than a *Singspiel* like *The Magic Flute*, with spoken parts as well as sung. It seems not to be a chronological account of the Diana story but more a series of episodes—some based on fact & others completely fanciful—designed to . . . designed to what, exactly? "Make a memorable evening's entertainment, of course," Gerry said in a surprised tone. Now Diana's sad, now she's frivolous, now she's earnest, now she's no better than she should be, now she's almost a religious icon, now she's practically a page 3 sex symbol. Marta says grimly, "She was not very interesting. She was only interesting because of other people's interest in her, & they weren't interesting people, either. So we must make her interesting." The result is a series of scenes, some funny and some tragic (in a stagey way), leaving you feeling Diana was a fictional heroine who never really existed at all but was just a lot of slightly footling component parts & who comes together in the end as a public myth. Anyway, that was my impression & as I said, this was just a run-through of an incomplete work for my benefit. Joan says there was a good deal of dykey sympathy for Diana (new to me) & wouldn't approve of her being mocked. This may yet cause friction because some of the bits sounded hilarious to me. I remember a duet for 2 wardrobe assistants complaining about Diana's clothing expenditure that was pure comedy. But that's merely on the way to the grand finale with her apotheosis as a people's saint or secular icon or similar. Even that may turn out to be tongue-in-cheek. There's probably something wicked up Gerry's sleeve.

Still, what do I know? I'm just someone who's unnaturally fascinated by very small crustaceans. But it's good to see Gerry at last completely swallowed up in a properly creative project instead of bleating about the horrors of having to write about people like Millie Cleat. It's also nice to have been able to tell my brother-in-law Max that not only is a lot of the opera already done but it does sound as though the finished article will be hot stuff. With a full orchestra, professional singers, some props & scenery & a succession of increasingly eye-catching outfits for the heroine, I can't see why *Rancid Pansies* (or whatever it's to be called) shouldn't be a success. Max was very pleased to hear this & became quite lyrical about Marta's genius as a composer. I tried to boost old Gerry, too, whose stock at Crendlesham is still not yet quite back to its pre-Great Puke days. Max softened & said how glad he was that Gerry had at last found a way to be serious. I'm not sure I dare ever tell Gerry that, given it's the complete opposite of the image he likes to project. Maybe he'd be secretly flattered. Anyway, I'm relieved to see him back in a house of his own & doing something he really wants to do. He & I got on extremely well & my disgracefully long absence was quite forgiven.

Gerry also dares me, when I'm in London, to eat a meal at the UK's first—& so far only—Voynovian restaurant. It's called "Danubya" & Marta's very complimentary about it though Gerry says having a resto for Voynovian cuisine is like building a concert hall for the deaf. It's somewhere up the Edgware Road, apparently, next to the wittily named Lebanese place, *Bonhommous*, where Gerry tells me they have an excellent Allah carte. So next time you're over here & feeling brave maybe we should try a Voynovian lunch in a spirit of scientific enquiry. According to Gerry, the aftermath of a Voynovian meal is very similar to the sensation of being goosed with Tiger Balm, so you're free to protest that eating should be a pleasure rather than an ordeal that leaves you feeling you've just done a month as an inmate in Abu Ghraib.

A lot of what pleasure there is in my life at present comes from nephew Josh, whom I see every other weekend, more or less. If you find small children at all interesting, Penny, do you think it's at least partly because you're a zoologist? I'm definitely touched by him, but I'm also fascinated to watch that little brain joining up the dots, getting better at hand-eye co-ordination, catching & kicking balls, lying, etc. His manual dexterity is amazing while his kicking is rubbish. Just as well he doesn't seem to be at all inter-ested in football. He likes small, intricate stuff he can fiddle with, such as Rubik's Cube-type puzzles. Maybe this is odd for a 6½ year-old. He has parked dinosaurs for the moment & is now pretty heavily into those Transformer things that look like vaguely ordinary model cars & helicopters but which unfold into Holly-woodian creatures with names like Scorponok & Bonecrusher. He witters on about Autobots & Decepticons which look & sound to me like glorified pieces of US military hardware (a brilliant bit of spin when you consider that the US military has hardly won a single real war since sharing victory in WW2). As far as Josh is concerned they're hi-tech dinosaurs. Just as a small boy who's been told to wash his hands before a meal could turn himself into a velociraptor who eats grown-ups for lunch, so he can transform himself from an ordinary-looking car into a space-going gunship that smashes planets with its armoured stinging tail. Inside impo-tent little Josh is omnipotent big Josh with unlimited destructive power. That's boys for you.

On the other hand, I can get him to forget his robots simply by getting out the microscope. I've taken to bringing him interesting specimens from the labs & have just introduced him (it had to happen!) to copepods. I explained that their name means "oar feet" & of course you can see why as soon as you watch them rowing themselves around with five pairs of legs (we were looking at a Calanoid). Showing small kids this sort of stuff does remind you how easy it is to become a professional bore simply by trying to explain too much. That's the worst of supervising PhD students (& I'm sure you felt the same about your tutor, oh dear, oh dear): it naturally turns you into a crashing didact. But Josh doesn't have exams to worry about yet, so rather than volunteer lots of stuff I tend just to answer his questions. If I can. "Adrian, s'pose you've got this giant copepod as big as a car, no, as big as a house, what will it eat?" "Small boys, exclusively." "That's silly. Go on, what will it eat?" Etc. (Actually, a carnivorous copepod the size of a house would almost certainly think a child the size of Josh would make an ideal snack.) My facetious answer probably does give him a moment's pause since his imperious little ego identifies with everything he sees, so maybe these weird & intricate creatures jerking swiftly across the lens remind him of Transformers (which some of them do quite resemble) which in turn makes him wonder what it would be like to be a copepod. I tell him it would be quite hard work because when you're that small water's pretty viscous stuff & it would be like trying to swim in treacle. Under slightly higher magnification some of the little beasties I've got on slides look downright terrifying—real ferocious space monsters. Josh gets slightly scared watching them & then reassures himself by looking at the dot on the slide that they're actually so tiny he could squash millions of them without noticing: i.e. pretty much what he already does to humans & monsters when he's in dinosaur or transformed mode. He did ask if there are lots of these creatures around, so I told him there are probably more copepods in the world than almost any other animal & you can find them virtually everywhere there's water & especially in the ocean. *Wow* . . . I'm thirsty, Adrian. When's lunch? That's when you know it's time to stop.

One needn't worry about telling children too much because they just switch off anyway. I'm afraid a lot of the time I watch Josh as if he were a lab animal instead of my nephew. He's constantly doing things that if he were an adult would land him in a neurological unit pronto. Peculiar gestures, spastic movements of the limbs, exaggerated facial expressions that have no obvious relation to external circumstances, odd gaits, sudden leaps, novel ways of going upstairs, looking at things upside-down from between his legs. All these things we take for granted in small children so we scarcely notice them. Are they involuntary? Are they signs of a young brain & body discovering what they can do? Are they sheer exuberance at being alive? When I ask him why he did that he might not answer, or he might say "dunno," or he might say "'cos it feels funny. You try." Or he might just look at me as if I simply don't know anything. But when does this familiar behaviour die away & stop, & why? When does one finally have to curb all these childhood tics & jinks? When you've done them all & got bored? Or when you acquire self-consciousness? Either way one still has to be a bit guarded. The other day at Southampton, on learning that someone from the Drinking Water Inspectorate had had a car crash on the M3 & would have to call off his meeting, I danced a jig in the middle of my office. It was unfortunate that Nick Vatican chose that moment to look in & I immediately felt embarrassed at having been seen. But why? Josh wouldn't have been. Nobody should have been, not in front of our Pontiff himself, whose own eating habits make Josh look like a master of dinner-table etiquette.

Well, OK, I suppose I've put off answering your entirely pertinent question long enough, & you certainly do have the right to ask it. Yes: ideally, I think I wouldn't mind a domestic relationship with someone, even someone with a kid or two—although if I'm a frustrated father I'm sure I can deal with that by being a devoted uncle to Josh & any other sibs he may acquire later. I don't want to *own* a child. At bleaker moments I can't really see making a long-term go of it with Gerry. We do get on very companionably & I find him as funny & odd & difficult as ever, but I'm not sure "relationships" (as opposed to friendships) ever survive physical separation undamaged for long. Unless something dire happens here—like my actually killing and eating a member of Greenpeace ("Eat up your Greens!" as Gerry would say)—I don't see myself leaving BOIS unless it's for a similar establishment elsewhere for a year or three. Woods Hole? Scripps? Oban? On the other hand I don't see Gerry leaving Italy, especially now he's just settling into his new house. Even if his fortunes change after *Pansies* I don't see why his domicile should. He's long since been a professional foreigner & probably always was from the moment that wave washed his mother & brother out of his life when he was nine. And there you have it, love or no love. Since there's never been the slightest pressure towards physical faithfulness for either of us there's always the possibility that somebody will drift in & usurp one or other of us. I mean, Gerry is quite a bit older. Between you & me, I went to a party the other night & although nothing *happened* it did remind me that the old flame burns higher in your thirties than it does in your fifties. True but sad, like so many true things.

Oh—& the BBC showed Leo Wolstenholme's Millie film last week. It was sort of all right though not a patch on Gerry's book. Just nothing like as much depth & interesting detail. I suppose they make these TV films so people won't have to read books. It was mostly stuff we'd seen a million times before: footage shot from helicopters of her conning *Beldame* through foaming breakers to victory, various interviews she gave in which—I'd

never realised it before—she both looked & sounded remarkably like Margaret Thatcher in her strident prime, although
minus an arm. And, inevitably, the zillionth re-run of Sydney Harbour. For the first time they also showed some of the Canaries
footage of Millie cutting up the EAGIS ramforms, which as I predicted has elicited zero criticism of her in the reviews I've seen.
Sport conquers all. But she's still too much the tragic heroine.
Give it a few years and maybe someone will do a documentary
on the unexpected environmental consequences of sport. I
mean, has anybody suggested fitting catalytic converters to F.1
cars? Or totting up how much water is lavished on golf courses?
Joan Nugent came over as good & fresh, while Gerry's bits of
interview also did him proud, perched on a lump of rock as he
was with a bright yellow digger trundling around in the background. He even looked quite stylishly butch despite a pair of
boots like orthopaedic clogs that didn't seem to belong to the
rest of him. He was loftily naughty at Leo's & Millie's expense, in
addition to quoting Millie's Aussie lover/sponsor Lew Buschfeuer
saying in an unguarded moment after her death that he felt as
though he'd lost his right arm. I'm amazed it wasn't cut. But TV
people are deaf to words, they only see images. I'm surprised
they weren't alerted by the guffaw Gerry gave on quoting it. He
almost fell off his rock.

I shan't ask retaliatory questions about Luke. You can supply
details or not, as you choose.

Cheers from a BOIS that might at last be getting back to
some proper science,
Adrian

8.

The last few months have whizzed by, and in a pleasurable way that reminds me how grim my life was for so much of this past year. From the moment Joan and Marta moved out and I had this house to myself things began to settle back into those half-forgotten routines that do so much to preserve one's sanity. Cooking and singing, to name but two.

The weasel (and putative *capo*) Benedetti found the perfect house for Marta. At least it's perfect from my point of view, being several hillsides away from Sciupapiedi. In the light of recent experience I can now say I don't think it's healthy for famous collaborators to live in each other's pockets. I can't believe Arthur Sullivan periodically moved himself into the Gilberts' spare room for months at a stretch, nor that mercurial Mr. Procter used to burst into the Gambles' marital bedchamber in the small hours with a brilliant new formula for soap powder. It's true that back in June I said proximity was important when a librettist and a composer were writing an opera. But I meant availability rather than actual cheek-by-jowl propinquity, especially if the jowls are Marta's. To be plainer still, after enough years on this planet we all of us tend to draw up lists of Things To Be Avoided At All Costs. Books whose title includes the word "Joy," for example; members of Amnesty International; any product with the word "Team" on it. To these I can add: sharing a house with a Voynovian composer and her nicotine-stained girlfriend.

And yet all this being said, it has to be admitted that Marta has done brilliantly. In early August she sent Max an electronic file of her score and he began raving about it soon afterwards. Within a fortnight he had taken the decision to perform it at the Haysel in the run-up to Christmas *this year*. Obviously this was prompted by his impresario's intuition that he is on to a winner but I think certain other considerations influenced him, such as his own Colchester Symphony Orchestra's availability. There was also the unexpected slot in the otherwise tight schedule of Tizia Sgrizzi-Pulmoni. Yes! TS-P herself, one of the great sopranos of today, is to première the part of Diana in my very own opera! That at least will guarantee it gets attention. Incredible luck, really. Max's first suggestion for the role was Dame Evelinne Cummeragunja, but I assume he was joking even though I realise she's an old friend of his. Never mind that she's really a contralto. The fact is that Dame Evelinne's being squat, black and proudly Aboriginal would make her task of convincingly impersonating the late Princess of Wales unusually taxing. But TS-P, being both tall and quite slender, will be perfection. The Di is cast, one could say.

The part of Prince Charles is written for a tenor, and Max originally tipped another old friend of his, Markus Strephon, for the role. He would have done marvellously, but within a matter of weeks a tragedy occurred that briefly turned into a major news item when he and a companion disappeared while walking in the Scottish Highlands. As you will doubtless recall, Strephon was eventually discovered after four days on the freezing, mist-shrouded slopes of Glen Gould having lost three fingers to frostbite as well as his mind and his friend. None of these has yet been recovered. It's a real tragedy: Markus had a lovely and expressive voice with acting talent to match. He also looked wonderful in a kilt, as anyone will testify who saw him from the front stalls in the Covent Garden revival of *Bruce and the Spider*, let alone from the orchestra pit. Never mind: Max has managed to get Brian Tydfil instead. It's a slight pity that this celebrated Welshman ("The Sweet Singer of Wysiwyg") is really a light baritone and Marta may need to modify some of the Prince's reedier outbursts, but this can only add much-needed dignity to the part.

Anyway, the signing-up of singers of such calibre ought to convey how seriously Max is endorsing this opera even if one hadn't already appreciated how his opening the Haysel for a special winter season—no matter how short—is itself an extraordinary new departure. But obviously he thinks he can guarantee audiences over the festive season, which these days is increasingly turning into the restive season with secular, sated people casting about for something to do that won't involve either children or Ryanair. When Max became so enthusiastic in August it never occurred to me that it mightn't take at least a year before the opera was performed—if ever. I suppose I was thinking like a writer, geared to book publishers' long lead times. But evidently producing an opera can be done in as little time as it sometimes takes to compose, always provided that enough weight is thrown behind it. So really, the five months or so between Marta's finishing the score of *Princess Diana* and its scheduled first performance is ample time to ensure the production goes smoothly. The only thing Max wants changed is my hard-hitting chorus of amputee children in "Sing a song of jubilance / For unexploded ordnance." He feels that apart from questions of taste (*that* old thing again!) it will be difficult to find enough mutilated kids who can reliably carry a tune.

An entire autumn is plenty of time for them to put together a collection of suitable dresses for TS-P to wear, whether by scouring Oxfam shops or by running up copies. The iconic "Elvis dress," as worn by my late bathroom's statuette, is one of those that will obviously have to be copied. Luckily, la Tizia is remarkably slender for an operatic soprano so the dress need not be of dimensions more suitable for its namesake. Dame

Evelinne, of course, is built like an oil barrel and I simply can't imagine how Max could ever have considered her, no matter how fleetingly, for the part. The time will also be needed to assemble a selection of boys' and youths' mannequins which will play Diana's two sons at various ages. Probably they can be borrowed from Selfridges or hired from whoever makes such things. The most realistic child mannequins I ever saw were in a Tokyo display window: just for a moment I thought they were little performance artists. But I think a William and Harry who look Japanese might be contentious. It would certainly make people wonder who their father was. Harry's ginger hair is bad enough as it is. The two mannequins will stand in the background fetchingly dressed in school uniforms, rugger shorts, etc. as they get progressively older. Their role is to be silent, unaccusing spectators of their mother's via crucis and, occasionally, of her via cruris also.

It's awful how obsessed I've become by production details that strictly speaking are none of my business. I wake in the night, suddenly worrying about where they'll find all the cameras to hang around the necks of the paparazzi for their big vindictive chorus in the final act. It's going to be highly effective because Marta has set it as *Sprechgesang*, as used by Schönberg and Berg, so the paparazzi neither quite sing nor speak but declaim with rhythmic menace:

It's as much as our job's worth
Not to get the pix.
We do it for the money and
We do it for the kicks.
Once you're a public figure
You're just fair game to us
'Cos people have a right to know
What makes you scandalous.

It's unfortunate that only the most musically literate will notice that Marta's orchestral bass line quotes the fugal motif *Laß ihn kreuzigen*—"Let him be crucified"—from the St. Matthew Passion. But I'm sure no one will miss the haunting sense of threat and impending tragedy. Anyway, how they'll get hold of the paparazzis' cameras is neither here nor there, it's just an example of the sort of detail that occupies my sleeping as well as waking thoughts. And here I must admit that Max, Marta and Adrian have all given me stern orders *not* to appear in Crendlesham—and preferably not even in the UK—before December 12th at the earliest. They evidently think I might interfere and pick holes and generally faff around in a state of high anxiety and drive everyone nuts, and they're perfectly correct.

In the meantime I have made sure of giving Derek plenty of warning. If he is not there for my triumph on the first night I can't guarantee to keep silent indefinitely about certain matters. The concept of "for old times' sake" will not necessarily be proof against his treachery. He knows exactly what I mean even if it conveys nothing to anybody else. So I expect him to be present and correct at the Haysel Hall on December 20th. "Correct" here means bringing the right person if he brings anyone at all. His current Mr. Wonderful, the Russian pianist Pavel Taneyev, fits that bill perfectly. Some awful pick-up he's met at work does not. My grandmother used to describe an aunt of hers using the conspiratorial code NOOTTDD. This stood for "Not out of the top drawer, dear" and referred to unsuitable suitors and the like. Although it's in Jermyn Street, Derek's barber's salon Blowjob attracts a certain residue of customers who most decidedly are not out of society's top drawer. I'm sure you will follow me if I say the phrase "bottom drawer" describes rather more than just their social standing, and I doubt if I'm telling unheard tales out of school if I observe that Derek has a regrettable taste for such low life. As

I say, if he turns up to my première with one of those creatures on his arm he will live to regret it, but turn up he must. I don't mind admitting his clicking with Taneyev has been a sore point with me. I mean, what on earth can a dazzling pianist of international stature possibly see in Derek, bubbly company though he sometimes can be? Well, if Derek thinks he alone has collected a free pass into the upper echelons of musical society he's got another think coming on December 20th.

Somehow the time goes by. Since I'm now living out of town I no longer get the paparazzi treatment myself in the way I did back in the hellish days of late spring and early summer. Not that the cult up at Le Roccie has diminished. Quite the contrary, as I discover in November when my curiosity grows too great and Joan and I drive up to take a look. Marta has already left for the UK to sort out a problem with the orchestral parts before rehearsals begin. Needing a disguise, I borrow a beret from Joan that smells of terriers and add a pair of dark glasses and a small brown moustache backed by sticky tape. This was brought me as a joke by Adrian when he came out in the summer. I think it originally came from a dressing-up set owned by Josh. It is unquestionably effective and the anonymity it confers greatly outweighs its hideousness. The complete kit makes me look like someone in a photograph taken in a Paris night club in the late 1950s: probably the man who's supplying William Burroughs, Gregory Corso and Alan Ginsberg (at the same table) with their hashish. At any rate I don't remotely resemble the suave and rather-too-well-known figure of Gerald Samper, the atheist who has unwittingly founded a local religion.

In the intervening months Le Roccie has been transformed. A steel barrier has been erected right across the edge of the precipice and the ad hoc shrine has, exactly as I predicted, turned into a fully grown grotto. This is now a considerable structure assembled out of large chunks of rock, in appearance somewhere between a stylised cave and the Hollywood Bowl. Inside it is about the size of a spacious living room. There is a back-lit altar supporting a careful hierarchy of images. On a small wooden plinth is a conventional brass cross. Behind and above this is one of those all-purpose faux-Renaissance pictures of the Virgin Mary with stars around her head. And in front of the cross, lower but even more eye-catching, stands a foot-high statue of Princess Diana. She is wearing her Elvis dress and the image seems to have been inspired by that infamous Franklin Mint statuette, but with her arms extended and wearing a manic come-hither smile. This arm gesture is not easy to read. It's less a papal-style blessing and more like something glimpsed by strobe light in a disco. However, the altar cloth is well strewn with roses—some wilted, some fresh, others costly fakes—so whatever the ensemble says to people they apparently treat it with reverence. There are some battered-looking supplicants hanging around as though waiting for something to happen: a materialisation, perhaps, or just a voice from a cloud.

In a prominent position on the back wall, lit by a small spot, is a rectangular gold frame containing some lines handwritten in illuminated black lettering as though on parchment and surrounded by swirls of coloured flowers and acanthus leaves. They are in English, with an Italian translation beneath. If they are not the work of Baggy and Dumpy I should be depressed to think anyone else capable of them:

> She gave us our sight back that we might all see
> The stairway to Heaven as clearly as She.

"Bleedin' arseholes," murmurs Joan incredulously in her forthright naval manner as we go back outside. I feel incapable of adding anything to this, not least because the sight of my old pear tree brings a lump to my throat as now being almost the only surviving landmark of my old property. Its autumn-stripped branches are even more humanly laden than before with twirling notes tied on with ribbon, fragments of cloth, cabbalistic signs, little dangling objects and mildewing stuffed toys. Gone is the stout wooden fence beyond it that I put up with my own hands a few years ago to demarcate my property from Marta's. Thirty metres away her house, newly exposed, has acquired the faintly heroic, hectic look of a patient putting a brave face on things after a punishing course of chemo. The doors and windows have been painted dark green, the roof scraped clear of moss and some bright copper guttering fixed around it, but it still looks unmistakably like Marta's hovel. Behind it, visible through the leafless twigs and bushes, some new concrete columns sprouting rusty tufts of steel reinforcing stand in what was recently her paddock.

But Joan is pulling firmly on my arm to turn me away. A gaunt, bearded fellow in a stained dressing gown has just appeared in the open doorway.

"That's him!" she says in a fierce undertone. "I don't want him to recognise me. That's the bugger I chivvied away. You know, the one I told you wanted to stay the night?"

"I don't blame you," I said. "He's not exactly the woodcutter's son, is he?"

"What?"

I'm forgetting that Joan is not privy to the fantasy I used to harbour about her new partner's sex life. "I wouldn't trust him an inch. Shifty-looking. Insanitary."

"He acts as though he's in charge of the site. Bloody hell. Let's get out of here. This place makes me feel like throwing up. When you think what it must have been like."

"I do," I say. "All the time."

Once I have dropped Joan off, reached home and soaked off my moustache I make a vow never to return to Le Roccie. There's no point. My home for years has been irrevocably erased, and that's that. Samper has moved on since those days of writing up taped interviews with dull people and turning them into books. These days he's writing stuff that puts him in the ambit of world-renowned artists and singers, the milieu he has always known was his birthright. There's no going back from that. I set about preparing an intriguing little dinner of buntings in savoury custard while singing Marta's setting of "It's truly a pathetic world." This has hooks, as they say in the world of commercial music. In fact, it's so catchy it wouldn't surprise me if it became a single once the opera's had its first performance. Diana sings in a fervent outburst:

> It's truly a pathetic world
> That needs a Sloane to say
> That landmines lie in wait for years
> Before they reap their crop of tears
> And children as they play.

Really, it *is* all a bit Amnesty International. But artistic reasoning dictated that at this point in the opera we needed some passion that had nothing to do with either marital breakdown or shopping, the two major themes thus far.

> Oh have you seen my little leg,
> My little eye and hand?
> A British shareholder's rewards
> Are ploughshares beaten into swords
> And blood upon the sand.

Awfully easy to write, this sort of stuff, and of course it will have absolutely zero impact on an audience whose own government has for years been raining fire and brimstone on the heads of "evildoers" and child shepherds for dastardly threatening the peace of a realm three thousand miles away. But what else can one sing to citizens who think they permanently represent civilisation's moral high ground? As I say, it's catchy stuff and will blend painlessly into the season of peace'n'goodwill. There remains, of course, the single nearly insoluble problem I've had as the librettist of *Princess Diana*. Namely, why should becoming a princess earn you tear-stained adulation merely for saying what any morally sane person knows: that it is wrong to kill innocent civilians with bomblets and that AIDS sufferers and lepers are merely ill people needing kindness and treatment? Is it because we no longer expect the slightest sign of humanity from our royals and celebs that we grovel and fawn on them for showing the most elementary evidence of decency? I describe this as a nearly insoluble problem, but I trust that between us Marta and I have successfully papered it over by means of jokes, spectacle, and some very diverting music.

More time speeds by and now at last it's December and I'm back in Crendlesham picking up the threads of a very different life. It gives me a lurch of excitement to see the playbills posted outside Haysel Hall and all around the village, knowing the announcement will long since have been in the national press. The name of Gerald Samper is right up there with those of Max Christ, Tizia Sgrizzi-Pulmoni, Brian Tydfil and, of course, Marta Priskil. This is the first time I have seen Marta's family name written in what must be its new international form, a spelling Joan tells me she has been obliged to adopt because the Voynovian original, Pŗškjł, was never going to trip off many tongues. The thrill of it all means something unmistakable to me. Samper has definitely arrived!

To their eternal credit and my considerable relief Max and Jennifer are as warmly welcoming as they were this time last year in the aftermath of the earthquake and the tragic loss of my home. The minor episode of the Great Puke really does seem to have been forgiven. As well it might, to be fair. After all, nearly a year has gone by and we've all had lives to be getting on with. This includes Josh, who has since aged by nearly a sixth of his entire life. He also seems pleased to see me, although probably as a figure he can assault with stuffed toys and impunity very early in the morning. However, when I go out for a short walk of reorientation and to take advantage of a bald and sunny December day, he insists on coming along. He is heavily armed with a futuristic pistol made of Lego he has invented expressly for our defence since, he assures me, there are evil minions everywhere. My religious step-mother Laura would undoubtedly agree. We amble past Crendlesham Church and I'm pleased to see the Rev. Daphne Pitt-Bull is still earning her stipend by putting up notices for her parishioners. Oddly, she's advertising for Pontius Pilates even as she's auditioning for Three Wise Men and a Virgin. It will make for a very distinctive sort of Nativity play. And a very new-looking poster pinned to her cork board announces "Birching and Parenting Classes."

"Why are you laughing, Gerry?" asks Josh.

"Just something on this notice that's spelt wrong," I say. "Although I expect it's really what she'd *like* to say."

"Gerry," he says in that tone that shows he has been listening only to his own thoughts.

"Yes, Josh?"

"Gerry, if I tell you a secret do you think it'll make you cross?"

"I very much doubt it. Why don't you try me and see?"

"But you've got to promise you'll never ever tell anyone. Specially not Daddy or Mummy or Adrian. Really *honestly*."

"OK Josh, I promise." What can a child rising seven years old possibly have to confess that would make it worth breaking a promise?

"Well, you know when . . . you remember when all those people came to dinner that night when the gorilla man came, and they all went off to hospital and Mummy said it was because of something they ate that you'd made?"

"Ye-es?"

"She said it was because of the mice."

"Did she? Well, that's certainly what some people said at the time." Bastards.

"Well, do you think it could have been my mouse?"

"*Your* mouse? But you didn't have a mouse, Josh." However, it turns out that he did. It turns out he had spotted me keeping the cadavers of the mice I'd trapped. Inquisitive little spy, he'd seen me putting them into the box in what temporarily became their mouseoleum, the fridge in the pantry that Jennifer seldom used. Thinking he'd be helpful he had secretly added the corpse of one he'd found in the potting shed. I come to a halt in the middle of the Suffolk lane. The potting shed was, of course, the place where that genius gardener had put down his squill.

"You're not cross, are you, Gerry?" he looks up at me anxiously. "It wasn't me that did it really. There was this giant minion *made* me do it. I morphed but my Zord didn't work."

Whatever this gibberish means it only makes me laugh helplessly. I put an arm around his shoulders. "I'm not a bit cross, Josh. In fact I'm really glad you've told me. It solves a tiny puzzle I've had all this time. I was pretty certain I'd only caught ten mice, but I definitely prepared and cooked eleven so of course I thought I'd just made a mistake and counted them wrong. But now you've told me about your mouse it all makes sense. Anyway, I'm sure it wasn't yours that made them ill, although we'll never know now. Let's just keep this our secret, shall we?" Who needs to enter his seventh year guilty of manslaughter?

"Not tell anyone at all, ever?"

"Exactly. We're the only two people in the whole world who know."

"Cool." He gives a little skip. "*Pew! Pew!*" He picks off a brace of incautious minions sitting in a crab apple tree. "I bet I've seen more copepods than you have."

"Lots more, if Adrian has been showing you."

And so the most momentous confession of his young life falls away from Josh, along with discarded dinosaurs that have lost a leg and expensive toys that never worked. I, however, return to the house thoughtful and vindicated. True to my oath, I shan't tell anyone because it will give me much deeper satisfaction to *know*—as I knew all along—that Samper is innocent and wronged. It won't be a grievance to nurse so much as another small superiority to cherish.

It is now December 14th and the première is on the 20th. Only six more days! Max invites me to sit in on the orchestral rehearsals which, on the 18th, will finally involve both chorus and soloists. On my last stay at Crendlesham I hadn't paid much attention to the Haysel Hall. It was just a vast expanse of roof somewhere on the edge of visibility among rook-filled winter mists. I have to doff my metaphorical hat to Max and his benefactor Sir Barney Iveson, inventor of the Shangri-Loo, who has so resoundingly demonstrated the affinity of muck for brass—not to mention strings and woodwind. Looking around inside at the acres of blond new oak and beech, at the raked auditorium and the futuristic shapes of the acoustic baffles on either side of the generous stage, it is an odd thought that all this has been made possible because enough people have enjoyed having their fundaments pampered by the "gossamer fingers" feature of Sir Barney's "Arabian Nights" model. Those naughty old Buddhists were absolutely right, and feeling you're whole *is* deeply refreshing. And to prove it, here we have a very beautiful private concert hall in the middle of a Suffolk field. I reflect that Mozart would have been hysterically amused at the thought of defecation enabling art.

Wearing rumpled corduroy trousers and shirtsleeves, for the hall's heating system is turned up high, Max takes the orchestra through the overture. Marta sits nearby. My well-known sense of delicacy stops me from joining her. Watching unobtrusively from the back of the hall I find myself—against all habit—moved by the sight of that familiar figure slumped in the stalls. The music, which I've only ever heard on her Petrof upright or synthesizer, is dramatic and impressive with full orchestra and I can't help a certain incredulity at the thought that these complicated, highly individual sounds all came out of that lone tousled head. I realise it's a hackneyed reflection, but you have to have experienced it. I also take a slightly less humble pleasure in thinking it was my words that started all this, that triggered these sounds in Marta's musical imagination. That counts for something, let me tell you, when you hear the solo trumpet softly announce the theme that will be associated with Diana throughout the opera. It's not in any way similar to Prokoviev's marvellous trumpet tune in *Lieutenant Kizhe*, being more of a leitmotiv, but it's instantly recognisable even when it appears in different instrumental guises. Depending on its orchestration and tempo it can sound lonely, amorous, entreating or triumphant, and Marta's use of this simple device is really inspired. Small wonder that Max is so enthusiastic about her.

Meanwhile, the stage curtains are closed and from time to time there are muffled sounds of banging and scraping and the curtains bulge and sway as unseen stage hands shift things around. As a concert hall and recital room the Haysel naturally doesn't have elaborate stage machinery, and any production is going to have to be kept simple with a few straightforward backdrops and a handful of props. The producer tells me that Max was toying with putting on Handel's four hundred and fifty-fourth opera next season to compete with Glyndebourne. The whole thing was to be done in lounge suits with the stage completely bare but for an immense flat TV screen on which static pictures of appropriate scenery were to suggest ambience. But the idea was swiftly dropped on closer examination of *Balbo in esilio*. Its plot concerns a depressed Roman general posted to Britain and homesick for Viterbo who orders a fort built on an Iron Age site, his "capital of misery," which one day will become Weston-super-Mare. Not a lot happens; and somehow the lounge suits could only have made things worse. Nonetheless, the Haysel's stage is well suited to minimalist productions and I am therefore all the more pleased that the production of *Princess Diana* is to be as elaborate as it possibly can be within the constraints of simple resources. The costumes have already arrived and are splendid, with Diana's dresses mostly excellent pastiches of her designer originals. So I'm quite sure that the production's flair and energy will more than make up for an overall simplicity. Plenty of time for the grand machineries of Covent Garden, where divas really can be borne heavenward on remarkably thin wires and chorusing sailors can stagger from side to side of a heaving deck onstage.

I begin to get nervous about my own lines. As I've already mentioned, the role of the Duke of Edinburgh is largely silent, consisting of a few more or less tetchy pronouncements and a good deal of shotgun-polishing. Whilst writing the libretto I thought it might be fun to design the part for myself, and Marta, Max and Adrian have all unexpectedly insisted I play it for at least the opening night. Still, it's one thing blithely to write oneself into a production and quite another to share the same stage with international stars like TS-P and Brian Tydfil. All of a sudden I'm falling prey to stage fright. I know it seems incredible: Gerald Samper, of all people, who for fifty years has played the lead in the story of his own life with such panache. How could he possibly be nervous of standing in the wings wearing lovat plus-fours and occasionally saying single lines like "I wouldn't buy a used camel from a fellow like that," or "Backs to the wall, chaps, it's that valet again." Not an unduly taxing role, in short, yet suddenly I'm worried I shall dry or fail to ad-lib convincingly.

On the 17th the great Tizia Sgrizzi-Pulmoni arrives in a Rolls Royce with a moustached chauffeur straight from central casting. As an old friend of Max's she has accepted his invitation to stay at Crendlesham rather than in a London hotel. Many white leather suitcases with gold fittings are carried up to the immense guest bedroom with its four-poster bed. Josh has been sternly bidden to be on his best behaviour but the famous diva proves quite at ease with children. When Josh and Luna the cat burst into the kitchen through the back door, both well spattered with mud, she greets him in excellent English with a smile and presents him with a very small Leaning Tower of Pisa made out of chocolate, explaining that all the First Class passengers on her flight this morning were given one. Josh is instantly won over. So am I, for it pretty soon emerges that Tizia (as she insists we call her) is anything but grande dame and has a lively sense of humour, which she is probably going to need. But I can feel myself expand. At last—the sort of company I have been craving all my life!

With the star's arrival things really begin to shape up and for the first time I'm required to take my place onstage. We run through the end of Act 1, finishing with the scene in Buckingham Palace in which Charles and Diana's marital discord is finally established. In the background the Queen is pretending to read the *Tatler* and the Duke is merely sitting with his head in his hands while Diana and Charles are singing their closing duet:

CHARLES: Look, Di, why can't we
Just have our own dates?
DIANA: Look, Chas, why can't we
Just agree to be mates?

When they have finished the final word comes from from the Duke, who bitterly observes "How are the matey fallen!" *Curtain*. Immediately, Tizia calls a halt.

"Sorry, Max, there is something here I am not clear about. Gerry, *caro*, your libretto is quite wonderful, but it leaves so much to interpretation. Your Diana, we can read her in two ways, *non è vero*? But is she *simpatica* or do you laugh at her secretly?"

"I agree," chimes in Brian Tydfil. "How are we supposed to be playing this opera—for laughs? Really, there's nothing inherently *funny* about a married couple falling out."

Sententious Welsh git (but a wonderful voice). Maybe he's a bit thick, this person from Wysiwyg, but on the other hand maybe he's a Squidgy loyalist and this really is something of a crux. Either way it's vital to get it out into the open and cleared up during rehearsal. In fact I've already had a session with Ken, the producer, about exactly this problem of how to pitch my complex work.

"Can you think of anything about the royals that *isn't* funny?" I ask. But catching sight of Tydfil's expression I think, Oh dear, she was after all the Princess of the Welsh and maybe we're also touching a nationalist nerve here. Better back off. "This guy you're singing, Brian—and very beautifully, if I may say so—don't forget he talks to plants and probably tucks his shirt into his underpants. He's also on record as likening himself to a tampon. 'My luck to be chucked down the lavatory,' he said, 'and go on and on, forever swirling round on top, never going down.' Now, you can't tell me that's not genius. By Windsor family standards that's a bona fide surreal imagination. And he said lavatory rather than toilet into the bargain. I adore him. His *tragedy* is he can only express himself intimately over an insecure mobile phone."

"Ye-es," agrees Tydfil thoughtfully. "I see what you mean. A tragic figure really."

"But with sublime comic overtones. Don't forget those."

"And Diana, we should play her as tragic, too?" asks Tizia.

"Certainly. Tragic, betrayed, worthy to be surrounded at the end by a quite unmerited aura of heroism as well as by tales of beatification and a probable ascent into heaven. In short, the whole operatic hog. Because while you're doing that, both the script and Marta's wonderful score are working to under-cut it. This was a lady who spent £3,000 a week on clothes and went around the world cuddling children who couldn't even afford underwear. It's a hoot. Remember that Act 2 scene of yours in the Karachi slum when she's talking to the mother? 'I'd love to take your pretty chicks / For a shopping spree in Harvey Nicks.'"

"But she is also spiritual."

"Exactly. Both she and Charles are. It's hilarious."

Silence briefly falls as Tizia and Tydfil digest this and I'm thankful old Joan has gone into Woodbridge for the morning because I have a feeling she might raise fierce, nicotine-stained objections to my reading of her blonde heart-throb, who any-way wasn't blonde by nature and had to spend £4,000 a year having her hair bleached. Then the divine Tizia says:

"I shall sing her as *simpaticissima*, then, but with tragedy inside. That is my Diana."

"You're the diva, Tizia. Whatever you do will be wonderful."

"So when in Act 2 she"—Tizia rapidly turns the pages of her score—"yes, here, she sings 'I feel tarty / And so party, / All disco and risko and free' and Marta has that brilliant *citazione* from *West Side Story*, Diana is going out for the evening to have fun and never mind what consequences? Even if one day they will be tragic?"

"Exactly."

"Very *simpatica*. I shall sing her as I feel her, then. Thank you, Gerry."

"Brian?"

"I think I understand what you're getting at. I'm not sure I approve, but I've been hired to sing Charles and I'm taking him at face value."

"That will be perfect. The soloists should sing their parts straight, as if they were doing Puccini, while it is the orchestra, the chorus and the words that now and then undermine them with satire and mockery. I'm so sorry, Max," I say, turning to the conductor who, like his orchestra, has been obliged to down tools. "I hope I'm not encroaching on your interpretation. Ignore everything I've said if I am." But at your peril, Buster.

"Not at all, Gerry. A very useful clarification. We have no disagreement. Marta's score speaks for itself." He slaps his baton on the music stand and turns to his players. "Fine, everybody. Could we go to Act 2, please, cue 46? We've got to be right on top of Brian when he's pointing out the different flowers or else it will sound ragged."

Ah yes: one of my favourite scenes. Charles and Diana are in their private garden at Kensington Palace, which is represented very simply on the stage by some shrubs in tubs and a heraldic pair of iron-barred gates (in front of which she will later sing "Don't Cry for Me, Kensington"). As the orchestra plays softly Charles wanders about, alternately speaking to the plants and explaining their history to Diana. "This mulberry was planted by George the Third." "Princess Romanovna gave us the original cutting of this Crimean rose in 1803." "These beauties were planted by my great-uncle Louis. He adored pansies." Meanwhile, Diana notices some children pressing their noses to the gates and exclaims: "Oh Charles, can't we let them in?" But Charles takes a stern view of intruders into his garden, like the late Sir Douglas Monteith into whose Suffolk demesne I blundered and whose bad-tempered shade probably inspired me to write this scene. "No!" he exclaims. "They don't understand such precious histories, / They'll just trample over our private mysteries. / They've the whole damned world as their playground, / Surely we're allowed one little compound?" And no, none of the children at the gates bears the wounds of crucifixion, for this is no nod to Oscar Wilde's lachrymose story of the Selfish Giant but an acknowledgement of certain people's obdurate need for privacy and beauty—a need that is always begrudged them, especially if they are princes. As Max hints, it is a difficult scene and not merely because the orchestra needs to co-ordinate its interjections with Brian's meanderings about the stage and his exclamations over each flower. It's written against the grain of expectation. Charles's music is gentle and soulful whereas Diana's is upbeat and a little bossy. But it goes well, and by the time we break for lunch I think we're all pleased by the way the opera's coming together.

Come Saturday and the evening of the first performance I'm all of a doo-dah. Adrian arrived late yesterday and sat through rehearsals this morning. From the tone of his enthusiasm I can tell he had misgivings. His sudden ardour has all the hallmarks of relief, frankly, which shows how little confidence he had in me, not to mention in his illustrious brother-in-law's musical judgement. But then of course he *is* a scientist and we must make allowances. Anyhow, he seems tickled pink after hearing only short and fragmentary excerpts and bets it will "divide the audience in an interesting way," whatever that means. But he has to acknowledge I am at last in my element. This is what Samper was born for. Last night I sat in the kitchen at Crendlesham Hall listening to one of the world's greatest sopranos swap reminiscences with one of its greatest conductors. Tizia was still wearing the red T-shirt she'd worn onstage in rehearsal with the slogan "It's Over. Fat Lady Sings." To think that less than eighteen months ago I was having to trail around after Millie Cleat and pretend to listen respectfully to her vainglorious blusterings! And before that I sat, glazed, while that odious little racing driver Per Snoilsson harangued me about the aerodynamics of Formula One racing cars. He later complained to my editor that I had nodded off during the interview, which was not strictly true because he had long since turned the interview into a lecture on something called—and I can remember it to this day—Computational Fluid Dynamics. Anyway, I was dog-tired as well as bored out of my tiny skull. Well, as I say, those days and that sort of company are over for good and have been decisively replaced by a scene more in sympathy with my true talents, where serious people discuss serious things like *portamento* and whether Tito Gobbi was incontinent onstage singing Scarpia to Callas's Tosca at Covent Garden in 1964.

The only person I feel sorry for—and even a little guilty towards—is Frankie. I could not have wished for a better agent, and this new phase of mine hardly seems a decent reward for his assiduousness over the years. After the rich pickings of *Millie!* in particular, a mere opera libretto will scarcely keep him in cigarettes for a week. Still, he's done very nicely out of my Champions Press books and if he dies a pauper as well as emphysemic it won't be my fault.

And now it is The Night and the car park is full and Haysel Hall is itself filling up nicely. You can tell they're the right sort of people because of their collective smell drifting up into the ancient rafters. This is a complex fragrance with top notes of Guerlain and mothballs, some spicy middle notes of gin-based juniper, and bass notes of foie gras discreetly emitted and filtered through upholstery. I prowl around restlessly backstage in my plus-fours and Duke of Edinburgh wig, wishing everyone good luck and constantly testing myself on my lines. It all takes me back to school theatricals. I don't think I've worn this much slap since I was fifteen. I risk a quick peep at the auditorium and to my relief I see Derek is there. What's more, he seems not to have anybody with him, unless his guest is either the oxidised-looking parson on his left or the mountainous lady in peach taffeta on his other side. As I have hinted earlier, one never knows with Derek. I now realise Pavel Taneyev was never going to be here in any case. Max tells me he's playing Rachmaninov in Boston tonight.

The orchestra is now assembling out there beyond the curtain. Their random tootlings and tunings are laid over the soft hum of the audience's conversations and provide that pulse-quickening atmosphere of pleasurable anticipation. In the occasional barking laugh I think I detect signs of pre-Christmas jollity. No doubt some of the audience came on directly from an office party. Suddenly there is a burst of applause as the leader of the orchestra takes his seat, followed by even louder clapping as Max mounts the podium. An expectant hush falls. Then as Marta's overture strikes up Ken appears in the Green Room and says, "Places, everyone, please." I walk out to my chair at left front. (This of course means the right-hand side of the stage as seen by the audience. We actors have our own point of view.) The music on the other side of the heavy curtain sounds very loud and close. Also thumpy. Right below me I've got the three timps and two squeezed-together bassoons, and beyond them the double basses, so I'm getting mostly bottom notes from my perch. Behind me on the set I see Diana, Charles, the Queen and a drugged corgi take their places in the drawing room at Balmoral. The dog is doped because for some reason it became hysterical when it caught sight of the mannequins of the two princes and obviously something drastic had to be done. The sight of them set it off barking furiously from the moment it was delivered backstage and I remember Adrian said some brave soul was going to push half a Valium tablet up the animal since this route provided the quickest absorption. This must have been done, because I've seen Josh's doggy pyjama bag look livelier than this animal. It looks to me as though the Queen may have something genuine to fuss over while she's on her knees on the hearthrug. She might even have to give it mouth-to-muzzle before this scene's finished, something that I'm sure wouldn't faze the real Mrs. Windsor for a moment. And then *woops*, right on cue as the orchestra plays the last five bars of the overture, the curtain is slowly rising and leaving me stranded on the edge of a dark abyss, dazzled by footlights.

But I don't have time to be terrified. There comes a rat-like scutter from the violins over on the right and the sad leitmotiv on a muted solo trumpet. Unaccompanied, Tizia sings her opening words as a great dramatic sigh: "This place is gloomy as a tomb." Ostentatiously but I hope silently, I turn the pages of *The Field* with what I hope is an expression of moody resignation on my face. Glued to one of the pages is a sheet of white paper on which some thespian humorist has written in large felt-tip letters YOUR WIG IS BEGINNING TO ITCH, and no sooner have I read this than it does. But no! I mustn't lose track of what Tizia's singing because here she is with the heavy men in heavy tweeds—not an easy word for an Italian to sing, incidentally. *Go*, Samper. "Oh Christ!" I hear myself declaim disgustedly at the darkness beyond the footlights, "Here we go again!" And out of the dark comes a gratifying titter of amusement. Hey, there are live people out there! By the time the scene ends with my slamming the magazine down on the chair, declaring "I'm off to the gun-room for a Scotch" and slipping behind the curtain, I feel sure everything's going to be fine. This audience appears responsive and willing to be amused.

By the interval at the end of the first Act I'm certain in my heart that we have a hit on our hands. The applause has been spontaneous and enthusiastic. Because I'm made up I can't sidle around the auditorium and bar like a legendary Middle Eastern monarch in disguise, listening to what the common folk are saying, but Max and Marta both come backstage beaming with encouragement and satisfaction. I catch hints that there have actually been one or two gratifying cries of "Shame!" that I must have missed. The subtlety of my concept will inevitably be too much for people of modest mental gifts. Also, even more than a decade after she died, Diana is still held in misplaced reverence by many of weaker intellect—which is after all what my opera is about. So I'm gratified rather than worried by the odd shriek of dissent. I just wish my blasted wig would stop itching.

Act 2 goes even better. The soloists and the chorus have now settled down and all stiffness has vanished. In fact the only thing growing stiffer will be the corgi from Act 1, which for yet unexplained pharmaceutical reasons has expired. It is lying in state beneath the stage in a small aluminium trunk marked "Wigzamillion Ltd, Covent Garden." From time to time I wonder how we will break the news to its owner, the Rev. Daphne Pitt-Bull. "The Lord hath called him hence," maybe? I do hope she doesn't become violent. Anyone whose unconscious replaces birthing with birching wants watching. Ken has already adapted the remaining scene involving the Queen and the hearthrug so Mrs. Windsor will now be sitting in a chair with a channel changer, trying to find *Neighbours* on a TV placed sideways on to the audience so no one will see that the screen is actually blank.

As the final Act begins the cast evidently feels we're home and dry. Their optimism boosts my own confidence still further. Surely these professionals wouldn't get something like that wrong? As if in instant confirmation the paparazzis' chorus is encored, just as "It's truly a pathetic world" was in the previous Act, precisely as I'd predicted. And yet I'm still a bit uneasy. This last Act is definitely the hardest of the three to bring off. So far, there have been plenty of laughs at Diana's expense, several of which might even have seemed rather cruel, but darling Tizia has played her so sympathetically that she has smiled with them in charming self-deprecation. She really is just right for Diana: about the same age, remarkably similar in looks under a blonde wig, and with the right degree of good-humoured common touch. But now things are about to turn more serious. "She whom the gods want to cut down to size / Allows commoners' hands to grope royalty's thighs." (Scriptwriting just is a gift that some have and some don't.) There is the final Vatican scene to come yet, dangling the idea that Diana may seriously have considered converting to Catholicism under the spiritual guidance of Mother Teresa. And following on from that there is the proposition that many of Diana's devotees are prepared to consider her as a kind of honorary saint. How receptive will the audience be to this notion, I wonder? But even though I have always thought Suffolk should erect roadside signs on its borders: "You are now entering Suffolk. Please put your watches back twenty years," today's newspapers do nevertheless penetrate and I have discovered that Diana's unofficial cult at Le Roccie has been very well reported in the British media. There have been interviews ad nauseam with Baggy and Dumpy and their now-sighted child. In this context it was never conceivable that Fleet Street would be able to resist punning on the word "vision" or making abundant references to miracles. Nor did they. The upshot is that I hope most of the audience are conscious of a vaguely mystical overtone sounding above the worldly pleasure of this evening's entertainment. I confidently expect they will also be aware that the accidental onlie begetter of the Tuscan branch of the Diana cult was none other than the librettist of the very opera they are now watching, and Samper is modestly prepared to take several curtain calls at the end.

As a result of all this I am acutely conscious that for the work to end in a proper blaze of grandeur there must be absolutely no more laughter in the last twenty minutes. People must leave the Haysel feeling exalted, conceding the bogus nature of the Diana myth yet having thrilled to her apotheosis as an icon and to the magnificent music that accompanies it. So as you may imagine, I'm a bit on tenterhooks. I am also still onstage in my relentlessly itching wig, unobtrusively prominent in my corner at the front. By now I represent the Windsor clan out of its collective depth. I have a shotgun (also borrowed from the Rev. Pitt-Bull) which I am mechanically cleaning with a rod and a swab soaked in Young"s "303" gun oil, a brown liquid that goes milky when diluted and has a pungent antiseptic smell. The cultural and emotional gap between what I'm doing and Diana's religious transfiguration centre-stage could hardly be more marked. At this very moment Diana is facing the audience with her right arm lifted, gazing upwards into a single spot while the rest of the stage is softly lit. Beside her stands the diminutive figure of Mother Teresa in her familiar habit, a quarter turned and holding Diana's other hand. Marta's music here really is sensational. At cue 81 the second violins and the violas are briefly muted, the first violins alone are marked *senza sordini*. I might once have joked about a possible element of *Parsifal* in this last Act, and although there's no trace of Wagner there is a radiant devotional atmosphere in common. A touch of Rossini's *Petite messe solennelle*, perhaps? Just the faintest hint, maybe, although there's not a harmonium in sight. Even the most delicate suggestion of Elgar's Gerontius as he speeds through oblivion towards that brief, searing glimpse of his maker? There are no Elgarian inflections in Marta's score; yet she has somehow managed to produce a contemporary version of what secular humility might feel like when it was not mere depression or self-disgust. "Nothing but doubt in my wasted life," Diana laments. "Good-time mother, failed wife."

I am staring sightlessly into the breech of the gun—and it is even possible that my eyes are a little blurred with the emotion of the moment—when to my horror I hear from somewhere out in the hushed audience a sudden murmur and a couple of distinct titters. I can't believe it. I glance up sharply, trying to see out into the auditorium, not daring to wipe my eyes. I am still in my role as the Duke and the Duke's severe eyes don't water. The titters coalesce, then grow in strength. This is awful. Frowning and stern I turn on my seat to check the stage and practically faint with horror. A large penguin has waddled up behind Diana and is caressing her bottom with its flippers. I glance aghast at Max but he is so intent on the score and watching his prima donna's mouth that he seems not to have noticed. The music and the aria proceed for a few more bars. The penguin's beaked head peers roguishly from beneath Tizia's raised arm. By now there are sounds of open merriment from the audience while others try to shush the offenders. The shushers must be puzzled by the incongruous apparition but are presumably assuming it's a scripted, if esoteric, intrusion. Maybe penguins had a spiritual significance for the Princess? But then comes the awful moment that finally breaks any remaining spell. The penguin slides a flipper coquettishly beneath Tizia's arm and her aria abruptly ends in a helpless wail of laughter as the great soprano hugs the flipper and spins around in convulsions of ticklishness. Oh, this is terrible! I can't bear it—my poor, poor opera, the atmosphere spoiled, the tension released, the whole evening ruined! Max is now standing helplessly with his arms spread as if in supplication. The music falters and poops out with some last ridiculous notes from the two bassoonists who can't see the stage. The audience is split into two factions. Half are laughing helplessly as at some uproarious farce. The other half are vainly trying to quell them and hang on to any shreds of the former intense mood. Furious with hurt I spring to my feet and stride with my gun towards the grotesque intruder determined, whether in my role as the Duke or as the librettist, to declare open season on penguins. At least—that is my intention. But what I haven't noticed is that one of my feet is entangled in a fold of the over-long side curtain which is itself trapped beneath a leg of the chair I'm sitting on. I give a great lurch and feel myself losing balance. I grab at the back of the chair but miss and trip back-wards over the footlights with a squeak and fall, still clutching the shotgun, into the nest of kettledrums below.

Yes, yes, yes: I suppose the sight and sound of an armed Duke of Edinburgh toppling backwards into some very expen-sive percussion might at any other time be thought mildly amusing. But frankly there is no excuse whatever for opera-goers and presumed music lovers to lose all sense of propor-tion as these boors do. It is as I feared, and this country no longer has any right to claim a serious interest in the arts. My deafening descent is greeted with near hysteria by the audi-ence, damn their eyes, as I writhe in agony trying to extricate my right buttock from the timp whose skin I have burst through, bruising my thigh on the steel tuning rim and almost certainly cracking some ribs on that of its neighbour. I am not sure whether the tears I shed are of rage or pain but they might equally be those of humiliation. The timpanist is separating himself from the wreckage of his chair. Some of the nearest musicians behave gallantly and come to my assistance but even at this moment I notice that one of them, a cellist, now and then turns sharply away with her shoulders shaking. I shall not forget *her*. And neither shall I forget the audience, slumped in their seats, their stupid faces buried in their arms or wadded-up coats. They are what I see most clearly as I am helped back on my feet, shedding a tangle of bent music stands. To hell with my ideal of *impassioned detachment*.

"Bring me that fucking penguin!" I demand as soon as I am free, my hand pressed to my side and my wig askew. But the rogue bird has disappeared. Max is now up on the stage talk-ing to Tizia who has recovered her composure, marvellous trouper that she is. Reeking of gun oil I myself clamber painfully back over the footlights with the aid of a chair. Marta is also here, white faced and in tears, poor thing. She slips a commiserating arm sheathed in midnight blue material around me and I'm afraid the famous Samper composure cracks because I let out an involuntary yell of pain. My side hurts so badly I can only take shallow breaths. "My poor Gerry," she says. "I'm so sorry. You're hurting." And only then does the treasonous idea flit across my mind that her own tears might also have been those of mirth. But no—surely not. No composer could laugh at the deliberate trashing of her new masterpiece. For I won't believe that bloody penguin's intrusion was anything other than purposeful and malicious. I am about to quiz Ken and some members of the cast pretty damned fiercely about how they could have allowed it to happen. It just isn't plausible that all these professionals were so entranced by TS-P's aria they never noticed someone hanging around in a goddamn penguin suit before he casually sauntered onstage. I'm about to demand that somebody gets on a mobile phone and calls out a police dragnet to hunt down and preferably shoot this prankster when Max turns to the audience and raises both arms. A chastened hush falls.

"Ladies and gentlemen," he says in his almost unaccented English. "I do not understand what has happened but I assure you an inquiry will be made. Not only do I apologise to you all but I deeply regret the disgraceful interruption of this beautiful new work." (Several cries of "Hear, hear!" from the auditorium.) "But too many people, first among them the composer herself, have worked too hard for this evening simply to be thrown away and the performance abandoned. After discussion, Marta and I have agreed that the atmosphere of these closing scenes has been too far destroyed for us to resume them from that point. We have decided that the only proper thing to do is to start again from the beginning of the last Act." (Here there is a spatter of applause that quickly swells into general approbation.) "Thank you for your encouragement and patience, ladies and gentlemen. Can we now pretend that the final interval has just started for the first time? This will give us the opportunity to reorganise a section of the orchestra and also enable those who sadly can't spare any extra time to leave. But I do most earnestly beg all of you who can to stay to hear this important work through to the end. I promise you will find it worth your while. Thank you again."

This speech earns Max prolonged applause and some cheers. The curtain is lowered and suddenly Adrian is hurrying across the stage towards me.

"Gerry, are you okay?" he asks anxiously. "From where I'm sitting it looked as though you took a hell of a tumble."

I essay a gallant, Samper-redivivus smile. "It hurts me to breathe and I'm a mass of bruises. Bloody but otherwise unbowed, I think."

"Unlike the timpani. You should see those. I'm afraid you've just put the drummer out of business." He moves to put an arm around me but I shy away in time, wincingly.

"Don't, Adrian, it's agony." Suddenly I feel quite unsteady and without warning a mysterious humming mist surrounds me in warm and soothing waves. I next discover that I'm on a chair being carried outside. The cold night air revives me but before I can protest adequately I am being loaded—brilliant pain!—into Adrian's car. Breathing is now so agonising I can only take shallow gasps but I manage to splutter out some objections. My opera! My bow! But in vain. The doors slam and Adrian starts the engine.

"Now it's *our* turn to take *you* to A&E," he says with a smile of pure mischief, sod him.

Adrian 8

email from Dr. Adrian Jestico (ajestico@bois.ac.uk)
to Dr. Penny Barbisant (penbar05@btinternet.com)

Thanks very much for yours, Penny. I note you're home for Christmas so will simply reply to this UK-based address. Let me know when I should revert to Woods Hole again. Surely you can't resist paying us a visit in Southampton? BOIS—and no doubt boys—will welcome you with open arms. Alternatively, any chance of meeting you in London? We could always try that Voynovian restaurant if you're feeling enterprising or suicidal.

Your idea of starting an email campaign to shame people into boycotting ICOC's Thailand extravaganza is a good one, although such things have been tried before & have fallen on largely deaf ears. Like everybody else scientists cherish their freebies, as I expect you've noticed. But I certainly agree that we ought to be setting an example these days, like doctors who give up smoking. Besides, I've never been convinced these thrashes produce much in the way of hard science. And somewhere at the back of my mind I've always felt it's incongruous that a devotion to the study of organisms a millimetre or so long can lead to gigantic Boeing-loads of people flying 6,000 miles to talk about them for five days on end. Anyhow, good luck with the campaign. I shall immediately nail my colours to the mast by declaring that I shan't be going myself.

And now I can no longer delay telling you about recent events here at Crendlesham, where Gerry's & Marta's opera,

Princess Diana, had its first momentous performance 3 days ago. To cut to the chase, it has turned out a huge critical success although there is marked dissent from a small but vocal minority. More of that later, although I might attach some representative newspaper reviews before sending this.

The first night was dramatic in ways its authors didn't intend & was an experience I wouldn't have missed for much fine gold. One day I hope to be able to tell my wholly imaginary grandchildren that I was present at the famous first performance of *Princess Diana*, an occasion on a par with that of Stravinsky's *Rite of Spring* in 1913 which caused its Parisian audience to riot. Checking back, I see I told you in my last email that I'd only ever heard a sketchy run-through of the piece in Gerry's house in Italy with Marta at the piano. I was completely unprepared for how good it is with full orchestra, bells, whistles, etc. I don't know about you but I admit I'm not normally keen on contemporary music, still less of the little I've heard of modern opera. But *Princess Diana* is surprisingly approachable thanks to very agreeable music & an entertaining—if occasionally bizarre—script that quite often is genuinely funny. I spent the first 2 Acts revising my view of Gerry as something of a fantasist. Of course I know he's an excellent sports biographer, but I also know he despises himself for it & has aspirations to be rated up there in the "serious" arts. I can't deny that at the back of my mind I've been thinking of him as someone who, when push comes to shove, probably lacks the creative talent or the right kind of energy or something. I realise his appearance of dilettantism & his frequent daftness are essential parts of his charm, but I think I've imagined they would always undermine any claims he has to be taken seriously.

Well, I was wrong. What he & Marta have tried to do in *PD*— & we must remember that it was entirely Gerry's idea in the first place—is actually quite complicated. So far as I can judge he's attempting to present this (to me) rather null creature both as averagely silly (by poking fun at her haute couture pretentiousness & humiliatingly public amorous carryings-on) & as a genuine icon. Somehow he & Marta manage to weave these 2 threads simultaneously & convincingly, which I think is quite a feat. As I say, the first 2 acts were entertaining & although there were definitely some members of the audience who didn't approve of the mockery, there were many more swayed by the charm Diana exudes through the music. In short—& as I never would have predicted—Gerry & Marta turn out to be a brilliant team. One really good idea of Gerry's was to have 2 mannequins representing the princes William & Harry onstage throughout. They were periodically replaced by larger models so you had these little children gradually ageing into youths & functioning as silent witnesses to events. It was an extremely effective continuity device.

But in the 3rd Act disaster struck & unfortunately right at the moment of maximum emotional tension. Diana & Mother Teresa were discussing the Princess's possible conversion to Roman Catholicism (*can* this really have happened? I must ask Gerry where he got it from). Gerry, in his role as the Duke of Edinburgh—he had written himself an occasional speaking part— was sitting on the right of the stage at the front in plus-fours & a wig pretending to clean a shotgun while Tizia Sgrizzi-Pulmoni as Diana (& you can hardly get a more famous soprano than her to launch your new opera) was bewailing her spiritual inadequacy or something. Suddenly, someone wearing a penguin suit just strolled on to the stage from behind & started feeling Tizia up with his flippers. Talk about wacky moments in grand opera— none of us knew what the hell to think. Could this really be part of the action? Some awful send-up of Gerry's, maybe? Or is a penguin perhaps the accepted modern version of one of those holy doves that flutter around the heads of the blessed in Renaissance paintings? There was a moment of bafflement when no one was sure whether we were meant to laugh open-ly. But being ticklish, the wretched prima donna broke down in giggles & the audience with her. Seeing everything being ruined, poor Gerry sprang up brandishing his shotgun & overbalanced backwards into the orchestra where he landed on three kettle-drums and much else.

To my eternal shame (eternity in this case lasting approxi-mately 3 seconds) I'm afraid I simply corpsed with most of the audience. However dire the consequences, the actual spectacle of the Duke of Edinburgh doing a pratfall into the percussion section was dreadfully comic. It sounded like the late signor Pavarotti falling 20 metres into a display of kitchen equipment & silverware & most of us simply gave up & howled. But I could see Gerry had probably been hurt so I went forward, by which time everything had broken down & come to a halt. Max made a speech & they started the last Act again. Unfortunately I wasn't there to hear it. It turned out poor Gerry had injured himself quite badly & came all over faint so I drove him off there & then to A&E in Ipswich. The sight of the Duke of Edinburgh still in character hobbling up to announce himself at the hospital desk ("Had a bit of a prang") caused consternation & I'm sorry to say that although Gerry was in quite a lot of pain it was again too much for me & I disgraced myself rather. Anyway, all was explained & he was X-rayed & found to have broken a rib badly enough to threaten puncturing his lung. So they took him off & did a small op—some new American technique, apparently, in which the splintered ends are pulled back out and clipped together with a metal sleeve.

I fetched him back to Crendlesham the next morning, still sore but immediately cheered by the early reviews I brought him. He said he'd seen Derek in the audience, about which he obviously had mixed feelings. On the one hand he was upset that Derek had been there to witness the disaster, on the other he was dead chuffed that he'd seen the eventual triumph. Those two certainly do have a weird relationship so I badgered Gerry a bit & he finally told me about their great secret from the past. You've probably forgotten but some time ago I mentioned I thought Gerry & Derek each had something on the other from way back & that it might even have involved something criminal. Well, I don't mind passing this on, a) because I know you'll be discreet & b) because it all happened so long ago & the villain of the piece is dead. What Gerry told me was that in 1979 he'd been working for Curzon TV as an apprentice scriptwriter. Owing to a senior writer's illness Gerry was included at the last moment in a unit sent to Morocco to film an episode of *Tulliver's Travels*. You won't remember it but it was a series built around roving reporter Frank Tulliver, a cross between Alan Whicker & John Pilger, currently to be seen in an awful series of ads for instant coffee. In Morocco Gerry was enlisted by a cameraman called Dave Barraclough to help with a scheme DB had employed before to smuggle hashish back to the UK in film cans. The cans were stuck all over with important-looking labels saying something like CURZON TV/EXPOSED FILM/URGENT/RUSH PROCESSING & no one ever stopped them. They went straight to the processing centre at Chorleywood where Barraclough's 17 year-old protégé, Derek, knew how to separate the cans with hash from the rest (they were marked so he could pick them out under UV light). On this occasion, though, the cans never reached Chorleywood. HM Customs picked them up & Barraclough went down. Both Gerry & Derek were prosecuted for their part but because they were so young & pleaded intimidation by Barraclough they got off with severe cautions & lost their jobs. Ever since then Gerry has nursed an unverifiable suspicion (based on something another member of the film crew said) that it was Derek himself who anonymously tipped off HM Customs & shopped Barraclough in retaliation for an indecent assault by DB when Derek was only 16. For a long time afterwards Derek suspected Gerry knew this & was terrified that he might one day tell Barraclough, who did his time & left Wormwood Scrubs stripped of his union card & full of resentment. So for years each was wary of what the other knew & might say, & a sort of fossilised friendship has grown up based on a wary conspiratorial amity from the past. Gerry says Barraclough died several years ago, making the whole thing irrelevant now although Derek and he are left with this sometimes petulant rivalry. So that's *that* little tale.

As for the opera's last act which Max repeated while we were at Ipswich Hospital, it seems to have gone brilliantly after all though Max said some of the prolonged applause & many curtain calls may have been down to the sympathy effect that favours those who Bravely Carry On. Still, the largely rave reviews have completely lifted the librettist's spirits & he is now basking insufferably. He has attended both subsequent nights, which have played with someone else as the Duke, & borrowed a silver-topped cane to lean on in order to appear in the curtain calls with Marta at the end. It's still too painful for him to actually bow, so he stood there in a cloak and gravely raised his cane, looking for all the world like one of those old-time impresarios—Diaghilev or someone. All he needed was an astrakhan collar & a top hat. I'm afraid Gerry's future in the world of musico-thespianism is now assured.

The mystery of the penguin was soon cleared up. The strange thing is that in the shock of the moment neither Gerry nor I immediately thought of the mad clarinettist who came to that fatal dinner a year ago dressed as a gorilla & was later sectioned, although Max says he realised at once who it was. It turns out the wretched man, a really talented musician who was a founder member of the CSO but who now has no job, was eventually "returned to care in the community" (in the touchy-feely phrase that actually means "Get lost & keep taking the pills"). It seems he was put up to the whole thing by a fellow we know as Spud. Spud was the servant or driver or partner of Dougie Monteith, the ancient near-neighbour who died of a heart attack on that same night of the Great Puke & who was yet another Crendlesham guest who has needed to be stretchered off to Ipswich A&E. Spud has apparently never forgiven Gerry, whom he blames absolutely for his friend's death, & he paid this loony out-of-work clarinettist to sneak onstage & bugger things up. Which he did magnificently. Spud was waiting for him out-side in a car & whisked him away again. But the fellow had a serious relapse that night (I almost wrote "went ape again") & has now been sectioned once more & the whole story has come out. No actual crime has been committed so nothing more will happen although Gerry talks darkly of suing for injuries sus-tained or otherwise wreaking some terrible vengeance on the delinquent Spud. He drops the names of some Lincoln's Inn bar-risters he knows & says he's looking forward to seeing Spud come up against men of the forensic calibre of Berndt Naught-en QC or Sir Julian Easte-Coaker QC. I shall do my utmost to talk him out of this idiocy otherwise it will all degenerate into a truly operatic vendetta. My job is being made easier by the way the other two performances have gone & the praise he's receiv-ing. In fact he's getting so mellow I'm confident I can prevail on him to be magnanimous. It's already a good sign of his recov-ery—though not necessarily good news for the rest of us—that he says he's feeling like doing some creative cookery again. Anything but that.

And so closes this chapter in Gerry's rise to stardom, as one might say. In my last email I think I bored you with my fears that simple geography might sooner or later drive a wedge between him & me. But from the way things are going it looks more likely that he will soon begin to tire of a humble boffin who likes cope-pods. Suddenly he's been catapulted into a world of musical grandees & it's all Tizia this & Brian that & Jeremy the other. I'm not really being mean—he's earned it. My hope is he'll calm down round about the time his stitches come out. My fear is he won't.

Do let me know about London. Having now sampled and relished Marta's music I have this odd & probably quite misplaced feeling that I owe it to her to try her national cuisine. I'm sure it's perfectly OK. Gerry always does exaggerate so. But in any case happy festive season, as we say in 2008 AD (Anno Dawkins).

Cheers,
Adrian

ABOUT THE AUTHOR

James Hamilton-Paterson is the author of sev-
eral novels, including *Gerontius*, winner of the
Whitbread Best First Novel Award, and
Cooking with Fernet Branca, nominated for the
MAN Booker Prize. His non-fiction books
include *Seven-Tenths: The Sea and Its
Thresholds*, to be published by Europa Editions
in summer 2009. He is also the author of two
books of poetry and is a regular contributor to
Granta. He lives and works in Austria.

Now Available from Europa Editions

Carmine Abate
Between Two Seas
224 pp • $14.95 • ISBN: 978-1-933372-40-2

Muriel Barbery
The Elegance of the Hedgehog
336 pp • $15.00 • ISBN: 978-1-933372-60-0

Stefano Benni
Margherita Dolce Vita
240 pp • $14.95 • ISBN: 978-1-933372-20-4

Timeskipper
400 pp • $16.95 • ISBN: 978-1-933372-44-0

Massimo Carlotto
The Goodbye Kiss
160 pp • $14.95 • ISBN: 978-1-933372-05-1

Death's Dark Abyss
160 pp • $14.95 • ISBN: 978-1-933372-18-1

The Fugitive
176 pp • $14.95 • ISBN: 978-1-933372-25-9

Steve Erickson
Zeroville
352 pp • $14.95 • ISBN: 978-1-933372-39-6

Elena Ferrante
The Days of Abandonment
192 pp • $14.95 • ISBN: 978-1-933372-00-6

Troubling Love
144 pp • $14.95 • ISBN: 978-1-933372-16-7

The Lost Daughter
144 pp • $14.95 • ISBN: 978-1-933372-42-6

Jane Gardam
Old Filth
304 pp • $14.95 • ISBN: 978-1-933372-13-6

The Queen of the Tambourine
272 pp • $14.95 • ISBN: 978-1-933372-36-5

The People on Privilege Hill
208 pp • $15.95 • ISBN: 978-1-933372-56-3

Alicia Giménez-Bartlett
Dog Day
320 pp • $14.95 • ISBN: 978-1-933372-14-3

Prime Time Suspect
320 pp • $14.95 • ISBN: 978-1-933372-31-0

Death Rites
304 pp • $16.95 • ISBN: 978-1-933372-54-9

Katharina Hacker
The Have-Nots
352 pp • $14.95 • ISBN: 978-1-933372-41-9

Patrick Hamilton
Hangover Square
336 pp • $14.95 • ISBN: 978-1-933372-06-8

James Hamilton-Paterson
Cooking with Fernet Branca
288 pp • $14.95 • ISBN: 978-1-933372-01-3

Amazing Disgrace
352 pp • $14.95 • ISBN: 978-1-933372-19-8

Alfred Hayes
The Girl on the Via Flaminia
160 pp • $14.95 • ISBN: 978-1-933372-24-2

Jean-Claude Izzo
Total Chaos
256 pp • $14.95 • ISBN: 978-1-933372-04-4

Chourmo
256 pp • $14.95 • ISBN: 978-1-933372-17-4

Solea
208 pp • $14.95 • ISBN: 978-1-933372-30-3

The Lost Sailors
272 pp • $14.95 • ISBN: 978-1-933372-35-8

A Sun for the Dying
224 pp • $15.00 • ISBN: 978-1-933372-59-4

Gail Jones
Sorry
240 pp • $15.95 • ISBN: 978-1-933372-55-6

Matthew F. Jones
Boot Tracks
208 pp • $14.95 • ISBN: 978-1-933372-11-2

Ioanna Karystiani
The Jasmine Isle
288 pp • $14.95 • ISBN: 978-1-933372-10-5

Gene Kerrigan
The Midnight Choir
368 pp • $14.95 • ISBN: 978-1-933372-26-6

Little Criminals
352 pp • $16.95 • ISBN: 978-1-933372-43-3

Peter Kocan
Fresh Fields
304 pp • $14.95 • ISBN: 978-1-933372-29-7

The Treatment and The Cure
256 pp • $15.95 • ISBN: 978-1-933372-45-7

Helmut Krausser
Eros
352 pp • $16.95 • ISBN: 978-1-933372-58-7

Amara Lakhous
Clash of Civilizations Over an Elevator in Piazza Vittorio
144 pp • $14.95 • ISBN: 978-1-933372-61-7

Carlo Lucarelli
Carte Blanche
128 pp • $14.95 • ISBN: 978-1-933372-15-0

The Damned Season
128 pp • $14.95 • ISBN: 978-1-933372-27-3

Via delle Oche
160 pp • $14.95 • ISBN: 978-1-933372-53-2

Edna Mazya
Love Burns
224 pp • $14.95 • ISBN: 978-1-933372-08-2

Sélim Nassib
I Loved You for Your Voice
272 pp • $14.95 • ISBN: 978-1-933372-07-5

The Palestinian Lover
192 pp • $14.95 • ISBN: 978-1-933372-23-5

Alessandro Piperno
The Worst Intentions
320 pp • $14.95 • ISBN: 978-1-933372-33-4

Benjamin Tammuz
Minotaur
192 pp • $14.95 • ISBN: 978-1-933372-02-0

Chad Taylor
Departure Lounge
176 pp • $14.95 • ISBN: 978-1-933372-09-9

Roma Tearne
Mosquito
352 pp • $16.95 • ISBN: 978-1-933372-57-0

Christa Wolf
One Day a Year
640 pp • $16.95 • ISBN: 978-1-933372-22-8

Edwin M. Yoder Jr.
Lions at Lamb House
256 pp • $14.95 • ISBN: 978-1-933372-34-1

Michele Zackheim
Broken Colors
320 pp • $14.95 • ISBN: 978-1-933372-37-2

Children's Illustrated Fiction

•
Altan
Here Comes Timpa
48 pp • $14.95 • ISBN: 978-1-933372-28-0

Timpa Goes to the Sea
48 pp • $14.95 • ISBN: 978-1-933372-32-7

Fairy Tale Timpa
48 pp • $14.95 • ISBN: 978-1-933372-38-9

Wolf Erlbruch
The Big Question
52 pp • $14.95 • ISBN: 978-1-933372-03-7

The Miracle of the Bears
32 pp • $14.95 • ISBN: 978-1-933372-21-1

(with Gioconda Belli)
The Butterfly Workshop
40 pp • $14.95 • ISBN: 978-1-933372-12-9